Again, My Lord

Historical romance… with a twist.

A *twist* SERIES NOVEL

AGAIN, MY LORD: Copyright © 2015 Katharine Brophy Dubois.

Cover design © Julie Schroeder Designs.

ISBN 9780991641239 (Paperback)

Published by Billet-Doux Books.

To Nyra, with profound gratitude.

Each of us when separated, having one side only, like a flat fish, is but the indenture of a man, and he is always looking for his other half.

Plato, *Symposium* (ca. 385–370 BC)

The Ancients were rarely wrong about Love. I have tried to teach him this, and hope that someday the lesson will serve him well.

Lady Mariana Dare,
private correspondence to her sister (1805)

Prologue

LADY CALISTA CHANCE had excellent teeth.

Tacitus Caesar Everard, the ninth Marquess of Dare, knew that a man should consider a lady's manifold assets before deciding upon her as his life's companion. But only one asset really mattered to him. All others had been rendered inconsequential on account of his parents.

Tacitus's mother had had horrible teeth. During her childhood in the West Indies she had chewed on the stalks of sugarcane as a distraction from the violent pain of a constitutional bend in her spine. By the age of seventeen, her teeth were a disaster. Nevertheless she'd had speaking eyes and a dry, clever wit that slayed the eighth Marquess of Dare. They had twenty-five years of bliss and one child—this, despite the marquess's insistence that they must have no children. Nothing, he declared, would jeopardize his wife's health.

Happily, Tacitus did not. A strapping, healthy infant, he grew into a strapping, healthy boy, with a fine mind to match his fine musculature. His spine, it should be noted, was ideally formed to support square shoulders and give direction to long, strong legs.

Therefore, his father lavished upon him all the attention an heir deserved and all the love he could spare from the enormous lot he gave to his wife. Together Tacitus and his parents were a most happy trio.

Then everything went to hell. Unable to eat much with the sorry stumps of her teeth, and unable to move from her bed due to the spine that had finally had enough after all, Lady Dare gave up trying. A woman of spirit and intelligence, she said, did not go along well in confinement. At the age of forty-two, she departed this mortal coil.

A month later, Lord Dare followed her to the grave, in his case perishing of a failed heart.

At twenty-four, Tacitus watched it all in tangled horror, helplessness, and grief. And on the day he buried his father he made two promises to himself: he would marry a lady with excellent teeth and he would never fall in love. He realized that this was insane idiocy. But a battered heart easily encourages even the best of minds to foolishness.

Ladies' teeth became the new marquess's preoccupation.

Calista Chance had exceptional teeth. Straight, neat, and improbably white, they appeared whenever her lips split into a wide smile, competing with candles and sunshine for brilliance and, frankly, winning. That those lips were delectably pink and maddeningly kissable was a trifling incidental. That the smile occurred in the vicinity of a pair of long-lashed and crystalline blue eyes meant little to Tacitus. That it occurred with remarkable frequency as he watched her across ballrooms and drawing rooms for three weeks during a London season was only significant in that he was able to study the teeth well enough to know she suited one of his requirements for a wife.

The other requirement—that he would not be in danger of falling in love with her—seemed even easier to meet. Dazzlingly gay where he was somewhat subdued, compulsively social where he was fond of his library, and as vapid as a seagull where he was rather prone to deep contemplation, Lady Calista did not have "Tacitus Everard's Soul Mate" imprinted upon her brow. He was not in danger of falling in love with such a woman.

She would be the ideal wife.

He set about courting her, to discover that the Earl of Chance had left town with his family and was not expected to return, perhaps ever. Something about a scandal at a card table. But Tacitus didn't care about gossip. He had chosen his wife. He would acquire her, fill his nursery, and that would take care of that. Then he could return to his life of running his estates and occasional politics when the Whig platform inspired him.

And the corridors of Dare Castle would no longer echo with unbearable silence.

In pursuit of his plan, he traveled to Dashbourne, the Chance estate, where the earl had sequestered his womenfolk in the middle of the season. Tacitus stood in the drawing room that was nearly empty of furniture as rain echoed throughout the house as though the rest of it were empty too, and he awaited his intended bride.

The Countess of Chance entered the room, followed by her two daughters. All three had inquisitive eyes. And all three peered at him as if he were a ravisher intent upon … ravishment, he supposed.

Lady Chance was quietly graceful and golden blond. The other sister was younger than Lady Calista, not yet out of the schoolroom, with black hair and an astute eye. They were both attractive females.

But at close range Lady Calista practically glittered. Her beauty seized his breath and stored it somewhere in the region of his boots.

He offered the usual pleasantries while they stared at him. That none of the three of them seemed to understand the purpose of his call proved disconcerting. His tongue stiffened and the interview swiftly descended into uncomfortable silence. Finally, he found the presence of mind to make his intentions clear.

"I would like to speak with his lordship," he said.

The countess's face appeared abruptly strained.

"I beg your pardon, my lord. My husband is not entertaining offers for my daughter's hand at this time."

Apparently she did understand his intentions.

Tacitus blinked. "But," he said, nonplussed, "I am Dare."

Lady Calista laughed.

Just like that.

She laughed at him.

And for the first time he saw a spark of defiant intelligence in her eyes that had nothing of frivolity in it.

"My lord." Her voice rippled over him. "It would not

signify if you were York or Hanover. In this house the only tonic of marriage we drink is true love. Can't you see it?" She gestured about her at the wallpaper that showed darker squares where paintings had once hung, to the empty mantelpiece and the single sofa and two plain wooden chairs arranged around a small side table. "My mother is so enamored of my father, and he of her, that they make a deliriously happy home even in the midst of our shame and penury."

"That is enough, Calista," Lady Chance said in a hush.

With a smile that lit the rainy day like a torch, Lady Calista beamed at him, curtsied, and pulled her gaping sister from the room.

"As you can see, my lord, my daughter is not yet aware of the honor a gentleman's notice brings her. I hope you will forgive—" Her voice broke, but she recovered swiftly. "I hope you will forgive me for her impertinence, and for my mistake in bringing her into your company."

His throat was full of moths, it seemed. He cleared it.

"On the contrary, madam. She is merely high-spirited." *High-spirited?* Where had he heard that term applied to a woman? And hadn't he scowled at the time? "May I have permission to return tomorrow? In the hopes of finer weather I would be delighted to take your daughters driving."

It was Lady Chance's turn to blink. "You wish to take Calista and Evelina for a drive?"

"I do," he said. "Lord Chance's refusal to see me notwithstanding, I intend to court Lady Calista."

"Here?" She was still staring at him rather blankly.

"Where else?"

"But Dare Castle must be a hundred miles away."

"I have taken a room at the inn in the village."

Various thoughts seemed to cross her eyes rapidly. Then, with the ghost of a smile, she curtsied.

"My daughters will be honored to drive with you tomorrow, my lord."

~o0o~

They were.

And they weren't.

Delighted to drive, yes. With him, *not precisely*.

In only one manner did he seem to please Lady Calista: he provided her with infinite fodder with which to whisper behind the rim of her bonnet to her sister outrageous comments about his horses, his carriage, his coat, his hat, his hair, his eyes, the breadth of his shoulders, and even his legs. He pretended not to hear her, and didn't know what to say in response anyway.

Aside from two satisfying and instructive affairs with discreet widows during his university years, he had little experience with women. And he'd had no extended commerce whatsoever with girls of eighteen, only occasional holiday visits to his school friends' houses where he briefly encountered their sisters and such. This sort of raillery was foreign to him. How was a man to respond? With like teasing or with sternness? His father had never been stern with his mother, but his mother had never teased his father in this manner.

And yet ... Tacitus *liked* it. It stirred him.

He wasn't certain this was a good thing.

Lady Calista's smile and brilliant eyes arrested his tongue each time he sought to speak. He could not believe that a girl hopeful of attaching herself to a gentleman would treat him with such blithe disregard for propriety. It seemed eminently clear that she was playing with him.

By the end of the drive his hands were sore from clutching the reins and his jaw was tight. One part consternation, one part anger, and a final part crashing disappointment, he bade them good-bye upon the drive.

Dashing toward the house, she halted abruptly and whirled around to face him.

"Will you call again tomorrow, Lord Dare?"

"I will not." This had been a very bad idea. Girls aplenty peopled London's drawing rooms. He would return to town and find a bride with good, if not excellent, teeth and a suitably even temper and offer his name and future nursery to her instead. Lady Calista and her twinkling masticators could go hang.

Her pretty lips closed. A crease in her brow marred the loveliness of her features—for the better, oddly. He felt something very tight in his chest *loosen.*

"I should like you to return, you know. We are frightfully bored here with nothing to do, and you are ever so fun to tease."

"As I did not enter this world to be your object of ridicule, ma'am, that logic does not particularly recommend itself to me."

Her crystal eyes popped wide. "Ridicule?"

He had nothing to respond.

She walked directly to him and stood before him. The light fabric of her gown ruffled about her legs and a wisp of hair the color of the dark, loamy soil at Dare and shining like satin crossed her lips that now parted. Her teeth peeked out and he could not seem to look away.

"If you will not come here for me," she said, "then come because Evelina is going mad, locked away like a princess in a tower. I don't suppose you've brought any books with you? She is eager for something new to read. And our younger brother is wretched too. He would adore your horses. Our father has had to sell ours to pay debts," she said simply, making him wonder if Lord Chance had sold the contents of his library as well. "Gregory is pining to ride. He is pining for male company, really, male company that is not our father."

Tacitus regarded her for a long moment and she regarded him in turn, directly, and without shame. Raised by a strong, intelligent woman, now he recognized that Lady Calista Chance was not the featherbrain he had believed her to be from studying her in the midst of society. Which meant she was worse. She was false, a woman who hid a good mind behind a pretty face in order to twist the world around her little finger.

"If your brother wishes," he said, "he may call at the inn in the village tomorrow and I will give him the loan of my saddle horse. Your sister too, if she cares to accompany him."

"Oh!" Her smile returned full force. "You have a mount suitable for a sixteen-year-old girl at the inn too? Do you ride a lady's saddle horse on alternate days then, my lord?" she said, her brows perking high as she scanned his shoulders. He had wide shoulders. He knew this. He was tall, too. A lady's saddle horse was entirely unsuited to a man of his size.

Impertinent minx.

"No," he said. "But I keep a magic wand about me that allows me to transform my horse into a lady's mount." He opened his overcoat and pretended to search inside it.

"Do you?" Surprise chimed in her voice.

Aha. The minx thought she had invented teasing.

"Usually, but I must have mislaid it," he added with a frown and gave up his searching. "Perhaps you should not invite your sister to call at the inn after all." The words came easily now that he had dismissed his foolish notion of courting her. Without waiting for her response, he turned to his carriage and climbed onto the box.

"If I call at the inn with my brother and sister," she said, "will you turn me away, my lord?"

"Should I?"

"Only if I beg you to." Her eyes danced above cheeks the color of rosy peaches.

He snapped the leathers and left, feeling peculiar, out of sorts yet pleased. An eighteen-year-old girl with less decorum than a milkmaid and less honesty than a priest held no appeal for him. He should not have pursued a beautiful bride. His mother had not been a beauty, but a truly wonderful person. His father had been wise.

But when Lady Calista appeared at the village inn the following morning with her younger siblings, Tacitus did not turn her away. He could not. Her smile made his stomach tighten and the movement of her hands, always in action like birds alighting, captivated him. She teased him again, and again he did not always know what to say in return.

She drove him a little mad.

A lot.

The following day was much the same.

And the following.

And for many days after that.

His manservant told him that the local gossips had got ahold of the news of his presence in the neighborhood.

"The young ladies for miles about have caught sight of you, my lord. They hope you will cast the net wider."

"That is a disgusting metaphor, Claude."

"Eh," he shrugged with Gallic insouciance. "It is always so with the most eligible of the bachelors. But with the ladies," he said with a sidelong glance, "the competition inspires them to fight for the prize. You should accept the invitations you have received from the others."

But he did not wish to waste time courting every maiden in the county. He had interest in only one.

He took her and her brother and sister riding about the countryside in his carriage and they told him stories of all the adventures they'd had here and there—in the woods, the lake, the ruins of the old abbey, the stables. And they regaled him with shocking anecdotes in which Lady Calista had been the instigator of the trouble on most occasions. He laughed, and he felt a burning in his chest from something he could not name. Envy, perhaps.

He had never had siblings, nor close cousins, and though he'd gone to school, he had spent most of his life with his parents, whom he adored and who adored him. It had been a quiet life, but he'd liked it well. Enormously well. It was difficult now to watch the three siblings' deep affection without the dull ache of loneliness crawling into his chest. Surrounded by servants and comfortable with his friends, he had more than enough companionship. Yet he did not now have that special, profound companionship he had known for two dozen years of his life.

At these moments, occasionally, Lady Calista would catch him staring. Then her lips that he'd been thinking were probably too kissable would curve into a grin, then split into a smile. Her teeth would shine and he would be reminded of his

original purpose in this county, which he still believed was
sheer lunacy. And he would once again lose the easy use of his
tongue.

Then her eyes would flash and she would laugh at him
until her cheeks glowed, and she would run away. Literally.
Across a field or down the street. He watched her skirts flutter
and wondered what they felt like, that light, insubstantial fabric.
And the girl beneath the fabric.

Nights in his room at the inn he lay awake for hours,
recalling the days. Her laughter. Her taunts. Her smiles. All of
it designed to at once shock and charm.

But perhaps her smiles and charm were *not* designed after
all, rather merely in her nature: audacious, vital, and desperately
testing life. He recalled the pleasure in her eyes on those
occasions when he parried her light jabs.

Each night when he slept he dreamed of her, vivid dreams
that seemed like reality. And each morning when he awoke he
took himself in hand and allowed the dreams to continue until
he was groaning her name.

Within a fortnight he was infatuated.

Within a month he was besotted.

On the thirtieth day since he had called at Dashbourne, he
arose early and dressed in his finest coat, with the Dare insignia
pinned in gold discreetly in his neckcloth. This time when he
called on the Earl of Chance, he would insist upon being seen.

Just as he prepared to depart the inn, she appeared in the
doorway.

"Good day, my lord," she said as though unescorted
maidens met lords in the doorways of roadside inns every day
of the week.

He bowed. "My lady," he murmured. The fantasy he'd had
less than an hour earlier had involved the generous application
of her lips to his skin, and he was having trouble dragging his
mind into reality now. He glanced behind her, pretending to
search for her brother and sister, but mostly to look away from
those tempting lips. The street was empty of Chance siblings.
"Have Master Gregory and Lady Evelina remained at home

today?"

His blood pounded. In the absence of her brother and sister, today he might take her hand. Kiss her enticing lips. Tell her what had come to be in his heart. At least until he'd driven her home. He could not allow her to remain here, alone. He was not actually a ravisher. He wanted her with a desperate sort of ache he had never felt before. But he wanted her validly and licitly before he actually *had* her.

"I have come before them," she said breathlessly, her eyes very bright. "You see, I am running away and I don't want them to know."

His tongue fumbled for words, his throat for sound. "Running away?"

"Yes. Isn't it marvelous? What an adventure!" She took a step closer to him. "But you see, I haven't a horse or carriage or even any money," she said more quietly and cast a glance over his shoulder. "I wonder if you might help me." Her sudden smile blinded. "Would you drive me away from here? Today? Now? Please? I—" She placed a slender hand on his forearm. "I simply *must* leave today. At once." After a brief silence she said, "I would be so very … grateful. I— I have— That is— I have missed London so— so dreadfully. Please, my lord?"

With a movement of deadened economy, he removed her hand from his arm and released it as his insides crumbled into pieces of dried clay.

"I regret, my lady, that unfortunately I cannot aid you in this."

She stepped closer and Tacitus's battered heart did a painful turn about in his chest.

"But you simply must," she said, her speech now a silvery plea. "I beg of you."

He wanted both to retreat a pace and to grab her up and demand that she retract her words. But he stood his ground and it was the most difficult thing he had ever done except for burying his parents.

"Lady Calista," he said, "you must go home now."

He had never seen her eyes wider. "Are you refusing me?" She looked surprised and Tacitus knew he really had become an absolute fool, ensnared by a girl who was, however, not ensnared by him. Not only had she not come to like him enough to wed, but she now hoped to use him to convey her to more appealing company.

He deserved to be used. All fools did.

But he was not a fool by nature. Only by inclination at present. He had fallen in love swiftly. He would endeavor to fall out of love swiftly too.

"I cannot drive you to London, nor indeed anywhere except to your father's house."

Her lashes swept down and up. Three times. More slowly with each sweep. Then she said simply, "Very well, my lord."

And that was that. He drove her home, deposited her with her mother, and in a blind haze drove away. Back to London where there were young ladies who would recognize the appeal of a man of wealth and position and accept his suit. None of them would probably have glimmering blue eyes. Or if they did, they wouldn't have sparkling white smiles. Or even if they had those they probably wouldn't have maddeningly kissable lips. Or perfect pert noses. Or laughter like sunshine and sin at once. Or hips curved so roundly and delectably that they begged a man to wrap his hands around them and drag her close. They probably would not throw their arms around their siblings and declare, "You are the most sublimely wonderful sister a girl could ever have!" and "I will love you, little brother, until the day I die and beyond!" or to Tacitus's face, "But I am *Dare*" in a deep voice, then dissolve into laughter that sounded like a brook in springtime. And they probably would not make him fall head over ears in love with them with the determined tilt of their chins.

But he did not go to London. He went home to Dare Castle. Amidst the memories of affection that surrounded him, he stared at the walls and was unreasonably cross with his staff.

Soon his old school chum Peyton Stark, the Viscount Mallory, appeared on his doorstep with a sixteen-year-old bottle of whiskey and eyes full of deviltry.

"What are you doing all shut up in this old pile, Tass?" he demanded and thrust a full tumbler into Tacitus's hand.

"It is not a pile," he grumbled. "It is a castle." A very nice one, at that.

"Your mourning period is long since over." Peyton sprawled his muscular frame into one of the library chairs and surveyed Tacitus from beneath brows black as Hades. His face had something of the look of Lucifer about it, angelically handsome in an arrogant, wicked fashion. "You are far too young to molder away in this house for the rest of your life."

"What would you have me do instead? Paint the town every shade of red as you do?"

"Works wonders for chasing away the goblins." His friend lifted a single, aristocratic brow. "Why the devil not?"

Why the devil not?

Tacitus had never been a gambler or cardplayer or womanizer or any other sort of rowdy. He had enjoyed the company of his parents and hadn't seen any need to gallivant about town getting into scrapes. He had been very, very happy.

Now he was not. Now the knot in his gut that had settled there upon their deaths had ascended to his chest and acquired a fiery patina. Now when the memory of Calista Chance's face hovered before his closed eyes—which it pretty much always did—he did not feel the twist of confusion and pleasure as he had in her company, but the stabbing pain of loss he recognized all too well; he had felt it when each of his parents had died.

He was grieving now. Again. This time over her.

It was ridiculous. She was a spoiled girl of little discretion who disrespected her parents enough to wish to run away from them. And she hadn't cared that he was falling in love with her. Nor had she fallen in love with him in return, which damned her twice over.

It hurt. A *hell* of a lot. A *hell* of a hell of a lot.

Because after weeks in her company he had thought she was more than that. He'd thought she was full of life and joy and affection. He'd thought she was clever and warm, and damnably alluring. And he'd thought perhaps that, despite their differences, she liked him.

Obviously he had been wrong.

He sipped the whiskey. It burned going down, momentarily masking the pain in his chest. The next sip burned less, but masked just as well. The third masked even better; it downright coated the pain.

"What say you, old friend?" Peyton's glass was nearly empty too. "Have a mind to paint the town with me before settling down to rickety old age here?"

Rickety old age at twenty-five? Tacitus looked around the library, his favorite room in the house. It held no comfort for him now. His chest ached fiercely.

He held out his glass to be refilled.

Peyton gave him a scoundrel's grin. "I thought you'd never ask."

They drank until dawn, at which point they called for their curricles and raced quite irresponsibly half the distance to London. Peyton won, but Tacitus vowed to beat him the next time.

He did indeed win the next time, and many times after that. Like the whiskey, racing dulled the pain. Peyton, who had lost two adored siblings some years earlier, assured him that he had not truly grieved until he'd done something very stupid, so why not keep on grieving and have some fun? Tacitus did not mention that he had in fact done something very stupid, which had only compounded the grief. But he went along with his friend's plan anyway.

When drunken carriage racing grew tiresome, Peyton took him to several disreputable hells and some very fine clubs too, and to any number of society fetes. At these venues they drank more and occasionally gamed, and Peyton flirted with every female he encountered, from common molls to the crusty old Duchess of Hammershire. He was a dashing fellow, scion of one of the finest, oldest families in Britain, and charming. The ladies loved him.

They seemed to like Tacitus too. It wasn't to be wondered at. He was a marquess and plump in the pockets. And Dare Castle wasn't anything to sniff at.

"Don't be an idiot, Tass. It's not only the trappings that attract them," Peyton said over tankards of ale at a pub they particularly liked. It reminded Tacitus of the taproom at the inn at the village of Dashbourne where he had treated the Chance siblings to lunch for a month. He had not mentioned that to Peyton of course, or even acknowledged it to himself except when he was very drunk and muttering unintelligibly into his cup. Like he was at present.

"M'not an idiot." He was slurring now. Best to head home soon. Too much ale spoiled ... well ... everything really.

"Clara," Peyton called to the barmaid. "Come over here. Now there's a good girl."

The barmaid planted her behind on Peyton's knee and gave his chest a vigorous rub with the palm of her hand.

"You be wantin' a bit o' Clara tonight, milord?"

Peyton smiled. "Actually I've got a question for you."

"It's a game you're playing, then?" She gave his chest another rub. "I like games."

"Look at my friend Dare here. What do you think of him?"

She gave Tacitus the sort of perusal he'd gotten a lot of since he'd been going about town with the Viscount Mallory.

"I think I could lick him like a spoon that's been in the pudding, milord," Clara said, and dragged her tongue across her lips as though to demonstrate.

Peyton chuckled. "If he didn't have a penny to his name, or a title, or those fine clothes and gold signet ring, would you still lick him like a spoon?"

"Every day of the week and twice on Sundays," Clara replied with a wink at Tacitus.

Tacitus stood. He bowed. "Thank you, Miss ... ?"

"Clara, sweetness. But if you've a mind to come on upstairs for a tumble, you can call me anything you like." She jumped off Peyton's lap and moved to Tacitus, her hand outstretched, presumably for the chest rub she intended to give him.

He backed away. "I appreciate the offer, Clara. But I've got to be going." His head reeled. His mouth was a cavern of hopelessness. And he had to walk off his erection before he got home and descended into dreams of a girl he should by now have entirely forgotten.

Peyton followed him to his feet. "All right, my lord," he drawled. "I've got your back."

As it turned out, Peyton was obliged to make good on that statement. Two blocks from the pub they encountered a lady of delicate years and her aged grandmother in the midst of cutpurses. Tacitus and Peyton beat the thieves to the ground. In the fray, Tacitus caught a knife's blade upon his jaw. But in the end they bested the blackguards entirely.

The next day everyone in town seemed to know about the scuffle. Nursing his wound at home with a glass of brandy and a book, Tacitus instructed his butler to turn away callers. When he finally left his library, he discovered a stack of calling cards in his foyer.

"It is remarkable, Claude," he said to his valet the next morning as the Frenchman carefully shaved around the wound, then applied salve to it. "I don't recall ever having gotten so much attention before this silly skirmish."

"The ladies, they will always flock to the men who display the acts of honor. And the violence," Claude said with a sage nod. "Eh, they adore the scars."

After the bandage came off, Tacitus attended a few balls, a handful of musical evenings, a picnic or two, and occasionally dined with friends at his club. Most often, though, he found himself at Westminster, where he appeared to pay close attention to the debates. But often, when some grizzled old lord in a wig was prosing on and on, he daydreamed. Of a girl. Months later already, and that damn girl was still in his head.

By the time the wound faded into a scar, mothers were practically throwing their daughters at him every time he walked out his front door. It was enough to drive a man to the countryside.

So he went. And saw to affairs on his estate. And visited his tenants. And planned some improvements with his land steward. And tried very hard to ignore the emptiness in his gut and chest as he walked through the house and saw the ghosts of his parents in every room, and imagined laughter rippling like a clear spring brook along the corridors.

Returning to town, he spent his days in the house he had purchased after his parents' death, which held no memories of them, and in Parliament. Reading, listening, staying out of the way of women in general. It was rumored, Claude eventually told him, that his recluse ways were due to a broken heart. The scar was apparently a memento of a duel he had fought for his ladylove, which he had lost to his opponent, and now he lived a lover's lament. Given that six months earlier everybody had known about the cutpurses, Tacitus thought this was positively inane.

"Ah, but the story of the lost love, it is *plus* moving!" Claude exclaimed in an unusual burst of feeling as he cut Tacitus's hair. "The heart, my lord, it requires more of the time than the flesh to heal."

Claude had been at Dashbourne with him. At that inn. Tacitus thought perhaps his valet did not offer this comment idly.

"Has there … Has there been any particular lady's name attached to this ridiculous rumor, Claude?"

"*Non*, my lord," he said curtly. "They say she was nobody. A commoner, pfft!" He gestured as though she was of no consequence. "Your heart was, *on dits*, smitten despite the vast difference in station."

He craned his neck to peer at his valet, who was obliged to swiftly draw away the cutting shears.

"To whom did I lose this battle for her?"

"*Un matelot*, my lord."

"A sailor?" He settled back in his chair again. "That is irrational."

Claude shook his head. "Ah, but my lord, the love, it

knows no reason."

No reason.

Tacitus thought of his father's adoration of a woman with rotted teeth who could barely walk. He thought of the present date, January 14, the anniversary of his father's death of a broken heart; of how it had been two years since his father had eagerly followed his mother into the hereafter. Two years now that he had been without family. Alone.

Then he thought of Calista Chance, and that perhaps he had been hasty in attempting to forget her. That, in fact, love knew no reason. That he should pay a call on the new Earl of Chance and inquire after his sister.

In the year since he had courted her, he had come to know the truth of her family's circumstances. The old Earl of Chance had been humiliated after a duke accused him publicly of cheating. Chance had sold everything unentailed to satisfy his debts, but it did not suffice. When society cut him, he had retreated to Dashbourne to drink heavily and torment his children. It wasn't to be wondered at that Lady Calista had wished to run away. Perhaps he should not have judged her so swiftly.

Now, however, the old earl was dead. If rumor were to be believed, his heir, the new Lord Chance was currently struggling to recover his family's fortune. He might welcome a generous offer for his sister's hand.

At breakfast, accompanied by these tentatively hopeful ponderings, Tacitus settled at his dining table with a cup of coffee to read the *Times*. Eyes passing desultorily over the society page, they arrested on one item: the announcement of the birth of a son to the Honorable Richard Holland and Lady Calista Holland, née Calista Chance.

The ache in Tacitus's chest threatened to suffocate him.

Setting down the journal, he made a promise to himself. Again. This time, however, he intended to keep it.

~o0o~

And that was how the wealthy, handsome, dashingly

scarred and occasionally political Marquess of Dare came to be one of the *ton*'s most confirmed bachelors.

Chapter One

Five Years Later

CALISTA HOLLAND NEVER WEPT, no matter how twisted her heart. So she did not weep now at the sight of her son's eyes, round and filled with tears as he stood before her in the inn's foyer.

"I want you to come with us, Mama," he whimpered. Whimpering was not permitted at home. But this was an extraordinary occasion, to be sure.

"You know that I cannot." She straightened his collar. "You will have a splendid visit with Aunt Evelina at Dashbourne. She will show you all the places we used to hide from Uncle Ian when he was in a teasing mood, and Grandmama will instruct Cook to bake your favorite biscuits." She forced back the prickles threatening her throat.

"Please come, Mama." Tears fell silently onto his hollow cheeks. Too hollow. Damn Richard for his miserliness. But at Dashbourne her mother and Evelina would see that her son ate well. In a month Harry would return to her as round and happy as a boy of five should be.

"Papa needs me at home just now." To sit by his bedside and endure his harangues as the gout throbbed in his feet. "Now, don't weep. Weeping is for foolish women and weak men, and you are neither of those, are you?"

"No, Mama." His chin wobbled. "I am a warrior."

She straightened his coat to have an excuse to continue touching him, her only light, her salvation these past five years.

"You are a mighty warrior," she said. "It will be a grand party at Dashbourne, won't it, Evelina?"

"Yes. We'll have a marvelous time, Harry." Her words sounded forced. Damn *her*. Harry was not an imbecile. He would know Evelina hated this parting too.

"Now, my heart," Calista said, "Run across the yard and make certain Mr. Jackson has moved your luggage onto Aunt Evelina's carriage. He's just in the stable, which looks warm and cozy in all of this rain. I know you must want to see the horses, and I have a word to say to your aunt before you depart."

"Yes, Mama." Sucking his lower lip between his teeth, he swiped the tears from his cheek with his sleeve, turned about, and went out the inn's front door.

As soon as he was gone, Calista rounded on her sister. "I am depending upon you, Evie."

"I know it." Evelina's eyes were clouded. "Of course I will keep Harry busy and happy while he's with us. But it is unconscionably horrid of Richard to forbid you to spend a measly month with your own family."

Calista dug into her cloak pocket and drew out a scrap of paper that she pressed into her younger sister's hand.

"Write to me at this address. You know that Richard is ... *particular* about the post. My housekeeper's sister is reliable."

"I don't understand why you must receive and send correspondence in this clandestine manner."

"When you have a husband and a household," Calista snapped, "I will welcome your opinion."

Evelina's lips became a line. She was twenty-two now, and since their father squandered the family's fortune, she had often said she never intended to marry, rather to pursue work instead. Calista used to laugh at that.

"You should leave now," she said to her sister. "The rain is falling harder. The water over that ford must be nine inches high already and you have at least two hours' ride to Dashbourne. And I'm sure Mama cannot wait another moment to finally see her precious statue."

"She is more excited to see her only grandson, of course," Evelina said and went past her toward the doorway. Behind them the taproom was busy with patrons taking shelter from the late-winter weather and the entire inn echoed with the drumming of rain on roof and windows.

Evie paused, looking out. "Good heavens, it has become a veritable deluge."

"Take this." Calista proffered her umbrella, using the opportunity to grasp her sister's hand tightly. It felt peculiar to touch another adult. It had been so long; even touching the edge of affection like this felt wrong, weak, like a prick hole in her armor. She snatched her hand away. "Send Harry back before you leave." She would kiss him and fill her senses with his sweet scent and hug him one last time before returning to Hell. But he would be well. He would be with her mother and sister, away from his father for a month—long enough for Calista to devise a solution for escaping from Richard forever.

"Of course, Callie." Evelina grabbed her hand again, squeezed it, then opened the front door.

In the middle of the inn yard, shrouded in sheets of rain, Harry stood as though paralyzed, eyes and mouth agape at the huge horse galloping straight for him.

"*Harry!*" Calista leaped forward. But she was too far away, the horse too close, Harry immobile, the rain driving down. Evelina screamed.

The horse shied, and reared, its hooves pawing the slanting rain above Harry's head.

Then its master was flying into the air, boots slamming to the ground, greatcoat swirling as he swept forward, fell to his knees and wrapped his arms around Harry, surrounding her son in safety. A shrill whistle pierced the downpour and the horse wheeled away.

Abruptly there was no movement in the yard except the rain pounding on the muddy ground.

Calista ran forward. Harry broke from the man's arms and flew straight into hers.

"Mama, did you see? Did you? It was amazing!" Words streamed from his mouth as he wrapped his skinny arms around her neck and she gripped his body to hers. "That man saved me from his horse! And then he made it turn away, with only a *whistle*."

"Yes." She pressed the word into his soaking hair, the raw terror of the moment subsiding and making her arms shake. "Yes, darling. What an adventure."

But he was pulling away already, turning to the rider. Calista rose to her feet, took hold of her son's hand, and lifted her eyes to the man.

In her life she had hated only one man as much as she had once hated her father and now her husband. Rather, almost as much: Tacitus Everard, the Marquess of Dare.

Now he stood before her, soaked by the sheets of rain that perfectly matched his beautifully intense gray eyes. Still as stone and severe of jaw and stance, he stared at her without speaking as water streamed off the brim of his hat and the cape of his coat. Even with rain washing across his features, he was as handsome as ever: tall and dark and broad-shouldered, with the sort of jaw a woman longed to stroke and lips that stole her reason. And as stiff as a steel rod.

"I beg your pardon," he said across the rain. "Is he all right?"

"Yes, sir!" Harry volunteered. "Grand horse you've got there, sir!"

"Yes, well, he's a goer." He looked at her. "Forgive me, madam. I was ... That is ..." He scowled.

A second horseman splashed into the yard and slowed instantly, drawing his mount to a halt and sliding out of the saddle. He tossed the reins to a stable boy holding the marquess's horse.

"Damn and blast, Dare," he exclaimed upon laughter. "I would've had you if it hadn't been for that coach blocking that last bend." He took them all in. "Good Lord, have you run someone over?"

Calista grasped her son's slippery hand. "Come now, Harry. We must dry you off before you depart." She drew him back into the inn as he craned his neck.

Evelina stood in the doorway. "It's *him*."

"Who?" Harry said.

Calista glared at her sister. "No one." Going to her sodden knees in the foyer she dusted raindrops from her son's coat, and removed his hat and shook it out.

"But, Mama—"

"Harry," she said firmly.

Her son's lips shut tight. "Yes, Mama."

Her heart twisted anew. Despite the Chance spirit he'd been born with, he had learned to be docile from necessity.

Ignoring every lesson about stalwart strength in the face of adversity that she had taught her son over the past five years, she wrapped her arms around him again and pressed her face into the crook of his shoulder.

"I will miss you, my darling," she whispered fiercely.

"I'll miss you too, Mama."

She drew away. "Now, listen to your aunt and Grandmama this month."

"And to Cook," he said.

"Yes, and to Cook, so she will bake your favorite biscuits and allow you to taste the bread as soon as it is out of the oven," she repeated the comforting words she had been telling him the entire journey to this tiny inn in this little village where Richard had instructed her to leave him in her sister's care. She looked into his sober face that had never resembled her husband's, rather featured the Chance black hair, blue eyes, and defiant chin. Harry would be better off at Dashbourne than at home, free to be a boy. It was she who would hate every day of this month apart. She stroked his cheek, then stood.

Lord Dare filled the inn doorway, his coat dripping, knees and boots muddy, and face inscrutable. A scar now cut across his jaw, lending an air of danger to his male beauty.

"My lord," she bit through tight lips.

His attention shifted to Harry at her hip.

"Do you *know* him, Mama?" her son whispered in the comically voluble whisper of the young.

She reached down and clasped his little fingers. "He is Lord Dare. Bow to him now, darling."

Harry cut a neat little bow, his eyes remaining wide.

"Why doesn't he come in out of the rain?" His whisper filled the foyer.

"Because he is a peculiar man," she said. "Peculiar men who are very wealthy do anything they want."

"Even stand in the rain?" Harry asked skeptically.

"You should see me when it snows," Lord Dare said, and stepped into the foyer. His voice was as deep and velvety as it had been years ago. Adorned with a caped greatcoat and tall crowned hat, his presence dominated the small space. Were he atop a mountain, Calista thought, he would still seem to command the peaks with his quiet authority and stormy eyes. How a man of so few words could radiate such strength, she hadn't understood six years ago. Her father had ranted and shouted to make everybody cower. But confidence rolled from the Marquess of Dare's shoulders and hard, scarred jaw. He needn't rant or shout. He knew he would not be questioned.

She tightened her fingers around her son's. "Come now, Harry. You and Aunt Evelina must be on your way."

"But Lord Dare is all wet, with no one to dry him off. Won't he take a sniffle, Mama?" Harry said, looking up at the marquess.

"I'm sure he would not allow a sniffle anywhere near him."

"I don't know about that." His companion pushed past him into the foyer. "I've even seen him sneeze on occasion. All the great men are doing it nowadays." He winked at Harry, whose eyes went wide.

"My lady," Lord Dare said, "May I present to you the Viscount Mallory, my traveling companion today," and added under his breath, "unfortunately."

Lord Mallory swept her an elegant bow. "Charmed, madam." He peered curiously over her shoulder.

"This is my sister," Calista said.

"Ma'am." He bowed deeply and grinned.

Evelina's eyes were sparks. "Were you racing on the road in this weather?"

"We were indeed," the viscount said. "Excellent sport. Sorry to have discombobulated the little fellow. You're all right now, my good man?"

Harry threw back his shoulders. "Right as rain," he said solidly.

"You might have overrun him," Evelina said.

"Oh, don't go overstating the thing." Lord Mallory leaned a shoulder against the wall and drew off his gloves. "Everybody's well now."

"Everybody is soaked to the bone, with two hours' carriage ride ahead of us before dusk." Evelina's lips pursed. "I am not impressed with your puerile indifference, my lord."

"Did you hear that, Tass?" the viscount drawled, giving Evelina an up-and-down perusal. "I believe the lady just accused me of immaturity."

"I wonder how she could have mistaken your character so entirely?" Lord Dare murmured. Calista's heart did an uncomfortable trip. He sounded exactly the same as he had six years ago: dry and wry and thoughtful and amused all at once.

"I am positively diverted," the viscount said, eyes slanted at her sister. "And what do *you* do for amusement? Catalogue molds and funguses?"

"Yes, in fact, among other flora."

"How utterly original," Lord Mallory said with thorough disinterest.

"I have no doubt that such a pastime seems tame to you, what with your preference for roguish disregard for others' welfare."

"She thinks I'm roguish and I've barely said twenty words to her," he murmured, eyes glinting. "Mission accomplished."

Lord Dare moved around him. "Shouldn't you be on your way, Mallory?"

"After I've had a pint." He passed them by to enter the taproom.

"Forgive me, Lady Evelina," Lord Dare said. "His bark is worse than his bite." With a glance at Calista, he bowed and followed his friend.

"Do not say a word," Calista whispered harshly. "Just go."

"I wasn't going to say anything, of course." Evelina took Harry's hand. "Come along, sweetpea. Let's see what treats Cook prepared for our snack on the road, shall we?"

Calista touched her fingertips to her son's head.

"Good-bye, Mama," he said with a smile now, his cheeks still pink from excitement. Lifting her hood, Evelina drew him into the rain.

From the doorway, as rain sprinkled her wet traveling gown Calista watched the chaise pull out of the inn yard and onto the rain-washed road and then, finally, out of sight, taking her heart with it.

She swallowed back tears yet again. But they bubbled up, threatening to overflow. *Not here.* Not where the poker-up-his-arse Marquess of Dare might come through that door at any moment. She hurried up the stairs to her bedchamber. Richard had not given her sufficient money to purchase more than a meager dinner, and nothing for tomorrow's long journey home. But her stomach was in knots anyway. Food would wait until breakfast.

Closing her bedchamber door, with damp fingers she began unfastening the buttons of her pelisse and her eyes alighted on a wooden crate at the foot of her bed.

Her mother's statue.

"No!" She darted to the window, but she knew it was already too late.

After retrieving the statue twenty miles south of her home that morning, she had told Jackson that he was to put it on the carriage to Dashbourne. Clearly he had failed in that task. She would have a sharp word with her husband's drunken coachman. But not until they returned home. Jackson had been especially surly lately. She didn't put it past him to drive her over every pothole in the country on their way home just to spite her.

She gripped the sill. Bringing the statue here from the auction had been her reason for making the journey, the excuse for taking Harry away from home. If she returned to Herald's

Court with it, Richard would be infuriated. And he would suspect her of subterfuge.

Staring out into the rain, she considered telling Jackson not to unharness the team now, and chasing after her family's carriage. Perhaps this was a sign: her opportunity to escape. *Finally.*

But Richard's threat glued her feet to the floor. If she ever complained to her family, he would send Harry off to live with his sister in York—his sister who liked to use the cane on servants and children as often as possible.

She would never complain. No one need know what her marriage truly was. And she had a plan: wrest Harry away from her husband by whatever means possible. If that meant returning to Herald's Court with the assurance to her husband that Harry needn't be a burden any longer, that he was remaining indefinitely with Evelina and her mother at Dashbourne, then so be it. That she might rarely see her son again was a misery she would endure for his sake.

With agitated fingers she pulled off her boots and sat on the bed beside the crate.

Her mother had written to her about this statue with such excitement. A private antiquities collector not far from Herald's Court had recently died, and all the art was auctioned off. But the collector's son knew that Lady Chance wanted that statue for the museum exhibit she hoped to mount in London someday, and he sold it to her via letter before the public auction. It was far too valuable to send by post, though. Calista had seized upon the opportunity to take Harry away: how wonderful, she had told Richard, that she could be courier for her mother, and then her mother and Evelina would entertain Harry for a month in return.

Hotly possessive of her attention, Richard perpetually imagined himself in competition with his own son. The arrangement had made good sense to him. Screaming from the prickling pain of his gout, and shouting at every tiny sound Harry made in the house, he had declared that his wife must go, but hurry home immediately. When she asked to be able to go all the way to Dashbourne to see her mother, he forbade her to take more than a single night away. He needed her. If she remained away any longer, she would pay.

She would pay.

The same threat he always leveled. The threat he always made good on. And so she had come as far from Herald's Court as she could in a single day, to this inn in this village a mere two hours away from the home she had returned to only once in six years: for her father's funeral.

She would find another way of transporting the statue to her mother. Until then, she would just have to hide it from Richard.

The crate was nailed shut, but the wood was soft enough so that with the side of her palm wedged under the edge she could shove the lid open. Inside, wood shavings made a bed for the statue wrapped in folds of felt. Brushing the shavings aside, she pried the bundle out and lifted it onto the bed. Approximately two feet long, it was astonishingly heavy and made a depression in the mattress.

Calista unfolded the felt. Almond-shaped eyes stared blankly up at her from a face of perfect classical proportions. Two thousand years old, the Aphrodite carved of alabaster was indeed a masterpiece. With cascading hair and a garment that caressed the goddess's curves as though it flowed from her very skin, she seemed almost alive. *Real.* Full of love and affection and desire and lust and all the joys that the Goddess of Love bestowed on mere mortals.

Foolishness.

Hauling the stone into her arms, Calista placed it on the dressing table, the single piece of furniture other than the bed in the room, beside a basin and pitcher of water for washing. What she had seen of this inn as yet seemed unexceptional. The stable and foyer were well kept, the rugs cozy and the bed linens clean. But the village of Swinly was so tiny and out of the way that its only inn was far from fashionable. Richard had counted on that, of course. A fashionable inn would have cost him more. Worse, she might accidentally encounter someone from the high society he had never taken her into since their wedding, and he could not allow that.

Yet she had anyway. She had encountered the one person she least wished to ever see again.

She looked about the plain room in which the gorgeous Goddess of Love was the only hint of luxury. An earl's daughter—an earl's *sister*—and she had come to this—this debased penury, this continual hidden shame, this pale, cold, hard woman with circles beneath her eyes and bruises on her body in places no one but she ever saw.

"You are a horrid liar," she said to the Aphrodite statue. Then, thinking of the man in the taproom downstairs, she said with pinched lips, "And a cruel tease."

Unbuttoning her gown, petticoat and stays, she used the water in the pitcher on the table to wash the worst of the mud from the skirts. Then she hung the damp clothing and stockings before the grate upon which the coals were already dying, doused the candle, and crawled beneath the coverlet.

Tomorrow she would return home to the man who two months earlier had begun to lay his hand not only on her, but also on her son.

"Tomorrow I will find a solution," she whispered to the rain beating on the window and roof of her little room. During the long, solitary ride home she would devise a plan that would free her son from Richard without bringing shame upon her mother, sister, brothers, or anybody else. Ian was only now beginning to wrest their family's name from the dirt their father had dragged it through. She would not follow her father's model. The Chance name and title would never be stained because of her. No one would ever know.

Pride was all she had left.

"Tomorrow," she said, and it felt like both a promise and a prayer.

Chapter Two

CALISTA JOLTED UP IN BED, the toll of an enormous bell crashing through her sleep. Clapping palms over her ears, she cast her eyes into the murkiness.

She was in her bedchamber in the inn. Her traveling case sat on the dressing table, the Aphrodite statue beside it, and rain pattered against the window as the bell's ring faded into silence.

Barely a moment of peace passed before it boomed a second time. It sounded like it was beside her ear. Climbing out of bed as the bell's third toll made the candleholder jitter on the dressing table, she darted across the chilly floor and peered out the window. Through the rain slashing over the rear yard of the inn, she saw a massive stone tower that even in the reluctant light of winter dawn was unmistakably a church. In the downpour last night she had not noticed it.

The tolls ceased at seven. Mumbling a curse, she stared longingly at the bed. Sleep was a luxury Calista Holland was never permitted, apparently not even in escape.

Except that at home, since Richard's gout had come on so severely four months earlier, she had been sleeping in the guest bedchamber. There her son often found her as dawn peeked through the draperies. Climbing under the blankets, he would cuddle his warm little body up to her and she would allow herself another thirty minutes of dozing until she had to leave him to see to his father's demands and the rest of the household.

She missed him already. How would she endure a month without his little hand firmly in hers, his arms around her neck as he hugged her, and his sincere eyes as he told her about his day spent following the maid on her rounds of the house when Calista could not be with him? She could barely endure a single night.

Dressing in clothes that had not dried entirely and were stiff with cold, she buttoned her pelisse up tightly over her growling belly while staring at the Aphrodite statue. Like a ghost, it was pale white in the light of the rainy dawn, its body as supply sinuous yet its eyes as lifeless as they were in candlelight.

Then she went in search of tea.

As she exited her room, a cat slinking along the corridor lifted its head and bounded toward her. Curling around her ankles, it meowed.

"Oh, go away, do. You will rub hair all over my hem." Gently toeing it aside with the tip of her boot, she went to the stairs.

As she descended, the innkeeper's wife bustled from the taproom toward a closed door off the foyer, her arms brimming with plates of eggs and bacon.

"Good day, milady!" She offered Calista a harried smile between bright red cheeks. "The inn's all filled up with the rain bringing people in off the road last night, and I've my hands full at present. But I'll be with you right quick. Will you be having tea or coffee?"

"Tea, please." Her head ached and her stomach was sick with hunger. "Does the church bell ring at seven o'clock *every* day of the week, not only Sundays?"

The round little woman bustled toward the closed door. "Oh, no, milady! On Sundays Old Mary doesn't ring till *eight* o'clock."

Calista turned toward the open taproom door, steeling herself. But *he* must have left already. Even if he had not, he certainly would not be eating in a common taproom; he was probably behind that closed door Mrs. Whittle had gone into, a private parlor, no doubt. Also, she was a grown woman now. Wherever the wretched Marquess of Dare was, nervous stomachs were for stupid young girls. Not for her. Not in years.

Not only had the Marquess of Dare not departed the inn, but he sat in the opposite corner of the taproom in a chair facing the door. Among the dozen other guests present—mostly tradesmen by the look of their clothing—his table alone had an empty place. News journal unfolded before him, coffee cup and empty plate at his elbow, he appeared perfectly at ease.

A marquess in a common taproom? Perhaps in dire straits, yes. But even then she would not have thought it possible of *this* marquess.

He lifted his gaze to her. Standing, he folded his paper and moved across the room toward her.

"Good day, madam. The table is yours."

"Won't Lord Mallory be breakfasting as well?"

He looked down at her with those stormy eyes and made a swift, open perusal of her features.

"He continued on to his destination last night. But if he were taking breakfast here now, I am certain he would be delighted to share the table with you. You've had a near miss. He never forsakes the opportunity to flirt outrageously with a beautiful woman." Almost—*almost*—amusement glimmered in the gray. He bowed. "I wish you a good journey."

"No one'll be making any journeys from here today," came a gruff voice at the door. A man with white whiskers and a crisp cap shook rain from his coat and wagged his head. "The ford's four feet high if it's an inch, and the north road's flooded out clear across the valley."

Calista pivoted to him. "The road is flooded?"

"'Fraid so, mum." He repeated the rueful shake of his head like a bad actor in a penny play. "Did the same after the storm of '09. Swinly might as well be an island today."

"What do you mean?" Lord Dare said. "This village is now encircled by water?"

Others were gathering behind him to hear the news. The innkeeper had come from the kitchen holding a pot of coffee in one hand, and a cup and saucer in the other.

"Like a sailing ship upon the ocean, sir," the man said. "Not only the village. Butcher's fields to the north and

Drover's field to the east as well. Hip deep, they are."

"Glory be!" the innkeeper exclaimed. "And Mr. Whittle still in Wallings. I told him he'd best return yesterday, but he'd hear nothing of it till he'd got that new milking cow he wanted. Stubborn man."

A serving maid came from behind the other door. Mrs. Whittle thrust the pot and cup into her hands.

"Here now, Molly, wipe that table over there and pour her ladyship a cup. Then fetch breakfast for her. My heavens! We're nearly run out of milk already and it's not even eight o'clock yet." She hurried back into the kitchen.

"Are you certain, sir?" Calista asked the whiskered man.

"Just come from Drover's place," he said with a frown.

"But how do you come to be an authority on the flooding?" Cold panic was licking at her. "Perhaps you are wrong."

His chest puffed out and his whiskers quivered. "I've been the constable of this village since '05, ma'am, so I think that gives me plenty of authority."

"Sir," Lord Dare said, commanding the attention of the constable and everyone else in the place with the single word. "I am D—" His gaze flicked to Calista. "I am Everard," he said. "You are soaked through and must be chilled to the bone. May I offer you a pint? Then you can tell me more about the flood at your leisure."

The constable gave him a short study. Extending his hand to shake, he nodded.

"Eustace Pritchard at your service, Mr. Everard. Glad to make your acquaintance." The onlookers were grumbling as they returned to their breakfasts, and he followed the marquess to the table. "Molly, bring over that coffee."

"I believe that pot is intended for Lady Holland," Lord Dare said smoothly. "Molly, if you'll bring another pot and cup for Mr. Pritchard, I would appreciate it."

"My lady." Now the constable bowed deeply. "Welcome to Swinly. I apologize for the rain that's delayed your travel. But there's Mother Nature for you, upsetting everybody's plans."

"I don't take coffee," she said. "I asked for tea. And you should know that this man is the Marquess of Dare."

His bushy brows popped up.

"My lord, it's an honor! What a stew we're in here. But the rain's already lightening up. If it ends this afternoon the ford should be clear by dawn. We'll have you out of here tomorrow, my lady."

"Is there really no way out of Swinly at present?" When she arrived home tomorrow night, a full day late, Richard would rage. "None at all?"

"Not unless you care to swim," the constable said with a wink at Lord Dare.

"Does anyone in the village have a boat?"

The constable chuckled. "Nothing more than the ferryman's raft, but that's on the other side of the river and it's far too high to use now, of course."

The marquess was looking at her, carefully it seemed. The constable was still chuckling. A pair of tradesmen were gawping at her openly and she feared that in her muddle after the bell shocked her awake she'd left something unbuttoned. Rain poured down steadily beyond the taproom windows and the church bell began pounding eight o'clock through the walls of the inn.

"There must be some way out of this village today," she insisted.

"Mum." Molly offered her a cup of coffee filled to the brim.

"I said tea, please. Twice."

"Beggin' your pardon, milady," Molly mumbled and backed away straight into a farmer rising from a table. Her arm jerked forward, the full cup leaped off its dish, and coffee splashed in a cascading arc all down the front of Calista's gown.

"Oh."

Molly gasped. "Oh, milady! I'm that sorry, I am! I'll fetch a rag right quick."

Calista batted at the drips on her only gown with her

palms. "Thank you. And perhaps while you are at it you could bring me some *tea*."

Molly hurried from the room past a woman entering.

"Lady Calista?" the woman exclaimed. "Lady Calista Chance?" She hurried forward. "It *is* you. Calista Chance—oh, but I'd heard you *married*, of course. Oh, what a delight to see you after all these years!" She had a round, ordinary face and yellow curls and wore on her head a glorious cascade of lace and chintz tied with a pristine white ribbon.

Calista dabbed at her skirt with a table linen. Coffee had soaked through the bodice and waist, but she could not attend to that yet. Her stomach twisted with hunger and she felt wretchedly faint.

"*Dear* Lady Calista, don't you remember *me*?" the yellow-haired woman said.

"I'm afraid I don't." It was hopeless. The gown was ruined, and probably the petticoat and her stays as well. And she only had these. She must wear them all day, wet and smelling like coffee.

Lord Dare and the constable had settled at a table with a handful of farmers and tradesmen and she heard words like "flood line" and "recede" and "downed bridge." She didn't bother listening. What did talking about it matter if she was trapped anyway? Her fate when she returned home would be the same tomorrow or any day after that.

"Where did that girl go?" she muttered and looked toward the door where Mrs. Whittle entered to set plates of food before other patrons. "Have you any soda, Mrs. Whittle? Or soap?" She was revealing that she must clean her own clothing. But after a full day in this tiny inn in this tiny village, everybody would know she traveled with no maid, only a drunken coachman. And that she could not pay for both breakfast and dinner, never mind lunch.

"Of course, my lady," Mrs. Whittle said with the same gamely harried smile. "I'll have Molly bring it up to your chamber."

"No." She'd had enough of Molly's help at present. "I'll

come for it myself."

"Dear, *dear* Lady Calista, you must remember *me*," the woman with the gorgeous hat insisted. "It's *Harriet*. Harriet Ryan! I'm married now, of course, as we *all* are, naturally. But you *must* remember."

Calista looked up from her stained gown. "Harriet Ryan."

"You *do* remember me. But I am Harriet Tinkerson now, of course. I *knew* you would remember. We sat beside each other in watercolors at the Bailey Academy for Young Ladies for two full years, after all."

"How nice for you." *School*. The exile her father had sent her into when she was fourteen, intending to make her a tasty prize for a wealthy man. A school of such low tuition that she had been surrounded by tradesmen's daughters and noblemen's illegitimate by-blows, ashamed and wishing she were back at Dashbourne, wishing she were already married, wishing she were *dead*—anything but this blot on her pride.

But her father's plan had worked. She had become a treat for a very wealthy man who paid generously for her, and then, as soon as the vows were said, hoarded his gold like Midas. And now she had one traveling gown, stained irreparably with coffee. When she returned home, she would dye it brown to match the stain and it would have several more years' good use.

"It *was* nice! Delightful, in fact," Harriet Ryan said at her shoulder. "Are you a guest here?"

"No, I am a chambermaid at this establishment, of course."

"Ha ha! You always were *wonderfully* diverting, Lady Calista. But of course you are a guest here. It is an inn!"

"I am just passing through," she mumbled and moved toward the doorway.

"And now with this flood you will be here until tomorrow." Harriet followed her. "How splendid! I have a shop now. A millinery shop. Isn't that *perfect*? You know I always did like hats better than painting or French or anything else those horrid spinsters made us study, didn't I? My shop is right in the middle of Swinly, on the high street, safe from the flood. I will adore giving you the *grand* tour of it today," she said with a horrid faux French accent. "Oh, *do* say you will come see my darling shop. I daresay it's as elegant as any shop in London you've ever seen."

Calista had seen precious few shops in London. During the three weeks her father had permitted them there six years ago, he had not allowed them to shop. They had barely afforded the servants and food, let alone clothing and other fripperies.

"I really don't see how I can, with my gown and what-have-you to see to." Calista smiled thinly. "Good day."

"But you *must*. I have a lovely little parlor in the next room. Come for tea. Oh, *do* say you will, dear Calista."

Tea. Free food. She might make it through this day without fainting from hunger after all.

"Thank you. Now I really should go see to this."

"Splendid!" Harriet Ryan clapped. "Until later."

Mrs. Whittle came from the kitchen with a tin and cloth. "Molly's all broken up about mussing your pretty gown, milady. I've told her she's to pay for it out of her wages."

"That won't be necessary," Calista said through tight teeth. "Is there a dress shop in this village?"

"Surely, milady."

"I will need a replacement from that shop for the day."

The innkeeper's smile faltered. "Molly will run straight over there with a message."

"When the dressmaker arrives, send her to my bedchamber."

"Of course, milady."

Snatching the tin of soda from the innkeeper, she hurried up the stairs, her stomach tight and empty, and alarm crawling all over her skin. Praying for the dressmaker to accept credit from a stranger, for a boat to materialize in the middle of farmer Drover's east field, and for her husband to disappear off the face of the Earth, she stripped to her shift and began scrubbing the stain from her clothes.

After the dressmaker brought her a clean gown to wear

temporarily, she would go to the stable and insist that Jackson find an exit from this village as soon as the rain ceased. Then she would return here and curl up in bed until it was time to go to tea at Harriet Ryan's shop. She wanted sleep. Here was her opportunity to steal some. And for a few precious hours she would try not to worry. If she managed for even a moment to forget what awaited her at Herald's Court tomorrow, it might be almost like a holiday.

Chapter Three

FROM THE TAPROOM where he had settled into a game of cards with several of the other guests, Tacitus saw when Lady Holland returned from tea with the milliner. He had been watching for her. Some habits, he supposed, died hard. Or never died. Or were thoroughly imprudent from birth to death.

Peeling off her gloves and cloak, she handed them to the innkeeper's wife and spoke to the woman closely. Mrs. Whittle nodded, her face a flush of obsequious good cheer and anxiety.

Over the course of the morning, the rain had tapered off. Now the clouds were tentatively parting, and pale winter sunshine cast the noblewoman's features in silhouette. Without the light full on her face, she looked just like the girl he had known six years earlier.

Quite obviously, she was no longer that girl. The smudged crescents beneath her eyes and the pinched V between her brows had not been there before. And yet a spark of defiance still lit her eyes. Indeed, the little he had seen of her now confused him. All fierce tenderness with her son the previous night, she had been prickly with Pritchard and the serving girl this morning. Given his own mother, he might expect tenderness from any woman toward her small child. But knowing Peyton's mother well enough, he realized this was not universally true.

He folded his cards. "Gentlemen, you have nearly emptied my pockets. I am afraid I must bow out now. Thank you for the game."

The accountant's clerk grinned. "Thank you, my lord. It was a pleasure relieving you of your gold."

"I'll wager it was, you blackguard," he said, and went from

the taproom into the foyer.

Lady Holland glanced at him, then turned back to the innkeeper. "As swiftly as you are able, please, Mrs. Whittle."

"Yes, milady." The innkeeper cast him an apologetic glance. "Milord, I'm terribly sorry, but the milk's all gone."

"Milk is highly overrated anyway," he said, smiling. "But that boiled beef at lunch was delectable. I must have that receipt for my cook, if you will share it."

Pride shone in her round cheeks. "You are a tease, aren't you, milord?"

"Absolutely not. If you refuse to furnish me with the receipt, I will go into that kitchen and find it myself this very minute."

Mrs. Whittle chortled. "Oh, I won't be having that! Dear me, milord, you've gone and cheered my day right up. And what a day it's been."

"But finally it looks as though the sun wants to shine. How was the state of the high street, Lady Holland?"

"Six inches deep in mud, even on the verge."

"How uncomfortable. But the constable assures me that if the deluge does not renew itself unexpectedly, the ford will be crossable by morning. Mr. Whittle will return before you know it," he said to Mrs. Whittle, "with the cow, one is assured."

"I do hope so, milord," the innkeeper said.

"If you will, Mrs. Whittle …" Lady Holland said, her hands clenched at her waist.

"Oh, yes! Right away, mum." Mrs. Whittle bobbed another curtsy and hurried off.

"I am just now venturing out for the first time today to study the situation," he said, trying very hard not to peer too closely at her. The sensation he was experiencing now was utterly disconcerting: as though he had been in a dark closet for months and was seeing the sunshine for the first time, or like a man with blocked-up lungs abruptly able to breathe again. Looking at her—at her pert nose, clear eyes, perfect teeth, and lips that were still damnably kissable—was a dramatic shock. He had forgotten how thoroughly her slightest smile had knocked him over.

But she was not smiling now. He had not seen her smile yet, in fact.

He wanted to. Quite a lot.

"Given the clouds and sun at once," he heard himself saying, "I daresay there is a rainbow out there somewhere that needs admiring. I am all prepared to gape and coo. Would you care to join me?"

"I've just said the street is six inches deep in mud. And a herd of sheep are wandering about with apparently no one to shepherd them." The V deepened between her eyes that were now crackling clear blue sparks. "Therefore, no, my lord. I do not care to traipse about this little village searching for rainbows. Most especially not with you."

He sucked in air. "Well, that's a clear enough rejection, I suppose. It seems that six years has done nothing to improve your manners." He took his coat off the peg by the door. "Good day, madam."

He left, striking out in the direction of the ford where he could assess the depth of water and determine if it were deep enough cast himself in, like the blasted fool that he was. Six years, and she had apparently not changed.

Most unfortunately, neither had he.

~o0o~

Calista grabbed up the mud-caked hem of her borrowed gown and swallowed over the burning in her throat as she hurried to her bedchamber, tracks from her boots following her all the way up. The promise she made to the dressmaker, that she would not stain or dirty the gown, had gone down the river the moment she'd stepped onto the street. But she had been too hungry to care about the consequences when she forged on to Harriet Tinkerson's shop. There, the horrid woman shoved bonnet after bonnet in her face and then served her a single cup of tea and two biscuits.

She had *tried* to appreciate the day's unexpected reprieve

from Richard, to allow herself a few hours free of the fear and worry that were her constant companions. Now she owed the dressmaker the price of a gown and petticoat, her stomach ached, and she was weak with dizziness and twisted with frustration.

As soon as Mrs. Whittle brought dinner to her room, however, she would revive, with the added benefit that she would not be obliged to sit in the taproom with the Marquess of Dare for the duration of an entire meal. Of all the discomforts of this day, *that* she could not endure.

Just as six years ago, when he looked at her with those beautifully intense eyes, she felt entirely lacking.

From across the bedchamber, the Aphrodite statue stared at her as though it agreed with the marquess's assessment of her.

Then it smiled.

It *smiled.*

A playful curve of sensuous alabaster lips.

And for a moment, as though a candle flickered beneath its surface, it glowed. Golden, fluid light stole from the stone and seemed to set the goddess's skirts to swirling with glittering warmth as the scent of freshly baked cakes teased Calista's nostrils.

Then, in an instant, the figure was again only a hard, white sculpture, and all Calista smelled was rain.

"Wh—" She blinked. *"No."*

She shook her head and blinked again. The statue remained merely a statue.

"I need food. That is all. Food and rest." She moved toward the dressing table. "And *you*." She grabbed up the statue, shoved it into the box, and covered it with wood shavings. Plunking the lid atop it, she pressed the nails back into their holes. "Take that, you wretched witch. That will teach you to tease a naïve, eighteen-year-old girl."

Tearing off the borrowed gown, stained petticoat, and her encrusted boots and stockings, she fell onto the bed and wrapped herself in the blanket. After she ate, she would scrub the gown and boots clean of mud, sleep through the remainder of this day, and tomorrow she would depart as soon as the sun rose. Then, back at home, she would devise a plan for wresting her son from her husband forever.

Chapter Four

THE BELL'S HORRENDOUS TOLL jarred Calista awake, crashing through her head like a mallet. She bolted upright.

She could not possibly have slept past seven o'clock. She hadn't done so in years. But she must have. According to the innkeeper, the church bell did not ring until eight o'clock on Sundays.

Yesterday she had told Jackson she would be ready to leave by half past seven. Today he should have inquired after her when she did not come to the stable. But yesterday he had been thoroughly intoxicated. He was probably drunk again. Rather, drunk still.

Superb. She could not drive anything larger than a gig. But she could not wait for Jackson to sober up to set out for Herald's Court. She would have to let him drive, and pray that they arrived home intact.

She rubbed her hands over her cold arms. Her bedchamber was frigid and nearly dark.

Sliding her feet to the chill wooden floor as the bell's ring continued to throb through the walls, she brushed aside the curtain over the window. From the dim gray dawn above, sheets of rain rushed past the glass.

No. *No.* This could *not* be. More rain meant the ford would not be crossable. But she simply could not spend another day in this village. Richard would wonder where she was. He would send to Dashbourne. Worse yet, he would go there himself via the direct route, despite his gout. He was obsessed enough with controlling her to do it. And when he arrived there to find her missing, her son would bear the brunt of his anger.

She *must* find a way to leave Swinly today, even it meant swimming across the swollen river.

Blowing on her hands to warm them, she went to her clothing hanging from the bedpost, and paused.

The Aphrodite statue sat atop the dressing table.

"I put you away last night." *Hadn't she?* Perhaps she had been so weary and hungry she only imagined packing it away, just as she had imagined it glowing and smiling.

Drawing her stays and petticoat off the bedpost, she felt their cold dampness. They should have dried by now. But the coal Molly had laid on the grate when she took the dinner tray away had probably burned out early. It had seemed like plenty of coal at the time. Perhaps the shadows and her worry had confused her. She did not remember Molly taking the dressmaker's garments away, either. But she must have. Undoubtedly the girl wished to make up for dousing her with coffee.

She buttoned up her gown and pelisse, glad at least that the scrubbing had removed all hint of stain from the fabric.

Glancing once more at the statue, she left the room. The cat was slinking up the stairs toward her. Its ears went straight up and it came at her ankles just as it had the day before.

"I told you, do not *touch* me. I don't like cats." She hurried past its curling tail.

A murmur of many people in conversation came from the taproom. It was Sunday. Perhaps all the other guests had overslept too.

The door off the foyer opened and she caught a glimpse of a neatly furnished parlor as Mrs. Whittle came from it, her hands loaded with a tray of plates.

"Good day, milady!" She smiled in her usual harried fashion. "The inn's all filled up with the rain bringing people in off the road last night, and I've my hands full at present. But I'll be with you right quick. Will you be having tea or coffee?"

Calista frowned. "Tea and eggs, just as I requested of Molly last night."

"Did you? That girl is as flighty as she is clumsy. I'll see to it."

"Mrs. Whittle." She lowered her voice. "Has Lord Dare departed yet?"

"Not at all, milady! His lordship told me as you're acquainted, he's glad to share a table with you, bless his heart." She hurried into the kitchen.

Calista set her shoulders back and went to the taproom door. Tradesmen again crowded the little room, and the Marquess of Dare again sat at the corner table, reading his journal. He looked up at her approach, unfolded himself from the chair with swift grace, and tucked the journal beneath his arm.

"Good day, madam. The table is yours."

"But you haven't finished your coffee."

He drew out a chair for her. "I have had enough," he said and glanced at her, then seemed to study her face.

"Say what you like," she said. "After yesterday I am certain you wish to."

"I was only thinking it's a shame that Mallory continued on to his destination last night. If he were taking breakfast here now, I am certain he would be delighted to share the table with you. You've had a near miss. He never forsakes the opportunity to flirt outrageously with a beautiful woman." He offered her a shallow bow. "I wish you a good journey."

"I ... Thank you." Calista blinked. *A beautiful woman.* He had called her that yesterday, too. How on earth hadn't she noted it then? Perhaps because her empty stomach had been full of nerves over seeing him. "I thought Lord Mallory went ahead the night before last. Didn't he, after all?"

"He left last night," he said with a slight frown and a tilt of his head, "shortly after we rode in and I nearly ran over your son, actually." His face had sobered. "Mallory has pressing business elsewhere and could not delay his journey any longer."

"No one'll be making any journeys from here today."

Calista pivoted with everybody else to the constable standing in the doorway. He looked about the room with the air of a man full of news. "The ford's four feet high if it's an inch, and the north road's flooded out clear across the valley."

"Again?" she said.

"'Fraid so, mum." He shook his grizzled head. "But I don't know how a young lady like you would be knowing it flooded up the same after the storm of '09. Swinly turned into an island that day too."

"What do you mean?" the marquess said behind her. "This village is now encircled by water?"

"Like a sailing ship upon the ocean, sir," the constable said. "Not only the village. Butcher's fields to the north and Drover's field to the east as well. Hip deep, they are."

"Glory be!" Mrs. Whittle stood in the doorway, laden with coffeepot, cup and saucer. "And Mr. Whittle still in Wallings. I told him he'd best return yesterday, but he'd hear nothing of it till he'd got that new milking cow he wanted. Stubborn man."

Molly appeared beside Mrs. Whittle and accepted the pot and cup thrust at her.

"Here now, Molly, wipe that table over there and pour her ladyship a cup. Then fetch breakfast for her. My heavens! We're nearly run out of milk already and it's not even eight o'clock yet." With a bustle of skirts, she went out.

Eight o'clock?

"But the rain was supposed to halt last night." Calista went toward Mr. Pritchard. "It did halt yesterday afternoon. The sky was clear when I retired."

"I don't know about that, mum. I've just come from Drover's place, and that field is filled halfway up the wall, so it must've been raining straight through the night."

"But I thought it was supposed to have ceased. Have you actually seen the ford this morning to compare it to yesterday's flood?"

"Yesterday's?" He frowned. "Now miss, I've been the constable of this village since '05, and I've only seen that ford up this high that once in '09."

"Sir," Lord Dare said. "I am D—" He glanced at her, just as he had the day before, then swiftly away. "I am Everard.

You are soaked through and must be chilled to the bone. May I offer you a pint? Then you can tell me more about the flood at your leisure."

The constable bowed. "Eustace Pritchard at your service, Mr. Everard. Glad to make your acquaintance. Molly, bring over that coffee."

"I believe that pot is intended for Lady Holland," the marquess said. "Molly, if you'll bring another pot and cup for Mr. Pritchard, I would appreciate it."

"My lady." Mr. Pritchard ducked his big frame into a bow.

Every hair on the back of Calista's neck was standing on end.

"Mr. Pritchard," she said, "you are saying that the ford is impassable today, again, and the river beyond the fields has flooded all exits to the village?"

The constable squinted at her. "Yes, ma'am."

"Still?" she pressed through her lips. "Flooded. Everything."

"Yes, ma'am." He glanced at the marquess, then back at her. "But the rain's already lightening up. If it ends this afternoon the ford should be clear by dawn. We'll have you out of here tomorrow, my lady."

"Lady Holland," Lord Dare said, coming to her side, his brow creased. "Would you care to take a seat?"

"I … Yes." She lowered herself into a chair.

"Molly, that coffee, if you will?" Tacitus called across the room.

"I take tea," the lady mumbled. Her eyes were peculiarly round and unblinking. She peered around the room as though she did not quite recognize where she was.

"Rather, tea for Lady Holland, Molly."

"Yes, milord."

"Lord?" the constable said.

"He is the Marquess of Dare," Lady Holland said in an odd voice.

"It's an honor, my lord! What a stew we're in here." Pritchard settled at the table across from her and shook his head. "A shame we've nothing more than the ferryman's raft, but that's on the other side of the river and it's far too high to use now, of course."

"You said that yesterday," the lady said, staring at Pritchard.

"I don't know if I did, ma'am." He chuckled with good nature. "There wasn't any flood until this morning, after all, now was there?" He smiled at her as though she were a simple girl. Tacitus could have told him that assumption was a load of grapeshot. He had learned that the hard way.

"Milady," Molly said, just as Lady Holland sprang up from her chair, knocking Molly's hand clutching a cup. Coffee sprayed everywhere—on his coat, the constable's moustaches, the maid's apron, but mostly down the front of the lady's gown.

"*Oh.*"

Molly gasped. "Oh, milady! I'm that sorry, I am! I'll fetch a rag right quick."

She stared at the maid. "You really are as clumsy as Mrs. Whittle said."

"Now there," Tacitus said as the maid hurried away. "It was an accident. She didn't mean to spill it."

She blinked at him. "You did not say that yesterday. You didn't say anything about the coffee spilling yesterday, though I'm certain you must have seen it happen. So I must be dreaming, inventing your concern about me to soften the distress of meeting you here. That's it. I am dreaming." She looked about the taproom. "Where has Molly gone? I need her. Or Mrs. Whittle. Is there no other woman in this inn at present?" She frowned and looked at him again. "It will have to be you. How Evie will laugh at me when I write to her about this. Pinch me, my lord."

"I beg your pardon?"

"Pinch me." She held out her arm. "Go ahead. I must wake up and this does seem the most fitting end to the dream, not to mention my awful tenure in this village."

"My lady, I'm afraid that I—"

"Oh, *please.*" She rolled her eyes. "Even in my *dreams* you won't touch me? Aphrodite, you are a horse's ass of the highest order!" she shouted to the ceiling, abruptly silencing every soul in the room. She grabbed his hand and smacked it to her arm. "*Pinch me,* my lord. If you don't, I shall ask this farmer beside me to do it instead. As he is already blushing to his red roots, it might cause him an apoplexy."

He pulled his hand out from beneath hers. "You are the oddest woman. I will not pinch you."

"The blushing farmer it must be, then." She turned away from him. "Sir, would you be so kind as to— Oh!" She smacked her hand over her hip and pivoted back around. Her lovely face was suffused with surprise.

"Well." Tacitus allowed himself a slight smile. "You did not specify where I was to pinch."

"Y-You— You—" she stuttered. Then her lips closed and she blinked. Then she blinked again. "I did not wake up."

"I beg your pardon?"

"I did not wake up. I am still dreaming. You pinched me and I felt it, but only in the dream. I am still asleep."

"On the contrary. You are awake and I did actually just pinch you. But if you've been dreaming of me doing so, then perhaps we should have this conversation in a more private location." Two could play at the game of teasing. That was one thing he *had* learned in six years.

But she did not respond like he expected her to.

"Excuse me, if you will," she said blankly. "I should return to bed so I can wake up." She went toward the doorway and nearly collided with a woman coming through it.

"Lady *Calista?* Lady Calista Chance? It *is* you. Calista Chance—oh, but I'd heard you *married,* of course. Oh, what a delight to see you after all these years!"

Tacitus swallowed over the anvil lodged in his throat. For a brief moment he had entirely forgotten she was *married.* And a *lady.* And entirely *unpinchable.* She had demanded that he pinch her and he'd done it, just as all those years ago he had driven her siblings around the countryside for a month, gave Lady

Evelina all of the books he'd had and ordered more from the shop ten miles away, and lent his saddle horse to a boy of fifteen. All simply because she wished it. For God's sake, he didn't even pinch barmaids. And in the middle of a taproom, no less. What in the hell was he thinking?

Nothing. In the presence of Calista Chance, his brain had always gone to porridge.

"Dear Lady Calista, don't you remember *me*?" the woman was saying.

"Harriet Ryan?" Lady Holland mumbled.

"Yes!" She clapped her hands covered in brilliant yellow gloves. "I'm married now, of course, as we *all* are, naturally. I am Harriet Tinkerson now. I *knew* you would remember. We sat beside each other in watercolors at the Bailey Academy for Young Ladies for two full years, after all."

"Do excuse me, Mrs. Tinkerson," she said, and pushed past the woman.

Tacitus crossed the room. No matter how strangely she was behaving, he owed her an apology. Mallory had been a wretched influence on him, obviously. His own mother must be rolling in her grave at present.

"With this flood you will be here until tomorrow. How splendid!" Mrs. Tinkerson hurried after her. "I have a millinery shop now. Do say you will come see it. I daresay it's as elegant as any shop in London you've ever seen," she said to Lady Holland's back as she went up the stairs.

"Yes, of course," she murmured without turning around, and disappeared on the upper landing.

"Lady Holland is a bit under the weather now," Tacitus said to the milliner. "If you will excuse her." He took the stairs two at a time.

She was standing before her door, a cat curling around her ankles.

"I don't care for cats," she said to it in a weak voice. "I have told you that twice already. Two days in a row. Now go *away*."

His footsteps sounded on the top riser and she turned her

head as the cat slunk away.

"Lady Holland," he said as he went forward, his cravat far too tight. "I beg your pardon for insulting you. I don't know what came over me." *Her*. She had come over him. As she had six years ago. But this time *she was married*.

"Insulting me?"

"Pinching you," he clarified, somewhat strangled.

"I asked you to." She shook her head. "Do you know, I am not entirely sure this is a dream after all. If it were, I'm certain I would not have you apologizing for pinching my behind when it was quite a lot more like a caress, now, wasn't it?"

His mouth, dry as an old bone, opened and nothing came out.

Her perfect teeth showed between her parted lips and her breasts rose upon a quick breath.

"I am dreaming," she said a bit raspily. "I am sleeping and merely dreaming now." She was staring at his mouth.

Quite abruptly he could not think.

"I have heard of this before," he managed to mutter. "Sleepwalking, I believe the men of science call it. Good God, what do they say to do with a sleepwalker?"

"Never try to wake a sleepwalking person," she said. "You must gently encourage him to return to bed, then he typically falls into deeper sleep quite readily. I read about it once."

"All right. Excellent advice." He moved toward her as footsteps sounded on the stairs. "Why don't you open that door and I will make certain you tuck yourself in nicely." The air was surely lighter upstairs than down. He felt downright dizzy. Good God, he had never in his life wanted to put a married woman to bed. Any bed. Anywhere. Any married woman.

Until this moment.

"Milord," Mrs. Whittle said behind him. "I saw that her ladyship is feeling poorly," she bustled toward him. "How may I help?"

"Do wait a moment, Mrs. Whittle," Lady Holland said and

took a single step that brought her right before him. She looked into his eyes. "I am most certainly dreaming. There can be no two ways about it. And while I would never commit actual adultery, no matter how evil Richard is, I don't think that doing this in a dream really qualifies as infidelity. I think. I hope. I don't know. It's just that for six years I have wanted to ... I ..." She took a mighty breath. And then she went onto her toes and pressed her lips to his.

It was over as soon as it began. She jolted backward, butted her shoulder into the door, fumbled for the handle, then opened it and slipped inside. Tacitus heard the lock turn.

"Goodness me," Mrs. Whittle said.

Tacitus swallowed. Then again. Tried to breathe. Found it a futile effort. And then tried to breathe out, to expel entirely from his senses the honey scent of her skin and the soft warmth of her lips and everything that *he* had been dreaming about for six years. But it was impossible.

"Yes," he said. "Yes."

Chapter Five

CALISTA REMOVED HER STAINED GOWN and climbed into bed, bemused and muddled from hunger.

She should not have kissed him. Even in a dream.

If she were dreaming.

She must be dreaming. But perhaps she had dreamed *yesterday.*

How on earth would she have dreamed yesterday almost exactly like today before she had actually lived through today?

Pulling the pillow over her head, she willed herself out of the dream.

The church bell started tolling. She counted. It ceased at eight. If Mrs. Whittle were to be believed about the bell's regular habits, it was not yet Sunday, but still Saturday. *Again.*

This could not be happening. Unless it was some sort of hypnosis. She had heard of stranger things. Evelina had written to her recently that their mother tried to take her to a *séance* in London, presumably to ring a peal over their father's ghostly head. But a person must agree to be hypnotized for that, or some such thing, she thought.

Perhaps if she simply went through this day calmly, it would all end and tomorrow she would be on her way. She could not return to the taproom, though. Not now that she had kissed him. Not even under hypnosis or in a dream was she prepared to see him again after that.

That.

His lips—soft and firm at once. His scent—warm and real and intoxicating, his scent that all those years ago had made her positively silly every time he had come close to her. If she had managed to convince him to spirit her away from Dashbourne, she might have already been enjoying that intoxication for six years. Instead, beneath his disapproving regard in the doorway of the inn that day, her resolve had crumbled and she let him take her home.

It was for the best, of course. If she had convinced him, she would not now have Harry, and that was not imaginable.

"Of course, Harry's mother is now a madwoman," she mumbled to the Aphrodite statue.

It did not reply. But something … something was different about the statue's face today.

The eyes.

Slowly Calista approached it, studying the beautiful face and sinuous body that had been carved from a single block of flawless alabaster. Up close, nothing was out of the ordinary. The limbs and gown still seemed to undulate with sensual delight even as the stone remained perfectly immobile, and the eyes were still as empty as Calista's stomach.

"You are not glowing. You are not smiling. You are not glittering and I do not smell cakes."

Hauling it up from the dressing table, she threw it into the box, packed the stuffing around it, clamped the lid down, and pushed it all the way under the bed with a loud scraping of the crate against the floor. This time if someone moved it while she was asleep at night, she would hear it.

Pulling an old magazine out of her traveling bag, she sat down for a long day of hiding from everyone until this strange hypnosis had passed.

Two hours later, as Old Mary was tolling the ten o'clock hour, a knock came at the door. The dressmaker stood in the opening, her compact frame draped in the same gorgeous walking gown and pelisse that she had worn to call upon Calista here yesterday.

"Good day, my lady. I am Mrs. Cooke," she said in the smooth, cultured tones of a lady of birth. She was no more than four or five years Calista's senior, with large hazel eyes and dark hair pulled back in a chignon. "Mrs. Whittle sent Molly to me with the request that I call upon you immediately this morning." She folded her hands before her and perused

Calista's stained frock. "What a shame," she said. "That is a very serviceable fabric, but it will have to be dyed entirely brown now if you wish to use it again. In the meantime, I will be happy to loan you a gown today."

They were *the exact words* Mrs. Cooke had said to her yesterday.

Untying her tongue, Calista admitted her. She would play this mystical game, go along with the hypnosis or dream or whatever it was, and do everything she had done yesterday. And tomorrow when she woke up, she would set her mind again to devising a plan for wresting both her and Harry from her husband's home.

For there was only one explanation to this repeated day: the misery of life with her husband had addled her brain so dreadfully that she was going insane. The sooner she permanently freed herself and Harry from that life, the better.

~o0o~

Old Mary's dawn alert tore through the little bedchamber and Calista's head, waking her to the gray of early morning.

Blinking her eyes open wide, she counted the tolls. The seventh faded into silence. No eighth ring came. Mrs. Whittle had certainly gotten that little detail of life in Swinly wrong.

Pushing the covers away, she set her feet on the cold floor. Then she saw it.

Across the room, atop the dressing table, the Goddess of Love's pale white face stared at her with blank eyes as the drumming of rainfall outside filled Calista's ears.

Chapter Six

LADY HOLLAND LEFT THE INN without speaking to or looking at anyone, and without opening an umbrella or donning a bonnet against the rain. Eyes blank, she looked like she had seen a ghost.

Tacitus had seen a sleepwalking person once with eyes like that, fixed in some invisible place that was part of the dream. Given the flooding, if she were sleepwalking someone needed to watch her to ensure that she did not accidentally drown herself. When through the window he saw her turn toward the high street, he abandoned his coffee, grabbed his greatcoat and hat, and went after her.

He remained at a distance. If a woman wanted to walk around in the rain, he didn't have any business spying on her. *Or getting caught spying on her.*

She walked all the way to the ford without once breaking stride or turning her head. Her cloak, sodden and dragging in the mud, clung to her arms and hips, defining her curves decadently. Motherhood had only improved her figure, giving a pleasing roundness to her slender shape.

Slowing his steps as she approached the ford, he watched her halt before the roiling water, and held himself in check from going forward. If in a sleeping daze she waded in, he was close enough to run and grab her from it.

Still, he felt like a voyeur watching her now. It was true, of course, that he had never really been able to help himself from watching Calista Chance. He had followed her even then, six years ago, from party to party in London, from London to her family's estate, and then around the countryside for an entire month, driving her and her siblings about, walking through woods and ruins and every village within miles, as the Earl of Chance's offspring sought amusement away from their house.

Just as then, he was captivated now. Calista Chance could be soaked in rain, with mud up to her ankles, shadows beneath her eyes, and lines creasing her brow, and he would still be captivated. Even a sharp word on her tongue like the night before when she had called him peculiar could not quell his interest. It was his sorry fate, he supposed, to find her more compelling than any other woman he had ever met.

Abruptly she pivoted away from the ford and her eyes came to him. As he was the only thing in the road, it wasn't to be wondered at. She moved toward him, and he met her in the rain.

"Good day, my lady," he said with perfect inanity.

Upon a gust of wind, the rain canted to the side, slanting down between them.

"I realize it was a mistake to kiss you like that," she said. "But you needn't worry. I won't do it again."

Rain dripped off the tip of his nose. "I beg your pardon?"

"How often do you say that? 'I beg your pardon?' Or do you say it only to me?"

"I beg—" He coughed. "That is, may I escort you back to the inn? I don't believe you have taken breakfast yet, and you must wish to change out of those wet clothes."

"I haven't any other clothes with me. There, I have said it. I have no other clothing and no money. I cannot afford both breakfast and dinner today, my lord."

Something in his stomach tightened. No *money*? The sister of an earl?

"Allow me to treat you to breakfast. But not until you have changed out of those wet garments, I think." He offered his arm, both hoping and dreading that she would accept it and after six years of drought he would again drink of the madness of her touch.

Her lovely brow furrowed and her crystal blue eyes seemed to glitter behind the curtain of rain.

"You don't remember that I kissed you, do you?"

Tacitus was fairly certain that if this woman had ever kissed him, he would not only remember it, he would very possibly have swooned and immediately thereafter written an epic poem about it.

He lowered his arm.

"I do not, in fact," he said. "But I see that in one manner you have not changed in six years. You still like to tease a man, don't you?"

"I am not teasing," she said without a smile, the shine in her eyes now brittle. "Yesterday, I kissed you. Very swiftly, of course. I thought I was dreaming, but even so I should not have. Yet you don't remember it. Do you remember Molly spilling coffee on my gown?"

"The gown that you wear now? Your only gown?"

"Yes." She parted her cloak further and spread her skirts with both hands. "Just here, on the skirt and all across the bodice."

"Perhaps the rain has obscured the stain," he said and dragged his eyes up from where her fingers were splayed across her breasts that were the ideal size to fit into a man's hands.

"There is no stain today," she said. "It hasn't happened yet. Not this today, yet." She blinked swiftly, repeatedly. "I think I would like that breakfast now, if you are still offering it. I feel remarkably light-headed."

"Of course." He extended his arm.

"No. No, thank you. I don't think I should touch you," she said, and started back up the road.

He came astride of her. "Had you plans to travel farther today, that this flood has ruined?"

"I was to go home." She flicked a swift glance at him. "You did not ask me about my travel plans yesterday," she said. "You gave me your table and were ready to ignore me. In fact, the day before that, you did ignore me, until later, and the rainbow."

"The rainbow?"

She halted in the middle of the road. "Why are you here now, away from the taproom?"

"I saw you leave the Jolly Cockerel looking … odd. I was concerned." More so now. This babbling did not bode well. Perhaps she was not in her right mind. But the night before she had seemed perfectly sane with her son and Lady Evelina.

"You were concerned? About *me*? I insulted you last night in front of the others, and yet today you followed me out here in the rain because you were concerned?"

"Yes."

"All right." She nodded, but her eyes looked even more distracted. She headed toward the inn anew. Just as they reached it, the infernally loud church bell began tolling the hour. A woman in a hat suited to Ascot twirled about in the foyer and her eyes popped wide.

"Lady *Calista?* Lady Calista Chance? It *is* you. Calista Chance—oh, but I'd heard you *married,* of course. Oh, what a delight to see you after all these years!" The ribbon tied beneath her chin quivered with her excitement. "Dear Lady Calista, don't you remember me?"

"You are Mrs. Harriet Ryan Tinkerson," she replied and walked past the woman into the taproom.

Mrs. Tinkerson stared wide-eyed at the doorway, then at him.

"What a delightful person she is." She smiled uncertainly. "How do you do, sir? Oh! You are the Marquess of Dare! I saw you in the prince's review two years ago. It is such an honor, my lord." She fell into a deep curtsy.

He bowed. "Pardon me, if you will, madam." He went into the taproom. A grizzled-looking fellow with white whiskers had joined the guests among whom Tacitus had breakfasted earlier. Lady Holland stood dripping before him.

"The ford is flooded and the north and east fields are flooded as well, all the way across the valley," she said to him. "And there is no way out of this village, no matter how eager one is to leave it. Is this not correct, Mr. Pritchard?"

He stood up. "Yes, ma'am. That's correct. Swinly might as well be an island today."

Tacitus moved forward. "What do you mean? This village

is now entirely encircled by water? Not only the flooded ford?"

"Like a sailing ship upon the ocean, sir," the fellow said. "Just as the lady here said, Butcher's fields to the north and Drover's field to the east as well. Hip deep, they are, though I don't know how she knew it."

Lady Holland grasped Tacitus's coat sleeve and dragged him to an empty table.

"Please, sit," she said, and released him.

"Just a moment." He turned away.

"*No.* Don't leave." Her eyes were fraught. "Please," she whispered.

"I am going to call up some breakfast for you. You are too pale." And obviously agitated.

She nodded. Moving swiftly through the taproom and foyer to the kitchen door, he poked his head in. The innkeeper looked up from her dishes.

"Milord! You shouldn't be in here." She bustled toward him.

"Mrs. Whittle, breakfast for Lady Holland, if you will. And coffee. Quickly, please." He smiled. "Thank you."

He returned to the taproom. The woman in the tremendous hat was standing over Lady Holland waving her hands about and practically giggling. Lady Holland's eyes rose to him shockingly bright. Panicked. Her hands were fisted in her lap.

"Why, isn't it delightful, my lord? This dear lady has promised to take tea at my shop today. How happy I am that the flood came so providentially and she is trapped here so that we can have a nice long cozy chat and catch up on all these years apart! Why, you know, Calista, how I always did like hats better than painting or French or anything else those horrid spinsters made us study. Didn't I?"

"You certainly did," she replied in a flat tone.

"My shop is right in the middle of Swinly, my lord, on the high street and safe from the flood. I will adore giving Lady Calista—oh! Lady *Holland*—the grand tour of it today. Do say you will come for tea too, Lord Dare. I daresay my darling little shop is as elegant as any shop in London you've ever seen."

"As I don't often have the occasion to visit millinery shops, Mrs. Tinkerson," he said, his eyes on Lady Holland's drawn face, "I could not say. Would you excuse us now?"

"Oh!" She looked back and forth between them curiously. "Yes, of course. Now don't be late, dear Calista. My lovely little parlor in the room next to the shop will be all ready for you at teatime. Adieu!" Smiling vapidly, she fluttered out of the room.

Tacitus took the seat beside Lady Holland. Molly came forward with a pot of coffee and a cup. A farmer leaped up from his seat.

"I'm giving this one a wide berth!" he said heartily to his tablemates. They all chuckled and Molly's cheeks flamed.

"She spilled coffee on him a quarter hour ago," Lady Holland mumbled. "Right about the time we left the ford."

"Did she?" Tacitus looked around. Sure enough, the farmer's trousers were splattered with a brown stain. "How do you know that?"

"It happened yesterday. And the day before. Only she spilled the coffee on me instead of him. I was standing just beside him."

"Perhaps you should eat before saying anything more."

"It won't make any difference. After I ate yesterday it was the same. The day before that, of course, I did not eat until dinnertime. *Tea*," she said firmly as Molly set the cup on the table and lifted the coffee pot. "I don't care for coffee," she added less steadily.

"Yes, milady." Molly scurried off.

"If you haven't been eating properly," he said, "it's no wonder you're not quite top of the trees today."

"Lack of food has never before made me relive the same day three times in a row. Or at all. And did you really just use the phrase 'top of the trees'?"

"I did. Do you have a problem with that?"

"I have a problem with all of this!" She cast her hands out to either side and Molly, carrying a plate and teapot, jerked abruptly, splashing tea across Lady Holland's lap.

The lady's nostrils flared. "Cannot you refrain from dousing me *any* day?"

"Oh, milady! I'm that sorry, I am! I'll fetch a rag right quick."

"Don't bother. Just set down the plate and pot and go." She snatched up a table linen and dabbed at her skirt. "I have a problem with *all* of this," she whispered when the girl had gone, and stared at the food before her. Then she looked up at him. "This is the third time I have woken up to today."

Tacitus studied her fevered eyes, her graceful cheeks that were decidedly pale, and her posture of impatient tension.

"You woke up twice before the bell rang this morning?" he asked. "That isn't to be wondered at. The rain made such a racket on my windowpanes all night long, I barely slept either."

"No. You're not listening. I have woken up today, on Saturday, February twentieth, at seven o'clock, to the ringing of the church bell, three times. I have already lived through this day twice."

He leaned back in his chair and folded his arms across his chest.

"You know," he said, "it really is a shame Lord Mallory continued on to his destination last night. If he were here now, I am certain he would be delighted to share this table with you. He enjoys a fine joke." He blew out a breath. "I am unfortunately not as susceptible to the delights of bald teasing." He stood up. "I bid you a good day, Lady Holl—"

Her fingers clamped around his wrist.

"Don't leave," she whispered harshly. "I beg of you. I— I need *help*."

He might have pried her hand off of him, no matter how much pleasure the mere contact sent through him. He might have told her precisely what he thought of foolishness like this. But something in her eyes, the panic, gave him pause.

"You expect me to believe this?" he said warily.

"Of course not," she snapped. "I don't believe it myself and I am the one living it. But I don't know anybody in this village except my coachman and I think I should probably see a physician."

He nodded. "All right. Stay here and finish your breakfast, and I will make inquiries."

Calista's tight chest loosened enough so that she could feel her heart knocking against every rib.

"Thank you," she forced through clenched teeth, and took up her fork.

By the time she had eaten everything on her plate, he returned, carrying a woman's cloak.

"I have the address of the local doctor. He comes highly recommended by several people in the village. I did not delay in vetting him for you first, but I sent a boy to tell him we were on our way. I thought you would like to see him sooner than later."

"Yes." She stood. "Immediately."

He wrapped the cloak around her shoulders. It was an elegant garment made of fine green wool, the likes of which she had not owned since she was a child.

"Whose is this?"

"I don't know. I did not see yours so I borrowed it from the peg in the foyer. I understand there is a party of means hiring the private parlor today. I suspect it belongs to one of them. But I don't suppose she is adventuresome enough to strike out in the drenching rain at present." A slight smile played about his lips.

She fastened the clasp. "Is that why you have taken dinner and breakfast in the taproom? Because the private parlor was already occupied?"

"No. I take my meals in the taproom because I enjoy it."

The stiff-as-a-poker *I am Dare* marquess?

"You *enjoy* breakfasting with laborers and tradesmen?"

The pleasure slipped away from his handsome face. "Indeed I do. Come now. Professional counsel awaits you."

She went before him out of the inn and they walked side by side along the village's narrow main street.

"You think that my mind is unsettled, don't you?" she said across the rain. "That I am mad. Or playing a jest upon you."

"I think either is likely, yes," he replied grimly.

"Then why are you helping me?"

"Because you asked."

"You needn't help. I will escape this village—*this day*—on my own." She halted and he came to a standstill too. "If you will give me the direction of the doctor, I will call on him alone."

"I don't think that is wise."

"I didn't ask what you thought, did I?"

His eyes were quite dark behind the curtain of rain. "No, you didn't." His scarred jaw looked taut and handsome and wonderful. "His name is Appleby. His house is the last on the left, just before the blacksmith's shop." He bowed. "The best of luck to you, madam."

Watching his back as he strode away, she gulped a full breath then continued down the street in the opposite direction from her only connection to reality.

Chapter Seven

DR. APPLEBY'S HOUSE was filled with vials of murky liquids and mysteriously labeled tins. The doctor himself was a thin man of seventy or eighty, with stark white hair and wise eyes. He examined her from head to toe.

"You say you are reliving the same day?" he said as he peered into her ears with a pointed tool. "Every day?"

"Yes." She swiveled to face him. "Have you ever heard of such a thing before?"

"I have not, unfortunately. But your cranial structure is sound and everything else fit. You appear to be in good physical condition, Lady Holland, except perhaps suffering from moderate exhaustion."

"Then, if I am simply going mad, have you any medicines to help me?" At least until she ensured that her son would remain safe with her family. Never with Richard.

The doctor regarded her thoughtfully. "I once cured a man who believed he was a seagull. He continually dug into the garbage. It was most inconvenient for his family and neighbors, as you can imagine." He smiled.

"Doctor, please."

"I apologize, Lady Holland," he said gently. "I hoped to dispel your distress with a chuckle. I don't believe anything is physically wrong with you, though I cannot entirely rule out a tumor within the brain, of course."

"A tumor?" Her wretched voice quavered.

"Such a lesion might press upon the brain and cause hallucinations. But you say you have had no headaches or difficulties with your vision?"

"A small headache two days ago, but that was only

because I was overly hungry. I have never had trouble with my vision." Hallucinations, however, were another story, like seeing a stone statue glow. "Can hunger cause a person to see things that are not there?"

"It can indeed. Has that happened to you lately?"

"Yesterday, when I was famished."

"Only yesterday? One hallucination?"

She nodded.

"Then the cause of it was most likely your hunger rather than a tumor, which would produce such visions regularly. As to your mental state, on such short acquaintance I cannot make a diagnosis beyond the unfortunate effects of exhaustion." He stood up, went to a cabinet, and drew forth a bottle. "This could be of use to you now." He dispensed some powder from the bottle into a small packet. "It should calm your humors sufficiently so that they can regain balance. Above all, however, I prescribe sleep."

The doctor accepted her promise to send payment after her return home, and Calista departed his house and slogged down the muddy high street in the drizzle, her head a tangle of confusion and stomach a mess of panic. She *could not* go mad or die of a tumor. Not yet. Not until Harry was safe from his father.

At the far end of the village, no longer obscured by dark deluge, the church arose in a resolutely square mass above all the other buildings. Its tower was twice its height, the bell visible through the belfry apertures.

A man stood on the threshold of the neat little cottage flanking the church. He wore all black and watched her approach. As she neared, he opened an umbrella and came forward.

"Lady Holland, I presume?" he said.

"Yes?"

"How do you do? I am Reverend Abbot. Lord Dare suggested that you might pay me a call."

"Did he?"

"Would you care to come inside?"

"I am all mud and rain, Reverend." She gestured to her hem and shoes. "I don't think—"

"The Lord cares nothing about mud," he said with a smile. "Do come in and have a chat."

She followed him into the church. Inside it was all mellow golden stone carved in the medieval style into florets and palm fronds and the occasional saintly visage where later reformers had not taken cudgels to them. The pews were of natural wood, gleaming in the light filtering through simple glass windows, and the choir benches in the chancel of a darker hue, but likewise plain.

She sat beside the vicar. He was roughly the age of her father when he had died. But where the old Earl of Chance had cold eyes and cheeks blotched from too much drink, the vicar's face was lined only with years and his eyes were gentle, his face warm.

"I understand that you are having something of an adventure today," he said.

She gripped the package of medicine between her cold fingers.

"I don't know why Lord Dare thought he had the right to tell you," she said tightly. "I am barely acquainted with him."

"I always find that emergencies make fast friends, Lady Holland. And I believe he is only concerned about you. Would you like to tell me about it?"

"No. I would like it to be *over*. Finished. In the past. I cannot wait until dark so that I can sleep and wake up tomorrow."

"Hm." He nodded thoughtfully. "Sometimes it does seem that we are not moving forward, doesn't it? That we are trapped in one place day after day."

"With all due respect, Reverend, this is not a biblical allegory. I am actually reliving the exact same day again and again." Except today she had not kissed Tacitus Everard. Today he did not even remember that she had. Today he had followed her to the ford in the rain and provided her with breakfast and sought out help for her.

The vicar nodded thoughtfully. "I wonder, my lady, if you have examined your conscience lately. Unburdening oneself of guilt can be liberating to the spirit."

She stood up. "I don't want to examine my conscience. I don't feel guilt over anything." Except kissing a man who was not her husband and *liking it*. "And frankly I don't think I believe in God anymore. No loving, merciful God would trap a person as He has trapped me." And her son.

"God does nothing contrary to our best interests. Are you quite certain that you haven't, in fact, trapped yourself?"

"Yes." Her father had, damn his soul.

"Perhaps I should rephrase that question," Reverend Abbot said. "Is there anything you could change in your life? Anything that you would change if you had the opportunity to do it over again?"

What would she have changed?

She would have insisted he take her to London that morning, despite his disapproval. She would have insisted that he help her to escape. *That morning.* The morning after her father told her he was selling her to the Honorable Richard Holland for fifteen thousand pounds.

"If I give you to Holland," her father had slurred over his claret that evening, "he'll clear my debt to him and give me five thousand extra in the bargain. So his wife you will be, missy."

"But Father, allow me another sennight. Even a few more days, perhaps. Lord Dare is—"

"Dare expects a dowry, you little fool. What's more, if you married *him* you would need a trousseau to rival the Duchess of Devonshire's. Holland is paying me to take you off my hands. Didn't that school teach you simple arithmetic?"

"Father, I cannot like Mr. Holland." She had met Richard Holland thrice: the first time when she was thirteen, the second when she was fifteen, and mere weeks ago in London. On all three occasions he had maneuvered her into shadowed corners to fondle her breasts, calling her "a tempting little puss" and touching the fall of his breeches until it bulged. The first time she had cried, the second time she spit at him, and in London she slapped his face. That he wanted her nonetheless frightened her.

"A man doesn't require his wife to like him, only to obey him," he said, with a narrow, bloodshot glance at her mother standing silently across the room.

"Father, I beg of you—"

"I'll not hear another word about it," he had bellowed, sloshing wine across his trousers. "Holland is coming here tomorrow to sign the contract. You'll be dressed as pretty as you can and prepared to flirt or whatever it is silly females do."

In desperation she had looked to her mother, but found only sorrow in her eyes. No hope. No help.

At the time Calista had not understood that her father had beaten his wife's spirit down so thoroughly she was barely able to speak, let alone defend her daughter. A woman of quiet, intellectual pursuits by nature, her life had depended on her loutish, drunken, gaming husband for nearly three decades. With no income of her own and no friends to appeal to without exposing the family's shame to the entire world and the earldom to derision, Lady Chance had lowered her tear-filled eyes and said nothing.

Late that night Calista packed a small traveling case and hid it under a shrubbery by the gatehouse at the end of the drive, then she stole back into bed without Evelina realizing she'd been gone. All the while she silently cursed her mother, vowing that she would never be weak and docile like her. And she would never, ever cry in response to a man's cruelty. She would be the agent of her own fate.

After six years of marriage to Richard Holland, she understood matters better now. She had forgiven her mother. But only her mother.

"I would have escaped," she uttered to the vicar of Swinly, the hard pit of anger lodged in her belly and weighting her chest. "And if God were truly benevolent, he would have given me my darling Harry anyway, somehow, even without Richard."

"Escape. Hm," the vicar said thoughtfully. "Think about

that desire for escape, Lady Holland. Running away never truly solves a problem, does it?"

"It jolly well solves the problem of having to hide one's bruises so that one can go to the shop without attracting the gossip of everybody in town. Not to mention hiding them from one's own son and servants. Oh, good Lord," she exclaimed. "Why am I here? In church, of all places? Why am I talking to you? How could you possibly understand the—" Her throat seized up. "Good day, Reverend." Sweeping her borrowed cloak about her, she rushed from the building.

The rain had ceased while she was indoors and the clouds were making a valiant effort to part and allow the sun's pale rays to sneak through to the sodden earth.

Rainbows. He had asked her to go searching for *rainbows* the first day.

Foolish man.

Foolish *men*.

She spun around on the street, clutching the bag of medicines to her. Where could she go? Not back to the inn, to *him,* the catalyst that had dredged up those horrible days, days of hope and then hopelessness, fear and heartbreak. Followed by six years of the same, only minus the hope. Except for Harry, her little boy whom she already missed as if someone had drilled a big hole right through her middle. At least he was safe now. At Dashbourne. With her sister who barely knew him, but adored him. And her mother who, without the earl's daily insults, was now flourishing, happy, alive again as a woman should be.

Harry was safe with them.

And she was trapped in madness.

She started walking and did not stop until she reached the swollen ford. Sitting down on the bank in the mud, she pulled out the packet of white powder. Emptying the mysterious contents into her palm, she scooped the powder into her mouth and licked the remaining bits from her skin. It was bitter, but she didn't care. She didn't care about anything anymore except ending this wretched day.

She had entered this village via this ford, and she would leave it via this ford. She would wait here and watch the water recede until midnight, when the bell in the church tower tolled twelve times. Then it would surely become tomorrow. *Surely.* If God did exist, He could not be so cruel to make this day last one second past midnight.

Pulling her cloak tightly about her, she settled into the chilly winter day to wait.

Calista started out of sleep upon the church bell tolling. Slumped against the rock wall that abutted the ford on the village side, face tucked against her shoulder, she brought her eyes up and then her chin. The sky above was cluttered with stars, not a single cloud marring the glittering black. Cold had crept beneath her clothes and into every one of her bones.

She counted the rings of the bell to eleven. And waited for a twelfth. And waited. And waited.

And sensed she was being watched.

She craned her stiff neck around and met the impassive gaze of the Marquess of Dare. Carrying a lantern, he walked toward her.

"Good evening, Lady Holland."

"Do go away, my lord," she mumbled. "As you can see, I'm terribly busy at present."

He halted before her. "I ought to have known you would be here. You are desperate to leave this village, aren't you?"

"More desperate than you can imagine." The water rippled over the ford in a sleek black river that glimmered gold now from the lantern's light.

"It seems as though it is receding. In the morning, you should be granted your wish. Have you been here all evening?"

"I have. And what have you been doing this evening? Fleecing the local farmers of the last pennies of their harvest income?"

"Looking for you."

She snapped her head around.

"When you did not appear for dinner," he said, "I imagined the vicar had invited you to dine with him. When you did not return after dinner, I went to the vicarage. Then to the doctor's house. Then to the pub and the dress shop and the bakery. Then to Mrs. Tinkerson's, who, by the way, is deeply disappointed that you did not join her for tea this afternoon."

"One tepid cup and two measly biscuits is not tea."

He chuckled. "How do you know she didn't have a banquet set for your ladyship?"

"Because I took tea at her shop yesterday and the day before that." She turned her face to the ford.

"You missed a lot of excitement over sheep," he said conversationally, as if he meant to ignore her nonsensical statements.

"That's fine. I saw them yesterday."

"Did you?" he said quietly.

She pressed her palm into the ground and unbent her limbs that were wretchedly sore from sitting for so many hours on the cold, damp ground.

"Yes," she said. "I did. The herd is comprised of roughly three dozen animals. Until five o'clock they were all wandering around the other end of the high street without direction, apparently having escaped through an unlocked gate. And yet, as the shepherd seemed to have gone missing, no one was able to drive them anywhere until he was found dozing under a tree on the other end of the village. But in the meantime they had eaten Mrs. Elliott's entire garden of winter greens. I actually witnessed them doing so on my walk back to the inn from tea at the millinery the day before yesterday. Have I got all the details correct, Lord Dare?"

"Yes," he said.

"Excellent. Now do go away. I am waiting here for tomorrow to arrive."

"You must return with me to the inn now."

"I mustn't do anything of the sort. You are not my husband, my father, or even the local law. You have no authority over me. And as I have already had my surfeit of living according to a man's will, I don't think I would be inclined to acquiesce to your demand at this moment even if I liked the idea of it. Which in this case I don't."

"The constable, Mr. Pritchard, is presently enjoying a pint in the pub yonder." He gestured. "Perhaps I will fetch him over here and you will listen to him."

"Go away. Please."

"You are soaking wet. You will awaken tomorrow with a fever and then be obliged to spend many more than one day in this village convalescing."

"If I awaken tomorrow with a fever, I will sing Hallelujah and dance up and down the high street, then leap into my carriage and leave this place forever."

The darkness was silent then, save for the burble of the water rushing over the ford. The night had grown frigid and her skin and bones were like ice.

"Please, Calista." The words, spoken deeply, carried the edge of calm authority that always made her feel hot. "Allow me to assist you."

"No. And I don't believe I have ever given you permission to address me by my Christian name alone."

"Not even when you kissed me?"

"Do not *mock* me."

"I wasn't mocking you."

"How could that be so? You don't believe me."

"Truth be told," he said, "I wish I could remember you kissing me."

"Just ... go."

"You know, you are condemning me to waking with a fever in the morning too," he said as he set down the lantern, then bent himself to settle on the ground two yards away from her. "It's devilishly cold out here. I should have brought blankets, or perhaps flint and tinder. Will you accept the loan of my coat?"

"No, thank you."

"Your teeth are chattering."

"My teeth are none of your concern."

"On the contrary. I courted you six years ago because I admired your teeth."

She peered at him over the lantern light. "Because of my teeth? That is perfectly absurd."

"Rather, your teeth are. Perfect, that is. At the time I considered excellent teeth the most important quality in the woman I intended to wed."

"How utterly nonsensical."

"Agreed," he murmured.

"I suppose you are still searching for the ideal set of female teeth to marry?"

"No. I ceased that search some time ago, actually."

Abruptly Calista's tongue went dry between her admirable teeth.

"Why—" She was obliged to moisten her lips to continue. "Why have you told me this?"

"Well." His eyes were nearly black in the lantern light. "If this day is to repeat itself again tomorrow, and again the following day, and so on, I won't remember I've said it, will I?"

"No. But I will."

He nodded. "That suits me well enough."

She turned her face away from him, back to the waters of the ford that were lower now even than when he had appeared in the dark with his lantern and worry and demands and peculiar revelations. He was a peculiar man all around. He always had been. She did not want to like him now. *Again.* She did not want to feel the warmth that gathered in her when he looked at her as he had just now. She wanted to drive away from this village in the morning and forget she had ever met Tacitus Everard.

She closed her eyes.

When the bell in the church tower began tolling its final hour of the night, Calista opened her eyes and stared fixedly at the water running across the ford. Upon the twelfth ring, a hard exhale shot out of her lungs.

She sprang up as the sound faded into the night. "I am still here! It is not this morning again."

"It seems so." Lord Dare climbed to his feet. "May I escort you back to the Jolly Cockerel now?"

Her joints were frozen, her lungs beleaguered, and her cheeks and fingers nearly numb. But she was *free*. The water level was already lower over the ford. When dawn came it would surely be passable. And not a cloud marred the starlit sky to worry her with additional rain before morning.

"I am happy to accompany you to the inn at this time, Lord Dare," she said with a smile, and set off toward the village center. The marquess took up the lantern and came after her.

In the inn's foyer, she removed the borrowed cloak and hung it on a peg, then turned to him.

"Good-bye, my lord. I wish you a safe continuation of your journey." She extended her hand to shake.

He did not take it. "I wish you the same, my lady." He bowed, and went up the stairs swiftly.

In her bedchamber, Calista packed away the Aphrodite statue one final time and hung her clothing on the bedpost to dry. Then she climbed into bed, pulled the covers to her chin, and closed her eyes.

She opened them to the rattle of the windowpanes as the bell commenced its morning greeting, and she counted the tolls as her eyes catalogued the bedchamber: dim gray light of dawn; rain pattering the windowpanes mercilessly; and Aphrodite's pale face staring at her from the dressing table with blank eyes.

After the seventh ring, the church bell went silent.

Calista opened her mouth and screamed.

Chapter Eight

"HER LADYSHIP IS UNWELL."

"That's no surprise, after the way she shocked everybody in the place with that hollering to raise the dead," Molly mumbled.

"I've just been up to her and she is in a rare state of agitation, to be sure." Mrs. Whittle bustled around the kitchen. "She wants a pot of tea, three eggs, bacon, steak, kippers, muffins and marmalade brought up."

"But we don't serve in the bedchambers, do we?"

"As Mr. Smythe's family has taken the private parlor, while she's a true noble lady, it's the least I can do, especially seeing as she's unwell. There's her tray."

"All of that for a lady who's ill?" Molly exclaimed. "Does she have somebody up there in that room with her?"

"Keep a civil tongue, child." The innkeeper shook her finger. "On top of the Smythes, I've got two dozen souls to feed, a lady invalid, and a lord in the taproom. I've no time for your impertinence. Go on now."

"Yes, Aunt Meg."

Tacitus pushed the kitchen door wide and cleared his throat.

"Milord! You shouldn't be in here." Mrs. Whittle hurried forward.

"Mrs. Whittle, the constable has just told us all that the village is encircled with flood and the roads entirely closed."

"Glory be! And Mr. Whittle still in Wallings. What am I to do?"

"The very reason I'm here. Last night I heard you mention his absence. I'm certain my manservant would be much more useful to you in practical matters, but alas I am traveling without him. However, I can shine boots and chop wood with the best of them. I offer my services to you, if you are in need of an extra hand."

"Dear me! Now I've heard something I never imagined: a lord offering a poor innkeeper help. And the village flooded, too. Glory be, the world's turned upside down today."

"In truth, it is either assist you or pass the morning losing every coin in my pockets at cards with Mr. Anderson and Mr. Peabody. They already lifted a pony off me last night and I've little left to spare. I should have suspected an accountant's clerk and a bookseller would know their way around a deck of cards. We politicians are much more honest, it turns out."

Molly giggled, bumped into a counter, and a dish slipped out of her hand and crashed to the floor.

"You clumsy girl," Mrs. Whittle scolded. "Clean that up and then carry that tray upstairs to her ladyship, if you can manage it without spilling it all over the stairs. Some girls aren't born with coordination," she said to Tacitus and scraped eggs from a skillet onto a plate already laden with food. "You're a fine gentleman to offer help, but I'm sure I can't think of a thing I could ask of you."

"Is that for Lady Holland?"

"Yes, milord." She set the plate on a tray. "Molly, go on now, before it all grows cold as stone."

He moved into the kitchen. "By the way, there is a lady by the name of Mrs. Tinkerson in the foyer asking to speak with you. About a bonnet, I believe."

"Oh, she's a pushy one. But I do like that chip straw hat with green taffeta she's got in the window."

"Also, there are a number of patrons in the taproom hoping to have their cups refilled. Allow me to save Molly the trip upstairs."

"Oh, no, milord. That wouldn't be proper—"

"Lady Holland and I are old friends." It wasn't entirely a lie. Not really. Except the part about being friends. "She won't mind it." Judging from her attitude toward him last night, she would probably bite off his head. The notion gave him enormous pleasure. It might be six years too late, but if he managed to get under her skin even a fraction of how she'd gotten under his at one time, he would consider the day a vast success.

"What if she's still wearing nightclothes, milord?" Molly whispered.

"I shall keep my eyes closed." He hoisted the tray. "Teapot?"

"Well, I've never seen the like and won't again, to be sure, a great lord carrying a breakfast tray," Mrs. Whittle exclaimed, but she gestured for Molly to set the pot on the tray. She beamed. "You're as fine a gentleman as I've ever seen, milord."

"Merely fortunate to have been raised by a woman as competent and generous as you."

"Oh, now none of your flattery. Those eggs are getting cold."

He went up the stairs with a light step, his heartbeat quickening upon every riser. This was *not* the behavior his mother had raised him to, volunteering to carry breakfast to a married woman. Keeping Peyton Stark's company was undoing all the lessons in gentlemanliness he had learned as a child.

When Calista Holland opened the bedchamber door and her glittering smile nearly knocked him against the opposite wall, he knew that even Peyton's bad influence had nothing on him compared to this woman's unguarded pleasure.

"Lord Dare! Whatever are you doing with my breakfast? I assume this is my breakfast."

"Yes. The innkeeper is shorthanded on account of—"

"Yes, yes, I know. The flood and the closed roads and the inn full of stranded guests and what have you. Come in, then, and set it down here."

"I don't think I should—"

"Then what are you doing bringing it up here in the first place unless you wished to see me? Don't be such a prig. Do you think a cat would prefer steak or kippers? Or bacon? I ordered the bacon for myself, but I don't suppose it cares what it eats."

A cat the color of the deluge outside sat on its haunches in the center of the room, staring at the tray in his hands. Its ribs poked out prominently.

"I suspect the kippers will meet with success. Truth be told, though, I'm rather more of a dog person."

"I might have suspected that, but only lately, of course. Not before," she said cryptically. "I'm not fond of any animals. But this one is clearly starving."

"So you have invited it to share your breakfast?"

"Well, I certainly cannot eat all of that by myself, can I? You look like one of the king's guardsmen standing there so unbending. Do set that down, will you?"

"Forgive me. I think I may be a bit bemused by your temper this morning. It does not entirely resemble last night's."

She set her hands on her delectably curved hips. "Well it wouldn't, would it?"

He placed the tray beside a statue of a woman sculpted in the Greek fashion.

"This is an impressive piece," he commented, to have something to say, to give him an excuse to linger. *Reprobate.* "Remarkable how she seems to smile without smiling."

"She does *not* smile. She only stares." She crouched before the cat and proffered a kipper with her bare fingers. She was dressed in a simple gown of unremarkable color that now cinched around her gorgeously rounded behind and sent the temperature in the chamber up twenty degrees. "Come now," she said to the cat, "don't be foolishly shy. I have gotten these expressly for you and if you do not eat them I shall have to feed them to that great big man there, and I don't know if he likes kippers either."

"I do, as a matter of fact."

"So does this one, it seems. You cannot have them after all, my lord." A smile pulled at the corners of her intoxicating lips as the cat nibbled at the fish right from her fingers. It was a simple, small smile, but it lit her eyes and sallow cheeks.

He had to turn away to find distraction.

"The statue does smile," he forced out. "Just look at her."

"Thank you, but I have already seen enough of her face to last me a lifetime." She straightened. "But I have seen little of this village except the ford, and the doctor's house and that wretched church, and Harriet Tinkerson's awful shop. If I am truly trapped here, I think I will go exploring this morning." She poured tea and took up a slice of bacon.

"I will leave you to your breakfast, then," he said, glancing at the untouched cutlery on the tray.

She laughed. "Haven't you ever seen a woman eat bacon without using a fork?"

"I beg your—"

"You really are an incorrigible prig. Look." She grabbed up the steak and bit off a hunk with her even, white teeth. "Delicious," she said around the mouthful. "I think I will slurp my tea now, too, merely for the diversion of seeing you shocked. It's downright refreshing, really. I feel like I'm eighteen again."

"If you set the plate on the ground," he said as he turned toward the doorway, "you'll be able to eat the eggs like that cat is eating the fish."

Her crack of laughter was muffled by the food in her mouth.

"I don't care what you think of me, Tacitus Everard. I don't care if you are considerate and protective and honest." She slurped the tea. "I don't care about anything at all, in fact. If the world refuses to live by its own rules, I don't really see why I should live by rules either. I have been living according to someone else's horrid rules for six years. Rather, twenty-four years. If fate is offering me this opportunity, I aim to seize it."

He peered at her. "Are you feeling quite the thing, Lady Holland?"

"Don't call me that. Call me Calista like you did last night, or nothing at all."

"I didn't—"

"Or, wait! Perhaps you should call me Your Highness.

Yes, I like that better." She lengthened her face by lifting her
brows, and thrust back her shoulders. "Your Highness," she
mimicked his voice perfectly, "are you feeling quite the thing?"

Tacitus fought to control the twitch of his lips.

"Clearly, I have my answer," he said, trying not to look at
her breasts that were decadently presented by her erect
posture.

"Today I will demand that everybody call me Your
Highness. Go now and tell them." She made a shooing motion.
"Tell everyone downstairs that I am a princess traveling
incognito, but that you have discovered my secret and they
should all treat me with thorough deference. That Tinkerson
woman will positively swoon. How delightful. I think it may be
illegal to call myself royalty. But nobody will remember
tomorrow, so it doesn't signify. Go now, my lord. Make it so."

"I will do nothing of the sort."

Her eyes rolled. "Oh, *do* try not to be so stiff, will you?
Play along."

"I really don't think my stiffness is the issue here."
Though the radiance of her eyes and slightly rabid gaiety on
her face was making one part of him rather stiffer than he
wished at present. She was far too pretty. "You have changed
in six years. And yet perhaps you haven't."

"You have *no* idea. Now, off with you! Do my bidding,
plebe."

"You do understand that I am a Peer. A relative of *actual*
royalty, albeit distant."

"Of course." Her lips curved into thorough wickedness.
"You are *Dare*."

He bit down on his molars.

Her eyes went positively round with mirth. And then she
commenced laughing so hard that tears ran onto her cheeks.
She clutched at her middle and waved him out the door.

"Go, go! I cannot stand this." She gasped, her entire face
overcome with hilarity. "Go now!"

He went. Hysterical laughter was a sign of madness, of
course. Perhaps she had gone mad.

But she hadn't seemed mad when she was holding her son close the night before, murmuring tender assurances into his hair, the sinews in her neck taut as she seemed to restrain her emotions. At that moment she had seemed like a fiercely loving mother, the same way she had been a fiercely loving sibling to Lady Evelina and Gregory over the course of that month six years ago.

Down in the kitchen Mrs. Whittle assured him that she and Molly needed no assistance washing up from breakfast. So he went into the taproom, found Anderson and Peabody and a third fellow, and settled into a rather cutthroat game of whist.

He wasn't a shabby cardplayer by any means, but he was two guineas poorer by the time he saw Calista Holland descend to the foyer munching on a slice of toast. Popping the remaining crust between her lips, she rifled through the coats hanging on pegs by the doors, pulled forth a green cloak, and slung it around her shoulders. Without an umbrella or hat, she walked out into the rain that was still falling generously.

Shaking his head, he returned his attention to the three sharpers waiting for him to make his play.

An hour later his pockets were empty and he was accepting a cigar from Mr. Anderson—intended, he suspected, to entice him to play again tonight—when a commotion sounded in the foyer.

"Mother," said a young lady gowned in frothy white up to her chin, "that woman out there is wearing my cloak. And look what she's doing to it."

A woman of middling years, wearing black feathers in her headdress and a gown far too elaborate for a day at a country inn, rushed to the front window. "Good gracious! Who is she?"

"I don't know." Her daughter pressed her nose against the pane. "But she has ruined my best cloak."

"Your father will buy you three new cloaks to replace it, Penny." A nattily dressed fellow craned his neck over her shoulder. "Why, that's Lady Holland. The Earl of Chance's sister. I heard she was stranded here today too."

An older man came from the private parlor. "Lord Chance's sister? I placed a bet on his stallion last autumn at Newmarket. Bucephalus, I think the beast was called. A superb runner. Won me a tidy bundle that day," he said cheerily. "Where is the lady, Alan? I should like Penelope to make her acquaintance."

"Just there, George. Splashing about on the muddy street. It looks as if she's *playing*, of all things."

Tacitus dropped the cigar, grabbed his coat and umbrella, and went around them and out the door.

Twenty yards from the inn, in the center of the street bordered on either side by neat two-story buildings with shop fronts, Calista Holland stood in the light rain up to her ankles in mud. Rather, she danced. Skipped. Pirouetted. She wore nothing on her head, and her dark hair hung haphazardly in long, sodden strands down her back and over her shoulders, and her face and neck were smeared with mud. The green cloak was now thickly covered as well. She had thrown it back over her shoulders, and beneath it seemed to be a white gown that had inevitably become brown.

As he neared her it became all too clear that the gown was not a true gown at all, rather an undergarment. Clinging damply to her breasts and thighs, it revealed ... *everything*: taut nipples, breasts round as peaches, slender waist, dark cluster of hair at the apex of her thighs, and long, shapely legs.

Look at her face.

"Lady Holland," he said and tugged his greatcoat together at the front. *Look at her face.* "Would you care to return to the inn at this time?"

"No, thank you, my lord. I am happy here." She bent and took up a handful of mud, and slapped it against her chest, then rubbed it around to the back of her neck. "Nobody else is using the street at present, as you can see. Oh! There is one of the sheep now. Already? I hadn't realized they entered the street quite this early. I shall have to jot that down, though of course the note will disappear by dawn. I shall simply have to memorize it."

"It's devilishly chilly out," he said in as common a tone as he could muster, moving closer to her. Eyes peered out of every window on the street and the other guests at the inn had clustered in the doorway. "Perhaps you should draw your cloak over your ... that is ... close your cloak." He glanced at her exposed body and regretted it. By God, she was beautiful. Perfectly formed, like the Greek statue in her bedchamber, but real. And smiling with thorough abandon.

"Should I?" she said. "Do you dislike a woman undressing on the high street and splashing in the mud?"

"Not particularly. But the constable of this village might."

"I haven't seen him since yesterday morning. I believe he spends his time mostly at the pub. It is over there, at the other end of the village, if you wish to retrieve him."

He removed his greatcoat. "You can put this on."

"You really do want me to cover up, don't you?"

"It would be wise, yes."

"Why? Because covered in all this mud I am not sufficiently appealing to your aesthetic senses?"

"Covered with mud or not, you are entirely appealing to all of my senses. However, I am not your husband. Nor are the various villagers and travelers staring at you now. It will be best for you to cover up and return to the inn."

"My husband demands that at home I wear gowns that barely cover my bosom. He likes to ogle and fondle. I might be in conference with the housekeeper, and he will walk by and caress my breast, while she is sitting right there. Honestly, I don't know why she remains, except sometimes I think perhaps she feels sorry for me. And of course the servants all adore Harry. I think they stay mostly for him. He is the sweetest child."

"I've no doubt." He wondered if she had been drinking at the pub today, and if her husband knew that he was a thorough knave. "Do put this on." He ventured close and she allowed him to drape his greatcoat around her shoulders.

"When I wish to leave the house," she said, looking up at him with eyes shrouded by rain-speckled lashes, "he demands that I cover myself from chin to toe. He is concerned that I will attract inappropriate attention. He is a very jealous husband."

"If you were mine, I think I would be too," came from his mouth without forethought.

Her smile faded. "Would you? How vile of you." She bent and scooped up another handful of mud. She slapped it against his chest. "There. You look much better now."

"You know, I liked this waistcoat without the mud."

"Did you?" She raised a hand dripping with mud and caressed his jaw. "Did you like that cheek without mud too?"

"I suppose so." The pleasure of her touch was hot and sharp and went through his entire body. "But then, I haven't seen it with mud. Not in twenty years, at least."

Now her eyes looked a bit wild. He understood. There was fire between them. He had convinced himself that he imagined it six years ago. Clearly, he had not.

"I misspoke," he said somewhat roughly.

"About what?"

"I think if you were mine, I would let you wear whatever you wanted, including a sodden chemise and mud-covered cloak."

Rising and falling swiftly, her breasts pressed at the wet linen. "You would?"

"Your own style clearly suits you." He willed his pulse to steady. "Now, will you return to the inn and put on some clothes?"

She backed away from him and cast off his coat. It landed in four inches of muddy water.

"No. I will not be confined!" she exclaimed. "Not today of all days. Today I aim to do whatever I wish, and defy the consequences. For there won't really be any, you know."

"If I weren't standing here, the consequences of this particular act of defiance might not be precisely what you wish."

"Again with the noble protector?"

"Yes."

"And where was that man when I *actually* needed him?" She swirled away from him and strode toward the inn. "Go away. I neither need you nor want you here ruining my fun."

"You are being childish."

"And you are being a prig."

"No, I am not. I am being really quite reasonable. And by the by, I admit that I was probably a prig six years ago. But I haven't been one in ages."

"You have a stick up your arse, my lord. It was there six years ago and it is obviously still firmly in place."

"Nicely graphic, thank you."

She laughed carelessly and started off toward the inn.

He followed her.

As she entered the inn she winked at two tradesmen standing in the doorway.

The girl in frothy white covered her mouth with her palm. "My cloak!"

Calista shrugged off the garment, effectively gluing every male eye in the place to her gloriously exposed body. That Tacitus wanted to immediately take the round globes of her buttocks into his hands and worship them did not make a damn bit of difference to the acute fury he felt seeing other men ogling her behind too.

She hung the cloak on the peg. "Thank you for its use, darling," she said to the girl. "Don't worry. Tomorrow it will be as good as new, I promise." With a saucy smile at the girl's menfolk, she took the stairs two at a time.

Now every eye, male and female, had turned to him.

"She is unwell," he muttered, and followed her muddy footprints up the stairs. Her door was shut and she did not answer his knock. Retiring to his own bedchamber, he changed out of his stained clothing and took up a book.

Reading never failed to steady his ill temper, and it had the desired effect now. By dinnertime he felt pacific enough to knock on her door before he descended for a glass of claret in the taproom. She did not answer, and he continued downstairs.

Within moments, without prompting, his companions

from earlier at the card table informed him that Lady Holland had gone to the pub. She was, apparently, the talk of the entire village.

He could not resist the temptation. He walked the length of the high street toward the ford, and found the pub. The place was packed with patrons.

In the middle of the room, she danced.

On top of a table.

This time she wore an unexceptional gown that nevertheless clung to her legs as she gyrated, and her hair flowed about her shoulders in spectacular abandon. She was not alone in her tabletop defiance of propriety and good sense. Several men danced jigs atop chairs, and a woman who looked as though she'd spent too many years in this pub was actually sitting on the bar, swaying to and fro to a fiddle's cheerful sawing.

But beautiful, mad Calista Holland was by far the main attraction.

Swallowing over the crushing disappointment rising in him—the sort he hadn't felt in six years—he went to her, remonstrated with her until she descended from the table, and eventually escorted her from the pub. All the way to the inn, as she sang aloud, twirled in circles, and kicked up mud from the soggy street, he silently cursed himself and her and most of all fate.

Obviously he had not learned a thing six years ago.

And obviously she had, in fact, changed.

Chapter Nine

CALISTA HAD NEVER before understood the challenges involved in herding sheep. The animals milled about in the muck every which way, groups of them hustling this way and that like ... well, like sheep, probably.

But her experiment was not a complete failure. She had devised the ideal costume: a gown of pale blue muslin with a thick white petticoat puffing out at the ankles; white stockings and sturdy leather shoes, all now covered in mud; a high poke bonnet tied about her chin with a thick blue ribbon; and a shepherd's staff. The staff wasn't an actual staff, rather a freestanding candlestick holder she had stolen from the church. But it suited the purpose well enough.

As a child she, Evelina, and Gregory had played dress-ups with the cast-off clothes of their parents and the servants' old livery, and she had adored it. But she hadn't dressed in costume since. Years ago, her father snatched her family from London on the eve of the first grand masquerade she had been invited to attend. Richard, of course, believed a disguise would allow her opportunity to dally in secret with other men, and never allowed her to attend such parties.

Now she was certain she looked a perfect picture. She only lacked company. She wished Harry were here to giggle with her. Evelina too. They both adored a good lark, Harry because he was five and Evie because she was Evie.

Apparently the Marquess of Dare did not adore larks. Today, at least, he was merely glowering at her from afar rather than dragging her back to the inn, no doubt because she was not behaving immodestly.

Despite his dark disapproval yesterday he had not scolded

her. It was only when she had returned to her bedchamber, washed, and climbed into bed that she realized she had been waiting for him to shout at her. To call her empty-headed. To strike her.

But of course he would not have. As he had pointed out, he was not her husband.

A sheep butted against her leg. She poked it with the candleholder and it moved. The sheep beside it moved too. And then the sheep beside that. And then a dozen sheep were moving in the direction in which she had poked the first one. Directly toward Mrs. Elliott's turnip greens. An hour before they usually discovered the greens.

She had changed something!

"I've done it!"

"Hurrah, my lady!" Harriet Tinkerson shouted from the doorway of her shop and clapped her little hands gloved in jonquil kidskin.

Calista gave the candlestick a triumphant shake. Harriet had liked the gift of delectable little French butter biscuits from the bakery that Calista traded for the use of the bonnet. She wasn't so bad, after all. And Calista was coming to truly like Elena Cooke. Her gowns were exquisitely made, including this one, and she was rational and serene. She lacked patrons, though, and had nearly admitted to Calista this morning that her experiment in owning a shop was not proceeding as she had hoped.

"What's this, miss? Trying to steel my flock right out from under me while I napped?" The shepherd waded through the sheep toward her, smiling with all three of his teeth in a pleasant, sun-swarthy face.

"No, indeed. I only hoped to keep them company until you woke from your nap. I am now in awe of your skill."

"'T'aint skill, miss." He doffed his cap and looked fondly about him at the milling bundles of white punctuated by black ears and noses. "'Tis affection."

"Affection? For the sheep?" She looked about at the animals. "You actually care about them?"

"Aye, miss. Like they was my little sisters. Ai! Ai!" he called out. "Come on now, girls. We'd best be on our way afore Mrs. Elliott discovers Sally's gone and et her turnip greens. Good day, miss."

While he ushered them away like the pied piper of cloven-hooved creatures, she untied the bonnet and walked to Harriet's shop.

"Dear Lady Holland," Harriet gushed, "*do* come in for a cup of tea and one or two of those tasty biscuits you brought me."

"I would be delighted to, but I have an appointment elsewhere." She gave Harriet the borrowed bonnet. "Good afternoon, and my thanks again."

Exiting the church several minutes later *sans* candleholder, she saw the marquess in the inn doorway. He watched her approach.

"Has Little Bo Peep lost her sheep?" he said as she passed by him. Today she had spoken with him only briefly at breakfast. He thought they were strangers, and yet still he teased. Either he had changed, as he had said yesterday, or she had not really known him six years ago.

Of course she hadn't really known him. She had believed he would run away with her.

She went toward the stairs. "She has given them over into their master's care, with alacrity."

"You might have been injured," he said to her back, his voice no longer light. "They are dumb animals, but not without power en masse."

"Ah. There is the old Lord Dare back again." She pivoted to him. "Were you born sixty years old?"

"Were you trapped at ten?" His expressive eyes were hard. "Because that would explain this." He gestured to her costume.

"I was only having a bit of fun. You might try it sometime, if you can unbend your forbidding lip long enough to smile."

"Do you know, last night I thought you merely rude—"

"You nearly ran over my son with your horse. I was upset."

"—but today I think you are simply childish. And unkind. I don't deserve your insults now, just like I did not deserve them six years ago."

No quick defense came to her tongue. She was stunned.

For a moment longer he stared at her, then he shook his head and disappeared into the taproom.

And quite abruptly Calista understood that she wanted him to argue with her, at least to chastise her. She had hoped he would call her out for dressing up in this ridiculous costume, and then she could quarrel with him, and he would say unexpected things and make unexpected revelations and look at her with his gorgeously thundercloud eyes like a war was waging inside of him.

Instead, he simply did not care. He thought her foolish and immature and unkind. But ultimately she meant nothing to him. Worse, she was no better than the girl he had disapproved of all those years ago.

"This is the worst day of my life," she said aloud to the empty foyer. "The very worst day."

She climbed the stairs to the bedchamber she had come to loathe, sat down on her bed, and dropped her face into her hands.

"The very, very worst day."

She fell asleep on the end of the bed, still wearing the shepherdess costume. She awoke to the throbbing of the church bell and the drone of pouring rain outside, in her nightgown, dry and tucked under the covers.

"The worst, very, very worst day," she muttered as the bell tolled on and on and on.

Chapter Ten

"SHE'S WON ALL of Peabody's blunt, three quarters of Anderson's ready cash, and nine guineas from Mr. Alan Smythe."

Standing beside Tacitus in the doorway, the constable stroked his white whiskers as they studied the tableau in the taproom. Behind a cloud of cigar smoke, Calista Holland sat at a table with three of the inn's other guests, all men. A fan of cards was clutched in her fingers. The arrangement of her satiny dark hair had disgorged tendrils that now hung loosely over her shoulders. To her right was a half-burnt cigar, its smoke rising in a white curl to join the smoke from the other cardplayers' cheroots. A pile of coins, bills, and scraps of paper—vowels, no doubt—graced the center of the table, and stacks of chips sat by each player's hands.

"They have been there all day?"

"Aye, my lord, according to Mrs. Whittle. None of them have moved in hours. She served them lunch some time ago, but they barely ate it. Shame to waste all that food." He gave his head a rueful shake.

"And you say Lady Holland is winning?" he asked. "Against all of them?"

"Aye. Nine out of ten hands."

Tacitus studied the men's faces. They were drawn, worried, frustrated. These men were not accustomed to being beaten at cards by a woman.

"Who is that one? With the fine waistcoat?" The only one of the three not frowning.

"Mr. Alan Smythe," the constable said. "Comes through here with his brother's family twice a year, on their way to

London in this season, and back home in the summer. The
brothers are importers, and very successful. Mrs. George
Smythe is a great hostess, they say."

Tacitus had never heard of them. Petty gentry, no doubt.
But this Smythe watched Calista like he had something on his
mind other than cards. And it made Tacitus unreasonably
cross.

But she was not watching Smythe. Her attention was fixed
entirely on the cards. There was fevered desperation in her
eyes, the sharp-edged gleam of the confirmed gambler.

Tacitus knew of her deceased father's reputation for
gambling beyond his means. The new earl, Ian, whom he and
Peyton had gone to school with back in the day, was doing
what he could to shrug off his father's unsavory mantle. Ian
still played cards, but moderately and honestly. Mostly he was
breeding fine racehorses. Ian was not political; Tacitus never
saw him at Westminster. But in his own way he was trying to
remake the earldom into a source of pride for his family.

Apparently, however, his sister was cut in the old earl's
style.

The serving girl, Molly, passed by them at the doorway
with a coffeepot and stacked cups. Setting them quietly on the
table beside each player, she poured Lady Holland's first.
Behind her, another patron scraped out his chair, Molly's hand
jerked, and coffee splashed over Lady Holland's hands.

"Oh!"

"Oh, milady! I'm that sorry, I am! I'll fetch a rag right
quick."

Lady Holland slapped her cards face down and snatched
up a table linen to wipe her fingers.

"From this day forward, you clumsy girl, I insist that you
not come near me with a pot of coffee. Not for any reason.
Have I made myself clear?"

"Yes, milady! I beg your pardon, mum." Molly's lips
quivered as she hurried past Tacitus and the constable toward
the kitchen.

As the dealer collected the cards and shuffled them, Lady

Holland lifted a hand to swipe a lock of hair from before her eyes, and her gaze followed Molly's flight from the room. Then it shifted aside to him.

It changed. For an instant, pleasure shone in the crystal blue.

Then—swiftly—bleakness.

She returned her attention to the dealer and Tacitus remembered to breathe again.

Since the previous night he had wondered why she let her son go off with Lady Evelina when the separation clearly pained her. Perhaps she knew she could not care for him, not when her attention was all for the card table. Perhaps she was voluntarily relinquishing him out of apathy, in the manner of most gamblers regarding all except the game, and only briefly the evening before had regretted the loss. Perhaps her husband thought her an unfit parent because of her gambling, and was separating her from their son for the boy's benefit.

Perhaps ...

Whatever the case, it seemed obvious enough that six years ago he'd had a near miss. But if fate had been kind to him then, why now, watching her in this state, did he feel like he was being punished?

Chapter Eleven

CALISTA SLEPT POORLY AND AWOKE to the gonging church bell crosser than usual. Turning over, she dragged the bedclothes over her head, waited for the bell to ring its seventh evil toll, and let herself fall into sleep again.

For most of the day she slept between tolls. When she finally climbed out of bed, sunlight slanted tentatively through the window. But she felt just as cross as she had at dawn.

She washed, dressed swiftly, did not bother packing away the statue, and descended to the ground floor.

She found the innkeeper bustling about the kitchen between pots and plates. She watched her as she dressed a giant slab of meat, set it in a pan, and put it in the oven, her round cheeks flaming even more than usual from the heat. Then she hurried across the room to another table, took up a bowl, and began stirring it vigorously, while her eyes darted from a pile of potatoes on the counter to several onions to a round of dough to three fat hens that had yet to be plucked. Her lips moved in silence as though she were cataloguing the tasks she must still do to prepare dinner.

"Mrs. Whittle?" Calista said, moving into the room.

"Oh, good day, milady!" She smiled. "I thought you'd sleep the day away, I did. I know you meant to drive out this morning, so I guess you've heard the news of the flood. I sent Molly up to knock on your door, but she said you must have been sleeping. May I pour a cuppa for you?"

"I'm actually famished," she said, thinking of how many breakfasts, lunches and dinners she could have purchased with the money she had won the day before if it had not disappeared overnight when the church bell reset her calendar yet again.

"But first I wonder if you could tell me where to find Molly. I've a—well—I have something to say to her."

"She'll be in the back, blubbering over that cow."

"Thank you."

Finding her way to the rear entrance of the inn, she went out into a small, enclosed yard oozing with mud despite a layer of straw. A handful of chickens and a cock pecked at the mud beneath the straw on the other side of the yard. A shed-like barn stood at a right angle to the back wall of the inn on the opposite end, flanking the tall stone wall of the church. Molly sat in the nascent winter sunlight on a stool about three feet from a piteously lowing cow.

Calista picked her way across the yard, her toes and heels sinking into the mud and ruining her slippers. It didn't matter, of course. They would be fine again tomorrow. And after the bath she had taken in the street three todays ago, the mud in this livestock yard seemed tame in comparison.

"Molly?"

The girl's head swung up. "Oh, milady," she said more wanly than usual, and popped up from the stool. "How may I be helping you?"

"Good day." Calista moved toward her, and the cow turned its big white and red head toward her. She shied back. "Does it bite?"

"Nell?" Molly said with obvious surprise. "No, mum. Nell's as sweet as a buttercup."

"A buttercup?"

"Surely." Molly moved to the hulking beast's head and cupped her hand beneath its mouth. "She'd never hurt a fly. You can pet her if you'd like."

"Um. No, thank you." She clasped her hands before her. "Molly, I said something to you yesterday that I should not have."

Molly's lower lip protruded. "I don't remember—"

"You wouldn't. But do trust me, I have not been entirely kind to you. Or, rather, kind *at all*. And I want to apologize for it."

"Apologize to *me*? If you're set on it, milady, I don't guess I can tell you nay."

"Thank you. I do beg your pardon for it, and I shall try to be kinder for the remainder of the day." As many times as the day happened. Lord Dare's words from two days earlier would not leave her. She had tried to forget them, to lose herself in activity and to ignore his presence in the village entirely. But even the satisfaction of winning all of that money at cards when Richard and her father had always told her she was a hopeless idiot at cards—a hopeless idiot at everything—even that had not lessened the nauseous sting she felt in her stomach remembering the marquess's eyes as he told her precisely what he thought of her.

She had never thought herself an unkind person. But at some time, she didn't know exactly when, she had grown so accustomed to misery, and so constantly furious at her father and Richard and—*yes*—Lord Dare for entrapping her in a life she hated, she had stopped paying attention to what she said to others. She had grown careless with other people's feelings. Selfish. She saw that now. With a few direct words, Tacitus Everard had made her see it.

"Thank you, mum," Molly mumbled, obviously uncomfortable.

Calista didn't know what else to say. She looked at the cow, then at the stool, then at the empty pail beneath the cow.

"Were you milking it?"

"I was trying, milady. With Mr. Whittle across the river and Mrs. Whittle over-busy with a full house and trying to fix dinner and everything else for everybody, I thought I'd help. We're out of milk, you know."

"I had heard that." She glanced at the pail again. "You are not having any success? Is it ... That is to say, is there any milk in the cow to be gotten?"

Molly giggled. "Yes, milady. She's got plenty of milk in her. But she likes a right-handed milker, like Mr. Whittle."

"Ah, you are left-handed, I guess."

"Not at all, mum." She held up her right hand. "It's only

that I can't get a purchase on her, you see." The hand lacked a thumb and forefinger.

Calista's throat seized up. "Good heavens," she said weakly. "How did that happen?"

"It was a cleaver. I weren't twelve at the time. The trouble of it is, I was terrible clumsy even before that. So now I'm a sore burden to my aunt."

"Your aunt?"

"Mrs. Whittle."

"Oh, I see." Her chest felt leaden. "Good luck with the milking, Molly."

"Aunt Meg'll have to do it herself after we've finished dinner. And by then poor Nell'll be moaning and groaning something awful."

"I daresay no sound can be worse than that horrid bell." She glanced up at the church tower that loomed over the yard. "I don't suppose anyone will mind a cow's groaning."

Molly shrugged. "No one but the cow herself, mum."

Calista returned to the inn in a muddled humor and immediately encountered Lord Dare in the passageway to the foyer. He filled up the space, a big, tall, handsome man of worth and position, and stiff as the statue on her dressing table in the room above.

"Good day," he said.

"Good day." Her cheeks were hot with shame, but not because he had seen her in her shift. She hurried past him.

"Lady Holland?"

She turned. "Yes?"

"I don't mean to pry, but I understand that you were abed all day. Are you ... well?"

Not remotely. "Yes."

"All right." He nodded. "Then. Good." He bowed. "Forgive my intrusion."

"It was kind of you to ask."

"Given your parting with your son last night, I thought you might be missing him today."

She stared. Not even Evelina understood how much it

hurt her to part with Harry.

"But perhaps I have made a hasty judgment." His stance became abruptly uncomfortable. "I was very close to my parents, you see, and they to me. We were rarely ever apart until I went to school. Good Lord, I will go on, won't I? Again, my lady, forgive my lack of propriety."

She caught her unbidden burst of laughter between her teeth. It was too rich, *him* apologizing to her for lack of propriety.

"I see." His lips tightened and he began to turn toward the stairs.

"No. Forgive *me*. You must not believe that I am laughing at you."

"Because I've no precedent for believing that, to be sure." His eyes glimmered.

Her heart did a hard thump.

"You continually surprise me," she said quietly.

"I do? Continually?"

"With your self-deprecating humor. I think … I think perhaps that you are a truly humble man."

"Not at all, madam." His back went rigid again, his shoulders perfectly square. "After all, I am *Dare*."

There was complete silence between them for a stretched moment. Then a crooked smile shaped his mouth.

This time she allowed her laughter. "Indeed."

He nodded, still smiling, and started up the stairs.

"Wait." She stepped forward. "Did you—"

He paused on the first riser.

This was ridiculous. "Did you know that Molly lacks two fingers on her right hand?"

"The serving girl? No, I hadn't noticed that." He tilted his head.

"I realize that was a non sequitur."

"Are you perhaps remembering a conversation you have had with someone else, yet thinking it was me?"

"No. No one else." Only he who made her heart feel both light as sunshine and as heavy as stone.

The door to the private parlor opened and the Smythe family moved into the foyer.

"Good day, my lord," Mr. George Smythe said affably. "Aren't we all a cozy little gathering here at the Jolly Cockerel?" He looked meaningfully at her.

"Lady Holland," the marquess said, "allow me to introduce you to Mr. Smythe, Mrs. Smythe, and Miss Smythe, of Hammershire."

The matron nodded, then lifted her chin and perused Calista's simple traveling gown. The maiden cast her eyes to the floor as she performed an admirable curtsy.

"Good day," Calista said with her best daughter-of-an-earl hauteur. She would curtsy for Mrs. Smythe when Nell sprouted wings and flew. From all Calista had seen of her, she seemed an atrociously puffed-up mushroom.

"My lady, my lord," Mr. Smythe said. "We would be delighted to have your company in our parlor for dinner this evening. Wouldn't we, Mrs. Smythe?"

"Of course, Mr. Smythe," she drawled and peered down her nose again at Calista. She needed only a lorgnette to be as stuffy as the Duchess of Hammershire herself.

"Thank you," the marquess said. "I should like that very much."

Calista was not surprised. He was unlike any man of birth and rank that she had ever known, but she was becoming accustomed to his peculiarities.

"My lady?" Mr. Smythe said. "What say you? Will you join our little party?"

"Yes, Lady Holland," Mr. Alan Smythe said as he came out of the parlor and around his niece to stand before her. "Do accept my brother's invitation, or you will condemn us to uneven numbers at the table."

She allowed herself to smile. "I cannot allow that, can I?"

"I was certain you would understand," he said with an appreciative smile. He was an attractive man, dressed in the high fashion she saw only in catalogues that her mother sent from town. And he looked at her now as he had yesterday, as gentlemen had looked at her during her all-too-brief season in London: like she was a beautiful girl of noble birth, not the haggard, unhappy woman she had become.

While playing cards he had said something about silk trading, and she thought he and his brother were perhaps in business together. It mattered little. His conversation was light and insubstantial and made her feel like this nightmare of endless repetition was only that: a very bad dream from which she would awake tomorrow.

"Thank you, Mr. Smythe," she said to George. "I will be happy to join you for dinner."

"Splendid, splendid," he said.

She offered him a nod, and a smile to Alan Smythe, and turned toward the inn door, catching for an instant Lord Dare's sober regard upon her before he pivoted and continued up the steps.

The stable was less than fifty feet from the inn. She walked across the yard, sidestepping puddles, with heated prickles climbing up the back of her neck.

He was displeased with her. That she knew this from a moment of his intense gaze proved only that she had become overly sensitive to a man's disapproval of her. Richard was forever finding fault with her, just like her father had. That the Marquess of Dare did too was only more of the same ground they had trod six years ago.

If she wanted to flirt very mildly with an attractive man who found her attractive too, there was nothing to stop her from it now. She believed in the sanctity of marriage, and though hers was a tragic mistake, she would never betray her vows. But flirting was not adultery. Anyway, she had kissed *him,* which was much worse than flirting.

But now she was trying to convince herself that she had been justified in kissing him, which was every sort of insane.

She pushed open the stable door and the scents of damp straw and warm horses surrounded her. She thought of her elder brother, Ian, who often smelled like horses when he was up at Dashbourne, which according to her mother and Evie was frequently now that he was building his stable. Ian was a roguish devil. But he was trying to repair what her father had destroyed, and for that she admired him. And because he was a good man at heart. He would never force their younger sister to marry if Evie didn't wish it.

On the last occasion when Richard had left a bruise on her that she could not hide, across her jaw, she had considered writing to her brother about her situation. But even in such an instance, Ian would have no authority over her son. Only Richard did. And so her pen had remained silent.

Straw and horse were not the only scents in the stable. The sharp tang of whiskey met her as well.

"Mr. Jackson?" She had not seen her coachman since the first today, when she had scolded him for drunkenness and taken away his bottle. She walked farther into the building. "Mr. Jackson?" she called.

The stable boy came running from the opposite end, his skinny legs carrying him with great speed past her.

"Young man," she called out. "Where is Mr. Jackson?"

Still running, he looked over his shoulder. "Sleepin' in the tack room, mum." He darted out the stable door and she saw him streak across the yard and away from the village center.

Mr. Jackson was indeed in the tack room, passed out. She had nothing really to say to him, and nothing that would not prove entirely irrelevant tomorrow—if tomorrow were today again. She only needed to speak with someone who knew Harry. Like most of the servants at Herald's Court, the coachman adored her son. She wanted to talk about her little boy with someone who loved him too. Missing him was an ache that widened inside her with each hour.

Instead she left the stable and turned toward Harriet Tinkerson's shop. Mrs. Whittle was far too busy preparing dinner to bother her with cooking breakfast at two o'clock in the afternoon. But her stomach growled. At least at the millinery she was certain to get two biscuits.

Harriet greeted her as the prodigal daughter, with surprise, then glee, then fawning enthusiasm. Calista pretended she remembered her from their school days, cutting through that foolishness, and soon Harriet had set an empty plate and cup before her. Shortly she began the wheedling, unsubtle speech about how a woman of creative and artistic *brilliance* really did need a *noble* patron to have *any* success in business these days … And wouldn't Lady Holland like a biscuit now?

Though Harriet's bonnets were arranged throughout the store more like meat in a butcher's shop than hats in a millinery, they were all fetching. A few of her hats were true works of art. It was a shame Harriet herself was such a ninny. It was an even greater shame that, if tomorrow never came, she would be one of Calista's few friends forever.

~oOo~

Dinner in the private parlor was not enjoyable.

Mr. George Smythe, indeed a silk trader in partnership with his brother, engaged the marquess in conversation about politics almost exclusively, despite Lord Dare's many polite attempts to turn the conversation to topics more suited to ladies. Their host would not oblige, nor would the ladies themselves. Mrs. Smythe divided her time between grilling Calista on information concerning every member of the *ton* that she, her mother, and Ian knew, and disapproving of her daughter's timid additions to the conversation.

Penelope Smythe was painfully shy, but trying valiantly not to be miserable in the company of two strangers. Her uncle managed to charmingly deflect his sister-in-law's barbs while flirting mildly with Calista too.

At first she found it flattering. But by the end of the evening a sour flavor had invaded her mouth that had nothing to do with Mrs. Whittle's excellent dinner. What sort of man made such a cake of himself over another man's wife? Lord Dare had said things to her that could be construed as inappropriate flirting. But it felt different. It felt genuine, not as though he said them for the effect they would have on her, but simply because it was the truth.

He found her entirely appealing to all of his senses. When she was covered in mud and splashing about on a high street.

Now, in unexceptionable circumstances, he barely glanced at her. Courteous, interesting, and pleasant, he was a perfect guest even to these upstart members of the petty gentry who thought that because they paid an extra guinea a night they owned this little parlor.

Claiming exhaustion, she excused herself immediately after tea and went to her room. Aphrodite's face shone in the candlelight across the room. Unbuttoning her gown, she began to draw it off when a soft scratching sounded at the door.

Only one person had come to her door other than the women who worked in this inn: the Marquess of Dare. But he was not the sort to scratch.

Hoping it wasn't Alan Smythe, she opened the door. The cat from the previous mornings sat on the threshold.

"You do not remember the kippers," she said. "So why are you here?"

It mewled.

"No." She started to draw the door shut. "You are probably riddled with fleas, and I don't fancy waking up with bites all over my—" She pinned her lips closed. And opened the door. The cat slipped inside, leaped onto the bed, and curled up into a tight ball at the foot, its open eyes on her.

"Yes, you may stay." She shut the door and bolted it. "But you won't be here in the morning, you know."

A rumbling purr sounded from its scruffy head. Calista removed her clothes and joined the skinny little creature in bed.

In the morning it was gone.

Chapter Twelve

CALISTA LAY BENEATH THE COVERS, trembling. The rainfall against the windowpane was the scratching of a thousand tiny claws. And that church bell ...

That church bell.

That hideous, diabolical church bell. It tolled and tolled and tolled, and although she counted to only seven it *felt* like seven hundred thunderous death knells crawling beneath her lungs and making her hate every unblessed reverberation.

Except that she would *never* actually die. She would never move on from this day, grow old, and someday be at peace. She would remain here in this room in this inn in this village forever with only that evil bell to remind her that she was cursed. Forgotten by time. Unloved by God. Destined to insanity.

That hateful, wicked bell.

She stared unblinking at the ceiling, every nerve jittering, every surface of her skin cold with sweat, every hair on her body standing on end, and she knew one thing with a clarity she had not experienced in many days.

That bell had to die.

Now.

And she would be the one to do it.

She had already tried earplugs. On her cardplaying day, she had called upon Dr. Appleby for wax and lambswool. The following morning she awoke with empty ears. But now it was suddenly so obvious. If she could not stop herself from hearing the tolls, she would stop the tolls from being heard *by anyone.*

She dressed, knowing exactly where she must go now.

Mrs. Whittle was exiting the kitchen when Calista

descended to the foyer.

"Good day, milady! The inn's all filled up with the rain bringing people in off the road last night, and I've my hands full at present. But I'll be with you right quick. Will you be having tea or coffee?"

"Whatever you have here." Calista took the pot from her and a cup, and poured. She drank as Mrs. Whittle watched with round eyes. Then she deposited the items in the innkeeper's hands, grabbed a cloak off the peg, and went out into the rain.

The blacksmith's shop was at the far end of town, on the other side of the pub and closest to the ford. The rain still fell heavily, but she pressed through it along the deserted high street until she came to her goal.

The smith was a large man, as smiths often were, she supposed, with a dark face and enormous arms. The flood had not stayed his work today; his forge was brilliant red already and as she entered he was setting a glowing horseshoe to the anvil with a pair of tongs, a hammer in his other hand.

"G'day, mum. How might I be helping you?"

"Good day. I need an axe. I've nothing to pay you with, but I am sure you will be tremendously happy with the outcome of my work with it, as will everybody. Except perhaps Reverend Abbot, of course. Ah, there is just the tool I require." She crossed to the axe leaning against the wall and hefted it with some effort. "Good heavens, it's quite a lot heavier than I had imagined. But it will do splendidly. Thank you, sir."

He set down his work and towered over her by a head and a half.

"Can't be letting you take my good axe, mum, especially as I've never seen you before."

"Then may I have your not-as-good axe? Only to borrow. I shall return it anon."

"Can't do that either, mum."

"All right." She returned the axe to him. "Good day." She left the shop, went to the bakery, and bought a sweet roll. Then she went to the church and waited. No one bothered her in the corner of the pew that she tucked herself into, and only two others came into the church: a slender, youngish man with yellow hair and a decent face, and the bell ringer before each hour.

At noon she went to the pub, ate lunch, read a bit of the *Book of Common Prayer* that she had taken from the church, and waited. No one bothered her here either. To these people she was not the woman who had played in the mud, danced on tables, and shepherded a flock, rather merely a traveler stranded overnight in Swinly and seeking escape from the inn.

When darkness fell entirely, she returned to the smith's shop, now uninhabited, took up the axe, and sloshed through the puddles along the high street to the church. No one in this miserable village ever locked their doors. Either they were hopelessly naïve or the flood gave them false assurance of safety from the intrusion of outsiders. Swinly was not on the main highway, of course. Perhaps they were trusting sorts and did not suspect strangers of ill intent.

Tonight she would change their thoughts on that.

The church was a high, airy place, even in the darkness. She walked around its interior perimeter to ensure that there were no worshippers hiding inside before she returned to the west end, where she hid in a shadow behind a column.

Eventually the bell ringer appeared. He was an elderly man, but wiry, and he made his way with an easy gait to a door at the base of the tower.

Calista waited a few minutes longer until he began ringing. She counted the tolls—seven—and grinned. It seemed right that seven would be the last number of rings Old Mary would ever toll.

When the ringer appeared again, walked the length of the church's nave toward the chancel, and let himself out at the north aisle door, Calista went to it and bolted it shut. Then she returned to the main door at the west end and bolted that too. Taking up the lamp just inside the door, she moved to the narrow, winding staircase that rose into darkness. Lifting the lantern before her and dragging the axe, she climbed the stone stairs.

From her studies of the exterior of the tower from the ground, she knew that at its top it opened into a vast belfry. Halting on the level beneath the belfry, where the stairs let off onto a floor upon which the ringer stood to pull the rope and set the bell in motion, she confirmed her conclusions. Now the rope hung lifelessly from the darkness above. Nothing else about the ringing chamber recommended itself to her: a metal placard with a Latin inscription and several English names, and a single chair were its only accoutrements.

It was clear that she would have to destroy her nemesis at its source.

Returning to the stairs, she climbed at least two dozen more to the belfry. At the top, she set her foot on the catwalk skirting the wall and heaved air into her lungs, startling a pair of doves nestled in a window. With alarmed coos, they fluttered off.

The space was open to the air on all four sides, without netting or any other enclosure. February wind batted at her as she crept around the edges of the catwalk, studying Old Mary from all sides. It was an old-fashioned rope and wheel construction, the bell not affixed in place with a moveable clapper but entirely free-swinging. More than half her height, the bell was not nearly as fearsome a beast as she had expected, fashioned of thick metal and inscribed along the edge with more Latin words. Still, as a whole, it defied easy disassembly. The clapper was fixed too far up into the monster to dislodge without hanging upside down inside the bell. Cutting the rope here at the top where it was easy to repair would be a temporary deterrent at best.

With a larger bell, the solution she had decided upon would not be possible; the beams would be far too well reinforced or perhaps even metal. But the wooden frame from which Old Mary hung looked as old as the rest of the church.

She set down the lantern. Dragging the axe up the ladder built into the narrow strip of wall between corner and open window, she turned around with awkward effort, braced her behind against it, and began to chop at the beam of the frame before her.

The wood was frightfully hard. It came away in only bits and chips. And she could not swing as widely as she wished for fear of losing her footing. But she still had almost an hour.

Several times the axe slipped in her tiring grasp and the blade came perilously close to her limbs. Occasionally, she rested.

By the time the beam had become a sideways hourglass, with only a fragment of hard pulp connecting its two ends, her arms ached viciously and her shoulders and hands were fiery clusters of cramped pain. Music from the fiddler at the pub rose upon the night air, and a breeze ran cold across her sweat-dampened skin.

A faint echo of pounding floated up the tower—pounding at the church door.

It must be eight o'clock. The bell ringer had come to ring the hour.

She swung a final time and cut through the last of the beam. As the two sides of the severed beam bent slowly in on themselves, and creaking and moaning and cracking filled the belfry, only then did Calista realize that when the bell came down, the belfry might too. At the very least, the now wounded frame to which the bell was still attached on one side might collapse.

With her in it. And the lantern.

Dropping the axe and hearing it thunk on the ringing chamber floor far below, she wrapped her hands around the ladder's shallow rail and in horrified fascination watched the weight of the bell drag down the framework bit by bit. The wind whipped at her hair, plastering locks across her face, and abruptly the lantern light snuffed out.

"Dear God, *save me*," she whispered.

Lit only by the starlight, with a vast, grumbling, creaking roar, the bell slumped, and then tilted. Finally the supporting frame broke free of the stone and the opposite beam snapped with a horrendous crack. The tower shook, her fingers gripped, and Old Mary crashed down—to the ringing room floor and through it and down—deafening bang after smash after crunch—an endless bellow of destruction into blackness.

Then, except for the wind humming through the belfry, there was silence.

Calista opened her eyes and found herself gripping the ladder railing. Her entire body shook. The broken frame shone bluish-silver, but she could see nothing below. Descent would have to be by touch alone.

Footstep by careful footstep, she found her way around the miraculously intact catwalk to the stone stairs. The tower, it seemed, had been sturdily built—all but the ringing room floor, apparently—and Old Mary, it seemed, had been obliging enough to fall straight downward. On wobbling knees, Calista reached the ground in one raw piece of shaking flesh and bone.

She unbolted the church door and opened it upon a cluster of villagers: the vicar in a dressing gown, the constable with glowing red cheeks from his regular Saturday evening sojourn at the pub, the bell ringer with horrified eyes, and a number of others.

"Well," she said, blinking in the torchlight and smiling. "That takes care of that."

Chapter Thirteen

TACITUS HAD NEVER before considered Lady Calista Chance odd.

Immature, yes.

Too blithe at times, certainly.

Fond of teasing, to be sure.

Irrepressibly high-spirited and tenderly affectionate at once ... *He had fallen in love with that.*

But never odd.

Lady Calista Holland, however, was odd. What lady of birth, when stranded by a flood in a small village several miles off the highway, became fast friends with the local dressmaker and then purchased several bolts of wool from the shop as well as a bundle of washed fleece from a local farmer?

Provided with this information by a woman Lady Calista had apparently been to school with, Mrs. Harriet Tinkerson, Tacitus chewed on the news as he sipped ale in the taproom and tried not to lose another hand of cards to Mr. Alan Smythe.

"Lady Holland, you say?" Smythe said with an appreciative perusal of Mrs. Tinkerson's impressive hat. "How charming. I wonder what she'll do with it all."

"Make dresses, one supposes," Mrs. Tinkerson said. "Oh! Mrs. Whittle!" She hurried across the room to the innkeeper. "I've finished that chip straw hat you admire so. Do come by to try it on. I think it will look positively delightful on you. I've even added a green ribbon to match your church gown."

"Oh, dear me, Mrs. Tinkerson," the innkeeper said, collecting empty plates from the tables. "I'm terrible busy today without Mr. Whittle. I'm afraid I won't—"

The foyer door crashed open and Lady Holland entered,

her arms full of bolts of cloth.

"Calista!" Mrs. Tinkerson said, rushing forward. "It's such a pleasure to see you again after only an hour's absence. Lady Holland," she said to anyone who was listening, "honored me with a visit to my shop this afternoon." She dimpled. "Whatever will you do with all of this cloth?"

"A project." She set down the bolts. "Mrs. Whittle, may I leave these here until later?"

"Of course, milady."

"Excellent." Turning about, she exited the inn with empty arms.

Through the window, Tacitus watched her walk up the high street, lifting her skirts to avoid muddying them, her dark hair without hat or bonnet shining in the sunlight that now lit the entire sodden village into sparkles.

"I don't blame you, my lord," Smythe said quietly.

He yanked his gaze away from the window. "Blame me?"

"She's a beautiful woman. And by the way she was looking at you this morning after breakfast, she clearly thinks you're not so shabby either." He nodded knowingly and shuffled the cards. "Stranded at an inn overnight ... If I were you, and I hadn't already got my eye on another sweet lady right here in this village, I would seize the opportunity."

Tacitus clamped down on the quick anger that arose in him. He stood up.

"I believe I've had enough of cards. Good afternoon, Smythe." He went to the stable and inquired of the ostler if there were a pub in the village. Then he headed in that direction.

He needed a drink, but not with Mr. blasted Alan Smythe.

Got his eye on? Seize the opportunity? What sort of scoundrel spoke with a stranger that way about a lady, however odd she was?

Discovering the pub to be a pleasant place, with comfortable chairs, clean tables, and a good-natured host, he commanded a glass of ale, pulled his book out of his pocket, and settled in to read.

When night fell, he stayed for dinner. He did not fancy returning to the Jolly Cockerel and watching Mr. Smythe flirt with Lady Holland during dinner, as Smythe had tried to do earlier in the day. She had been pleasant to him, but she hadn't taken up the flirtation. Nevertheless, Smythe had persisted until she asked him to go to the dress shop and invite the dressmaker to pay a call on her at the inn. He'd left the inn like he was a knight heading out to do battle for his lady.

Some men had no honor.

But Tacitus realized he wasn't being entirely honest. He did not want to return to the inn just yet because *he did not trust himself.*

Smythe was right. That morning she *had* looked at him warmly. Too warmly. Briefly, thank God. But even that brief glance, coming suddenly as it had after her sharp words the night before, had rocked him to the soles of his boots. It was best if he stayed as far from Calista Holland as possible while stranded in this village.

When the fiddler had wrapped up his playing, and the tolls of the God-awfully-loud bell in the church tower on the other end of the village struck twelve, he shrugged into his greatcoat and headed back to the Jolly Cockerel. She was certain to be abed now; there was no danger of accidentally encountering her. And tomorrow when he left Swinly he could relegate this chance meeting to the realm of unfortunate episodes he hoped to never, ever repeat.

Unless she was indeed odd and at this moment was lugging four huge bolts of fabric and a bag of wool into the church.

Go to the inn.

What in God's name was she doing, entering the church at midnight with all of that cloth?

Go to the inn.

Go to the—

He reached the closed church door in time to hear a thumping clunk on the other side. The sound was like a heavy bolt sliding into place. But if it weren't ... If burdened by all that cloth she had tripped … If she had fallen …

If someone had been lying in wait for her…

Like many medieval churches, the door had no handle on the outside. He pounded on it.

"Lady Holland," he shouted at the thick wood. "Lady Holland!"

The thunking sound came again and the door cracked open.

"Shh!" She opened it only a crack. "Do you want to wake everyone in the village?"

"I— I—"

"Well, what is it?"

"I saw you enter— I was afraid that you …" He sounded like a perfect idiot.

"You were afraid that I what?" She looked directly into his eyes and he lost all thought.

"What are you doing?" he mumbled.

"Nothing that concerns you." She pushed the door closed. "Good night, Lord—"

He stuck his boot in the crack. "Let me enter."

"No. Go away."

"I think you might be doing something clandestine, and I cannot allow that."

"I am definitely doing something clandestine, but it still doesn't concern you."

His anger from earlier boiled anew. "Is Smythe in there?"

Her brow screwed up. "Mr. Smythe from the inn? Why would he be in— *Oh.*" Her eyes seemed to dim a bit, and then her lips hardened. "You really do have a low opinion of me, don't you? Well, my lord, come right in and join the orgy, why don't you?" She opened the door wide and made a sweeping welcome gesture. "Someone or other in here was just asking after you, in fact, but I was too engaged in flagrant disregard for my marriage vows to notice who at the time."

He stepped inside and allowed her to close the door. Then he turned to her.

"I beg your pardon," he said.

"I know." She bolted the door. "You beg it all the time. But I'm still not really convinced you've yet meant it." Hefting two of the bolts of cloth, she started toward the opposite corner lit only by the single lamp at the door at which he still stood. "Bring that cloth, will you? It will save me a trip," she called over her shoulder.

"I don't—"

"No questions," echoed back to him. "If you insist on being here, you must promise not to speak."

"I will make no such promise." He took up the bolts of cloth and the bundle of wool and followed her.

"Suit yourself. But if you object to my project, do not expect me to obey your demands this time." She stopped at a wooden door, lodged the bolt in her right arm against the wall, and opened the panel.

He followed her into a narrow tower that was entirely black. She started up the tightly winding stairs.

"Would you like me to bring the lantern from the—"

"No. I know my way. At the top, the stars provide sufficient light."

He went cautiously behind her. Despite the heavy cloth in her arms, she climbed swiftly. He listened to her in the darkness and felt carefully for each step until the rhythm of their height and depth became familiar.

"What exactly is your project?"

"You'll see. If you wish, you can assist me."

"Does the vicar of this church by chance know what you're up to?"

"Of course not. He would not understand."

"What a surprise."

"If you don't want to help, go back to the front door. But don't leave. I need that door to remain locked until after seven o'clock tomorrow morning."

She was mad. And yet, at the top of the stairs, as the starlight shining in through the belfry apertures settled on her lovely features, he could not look away from her. Her eyes were not the eyes of a madwoman. Instead they were crystal clear, as always, and thoughtful. And his heart was a miserable betrayer; it thumped far too hard. He could put it off to the climb up dozens of steps. Or he could admit the truth to himself.

No. He would blame the steps and leave it at that.

She set down the bolts and fisted her hands on her hips as she walked confidently onto the catwalk, studying the bell. "I think the wool first, then the cloth. Yes. That should do it."

He remained in the doorway. "Do what?"

She reached for a great coil of rope on the narrow catwalk. "Mute it sufficiently."

"Sufficiently for what?"

"So that I won't hear it in the morning."

He watched her pull the wool out of the sack and unwrap the rope.

"You are muffling the bell so it won't ring in the morning?"

"Yes. Don't just stand there. Help me with this."

He did. He could not do otherwise. "This reminds me of the sorts of stories your sister and brother told me."

"I'll wager it does," she said, stretching to toss the rope over a beam and pulling the fabric of her gown so that it revealed her sweetly rounded behind. "Those stories shocked you."

"No." He grabbed the end of the rope she tossed to him across the bell and tied it off.

"Don't bother trying to be gallant."

"They didn't shock me. They made me jealous."

She stopped wrapping cloth around the bell and peered at him. "Jealous of what?"

"Of your companionship."

She blinked rapidly several times. "My companionship?"

"The three of you, together," he said, tamping down his discomfort. "I have no siblings. I had only my parents growing up, and that was more than sufficient for me. But seeing you and Lady Evelina and Gregory together ... I wished that I'd had that."

"I see," she said quietly. "You know, in truth, we plagued each other more than we cared for each other."

"I doubt that," he said.

She reached for the last bolt of cloth. "Take this. You are tall enough to run that end over the top."

He did as she requested and they cinched the final length of rope about the whole. She folded her arms and looked upon their work in obvious satisfaction.

"I wish we could wrap the clapper," she said. "But I think this should do it."

"This is the oddest evening I have spent in some time."

"What? Don't you and Lord Mallory climb church towers every Saturday night to wrap the bells in cloth?" She offered him a smile and Tacitus's heart fell into his shoes.

"Not lately," he murmured. "Are you mad?"

"No. Rather, perhaps. I'm not certain. But nothing else has worked yet, so I thought I would try this." She gestured to the bell.

"This, what?"

"Wrapping it in cloth to mute it. I tried destroying it, but that didn't work. The local carpenter required more than a single day to block up the windows, no matter how much gold I promised him. And though I plied him with drink, I could not manage to get Mr. Pimly disguised enough so that he was unable to ring it. For a small man he has a remarkably strong constitution when it comes to spirits. I even suggested to Reverend Abbot that he give Mr. Pimly a holiday from ringing, on account of the flood. But he said Mr. Pimly has not missed a single hour in forty-eight years. Can you imagine that sort of loyalty—loyalty that does not waver no matter what happens?"

"Yes," he said, his chest too tight for more air to make words.

She looked at him. "Thank you for your help. Would you like me to let you out of the church now?"

"Are you intending to stay? Locked inside all night?"

"I must. I cannot let Mr. Pimly enter with time to unwrap it before seven o'clock."

"Really?"

"I'm not mad," she said more subdued now. "Not in the usual way, that is."

"Then perhaps ... explain this?"

The smile she offered him now was small and oddly resigned. "I cannot. You can either trust me, that I must do this, or go tell everyone I'm mad."

"What if I only tell the vicar?"

"As you wish. I cannot stop you from it. But I hope you won't. I would like to know if this kinder, gentler method of silencing this dratted bell will please the gods or whoever it is that must be pleased. God, perhaps. I don't know. I just know that I hope you will not reveal me."

He shook his head. "Perhaps you aren't mad."

"Why do you say that?"

"You sound just like you did that morning."

"What morning?"

"The morning you asked me to help you run away."

Her eyes shone in the starlight. "Do I?"

He nodded.

For a long moment he heard only the whistling of the cold wind in the belfry rafters and his own tight inhalations.

"Do you intend to remain on this frigid catwalk until dawn?" he said when she did not speak. "Because I noticed that the pews below look quite comfortable. A man might even sleep on one if he likes."

Her face broke into delight. "You intend to stay? Until dawn? Because you think I am mad or because you think I will fall asleep and then you can betray me to Reverend Abbot without my notice? I won't sleep, you know. I will remain awake until dawn."

He turned toward the stairs. "I will not betray you. But it's getting colder up here each minute." He gestured to invite her to descend before him.

"Thank you, my lord. You are truly gallant."

They descended, and Tacitus did not allow himself to consider that this was unwise or to berate himself for weakness. For the first time in far too long, he felt happy. Even if only for a stolen moment, he would take it.

Chapter Fourteen

CALISTA TUCKED THE FOWLING PIECE against her shoulder, pointed it at Old Mary, and set her finger to the trigger.

"Wait! Good God, wait, woman!" Lord Dare stumbled into the belfry, his hand outstretched and eyes fraught. "What are you doing?"

She turned her attention back to the bell.

"I know how to shoot." She dug the stock more tightly into her shoulder. "My brother taught me years ago."

He came forward and knocked the barrel aside, then grabbed her wrist.

"What—"

His eyes flashed with fury as he wrenched the weapon from her hands. "He obviously didn't tell you that solid metal will repel grapeshot right back at you. Good God, it's a good thing I saw you coming in here just now." Holding the rifle and her wrist both tightly between them, he gaped. "What were you *thinking*?"

She tugged out of his grip and backed away from him.

"I told you at breakfast. I cannot bear to hear this bell ring at dawn one more time. Not even *one* more time. If I have to hear it again, I think I will go mad. Truly mad."

"And you don't think shooting at it with a hunting rifle is already a sign of madness?"

"Yes! *Yes*, I do. But I haven't any other choice in the matter. I have no choice in *any* matter. No matter what I do, nothing changes. Every act I make, every plan I devise, every word I utter disappears as though it never existed. I thought that if I shot at it—"

"You would accidentally shoot yourself and not have to take the blame for having done so?" he demanded.

"*What?* No. No, I didn't— I never would— My son needs me—"

"Because I'll tell you, after my parents died, I went down that ugly road. I thought through the entire thing logically and rationally, again and again. And again and again I came to the same conclusion: I was the worst sort of coward for even entertaining the idea." His eyes were thunderclouds. "And if there is one thing I am certain about, it is that you, madam, are not a coward." He gestured with the rifle toward the bell. "I don't know what this is about. But it has been clear to me all day—even since last night when I arrived in this village—that all is not right with you. Whatever is going on, I needn't know the details of it to know that you are made of stronger stuff than this. You can conquer it."

"I don't know if I can," she said.

"You must. You will."

"How do you know that? You don't know anything about me. Not for years."

"Perhaps. But I don't think a person alters her character so severely, not in so few years."

"You disapproved of me then."

"Yes," he said. "And no."

"You had no right to."

He seemed to draw a deep breath. "Whose is this?" He gestured with the rifle.

"Reverend Abbot's." It had taken her all day to locate a firearm, shot, and powder that she could borrow without notice.

"Come with me," he said, and disappeared into the stairwell.

Calista followed him down the stairs, from the church, and along the soggy high street in the dark toward the opposite end of the village. He strode with purpose, not looking back at her, and directly to the pub. He halted at the door.

"Wait here," he said. "Don't move. Can you do that?"

She nodded.

"Keep this." He handed her the rifle. "But, for God's sake, don't go back to that church and try to shoot that infernal bell."

"You trust me not to?"

"Yes." He went inside and returned shortly with a stack of glasses and bottles lodged beneath his arms. "Bring the piece." He set off toward the blacksmith's shop and then walked past it to the ford.

"Where are you going?"

"Here," he said above the rippling rush of the water. He halted before the stone wall that bordered the swollen creek on the side of the smith's shop, and set down the bottles. One by one he arranged the glasses along the wall at intervals of a few feet.

Calista watched in wonder. He surprised her every day. She never anticipated him. The night before, when he sat on that hard wooden pew and talked to her until dawn, as the hours passed and she told him about Harry and he told her about his parents, she'd felt happy for the first time in days. Simply happy. And as the night passed she had become certain—*certain*—that the bell would not wake her in her bed at seven o'clock.

Yet it had.

And she had gone a little insane. Rather, *more* insane.

"All right." He came to her side. Starlight glimmered off the water and the empty glasses and full bottles standing like soldiers in a row. "I assume this is loaded?"

"It is."

"Do you have more shot and powder with you?"

"Yes."

"Good. Now, my lady, you may shoot."

"At those?"

He nodded, his face serious. "It should help."

"To shoot *those*?"

"Yes, woman." He snatched the rifle from her hands, took a step away from her, raised it to his shoulder, and a deafening blast sounded as smoke arose from the barrel and a bottle exploded into splashing shards. He lowered the rifle. "There. I feel better already." He glanced at her. "Where is that shot and powder?"

She laughed.

"The shot, madam?" he urged.

She gave it to him, and the powder horn. "You are an extraordinary person, Tacitus Everard."

"Because I can shoot a bottle of whiskey at four yards out?" he said as he poured shot down the barrel.

"Yes," she said, biting her lips.

"Your standards are far too low." He handed her the rifle. "Now it's your turn."

She shot and missed. After reloading, he adjusted her grip and Calista tried very hard not to pay attention to the pleasure of his hands on hers while silently cursing the acrid gun smoke that overpowered his scent.

The next try went better; she nicked a glass.

On the third try, she hit a bottle and it burst in glorious abandon.

"Brava," he said. "And just in time for us to be reprimanded by the local law."

The constable's bulky silhouette lumbered toward them from the direction of the pub. Calista held her breath. She had already spent several hours in the tiny Swinly jail after she chopped down Old Mary. She would rather not repeat that particular detail of her day.

"Good evening, gentlefolks," he said pleasantly, a roll in his tongue from his tenure in the pub. He stuck his thumbs in his waistcoat and rocked on his heels. "Having a bit of target practice, are we?"

"Yes, sir," Lord Dare said with a conspiratorial smile at her that dove straight into Calista's toes. "Would you care to join us?"

"Don't mind if I do." The constable accepted the rifle and promptly sent a glass flying from the wall.

"Well done, Pritchard!" Mr. Alan Smythe came toward them. Beside her, the marquess seemed to stiffen. "What are you all at, shooting at midnight?"

"Simply shooting at midnight," she said. "Will you take a shot, Mr. Smythe?"

He smiled charmingly, but it was a different smile than usual. Tonight it did not invade.

"No, thank you, my lady. I'll leave that to men who actually possess that skill. But while my lord and the constable are at it, might I have a private word with you?"

"Her ladyship is shooting too, Smythe," Lord Dare growled. "She is getting quite good at it."

Mr. Smythe's chin seemed to tuck inward. "Of course she is. Forgive me, my lady."

"You are forgiven, Mr. Smythe," Calista said, "and I will be glad to speak with you. Lord Dare, save me a bottle." She took Mr. Smythe's arm and walked a few paces away. "How may I help you?"

"At the risk of seeming atrociously indelicate, I wonder if you might share with me what you know of Mrs. Cooke."

"Mrs. Cooke? The dressmaker?"

"The very lady. I made her acquaintance briefly today, when I went to her shop on your behalf. And may I say, this gown suits you superbly. I would not have thought worsted wool would do justice to your beauty. But it is a remarkably clever design, and the embroidery is superb about the collar."

"Thank you." She studied his intricately tied neckcloth and the fine fabric of his greatcoat that sported three capes. "You are an admirer of fashion, I think. Do you wish to consult Mrs. Cooke on patterns and fabrics and such?"

"I do indeed. But before that ... that is to say, my lady ... I should very much like to know if there is a *Mr.* Cooke in the picture."

Of course.

"Mrs. Cooke is a widow. Her husband of only two years perished at Waterloo."

"A widow of some time already, then." His shoulders seemed to loosen. "That's good news. That is, terrible tragedy, of course," he amended swiftly.

"Mr. Smythe, are your intentions towards Mrs. Cooke honorable?"

His eyes popped wide. And then his mouth twisted into a sheepish grin.

"Lady Holland, I am honestly shocked to admit that they are."

She smiled. "Then I wish you success in your courtship."

"Courtship?" the marquess said, coming to her shoulder.

Mr. Smythe's cheeks filled with red. "Thank you, my lady. Good evening to you both." He bowed and hurried back toward the pub.

Lord Dare looked after him. "What was that about?"

The silvery blue light of the stars cast his face in shadows and the scar looked especially dashing. She wondered how he had acquired it. She wondered if it had hurt him terribly and if anyone had comforted him in his pain. Last night he had told her things she had not known about his family and his life, things she had not bothered learning from him six years earlier. Now she wanted to know so much more.

"It seems that Mr. Smythe fancies Mrs. Cooke," she said.

"The dressmaker?"

"Yes. He intends to court her. It's marvelous. If I had not fed the cat and so gone in to breakfast late, and if Molly had not spilled that coffee on me instead of Mr. Dewey at just the moment Mr. Smythe came through the foyer, and if he had not offered to ask Mrs. Cooke to call upon me, he might continue to pass through this village twice a year and never meet her, though she is only one hundred yards from him every time. Isn't it delightful what an accidental happenstance can lead to?"

He was silent, only his beautiful eyes intent upon her features, one feature after another.

"Yes," he finally said. "I wish him well in it. Now, there is one bottle left to be destroyed. Will you do the honors?"

She smiled; but now, strangely, it was an effort to do so. "Thank you, my lord."

She shot the bottle. And for a few precious moments she did feel better.

Chapter Fifteen

CALISTA AWOKE GROGGILY, cracking her eyes open to the gray dawn and slowly drawing in a lungful of cold air. She counted Old Mary's tolls, but she already knew when they would cease. Turning her head aside on the pillow, she watched the rain run along the pane, an endless stream of heaven's tears.

No tears threatened her eyes. What was the purpose of weeping when it would have no effect? What was the purpose of doing anything when nothing had any effect? She had never had much influence on anything; not on her family's scandal or its recovery under Ian's guidance, not on her father's decision to sell her to Richard, and not on her husband except to rouse his jealousy and possessiveness.

Now she was thoroughly impotent. She had no power to wrest Harry from her husband's control, and no power to end this endless day. She understood that finally.

She supposed she ought to thank God that she would never be obliged to return to Richard. Yet without her son, it was a hollow, horrible prize.

She dressed, and when she opened her bedchamber door the cat bounded in and straight to her dressing table. Leaping up beside the statue of Aphrodite, it curled its body around the stone, rubbing its brow against the goddess's knees and twining its tail around her lovingly. It purred.

"I don't like her, you know," Calista said. "You cannot change my opinion."

The animal meowed.

Jumping down from the table, it followed her to the kitchen for its breakfast. Accepting from Mrs. Whittle a slice of buttered bread for herself, Calista took up an umbrella and escaped the inn before Mr. Pritchard and Harriet could arrive, before Molly could douse her with coffee, and before she could see the civil distance in the Marquess of Dare's eyes.

She had no further desire to try to silence Old Mary. That madness had passed with the shattering of whiskey bottles.

She crossed the rainy yard swiftly and ducked into the stable. Shaking her skirts, she went in search of her coachman and found him feeding the carriage horses.

"Mornin', milady."

"Good morning, Mr. Jackson. We shan't be traveling home today. The ford has flooded over."

Distress clouded his eyes.

"Are you— What is the matter?" she asked.

He turned from her and his trembling hands made the pail rattle. Perhaps he had already taken to the bottle this morning.

"Nothin' a'tall. The horses'll be well-rested to go tomorrow."

"Mr. Jackson, I wish you would tell me what your trouble is. In my husband's absence, it is my responsibility to take care of such things."

"T'ain't nothin' you can take care of, milady," he grumbled, and left the stall.

"Come now. Why don't you try me?"

He set down the pail and heaved a great sigh. "My Petey, my second boy, he's been off in the East Indies for some time now."

"In the Army?"

"Aye. Signed up the very week his mum passed four years ago. I haven't seen him since."

"You must miss him dreadfully." She knew that ache well. He nodded, then his face crumpled.

"Oh, dear." She reached out to touch his arm. "Why don't you sit down?" She urged him to a bench and he slumped upon it, then she joined him. "Has something happened to him?"

"I'd a letter ten days ago," he said dully. "My boy sickened with a fever. It— It took him quick, his captain said. He didn't suffer too much." Tears fell onto his cheeks.

"I am so sorry," she said. "So very sorry." But this was too painful. Much too painful for her. This was the reason for his drunkenness in the past sennight, and it dug too deeply, too swiftly. She stood up. "If there is anything I can do for you, you must let me know."

"My older boy, Bartholomew, he don't know about Petey yet. With the master doin' so poorly of late, Mr. Baker's been too busy to write to him."

"Mr. Baker? Why would my husband's valet write to your son?"

"He's a good soul, Mr. Baker is. He does it for me, seein' as I can't."

"You cannot write?"

He shook his head. "Can't read neither."

"Oh. I see."

"I'd like to tell Bart about our Petey. They were thick as thieves when they were lads. Then Bart went off to serve a gentleman in Leeds and Petey couldn't bear staying at home without his brother and mum both. It'll break my boy's heart to hear his brother's gone. But I'm anxious to tell him. Then, I suppose, we can comfort each other."

"I daresay," she whispered. She clutched her hands together at her waist. "Do let me know if I can assist you with anything ... here." She looked around. "Not that I really could. I don't know how to care for horses."

Jackson nodded somberly.

"I am so terribly sorry, Mr. Jackson. Truly."

She fled the stable. But there was nowhere to go to escape her fear of never seeing Harry again. Of all of the horrors of this curse, that fear was by far the worst.

~o0o~

Through the taproom window, Tacitus watched Calista Holland leave the inn, walk up the high street and disappear from view, and then return an hour later carrying a wrapped bundle. Crossing the foyer, she ascended the stairs, leaving a trail of water dripping behind her.

Shortly, she came down the stairs in a dry gown and cloak, took up an umbrella, and went out again.

An hour later, she returned, this time empty-handed, and the entire process repeated itself.

Then again.

The fourth time, he donned his coat and followed her. The rain had finally ceased but the roads and paths she took were sodden. From twenty yards behind her he admired her even stride despite the mud, the set of her shoulders, and the fall of her wet hair down her back. She wore no bonnet and had left her hair unbound.

She seemed to have no destination. She walked to the ford, then behind a smith's shop to a path that wended along the swollen creek, then across a field and up a hill. Descending, she climbed over a stile, crossed another field, this one peopled with sheep, and, after she passed through it, closed a gate that had stood wide open. When he opened it to follow her, she halted.

"Do make certain to fasten the latch firmly, my lord," she called back to him. "The sheep will escape if you don't."

He did so, but before he could walk to her she started off again.

She was an odd, mysterious woman.

"Have you a destination?" he called forward.

"No," she shouted back, and turned from the path onto another that led up another rise.

He jogged to catch up with her, the muddy earth splashing on his boots. She did not break her stride or slow for him.

"What are you doing, then?" he said, coming to her side.

"Strolling. Obviously."

"Have you taken this same path on each of your four previous strolls?"

"The first time I stopped at the dress shop on my return route to the inn. And I had forgotten about the sheep gate until this time. Have you been watching me, my lord?"

"I have. From the taproom at the inn where I was losing at cards to the sharps disguised as our fellow guests. It was a welcome distraction to follow your progress, or lack thereof, as it were."

"Why did you decide to follow me?"

"I suppose I should be embarrassed to admit that my curiosity overcame me."

"Well, there is really nothing interesting about this. I am sorry to disappoint your curiosity."

He walked apace with her a few strides. "You must be tiring."

"A bit."

"Have lunch with me at the pub."

She halted and faced him. "Why?"

"It's lunchtime."

"I saw a rainbow," she said.

"Did you?"

"Yes, for the first time today. I never saw one before today, though it must have been here all along."

"Then I am glad you have finally seen it."

"I will have lunch with you. Thank you." Her words were subdued and she did not smile. She seemed a changed woman from the girl he had known six years earlier. Still beautiful—despite the gray circles beneath her eyes—so beautiful that looking into her face made his chest ridiculously tight. But now she was too somber, her features entirely lacking the joy that had lit her smiles and laughter that month.

They walked in silence to the pub, took a table, and ordered food. He instructed the serving girl to bring tea as well. Lady Holland's hair was wet and her skin too pale.

"I should have known that you would be kind to me today, even after my sharp words last night," she said, stirring milk into the tea.

"Curiosity is not kindness," he said, his voice unaccountably scratchy.

"Call it what you will." Then her eyes came up suddenly to his. "I have never asked you where you are traveling now."

He tilted his head. "No, you haven't."

"Where are you going?"

"My cousins from America have made the sea journey and will be arriving in England momentarily. Their ship docks at Bristol."

"You have American cousins? I didn't know."

It was a moment before he was able to say, "How should you? I barely know of them myself. But they are all the family I have now. So I thought it time for a visit."

"That's good of you."

"I hope they don't turn out to be insufferable." He smiled. "They wrote that they intend to remain in England for several months before continuing on to tour the Continent. How horrid it would be if I have damned myself to poor company for months."

"I daresay." Only the corner of her mouth lifted.

He took up his glass. "Is the journey that brings you through Swinly a lengthy one?"

"Only two days. I came here to meet Evelina so she could take my son to Dashbourne for a holiday. But I must return home tomorrow."

"You are not to have a holiday as well?"

"My husband is ill. He needs me at home."

He found he had to look down. "I'm sorry. Forgive my prying."

"Pry all you wish. It won't change a thing. My single reason for living these past five years has been taken from me and I honestly don't know when I will ever see him again. I am hopeless, my heart is aching so fiercely that it fills up my entire body and soul, and yet I can do nothing about it." Her words were desperate, but her tone was too bland, her eyes empty.

Tacitus recognized these signs. Once, he had lived them.

He stood up, went to the bar, and commanded two ales and a bottle of whiskey. Returning to the table, he set an ale and an empty glass before her.

"Spirits won't change anything either," she said.

"But they will temporarily dull the pain." He poured whiskey into her glass. "Drink up, my lady. We've an entire bottle here and only an afternoon to drink it."

The ghost of a smile teased her beautiful lips. Then she lifted the glass to her mouth and swallowed the draught.

~o0o~

He got her drunk.

She allowed it. She welcomed it. She had nothing better to do and she had never been truly foxed. He drank along with her, noting that it would be rude of him not to.

They talked of thoroughly inconsequential matters, neither of them introducing any topic of weight or personal relevance. He described to her every minute detail of the fine carriage and horses that he used to race against Lord Mallory when they were in their cups, and the outcome of every such race. Finally she begged him to cease, at which point he regaled her with stories of his friend's scandalous losses at the gaming tables in London. He himself never wagered more than he had in his pockets at the time, which he realized was dreadfully tame, but he rather liked his fortune and preferred to keep it. They spoke of grand society balls that gossips talked of for weeks, but that neither had attended, a balloon ascension she had once witnessed, and books he had read, and her mother's plans to someday mount an exhibition of ancient Greek statuary at the museum in London.

He was a charming companion, attentive and amusing. At some moment over the course of the afternoon she asked him if he had always been thus.

"Yes." The drink had made his voice slow and husky. "I have always been charming and pleasing, albeit in a somewhat bookish fashion. Next question?"

"Six years ago I thought you unreasonably stiff."

"You weren't the only one."

That another woman might have teased him for his rectitude made her angry at that anonymous woman, though even in her cups she realized this was hypocrisy of the worst sort. "Who else?"

"Mallory." He crossed his arms over his chest. "But he is a confirmed scoundrel. What was your excuse?"

"You told me I was childish."

"*Never.*"

"Yes. You did. And you were right, at that moment."

"Was I?" His eyes squinted as he studied her. "You don't seem like a child now. If I weren't three sheets to the wind, I would say you are lovely. I would have said it then too if I hadn't been so—what did you say?—unreasonably stiff."

Butterflies fluttered through the fiery spirits sloshing around her stomach.

"If I were Lord Mallory," she said, "and you were drinking with him now, without a curricle in sight, of course—"

He nodded.

"—would you be flattering him?"

"That wasn't flattery. That was the truth." He parted his lips as if to say more, then clamped them shut.

"What? Tell me." She feared she slurred.

He shook his head. "Can't. Wouldn't be right."

"What wouldn't be right?"

"Saying what I'm thinking." His gaze slipped across her face, her shoulders, and ever so briefly her breasts. "It would be the height of dishonorableness."

The fluttering butterflies became diving swallows.

"You should say it," she said. "You must. I'm having the worst day of my life and I want to hear it. Please."

Beneath his folded arms his chest seemed to rise upon a breath. Then he said roughly, "I wish you weren't married. Now. Today. Tonight."

She forced her gaze down to the table. "You are correct." She stared at the table rather than his expressive eyes. "You should not have said that. So let's forget that you did."

He said nothing.

She chanced looking at him again. He was not smiling now.

"Forget that you said it, my lord," she said. "That is an order."

"As you wish, my lady," he murmured.

By dusk they had finished the bottle and dinner as well.

She suggested buying more whiskey.

"That would be unwise," he said.

"Why is that?"

"When one feels more inclined to set one's head down on the table than to converse, it's generally time to stop drinking."

"Have I been napping on the table?"

"Not yet. But I can see it in your eyes."

"Do you know what I see in your eyes, Lord Dare?"

"Thorough bemusement?"

"Goodness. You are a truly good man."

He hauled himself to his feet. "When a beautiful lady whom I've gotten drunk starts telling me I'm a good man, then I know I'm doing something tragically wrong." He offered his arm. "Come, madam. To the inn and bed you must now go."

Her eyes snapped up to him. The room spun. "To bed?"

"Not," he said slowly, "with me." He laid her cloak around her shoulders and his hands rested there briefly. "Unfortunately," he said close to her ear, then he released her.

They stumbled to the inn. Rather, he walked in an exaggeratedly straight line and she wove back and forth. Halfway there, she fell on her behind.

"I slipped," she said when he stood over her.

"It seems so." Heedless of the mud, he picked her up and carried her the remainder of the way.

She told herself not to put her hand on his chest, not to wind her arm about his neck, and not to rest her cheek on his shoulder. And remarkably, she obeyed herself.

"If you had been drinking to excess with Lord Mallory, would you do this for him?"

"Of course not. He's far too big for me to lift."

The church bell boomed and her eyes popped open. She was lying on her bed. Lord Dare was sitting beside her.

"Oh— Oh—" she gasped. "Is it *tomorrow*?"

"It's ten o'clock tonight. Drink this." He wrapped her hand around a glass. Head awhirl, she gulped the water. As he removed the glass, she saw before her white. A lot of white. Her lap. Her legs. All white. The *bedclothes*?

Her muddy gown, shoes, stockings and petticoat were gone. She wore only her shift beneath the bed linens.

"Did you—Have you *undressed* me?"

"Molly did, while I waited without. She's still here."

"Evening, milady," came from the doorway.

Calista gathered the blanket higher. "Thank you."

"You will have a nasty head in the morning," he said.

She wouldn't. But she nodded.

"Coffee helps with that," he said. "And if you are very miserable, an ale."

"All right."

He gazed down at her. "Good night, Calista."

She released the covers and grasped his hand. "Sometime ... I don't know when ... But sometime I should like to do this again, my lord."

His fingers tightened around hers. "I would like that too." He released her and offered her a sideways grin. "You are a much less expensive drinking partner than Mallory, after all. With him, it's never fewer than three bottles."

They left. Calista tucked her face into the pillow and passed out.

Chapter Sixteen

SHE AWOKE WITH AN ALERT, clear mind. Rain drummed on the windowpanes as Old Mary welcomed the dawn.

Seven rings. Only seven. Forever seven.

Inside she was anguish.

"Goddess of Love," she said to the statue on the dressing table that she had not bothered packing away lately. "Would you grant me two wishes? Two small wishes only?" She closed her eyes and gripped the blanket. "Would you remove him from this inn and replace him with my son? Please? I beg of you. I will do anything you wish if you grant me this. Anything. Just take away that man I cannot have and bring me my son."

She opened her eyes. The statue's face remained blank, beautiful, and stone hard.

Eventually Calista arose, dressed, and beckoned the cat to the kitchen, where she gathered a plate of food. Enduring Mrs. Whittle's regular surprise at a lady doing such a thing, she fed scraps of egg and bacon to the animal. Waiting until the innkeeper left the kitchen to speak with Harriet in the foyer, and then waiting until she heard Harriet leave the inn, Calista carried the remnants of her breakfast to the taproom. The constable was well ensconced now, and conversation was all about the flood. The Marquess of Dare cast her a brief glance. But as Molly had already cleared the table at which he had breakfasted and he sat now with others, he did not offer it to her.

She sat down, drew the journal he had left there under her nose, and read the news she had already read many times while the cat sat by her ankles waiting for more bacon. With little appetite herself, she set the plate on the ground and swallowed the remainder of her tea. When she saw Molly enter the room, she walked right into the cup of coffee. Assuring Molly that it was entirely her own fault, she went into the foyer where the Smythes were just exiting the private parlor. Ducking out the front door, she hurried to the stable.

Mr. Jackson told her about his son. She sat with him for a time, and he talked about how Petey and Bartholomew were as different as night and day—one an adventurer, the other a solid worker—but their bond was as strong as steel. Watching him wipe tears from his weathered cheeks, she thought perhaps she was intentionally torturing herself now. But once he had begun speaking of his sons, he needed no encouragement to continue. So she sat and listened until a horse nickered and Jackson seemed to snap out of his reminiscences.

"I should be seein' about the animals, milady. With that boy runnin' off every hour, and them other fine animals crowdin' up the place, I've got to do it all myself. Don't mind it, of course." He stood up and tugged at his cap. "Thank you, mum."

"I have done nothing, Mr. Jackson." She watched him return to his work, then she drew her hood over her head and went out into the rain again.

Just as she had the day before, she walked. This time she did not stop to gather a new gown from Elena Cooke's shop. And she did not return to the inn to dry off after each perambulation of the village. She did not want Lord Dare to see her and grow curious. She did not want to see him or speak with him or drink with him or touch him. When he noticed her, he inevitably came after her. But she knew his schedule now: cards at the inn all day, dinner at the pub. She could avoid disturbing it. The farther she stayed from the inn, the more likely she would be able to avoid him.

The walk took her over several low hills, through five fields and the sheep pasture, and along the overflowing creek. She strolled it three times as the rain came down on her head and shoulders. She considered pausing to visit Elena, or even Harriet. But the prospect of becoming acquainted with them yet again depressed her.

She went to the ford.

Roughly twenty-five feet wide, in most weather it was covered by no more than a trickling stream. The villagers said that when regular rain fell, six inches or so of water would top the pavement. Now water rose to the banks on either side. Mr. Pritchard insisted it was at least five feet deep, while other villagers estimated four and a half. She stared at the rushing water pelted now with rain and wondered if they were all wrong. What if it was actually passable? It wasn't far across, after all. What if she could wade to the other side? What if she waded to the other side and walked right into tomorrow?

Her heartbeats were like knife jabs beneath her ribs.

She must try it. Perhaps she had been meant to try it from the beginning. Perhaps she had perished on the journey to Swinly and she was actually already dead. Perhaps this was her River Styx, or whatever that mythical river to Hades was called. Perhaps if she waded across, she would finally reach the hereafter.

Or Harry.

She had considered many times that this was the hereafter, that on the road to Swinly, poor, grieving, drunk Jackson had run the carriage into a ditch and she had perished. It seemed a reasonable enough explanation. Perhaps she only needed to cross this water in order to find peace.

Unclasping her cloak and letting it fall to the ground, she felt the cold raindrops drop onto her cheeks and lips, and she closed her eyes. Drawing up her courage, carefully she stepped forward.

Frigid water consumed her ankles, but the stones beneath her feet were not slippery. She took another step and the current caught at her hem. It seemed mild, though, not at all quick or strong like it looked from the bank. Her foot moved further and she lurched forward and down. Thrusting out her arms to steady herself, she opened her eyes.

A gasp jerked from her. From here, only two feet across, the pass looked much wider than twenty-five feet. Rather, thirty. Perhaps even forty.

She took another step, more carefully now, and the creek rose to her knees. The current tugged at her skirts. She should have removed her gown first. But she was more than a yard across already. A dozen more yards and she would be on the other side.

Feeling the bottom of the ford with her feet, she shuffled forward as the water rose to her thighs. She wavered, pressed her toes into the stone, and made her palms flat to use them as paddles. Another step across took her down abruptly; the water sank into her gown at the hips. Her skirts were heavy. Remarkably heavy. But they were entirely saturated now; they could not grow heavier than this. Her heartbeats were too swift.

She must remain calm. A lesson she had learned at Richard's side: if she remained calm, she would survive. Drawing air into her lungs slowly, she tried to relax her pulse as the rain fell steadily about her. Then, leaning forward, she used her hands like oars and forced herself forward against the lateral pull of the water.

Arms banded around her waist and dragged her off her feet. Backward she went, stumbling, floating, grabbing the iron muscle cinched about her.

"What are you—" she shouted. "Stop! Let me go!"

In knee-deep water he twisted her around and pulled her hard against him.

"What in the hell are you doing?" Lord Dare's furious eyes matched the gray water, the rain, the entire day, and Calista knew finally that this *was* Hell. She needn't cross any mythical river to descend into Hades. She was already there.

He gripped her arms. "Are you trying to kill yourself?" he demanded.

"Release me."

One of his hands fell away, but the other stayed clamped about her arm. "Not until you tell me exactly what you hoped to accomplish wading into this river."

"I wanted to see if I could cross to the other side. It isn't so wide. It is swimmable."

"If it were swimmable, don't you imagine someone would have already swum a *horse* across it? An animal that is considerably stronger than a wisp of a woman. For God's sake, haven't you any sense?"

"I didn't know that horses could swim."

He stared at her as the rain fell between them. "You would have drowned."

"I guess I would have." She shivered, chilled and burning up both at once.

"Did you intend to?" he said, as if he spoke around gravel.

"No. *No.* I don't want to die. I want to *escape.* I want to see my son again. I want to be gone from this place. And from you."

He released her. "Me?"

"Yes."

Rainwater ran in rivulets from his perfect jaw. "Like you wanted to escape me six years ago."

"What? No. Nothing like then. This time I want to run away *from* you. Seeing you—speaking with you—touching you—it's torture. Sweet, horrible, awful torture. I want it so much, I cannot bear it."

His throat jerked in a hard swallow. "Calista Chance, I have never met a woman who made less sense than you."

"Well, then I am sorry for you, because I am suddenly finding lack of sense to be a remarkable advantage after all. If I had not irrationally believed I could wade across this creek, you would not have rescued me, and I still would not know what it is to feel your arms around me or your body against mine. And that would be a shame because I adored it, even if you yanked me backward and I screamed at you. It was perfect and I never wanted it to end. But that would not have happened if I hadn't—"

He dragged her into his arms and covered her mouth with his.

The kiss was nothing like the quick peck she had planted on him at her bedchamber door. It was hot, deep, and instantly drugging. His lips were soft and demanding at once. They parted and she eagerly followed his lead. Again and again they met, and she let him taste her and take more with each meeting, each taste. She had never been kissed like this, with such seeking urgency, as though her mouth were something to be pleased, treasured, *taken*. His hands were splayed across her back and she let her fingers steal into his wet hair and down his neck, and she gripped taut sinews and beautiful man. Touching him like this—kissing him—she had never thought she would know this. He felt like sin and tasted like every dream she had ever had of him. She pressed onto her toes, he pulled her up against him, and his tongue stroked hers, and pleasure rushed through her. She moaned against his lips.

He broke away and jolted back. Across the rain, his eyes filled with shock.

"Good God," he said, breathing hard. "What have you made me do this time?"

"*This* time? I haven't made you do anything. You grabbed *me*."

"Right. Yes. I know. I'm sorry. It was my fault. And yours. You kissed me back. Both of us did it." He slashed his hand through his dripping hair. "It was a mistake."

"Yes. I goaded you." She bit her lower lip and tasted him there and ached all over her heated, sodden body. "Do you usually kiss women you don't know? Rather, women you haven't seen in years?"

His eyes flashed. "No."

Blooms of wicked joy burst all through her. "I didn't think so."

"Why not?" he demanded. "I might be as loose a screw as my friend Mallory. Why wouldn't you think it?"

"Because you are a good man."

"Good men do not haul other men's wives into their arms and kiss them."

"Other man's wife."

"What?"

"You said you don't usually do that. So … wife. Singular."

Anger sparked in his eyes. "Are you making sport of me? *Now?*"

"No." She bit both of her lips together. His gaze dropped to them, and the sparks of anger turned to fever.

"You must stop staring at my mouth," she mumbled.

He turned away from her. "My God, this was an unfortunate coincidence, meeting you in this village."

"If you weren't here, I would have drowned, so I am glad for this coincidence, at least at this moment," she said, dragging her soaked skirts out of the water and up to the bank. "Thank you for saving me."

He grasped her arm and rotated her toward him. His face was stark.

"I beg of you, forgive me." His hand fell away from her. "I am mortified to have insulted you."

"I would forgive you if you had actually insulted me. As the opposite is true, I cannot offer you my forgiveness. I enjoyed it. I enjoyed kissing you more than I have enjoyed anything in a very long time." And she wanted to do it again and again and again. "It was wrong of you, of me, of both of us. But I refuse to regret it. Good day, my lord."

She went to Elena Cooke's shop, borrowed a gown and dry undergarments, and returned to the inn to change her clothing. She could not remain where he was today; she feared her own weakness in wanting him more than the embarrassment. So she set off to the millinery.

Harriet greeted her like the long lost friend she was not. Calista tried to attend to her conversation but had little mind for anything except the memory she should not have at all.

If she had done that, *kissed him*, on any other day, Richard would discover it. Four years ago he had hired a footman as his personal spy. Now he always knew of every little thing she did, at home and in the village: each moment she lingered in conversation with a neighbor at a party, each exchange she shared with a farmer or shopkeeper, each glance she innocently cast at another man at church, he knew it. Occasionally he even accused her of consorting too freely with their menservants.

Reprimands followed, sometimes verbal, often with the flat of his hand or his fist. Soon after marrying him she learned to avoid the sort of flirting that the gentlemen she had met in London seemed to like. Of necessity she had become docile and subdued, passive.

Especially in intimacy. Richard's kisses had been thick and sloppy. After the first time, when she suggested that he kiss her differently and he slapped her for insolence, she never again complained. But for some time now he had been more interested in pawing at her while pleasuring himself, anyway. He said he didn't like the way she stared blankly at him as he had her; he preferred it when she fought. So passivity, foreign to her nature, had become her armor, donned each day like an ill-fitting coat in order to survive.

She had never done anything in her life to deserve a man like Richard Holland.

But, she thought as Harriet prattled on, she had never done anything to deserve a man like Tacitus Everard either.

Now she had used him. Against his morals and her own. For a few minutes of decidedly unsubdued pleasure, and she had been an eager participant.

She should have pushed him away. She should have thanked him for dragging her out of stupidity born of desperation, and fled. She should not have welcomed his kiss.

"Mrs. Tinkerson," she broke into Harriet's monologue and set down her teacup. "I'm afraid I must depart. I have business with my coachman." Beyond the parlor curtains, dusk was beginning to fall.

"You simply *must* stop by before you depart in the morning. I will make up this adorable little hat to match that gown—oh! That is one of Mrs. Cooke's gowns, isn't it? How *talented* she is with a needle. And how tremendously fetching it is on you, dear Calista. And this hat suits it so well, don't you think?"

"It is a very clever hat." She fingered the stiff satin bow atop the wool cap meant to dip low above one eye. "I haven't been to London in years, but I daresay this design would catch on splendidly there."

"*Do* you say so?" Harriet's eyes popped wide. "Oh, my dear friend, how delighted I would be if you wore *my* hat on your next visit to town."

She returned the hat to the milliner. "I don't expect that will be any time soon." Ever. "But if I do travel there, I'm sure I will keep you in mind."

Harriet effused a bit more and finally Calista left. Ignoring her protesting belly, she went around to the back of the inn, entered through the rear entrance, slipped into the kitchen, and closed the door behind her.

"Milady!" Mrs. Whittle exclaimed. "You shouldn't be in here. But I suppose you're just like his lordship." She smiled with her apple cheeks.

"Like his lordship?"

"Not so high on your consequence that you can't poke your nose into a kitchen and see what needs to be done to help in a pinch." She nodded cheerfully. "A person would never know he's a grand lord, for all the fetching and carrying he's done for me today in Mr. Whittle's absence, and all those other men just sitting in there playing cards and making demands on a body. And here you are, a grand lady, coming right in like anybody."

"I wonder, do you have a pen, ink, and paper, by chance?"

"Mr. Whittle keeps some at his accounts desk. I'll have Molly go and fetch it to your chamber—"

"I will be glad to fetch it myself."

The innkeeper led her through the kitchen to a minuscule room dominated by a desk. Mrs. Whittle pulled a sheet of paper out of the drawer.

"If you'd like to write here, you're welcome to it."

"Actually, I need to write elsewhere. But I promise to return the ink and pen before Mr. Whittle comes home tomorrow."

With the writing tools in hand, she went to the stable. It was a small gesture of defiance to spend as much time talking with her coachman as she wished without her husband ever discovering it. But she knew her guilt propelled her now more than anything. Even if God had already forsaken her, and even if Richard did not deserve it, she needed to do something now to atone for the wrong she had done in lusting after a man who was not her husband.

The inn's ostler sat in the light of a lantern at the entrance to the stable on a bench with a smartly dressed groom she assumed must belong to the Smythe party. She asked after her coachman.

"With the animals, mum," the ostler said.

She told him she could find her way and hoped that the ostler's easy manner suggested that her coachman was not sleeping or foxed.

He was neither. Bent over the hoof of one of the carriage horses, he was picking at it with a tool.

"Mr. Jackson? Have you a moment?"

He set down the hoof and tool and wiped his hands on a cloth.

"How can I help you, milady? After the good turn you did me this morning, listenin' to my stories about my boys, I owe you a debt of gratitude."

"I enjoyed hearing about them." She glanced about the stall. In the corner, a bottle of whiskey was tucked behind a pail. It was full to the cork. She looked at his eyes: the whites were clear. "I was hoping to help you. I've brought pen and paper. If you like, you could dictate to me that letter to Bartholomew, and I could write for you. I would be glad to post it before we leave Swinly tomorrow morning."

His face crinkled into a surprised smile.

"That'd be the kindest thing a lady's ever done for me, 'cept my own departed Bess, bless her soul."

Relief stole through her. "Shall we get started?"

Some time later, settled on the bench with a length of wood on her lap serving as a desk, she dipped the pen into the inkbottle a final time.

"There now, sign your name if you are able here at the bottom. An X will do as well."

"I'm grateful for this, milady. Mr. Holland'll surely think you've stooped low to help me."

"My husband needn't know. Perhaps we can keep this between us and then no one will get into trouble," she said with a rueful grin.

A high-pitched gasp sounded from nearby. She looked up into the round eyes of the stable boy.

"Yes?" she said.

"On my gram's honor, mum, I plumb forgot!"

"Don't be botherin' her ladyship, boy. Get on with you," Jackson said.

"But I've got a letter for her."

"A letter for me?"

He dug inside his filthy waistcoat.

"Aye, mum. A man come racin' in here late a' night, said the ford just about took him and his horse comin' in, and he couldn't stop to find anybody else to give this to, that he had to turn right 'round or he wouldn't make it out." He produced a well-crushed envelope and thrust it toward her. "I said I'd see as you got it."

She accepted the envelope. On its smudged face her name was written boldly in a hand she did not recognize.

"Seein' you writin' here reminded me of it," the boy grumbled.

"I haven't a coin at present for you," she said. "But given that it has taken you a day to remember to give it to me, I might be forgiven for not thanking you with copper."

"Aye, mum. That's the truth." Shoulders slumped, he shuffled away.

"That boy's been scamperin' out of here all day at any excuse to be away," Mr. Jackson said with a scowl.

"The flood has made it a peculiar day for all of us." She tucked the letter into her sleeve. "As to your letter, I promise to post it to Leeds first thing in the morning." Except that the page covered with tender words of a father to his beloved son would not be on the dressing table of her bedchamber when she awoke in the morning. It would be lost to today.

Her coachman thanked her and she returned to the inn. The Symthes were at dinner in their parlor, and only a handful of guests were in the taproom. In the kitchen, she returned the pen and ink to Mrs. Whittle, took two pieces of bread and some cold meat wrapped in a cloth, and went to her bedchamber. Tearing off a bit for the cat and opening the door a crack so it could enter as it liked, she sat on the bed and opened the letter.

As she read, she ceased breathing.

Dear Lady Holland,

It is with great distress that I write to you in haste. Late this morning, Mr. Holland received a gentleman caller in his chambers, Mr. Absalom Grange. I waited just without, as I always do when the Master has callers, and I was dismayed to overhear raised voices and a quantity of shouting. When Mr. Grange departed, the Master beckoned me in. His face was red and he was clutching his arm. He said it gave him pain and I could see that he was having trouble breathing. I fetched smelling salts and sent John off swiftly to Dr. Carver. But I am devastated to tell you that the Master's life fled him before the doctor arrived.

Dr. Carver believes that the Master's heart ceased functioning due to the Severe Agitation he suffered during his interview with Mr. Grange. Mr. Billicky says that I am to blame. I told him what does an ignorant footman know about anything? I have told Mrs. Pinker that I am devastated by this turn of events, as well as Mr. Preston, who called soon after the doctor's departure, indeed as I sat down to write this.

Mrs. Pinker is overset and, in lieu of a butler, which we have not had at Herald's Court in two years, since the Master released Mr. Frost, she begged me to write to you. We will send John with the fastest horse to convey this letter to you in the event that you intend to continue on to Dashbourne rather than return home immediately.

Mr. Preston wishes to speak with you at your earliest convenience.

I speak for the entire staff in saying that we eagerly await your return, as well as the return of our dear, now fatherless, Master Harry.

In deep sorrow and greatest sympathy,
James Baker

Calista read the letter twice. And then a third time.

In her lowest, wickedest moments she had imagined Richard's early death. Each time she had worn long sleeves or a high-necked gown to cover a bruise, or powdered the mark left by a slap on her cheek, she had dreamed of life free of him. And upon each of those occasions she felt evil for imagining and dreaming of any man's death. She was more fortunate than most women, with a fine house, servants, and a wonderful child. That she must endure the cruel possessiveness and hard hand of a husband she loathed was nothing worse than her mother had endured for twenty-five years. Only when she learned that he had struck their son and knocked him down had the guilt over her dreams turned to fury.

Now the dream was real.

Richard was gone.

She was free.

She was free.

"I am free," she whispered. And then upon a choking sob: "Harry is *safe*."

Crushing the letter to her face, she laughed and sobbed at once. The cat wound its way about her ankles, curling its body around her. She bent over, brandished the letter before its whiskers, and whispered, "We are free!"

Only slowly did the hilarity of her relief fade into calm.

Then, even more slowly, she returned to reality, *her* reality that was not in fact reality.

She raised her eyes and looked about the room, at the pale blue draperies, the simple globed posts at the four corners of the plain wooden bed, the small woven rug in the middle of the floor, the statue that greeted her every day, and at her own single gown and undergarments still dripping from her foray into the ford.

She was a widow. She had been a widow for many days already. She simply had not known it.

And every today she subsequently lived, she would still be a widow.

Her mouth split into a smile.

A happy, happy widow.

She laughed aloud. Then she laughed again simply because it felt so good to laugh aloud. It was wickedness to rejoice in Richard's death so thoroughly. Or perhaps it was not wicked. Perhaps it was simply her fate. Or her destiny. Or a twist in the curse. But at present her widowhood felt like a glorious blessing upon this endless, awful day.

I wish you weren't married. Now. Today. Tonight.

She was no longer married. She could do as she wished, as she had wished for fifteen days already, unknowing that all the while she had been free.

Chapter Seventeen

CLIMBING THE STAIRS TO HIS BEDCHAMBER, Tacitus heard laughter coming from the open door of her room.

He should ignore it and walk past. Three fingers of whiskey at the pub had done nothing to reconcile him to what had happened, the why, the how, the *wrong*. He had not seen her in six years and yet he was drawn to her now as powerfully as then.

But she was clearly no longer that girl. Years ago he had seen in her eyes determination, deep affection, and bright, reckless joy. He had wanted to touch that, to taste it, to be part of it. He had never imagined Calista Chance could become a quiet, withdrawn woman. Her contained anguish while bidding her son good-bye the night before had gone. This morning in the taproom during breakfast she had been subdued. And earlier at the ford her eyes had held both desperation and sorrow.

The laughter tumbling into the corridor now was open, wild, and full of pleasure.

Perhaps in the six years since he had last seen her, she had gone mad. It would explain her swim in the ford and violently changeable tempers.

He paused at her doorway. Alone in the room, she sat on the bed, laughter shaking her shoulders. Her hands covering her eyes gripped a wrinkled sheet of paper. A sleek gray cat sat at her feet.

He mustn't interrupt. He should walk away.

Perhaps she had not meant to leave the door open. He should quietly close it and protect her from strangers' prying eyes. Like his.

Walk away.

The music of her laughter set his entire body on fire.

Walk away.

He knocked. She twisted around. Her eyes flew wide and her lips clamped shut.

"Forgive me," he said, repeating those words to her for what seemed like the twentieth time since yesterday. "I noticed your door open and I thought— That is ..." He had nothing to say. *Nothing honorable.* "Would you like it shut?" he finally blurted out.

"No." She swiveled off the bed and came to the door. She wore a gown of some mild hue that covered her from chin to wrist, and yet his heart pounded like a fifteen-year-old's at his first hunt. Her fingers gripped the doorframe. In the other hand she held the paper. "I am sorry about earlier," she said. "I was distressed. I was not thinking clearly."

"But now you are?" He could stare at her face forever. Even with smudges of gray beneath her eyes, she was more beautiful now than as a girl, as though womanhood had settled her more gracefully into her features.

"I—" She pinched her lips together, lips that tasted like honey, like the way she smelled. "I have received a letter. The stable boy had it from a messenger last night, but forgot to give it to me until just now, and— and—" Her gaze dipped to his mouth. "My circumstances have changed abruptly. Dramatically."

Walk away.

He glanced at the paper in her hand.

"Is that the letter?"

She nodded and offered it to him. "Read it." A rosy flush now sat high upon her cheeks. "Please."

He took it.

Soon, his heartbeats were not only quick; they were each painful explosions against his ribs. He lifted his eyes to her.

"I am very sorry for your loss. I offer my deepest sympathies."

She blinked several times.

"I did not love my husband," she said. "In fact I disliked him. Excessively. I was faithful to him for the sake of my marriage vow. For that reason alone."

He felt like someone was pressing an anvil down on his chest.

He shook his head. "What do you expect me to do with that information?"

She seemed to draw back from him. "I thought ... I—"

"You thought that I was the sort of man who, upon learning that a woman has just discovered that after six years of marriage her husband no longer lives, would seize the opportunity to immediately seduce her?"

"No, I did not think it. I *depended* upon it."

His teeth would barely part to allow speech. "Thank you, madam, for that flattering assessment of my character. And for your candor." She had *disliked* the man she had run off to meet after rejecting him? Perhaps she had wed Holland for money. Perhaps for the adventure of it. It didn't matter. "Good night."

He moved away.

"Does this mean you won't?" she said to his back. "Despite what I have told you?"

He turned to face her. "I don't know you. I see a woman before me that any man would desire, a woman so beautiful that I did something today, impulsively, that made me furious with myself. But that beautiful woman is a stranger to me. And as remarkable as it may seem to you, I don't share my bed with strangers. Good night, Lady Holland." He made himself walk away.

"Oh, my God. It cannot—" Her voice broke. "I *am* in Hell."

He paused. But only the quiet click of her door closing sounded behind him.

Chapter Eighteen

CALISTA STARED AT THE CEILING and counted seven tolls.

An hour later she counted eight tolls.

An hour later she counted nine tolls.

There was little sense in rising when she knew everything that was to be known in the little village of Swinly beyond her bedchamber door on this cold and rainy February Saturday. She knew that Harriet Tinkerson would be dressing bonnets in her shop, that Elena Cooke was sewing the hem and cuffs of a blue muslin round gown, that the baker had burned his first tray of cakes, but the second batch tasted divine, that the vicar was at his desk preparing his Sunday sermon, that Mrs. Whittle would run out of milk at precisely nine thirty-eight, that sheep would begin wandering onto the high street at noon, that they would eat Mrs. Elliott's winter greens at half past two, that the bookseller, accountant's clerk, and Mr. Alan Smythe would cheat the Marquess of Dare out of four guineas before dusk, that the fiddler would begin playing "My Bonnie Lass" at the pub at quarter past six, and that a gray cat would expect its dinner—

The cat.

She had not fed it breakfast.

Bolting out of bed, she fastened her stays over her shift that was fresh each morning, donned her petticoat, stockings and gown, and threw open the door.

The cat sat on its hindquarters in the middle of the corridor, staring at her.

"Good morning," she said, pulling on her slippers and hearing the familiar drumming of rain on the roof above. "You are patient. Much more patient than I am, it seems." She started toward the stairs. "But you will see: if given the right motivation, I can be patient too." At the base of the stairs she glanced into the taproom, then back up at the cat still watching her. "And I do have excellent motivation, don't I?"

Sleep, and waking with the knowledge that Richard was gone, had done wondrous things to refresh her spirits. The truth of it was that she had as many days as she needed to seduce the Marquess of Dare. Delving into challenging projects had long been one of her best distractions from unhappiness. She knew he desired her. He merely needed the right sort of encouragement.

After seeing to the cat's breakfast and visiting Jackson in the stable, she went into the taproom for her gown's daily dose of coffee. Molly obliged, and while the men around the card table tried not to notice it, she dabbed at the stain with a cloth and pleasantly invited herself to play.

Lord Dare stood up to push in her chair.

"I did not know you were a cardplayer," he said.

"I'm not much of one, in truth." Men didn't like it when women bested them at cards. She had learned this not only from Richard but from nearly every man she had ever met. "But there is so much time to be passed today, isn't there? And what better way to pass it than with four handsome men?" She offered him a pretty smile. She hadn't been allowed to flirt in years, but she had not entirely forgotten how.

He introduced her to Mr. Anderson, the accountant's clerk, Mr. Peabody, the bookseller, and Alan Smythe, who smiled charmingly and gave up his hand to her.

"You mustn't, sir," she said. "I will wait until one of you loses everything and then take that place." She hoped her eyes could still sparkle as any number of gentlemen in London years ago had reported.

From Mr. Smythe's appreciative grin, she supposed they still did.

"I insist, my lady," he said, and passed his cards to her.

Throughout the game she allowed him to give her whispered recommendations. The others did not object; she was a neophyte, Mr. Smythe said, and needed instruction, and this was a friendly game, not a London club. Under the silk merchant's tutelage, she won four shillings, though she could have won more playing without his assistance. She thanked him, but offered her most taking smile to the marquess.

When she could, she watched Lord Dare's hands. She liked them. Years ago she had liked them too. They looked strong, the sinews pronounced and movements fluid, as though he were accustomed to working with them—a peculiar characteristic for a bookish lord, to be sure. Widowhood had awoken the woman inside her that wanted a man's touch. His strong hands had touched her quite nicely already. She wanted more.

She intentionally lost the next game to him.

"It's a pity you discarded that king, my lady," he said with a glance at her. "You might have taken that last trick otherwise."

Calista's cheeks felt warm. Pretending had never been difficult with Richard. She had never flirted with him or tried to manipulate him. She had simply remained silent. But a hint of suspicion glimmered in the Marquess of Dare's eyes now.

He was far too intelligent to blatantly cozen.

She allowed herself to win the next game.

When Mrs. Whittle served lunch, the game paused. Calista suggested a stroll to the ford since the rain had ceased. Mr. Peabody and Mr. Anderson declined, and she happily donned her boots and took to the outdoors with Lord Dare and Mr. Smythe. A stop at the dress shop, and a lengthy perusal of a series of fashion plates gave Mr. Smythe sufficient time to notice Elena and draw her into a conversation that wasn't quite flirtation. Elena apparently did not flirt. But she seemed to enjoy talking with him.

Eventually Calista and Lord Dare left their cardplaying companion at the dress shop and continued on to the ford. She mentioned a book that he had told her about during the afternoon they had spent at the pub, before she'd gotten too intoxicated to remember much. He seemed surprised, but pleased.

"Forgive my assumption, but I did not take you for an avid reader, Lady Holland," he said as they stopped not five feet from the place he had kissed her as if she was the only thing in the world.

"I haven't been, but I should like to read more," she said. "Now that my husband is gone, I would like to spend more time in pursuits that interest me."

His gaze had arrested. "Your husband is no longer with you?"

"No. I am a widow." It was wicked how much she liked speaking the words aloud.

"Recently?"

"Quite recently, in fact."

"I am terribly sorry. Please accept my condolences." He glanced at her gown, which was a modest shade of green like the ribbon on her bonnet, and she realized her mistake.

"My husband did not want me to wear black forever," she said swiftly. "He did not care for that habit of mourning."

"He seems to have been a considerate spouse."

Hardly.

"I would rather not discuss him," she murmured.

"Of course, I understand." His shoulders seemed especially rigid. "It must be very difficult for you. When I lost my parents, I found conversation about them with strangers intolerable. Forgive me."

"Thank you." Calista turned her face away and bit her lip. This was *not* going as she had intended.

A minute or two passed as they each silently studied the swollen creek before them and she cast around in her mind for safe topics.

"I wonder what pastime I should take up," she finally said. "There are so many to choose from. Do you have any particular favorite pastime, that is, when you are not seeing to your estates or in the Lords?" She chuckled. "But I suppose those would keep you sufficiently occupied, wouldn't they?"

He nodded. "Indeed, they do."

She felt his attention upon her and she looked up at him. A tentative smile lifted one corner of his mouth.

"Your laughter is as lovely as it was six years ago," he said.

Calista's heart shoved aside her lungs and commenced thwacking her ribs.

"You remember my laughter?"

"I do," he said. "I make furniture."

"I beg your pardon?"

"As a pastime," he said with that same slight smile. "I make tables and chairs. Once I made a display case, but the glasswork gave me such trouble, I've never tried that again."

Every moth in Swinly was fluttering around in her middle.

"You make furniture? With your own hands."

"And with wood, of course. And tools." He folded his hands behind his back and his stance as he looked across the ford was relaxed. "It isn't a particularly lordly occupation, I realize. You would not be the first friend to chastise me for wasting my time in laboring like an artisan. But I quite enjoy it. It has nothing to do with the concerns of my responsibilities. And I believe my great-great-grandfather on my mother's side was a cabinetmaker, so I suppose it is in my blood."

Friend.

He called her a friend. Why that should make her suddenly feel wretchedly ill, she could not understand.

After some conversation regarding the depth of the ford, they returned to the dress shop to collect Mr. Smythe, who convinced Mrs. Cooke to join them as well. The village was perambulated, with the dressmaker giving them a tour of its highlights: the pub; the millinery, where they endured Harriet's effusions over Calista and Lord Dare's presence in their little village, and paused to admire her hats; the church at the other end of the street where Old Mary now boomed three o'clock. The shepherd was still asleep, of course, and Calista suggested that they avoid the milling herd by walking along Farmer Donovan's east field.

"You seem to know almost as much about this village as Mrs. Cooke does," the marquess said as they walked behind the other pair. "Have you been here often?"

"Oh, several times."

They dined at the pub and Calista could not recall when she had enjoyed another evening in mixed company so thoroughly. But by the end of the night her head ached. Maintaining the pretense of knowing little about all three of them, and constantly editing her words before she spoke so that she would not reveal herself, proved exhausting. And her principal object seemed as far away as it had been the day before. Even farther, perhaps. As she already knew, the Marquess of Dare was an ideal companion. But other than complimenting her laugh, he had done nothing beyond the bounds of propriety, nothing that convinced her he would welcome her throwing herself upon him at his bedchamber door.

Instead, at her bedchamber door he offered her a bow and the same slightly surprised smile he had throughout much of the day.

"Good night, Lady Holland. I have enjoyed spending time with you."

Calista balanced on her toes. If she grabbed him and kissed him now, he might welcome it. But abruptly the alternative, his revilement, seemed unendurable.

She liked having his friendship. She wanted his friendship. She did not want to ruin that. She could not bear ruining that, even if he would forget it.

"Good night, my lord. Thank you for today."

Then he took her hand, lifted it, and brushed his lips across her knuckles. "And I thank you." He released her and walked away.

Inside her room, she fell against the closed door and allowed herself a long, deep groan. Then she opened the door again to admit the cat and watched it leap onto the bed.

"Tomorrow, cat. Tomorrow I will have my widowhood story straight, and start things off properly," she said firmly.

It meowed.

"Did you eat dinner?" She went to it. "I am sorry I wasn't

here to feed you." And she had not written Jackson's letter to his son, either. But she might tomorrow, or the next day, or any day after that. He wouldn't remember, so it didn't matter anyway.

No one but the cow herself, mum.

She frowned and pushed away the unbidden memory of Molly's comment. She stood up. "Let's go see what we can find for your dinner. Though it looks as though you've been eating well enough lately." It was true. The ribs that had projected from the cat's shaggy sides barely showed beneath the shiny fur. "You were little more than skin and bones the first time you bothered me. Weren't you?"

With an impressive display of tongue and teeth, it yawned. Then it mewled its usual hunger signal.

"I am mistaken. Aren't I? You were exactly like this sixteen days ago. Weren't you?"

In the corner of her eye, a light flickered. She glanced at the candle on the dressing table. But it was not the candle that had glimmered.

The statue glowed. Again. For the first time in a fortnight. *Unmistakably.*

A warm golden aura emanated from the alabaster, swirls of darker gold twining about the figure and glittering in her filmy skirts.

Then it ceased. The statue was plain, pale stone again, and staring blankly.

Calista stared.

"I might have had too much wine with dinner." She rubbed her eyes then again studied the statue. "Or ..." She walked toward it. "Perhaps it *is* you. Perhaps it is not my eyesight or a tumor inside my skull or madness or any sin I have committed. Perhaps this isn't actually Hell." The statue remained passive. "Perhaps *you* have done this to me, entrapped me here. Is that it?"

She peered into the passionless eyes of the goddess.

"It *is* you, isn't it? You are playing a game with me for your own amusement, and you have given me a *cat* as my only companion in this nightmare because you are the most awful, horrible, wicked, evil, unkind, miserable creature to have ever descended from Olympus. Isn't that so?"

The statue did not reply.

Grabbing the cold stone around the neck, she hurled it to the floor. It made a mighty thud and the wood splintered.

The stone remained unharmed. And Aphrodite's eyes stared up at her without sympathy.

"I refuse to be beaten by you," she exclaimed, renewed purpose pounding through her blood. "You will see. I will have him whether you want me to or not. I will win."

Calista turned her back, leaving the stone goddess on the floor where it lay.

Chapter Nineteen

HE LIKED PLAYING CARDS, although he did not always win. But when she let him win, he seemed to know she had.

He liked books. But when she mentioned titles that she knew he had read, he appeared perplexed. It seemed he had a difficult time believing that she was a reader. She was not a reader, in fact, but that was easily remedied. She visited the doctor, vicar, and Elena Cooke to borrow books, and spent time reading each morning.

He liked furniture carpentry. But when she introduced him to Swinly's carpenter he had no more to say than any other gentleman she knew, at least not in her presence. When she revealed to him that she knew of his pastime, that he must have told her about it six years ago, he replied that he had only taken it up five years earlier.

He preferred coffee to tea. She taught herself to choke down the bitter brew without cringing.

He preferred brandy to whiskey and whiskey to claret. But whatever she tried, she could not seem to entice him to drink alone with her again.

He was unfailingly patient with Molly and always gracious to Mrs. Whittle.

He treated Mr. Peabody and Mr. Anderson as near to equals as a man of his status could without embarrassing them with inappropriate familiarity.

He seemed suspicious of Alan Smythe's flirtations with her, though he never spoke a word about it, and he was sincerely interested in the political theories of George Smythe.

He was very kind to Penelope.

Calista wondered about that. Penelope Smythe had

neither beauty nor apparently much personality. The daughter of a vastly prosperous merchant, she was nevertheless beneath the notice of a wealthy marquess. Yet each time Calista saw him in the Smythe family's company, he made a point of speaking with interest to Penelope, to which the girl responded with exasperating shyness.

"My sister-in-law's hopes for poor Penny aren't what my niece wishes for herself," Alan whispered to her at tea as Mrs. Smythe forced her daughter into conversation with the marquess.

"Oh?"

"But my niece is terrified of displeasing her parents. She'll go along with it, I suspect, whoever they manage to corral for her."

Calista understood. Six years ago she had been young and foolish enough to bow to the wishes of others. She wasn't any longer. And she refused to lose this battle.

She doubled down on her seduction of the Marquess of Dare.

She told him directly at breakfast that she was a widow, and then she made her wishes indisputably clear. He avoided her for the rest of the day.

The next day she allowed him to learn of her widowed status from someone else, and then she spent the day doing things she knew he liked. He bade her good night at her bedchamber door with the hope that he might see her again soon.

Apparently he was more cautious with her when she had no husband.

The following day she did not tell him that she was a widow until the end of several hours filled with pleasant activities. His good night was warm, but definitely good night.

"Nothing I do suffices!" she shouted into her pillow.

The cat meowed.

She sat up and looked into its eyes. "He will not be won over in a day. He is too principled. And I think he cannot shake his unflattering memories of me. I hate him for it." She dropped her face into her hands.

The cat crawled onto her lap and rubbed its head against her knuckles. She uncovered her face and it butted up against her wrist.

"This is unprecedented. What are you doing? Are you trying to hug me? No, of course not. You want to be caressed, a desire I sympathize with fully, of course." The memory of his hands on her back was so strong. And his mouth ... *his mouth.* Her breaths deepened and she felt the memory to her toes.

Now the cat used her knuckles as a rubbing post. But passivity was not in her nature; she turned her fingers around and scratched its neck beneath the ear. It purred.

She wanted to make the Marquess of Dare purr. She wanted to make him kiss her again like there was nothing else on earth but her lips to kiss and her body to flatten against his.

"He senses something isn't right," she murmured to her companion. "He has probably become an expert at avoiding women who try to entrap him into marriage ... or into anything. Probably."

The cat's fur had grown soft, and it seemed much warmer than her own body. It was so slight, despite the steady strength of its heartbeat beneath her hand. For a creature of such unruffled attitude, it was practically a wisp.

She ran her hand along its back and it curled its tail to guide the caress. She missed touch. Sustained touch. She missed holding her son in her arms or holding his hand or even briefly stroking his hair. She missed *intimacy.* All intimacy. She missed intimate human contact. The brief taste of it with the marquess had only made her crave it more.

"I do not hate him," she murmured. "Rather the opposite. But I will never be allowed to touch him, no matter what I do. It is her punishment to me, you see, or perhaps merely her game," she whispered to the cat as she made lines through the fur on its back with her fingernails. "It seems that I have you, though." She drew a long breath and looked across the room at the statue. "At least she gave me you."

She fell asleep with the creature tucked against her side.

Chapter Twenty

SHOULDERS SQUARED AND BACK STRAIGHT, she stood before the ford and the rain beat upon her umbrella. But her gown was sodden from the knee down. She did not wear a cloak or coat. From his table in the taproom as he watched her progress up the high street, Tacitus had wondered why. So he took an umbrella and followed her to discover her now, motionless, studying the water that passed along the creek-bed like a river.

He had no business following her or speaking with her like this. But today—this—her, here at this place, in the rain— he could not resist.

"Have you come here with the hope that the rain has made the river disappear rather than the opposite?" he said across the rushing sounds of the rain and creek as he joined her at the edge of the ford. "Or are you considering building a boat to sail to the other side?"

"I came here to remember an experience I enjoyed." She turned her face to him. "My husband died three weeks ago. I married him three weeks after you left Dashbourne. Isn't it a peculiar coincidence that I should meet you again now for the first time since then, just on the other side of my marriage?"

Oh. God.

"I am terribly sorry for your loss."

"Thank you. I am sorry that I spoke of you to my son last night in the manner that I did. It was unpardonably rude."

"And yet I must pardon you for it, nevertheless." His cravat was three knots too tight. "I almost ran him over."

Astonishingly, she laughed. "So you did. But, as Lord Mallory said, he was well. He is a very sweet boy." She returned her attention to the river.

"Lady Holland." He did not know how to say this, or whether he should say it at all. It was foolishness. But the water gurgled and the rain droned and it felt so real. "I wonder if you would care to take a stroll with me."

"Now?" Her gaze jumped to his. "In the rain?"

"If you prefer to wait until—"

"No, thank you. I don't mind the rain. But I don't think I will stroll with you, my lord. It seems that reliving enjoyable memories is not as satisfying as I had hoped. But thank you for the invitation." She offered him a smile that had something more than gratitude in it. Something warmer.

"I should return to the inn now," she said. "I must have a word with my coachman, and I would like to finish a book before the end of the day. Good day."

He watched her go, her stride swift and even along the edge of the muddy street.

A *widow*. And so recently. He was the worst sort of scoundrel to feel positively buoyed by the news. It mattered nothing anyway. She was in mourning. And, apologies notwithstanding, she had attached the word "peculiar" to him too often in the past twenty-four hours. She thought him a bookend on either side of her marriage. A curiosity.

After a lone walk through the rain in an attempt to clear his head, he returned to the inn as well. In the foyer he met Mr. George Smythe, who invited him to dine with his family that evening. When Smythe added that Lady Holland was to join their party as well, the surge of anticipation he felt was so acute that he could not ignore it. The bookend coincidence was too much. And the other ... the thing he felt compelled to tell her, despite how inappropriate it would be ... At the very least he could not let this opportunity to know her again pass.

"Did you finish your book?" he asked later, after she entered the private parlor and their host offered her a glass of wine.

"I did not. It's a very exciting story. But I am not a particularly quick reader. Perhaps I will finish it tomorrow."

"I don't care much for reading myself, my lady," Smythe's card-sharper brother said with a toothy grin. "Too taxing on the brain, I say."

She chuckled. "I know you must prefer fashion, sir. The arrangement of your neckcloth is superb."

"I arranged it in your honor, madam." He made a flourishing bow.

Flirtatious coxcomb.

Tacitus suppressed a scowl. But her eyes sparkled and he could not blame the coxcomb for making that happen. He wanted to do that to her. He wanted to make her sparkle.

"That is a fine muslin, Lady Holland," Mr. George Smythe said with an eye on her skirts. "Where did you come by it?"

"Mr. Smythe," his wife said in a dampening tone. "I'm sure she doesn't have any idea. Do forgive my husband, Lady Holland. His mind is unfortunately always in the shop."

"That shop is the reason you've got those baubles hanging off your ears, m'dear!" Smythe chortled.

"This gown came from a clever dressmaker here in Swinly," Lady Holland said. "Her name is Mrs. Cooke." She turned to his brother again. "I daresay even you would find her fashions au courant, sir."

"With such a recommendation, I shall have to pay a call on clever Mrs. Cooke before we depart tomorrow. But I've no doubt the lady wearing the gown is the principal reason it is so taking. Don't you agree, my lord?"

He wanted to say something charming, something mildly flirtatious that would make her smile and show her pretty white teeth. He said, "Of course."

She turned to the Smythes' daughter. "I saw you with a sketchbook earlier today. Would you show me your drawings?"

"Penny is a splendid artist," Mr. Smythe said as his daughter reluctantly passed the book to Lady Holland. "Just like all the grand ladies. Do you have sisters, Lord Dare?"

"I'm afraid not, or I am certain I would be a better man."

With her head bent to the sketchbook, Lady Holland said, "I don't know how anyone could make you a better man than you already are, my lord." And then, without pause, "Oh, Miss Smythe, this is breathtaking. It is the dome of St. Paul's Cathedral, is it not? How talented you are."

"Do you draw too, my lady?" Miss Smythe said.

"Only portraits. Why, look at this. St. George's, I think? What a fine eye you have for detail. And a fondness for church architecture, it seems?"

Tacitus gave half an ear to Mrs. Smythe extolling the virtues of the elite finishing school to which they had sent their daughter to achieve the airs and skills of a lady. He had long since become accustomed to hopeful parents cataloguing the assets of their marriageable daughters. He knew when to nod and smile and insert an appreciative "How impressive" when appropriate. But the only woman he had ever actually cared anything about now sat across the parlor, eyes lit with pleasure as she paged through the sketchbook.

People did not change dramatically. Perhaps over a lifetime, yes. But not in six years. He had no reason to believe she was anything other than what she had been then. He only knew that her beauty still captivated him, that her smile now mingled sweetness and contemplation, and that once again he was in danger of losing his head in a single day.

~o0o~

Penelope's book was filled with landscapes and architectural structures: the high street from the viewpoint of the inn, a posting house on the road, and many images of London—the park, several prominent greens, grand buildings, and thoroughfares.

"You are very good."

"Thank you," Penelope said, but her face remained bland.

Calista paused on a drawing of a doorway sketched with such great care that it seemed real wood and stone.

"What is this?"

"Oh." Penelope reached out to cover her sketchbook. "That is nothing."

Calista drew it from the girl's grasp. "You have captured

the destitution of this alleyway perfectly, even in so few strokes." She turned the page and discovered another drawing of the doorway, from a different angle. The next image was of the entire building: a church rendered so clearly in simple pencil that Calista could nearly hear its bell ringing. There were at least a dozen drawings of the church, each done with care, and a number of interiors as well. "What a remarkable talent you have, Miss Smythe. You must be so proud."

"I suppose I am," she said dully.

"Don't you like drawing?"

Penelope shook her head, her eyes darting to Mrs. Smythe. "Don't tell Mother, please. She says that every lady must draw, and also paint watercolors. She says that men of worth expect it of a wife."

"Hm. My experience is that men care about two things: beauty and money. The rest is window dressing. But I suppose your parents intend a grand match for you."

"At least I have one of the two," Penelope said glumly.

Calista laid her hand on the girl's and squeezed it. "A good man cares about a woman's character more than her face or her purse."

"Does he really?"

"Yes." The man sitting across the room was proof of it. She paged through the images of the church. "What is this place? You seem to know it well."

"It is in Leeds, where we live. Mother and Father send me to church each week to learn French from the rector. During the war he was a chaplain with the army for several years. But . . ."

"You don't like French either?"

"I don't mind it, especially because after my lessons Reverend Greer allows me to assist him at the orphanage. Sometimes I serve lunch, and I read to the children. He has allowed me to take them to the park, too." She was actually smiling. "It is the most fun I have ever had, Lady Holland."

"Is it?"

"Oh, yes. Reverend Greer knows how happy I am with

the children, and he says I am very gifted with them. But he insists that I must be a dutiful daughter and do as my parents wish and marry, and then I can have children of my own. But how I wish I could spend every hour of every day of the week exactly as I do at the orphanage."

Calista closed the sketchbook. "I know something of entering into a marriage against one's will. I don't wish that on any woman. You should tell your parents."

The light faded from the girl's eyes. "I cannot."

"You must do as you will, of course." She glanced over at the marquess in conversation with the others. His gaze came immediately to hers.

"Do you admire Lord Dare?" Penelope whispered.

Calista snatched her attention away from him.

"What lady wouldn't?" she said.

"Mother told me that I must capture his interest. But I believe he admires you."

"I don't know why you would think so."

"The entire time you have been looking at my pictures he has been looking at you."

A tiny thread of pleasure wound through her. It didn't make any difference, of course. She already knew he desired her. His interest now changed nothing.

"You mustn't make anything of it. He and I have been acquainted for some time, Miss Smythe."

"Do call me Penny. But don't tell Mother. She would scold if she knew I asked. But you don't seem at all like the grand ladies I met in London."

"Don't I?"

"You haven't snubbed me. You are very kind to speak to me and to admire my drawings."

Kind. She had not always been kind to Penelope. She had ruined her cloak several times, and in three weeks had not bothered learning anything about her.

"Did I hear that you draw portraits, my lady?" Mr. George Smythe said from across the room.

"Years ago," she said.

"Years? Why, you're no more than a girl now! It couldn't have been long ago. You must do a portrait of my Penelope."

"*Father.*" Penny's face flamed.

"Why did the Almighty give us talents if not to share them with the world?" he said with a broad smile. "Lady Holland, I insist."

She chanced a glance at Lord Dare. He was quite obviously biting back a smile. The silk merchant was presumptuous, but he was sincere and honest.

"I will be glad to draw your daughter, Mr. Smythe. May I borrow your sketchbook?" she asked Penny.

"I would be honored, my lady."

"If I am to call you Penny," she said quietly as she took up the pencil and turned to a blank page, "Then you must call me Calista."

"I couldn't!"

"Then 'Miss Smythe' it will have to be." She set the pencil to the page.

"Yes … Calista."

Penny's face was simple in its lines, with a small nose and slightly protruding eyes. Calista had not drawn anything since before her wedding, and now she found the pencil fresh and pleasing between her fingers.

When she finished Penelope's portrait, Mr. Smythe insisted on showing it to everyone.

"A remarkable likeness! Extraordinary!"

"I beg of you, Lady Holland, allow me to be your next subject," Alan Smythe said.

"Whyever do you want a portrait of yourself, Uncle Alan?"

"I don't. While I appreciate the lady's skill, Penny, I admit that the request is entirely to ensure her attention for the minutes she draws me."

"You are making her blush, Uncle. You mustn't."

"Attractive women are accustomed to flattery," he said with a grin. "Aren't they, my lady?"

"I cannot say, Mr. Smythe." Calista sketched the curve of

his brow on a fresh page. "I was married for six years to a man who, I suspect, never flattered anyone in his life. You must find an answer to your question elsewhere."

"But he could not have kept you locked in a closet." He laughed. "You must have had ample opportunity to be flattered by other men."

"No."

"No?"

"No." Her pencil moved swiftly. His neckcloth was a delight to fashion, as well as the curling lock over his brow and the crease in his cheek. "You mustn't turn your head like that, sir, or I will accidentally give you jowls."

He chuckled.

After she finished the picture, Mr. George Smythe demanded a portrait of his wife, and then of himself, and then of Lord Dare as well.

"Of all the subjects in this room, I suspect his lordship is the most accustomed to having his likeness made," Mr. Smythe said.

"Only once, when I was at university," he said, his eyes on her as she drew the angle of his jaw and her stomach tingled with foolishly girlish nerves. It felt intimate drawing him now when he did not know that she had spent weeks admiring his features. As her pencil shaped the curve of his lips and his eyes—eyes that masked passion she knew was there—she drew slowly. She did not want to finish this portrait. Ever. But their host stood behind her shoulder, making appreciative, impatient noises. When she could delay no longer, she carefully tore the picture from the book and gave it to Mr. Smythe.

"Well, well, I thought the other pictures were all topnotch," he exclaimed. "But she's done you the best of all of us, my lord."

Lord Dare came forward and took the portrait. Finally he looked at her, but he said nothing.

"By Jove, I've never felt so depressingly mortal," Alan said, peering at it over the marquess's shoulder. "You are nothing less than godly in this picture, my lord. I'm so jealous,

I have half a mind to call you out." He chuckled.

"It is a perfect likeness," Penelope said.

Calista folded the sketchbook closed. "It is really nothing to remark upon. I am better acquainted with Lord Dare than I am with everyone else here."

"How should that matter?" George Smythe said.

"When an artist is familiar with her subject, Father," Penelope said, "she is often able to render it with greater depth of emotion and much greater intimacy."

"Good gracious, Penelope. Such talk for a lady!" Mrs. Smythe bustled forward. "I daresay it's time you called for dinner, Mr. Smythe."

Penelope cast Calista a resigned glance and tucked her sketchbook away.

They dined, and Lord Dare was as pleasant company with their hosts as ever. But throughout dinner she found him watching her. After dinner, when Molly brought tea and Alan suggested brandy for the gentlemen, she did not retire to finish her book as she had planned. It gave her too much pleasure to feel his gaze upon her.

"Capricia, my niece is drooping," Alan said to Mrs. Smythe as the last log upon the grate crumbled into embers with a rustle. "The poor girl must be allowed to sleep before we travel tomorrow." He stood and offered his arm to Penelope. "Allow me to escort you, my dear."

"Thank you, Uncle." She offered Calista a grateful smile. "My lady." She curtsied. "My lord."

"Well, it's been a great pleasure, to be sure," their host exclaimed upon a smothered yawn. "I've never yet taken to fashionable hours and I'm drooping as well. Ha! You can take the boy out the countryside, and all that. No, no, don't go on my account, my lord! Continue on here if you'd like. It's all paid up through the morning." He looked about the modest chamber with pride, then departed with his wife.

Calista stood and took up the shawl Elena had lent her earlier in the day and wrapped the soft cashmere around her shoulders. Against her arms in the borrowed gown it felt almost as good as the cat's fur. She had never before appreciated simple pleasurable sensations on her skin. Now she craved them.

"Will you drink a brandy with me?" The marquess poured from a carafe into two glass tumblers. In even this simple action his hands were beautiful, strong and capable, the hands of a man who actually did something of use with them. She wished she could draw them. She wished she could draw all of him.

Good Lord, she was all weakness for him. No matter how she tried to defy her fate, Aphrodite would tempt her cruelly.

"It seems that I must, unless you intend to drink both of those," she said, moving toward him. Soon, no doubt, the goddess would throw up a barricade. She may as well play along with it and suffer her daily dose of pain more quickly.

He gave her the glass.

"Thank you." She peered into it. "I don't typically drink brandy."

"Never a bad time to start." He tilted his glass to his mouth.

"You are fond of it." *She knew.* She sipped.

"Yes. Though in offering it to you now my interest is less in the brandy itself than in finding a justification for continuing the evening with you."

She choked on the sip.

"Are you all right?" He set down his glass. "I did not mean to—"

"You merely surprised me." *As always.* She backed away a step. Perhaps it was unwise to so eagerly throw herself into the torture.

Every bit of his tall, broad frame seemed too still as he remained where he stood.

"And yet," he said, "you are not hurrying away as you did earlier today. Despite what I have just said."

"I think I am staying because of what you have just said." Staying for the pain. Then she could go to sleep and start the day all over again. And again. And again.

She swallowed the remainder of the brandy and placed the empty glass on the table.

"That picture you drew of me ..." he said. "Your pencil was generous."

Her pencil was *unruly*. "You are too modest, my lord."

"It is uncanny."

She should not have done it. She should have drawn him as dispassionately as she had drawn the others. She should have known that Aphrodite would make her pay dearly for her honesty.

"I had the occasion to study you closely for an entire month." She could not look at him now.

"Ah, yes." His voice dipped. "The endless teasing."

"I was little more than a child then. I was poorly behaved to tease you so. But you were arrogant, and far too reserved. I know I have changed. Have you?"

The side of his mouth crept up. "Possibly."

She could not repress her own smile. "For the better?"

A glimmer of bemusement shone in his eyes. "No other woman speaks to me as you do. No other woman ever has."

"Because you are *Dare*?"

He laughed, a deep rumble of amusement, and pleasure went straight to her belly. Now it was close: the reversal. She understood Aphrodite's pattern now. The more pleasure she felt, the happier she was with this man, the closer she was to the disappointment.

"Undoubtedly," he said, his shadowy eyes reminding her of those days spent in his company, one after another of easy enjoyment, shared so innocently and with such hopeful expectation.

She could not bear it.

She must hurry this along. "You are staring at my lips."

"I beg your pardon."

"You are still staring."

"In one manner you have not changed. Your smile is equally as beautiful now as it was then."

She spread her damp palms over her skirt. "Would you

like to kiss me?" *That ought to do it.*

His gaze snapped to her eyes. But he did not break for the door. He came to her, closer than he had come in days, until he stood not a foot away.

"Yes," he said. "I would. But I don't wish to impinge upon your grief."

Damn goddess.

Calista sought words that would end this.

"My husband was ill for some time." It was not untrue. "I have not been touched by a man in many months." No other man than this one. But this would serve its purpose. Now he would recoil, or at best retreat. She steeled herself and let her tongue have its way. "I miss being touched." It was entirely true. "I miss intimate touch. If you wish to touch me now, I would welcome it. In fact I would appreciate it."

"I don't know if I want to be appreciated, exactly."

"What would you prefer?"

He lifted his hand and stroked his knuckles along her cheek so gently, tantalizingly.

"I would prefer to be desired," he said. "As I desire you."

"Then you have your preference, my lord," she said with a catch in her throat.

He set his fingertips beneath her chin and she lifted her face. He bent his head. Her eyelids slipped downward, her breaths disappearing.

"I have wanted to kiss you for six years," he whispered over her lips.

"Then what are you waiting for?" *What was Aphrodite waiting for?*

"Last night I dreamed kissing you. At the ford. In the rain."

"What?"

He drew back a bit to look into her eyes. "The dream was so vivid that I followed you there this morning. Everything about it was almost the same as in my dream. But—"

"Today I carried an umbrella." *This could not be.*

"Yes." His gaze scanned her face. "How did you know?"

"I—" She must not hope. She *must not.* "I—"

"And in the dream, your hair was unbound. Wet."

"Touch me." Prickles of desperation tangled with excitement. "Now."

His fingertips braised her brow, strafing her hair. His other hand rose to do the same and he tilted her head back. His hands were warm, and strong and gentle. *Heaven.*

His dipped his head and his lips brushed hers. She swallowed the sensation of delicious man against her lips, and his scent.

Then it was gone.

"That wasn't enough," she whispered.

"That was a test."

"You passed it. Kiss me again."

"A test of myself. To see if I could halt at that." His voice was rough.

"Can you?"

"Absolutely not." He sank his hands into her hair and brought their mouths together.

Chapter Twenty-One

HE TASTED HER, as though he wanted to learn her lips, her texture, her flavor, one moment at a time, one kiss, one caress. Then again, and again, slow kisses that explored, that teased until she was drunk on anticipation and the euphoria growing in her body.

She gripped his coat sleeves, pushing onto her toes to meet him closer, to feel him, to know him. It wasn't enough. Aching in places that had never ached for any man but him, she wanted to feel him everywhere. She parted her lips, tasted the heat of his mouth, and a moan escaped her.

"Calista," he said upon a ragged breath.

Then he delved. Seeking her deeper, he trapped her mouth beneath his. Twisting her fingers in his coat she felt his tongue and hot pleasure went through her. But his arms were locked, holding her at a distance when she was all heat and hunger and desperation for more. For *satisfaction*. She needed his hands on her. She needed her hands on him. If she was allowed this, she wanted it all.

He drew his lips away and his hazy eyes slewed over her face.

"It still isn't enough," she said upon an ecstatic quaver. "Not nearly enough."

His mouth took hers again, and finally his hands descended. Strong and certain they curved down her neck and over her shoulders, then around to her back. Bracketing her hips, he dragged her against him.

She freed her mouth to draw desperate breaths and he kissed her throat, his lips and tongue making her press to him. His hands spread over her behind, his hard thighs were flush with hers, and his arousal was entirely apparent. This was real. Not a dream or fantasy. Real.

She was being allowed this pleasure.

She felt him with her hands, her fingers and palms caressing hard muscle, then the sinews of his neck, and sinking up into his hair as he brought their mouths together again.

"Stop me," he growled against her lips. "Stop me now."

"No. I want this. I want you."

She nipped his jaw and then his lower lip and he caught her mouth and made her kiss him. Then he was pulling up her skirts, grabbing her thighs, and bearing her back up against a table, and lifting her onto it. Their kisses were wild, urgent, as he pressed her thighs apart to move between them. He tugged at her stockings and his hand found skin, and he stroked, caressing her until whimpers broke from her throat. He pushed her skirts to her hips and she could not believe she was feeling this, feeling *him*, that his hands were on her, touching her. Sweeping up her waist, his palm covered her breast.

"Yes."

His mouth descended, hot and hungry like her flesh that he lit aflame with his kisses on her throat, her neck, the gully of her collar. His hands cupped her breasts and then his mouth was there, tasting and caressing and making her lean into him and beg him for more with the movement of her body. His tongue teased the edge of her bodice, his lips so close to the center of her pleasure where his fingers stroked. It felt so good, deliriously good, a universe of sensation she hadn't ever imagined. She wanted it to go on and on and on.

And then he released her breast from its confines. Hot, wet, searing pleasure jolted through her from his lips on her bared nipple. She moaned and clutched at his shoulders. This was wicked and real and wanton and all she ever wanted now. How she had ever lived without this—his tongue, his lips on her—she didn't know. The intensity of it was almost too much. She needed it, needed him, his body against hers. She needed him inside her.

"Kiss me," she groaned.

He complied, meeting her mouth entirely, and she tightened her thighs around his hips.

"I want to kiss every inch of you." He traced his thumb over her nipple that was damp from his kiss. "Every beautiful inch."

"Your bedchamber, or mine?"

"Are you certain? If it's too soon—"

"I want you to take me upstairs now." Wild pleasure and hope and joy spun through her. "Then I want you to take me into tomorrow."

~o0o~

There was no hesitation now, only urgency. His bedchamber door closed and he trapped her between it and his hard body and fed her need with his mouth on her throat and his hands everywhere.

This was her dream. *This*. Being touched by him. Caressed. The violence of her need shocked her, but she let him touch her everywhere, whispering, "Yes," when his hand came between her legs. Her hunger for it was overpowering. She thrust her hips into his caress and a moan escaped her. Then whimpers. Pleasure built in her where he touched her, coiling tighter and mad for release.

She gripped his arms. "Take me to the bed."

"Come for me," he said against her throat, his hand working her. "Come for me here, and then I will take you anywhere you like."

The pleasure crested, clutching like a fist inside her and then cascading in a thick, hot wave. She gasped, groaned, and clamped her lips shut.

"No," he said. "Don't silence yourself. I want to hear your pleasure."

"But I don't know—" She struggled for breaths, closing her eyes, trying to shut out the memory of chastisements as the convulsions rippled through her. "I don't— Perhaps I am frigid."

He laughed.

Her eyes flew open. Was *this* the end? *Now?*

"Why do you laugh at me?"

"The woman who just came against my hand in less than a minute standing up at a door is frigid? Tell me another story."

A smile pulled at her lips. "You inspire me."

His hands swept into her hair and his body came against hers, and he surrounded her. He held her to him and kissed her deeply. It was a carnal kiss of lust and desire, and Calista discovered a new sort of need: the need to give a man pleasure.

"I want to make you to feel what I just felt," she said.

"That won't be difficult to accomplish." He kissed her mouth again, as if he were drinking from her. "I cannot seem to get enough of your lips. They entrance me."

"Remove my clothing," she said unsteadily, "and perhaps other parts of me will entrance you as well."

"An ideal plan. But allow me to explore this perfect lower lip for a bit longer." He drew her lip between his teeth and then used his tongue on it to brilliant effect. She felt it everywhere. "We've no need to hurry," he said.

She closed her eyes.

"Yes," she murmured, smiling as his mouth traveled to her neck. "We have all night." And, after that, if she understood one merciful goddess's game, finally, *tomorrow.*

~o0o~

She was soft and sweet everywhere, from the tip of her pert nose to the ends of her naked toes.

Her toes. He had never even imagined seeing this woman's toes, let alone laying kisses in the arch of her foot while her barely clothed body undulated in pleasure on his bed.

"I didn't know my foot could be so sensitive," she sighed and laughed at once, her eyes closed, lips smiling. "I am discovering all sorts of delights tonight."

She was unlike anything he had known of her before. Gone was the girl who had teased him, then fled from him years ago. Gone was the pensive woman at the ford that morning. And gone was the quietly elegant widow at dinner with the others. Now she was all languid heat and questing hands. He had descended to her extremities as much to escape the torture of her hands exploring him when she removed his coat and waistcoat as to make good on his word to kiss her everywhere.

But her lips were too ripe, too pink and delicious to stray from for long. Now, smiling, they made him mad for her.

Surrounding her calf with his hand, he left her perfect foot behind and climbed upward, drawing up her chemise slowly, baring her to his eyes.

"When did you acquire this?" He caressed a scar across her knee as he slipped his other hand along her thigh.

She breathed deeply. Her breasts pressed at the fabric of her chemise, the nipples two taut points, proof of her desire.

"I was nine. Chasing after Ian, I tripped over a stile. He had stolen my— Oh, *my lord*."

The inside of her thigh was like butter, silky smooth and hotter the higher he went.

"He had stolen your ...?" he prompted, leaving her knee to caress the sweep of her thigh and curve of her hip.

"My ribbon," she panted as he bared her to the waist. She was dark below, like the long, lush satin cascading over the pillow now, and her hips and belly were soft with the beauty of femininity. He kissed her there, where her waist flared to her hip.

"What are you doing?" she said in a raspy hush, her fingers gripping the bed linen to either side.

"Admiring this inch of you. And this inch." He pressed the garment higher to lay his lips upon one delicate rib, and allowed his hands to cup her breasts through the fabric. "And this inch." He ran his hand beneath her soft buttocks, and she arched to allow him to draw the garment higher. He uncovered her breasts entirely and nearly groaned aloud. They were perfect, round and full, the aureoles dark and peaks primed for his mouth again. He trailed the tip of his tongue around one and she went perfectly still. He paused.

"Please," she whispered.

He stroked his tongue across her nipple and she gasped, and her entire body shuddered. He lingered, tasting the salty sweetness of her skin, memorizing the texture of her arousal until his own was unbearably hard. Tugging the chemise higher, he drew it over her head and she was entirely naked before him, in his bed, her brilliant eyes fogged with pleasure and need.

"You are exquisite," he breathed.

Her lips quivered into a smile. "Yet you remain dressed. Why is that?"

"Body armor."

She grinned. "I have no weapons."

This was a mistake. After this, there would be no going back for him, no return to the empty comfort of rationalizing that she was another man's, that someday he would experience with someone else what he had felt with her from the first. In this moment he was condemning himself to a future alone. But he could not halt it now.

"You are a weapon," he uttered.

Her smile disappeared. Panic glinted in her eyes. She sat up and her hands went to his shirtfront, swiftly unfastening the button.

"You mustn't say such a thing." She tugged the shirttail from his breeches and he allowed her to pull it up and off. She tossed it aside and looked directly into his eyes. Hers were hot with alarm. "Do not think this—here—us—now is anything but right. Anything but— Oh, my." She stared at his chest. "Look at you." Five soft fingertips ran from his collarbone down his chest to strafe his abdomen. Then, with apparent resolution, she set to the fasteners on the fall of his breeches.

He reached to her face, curved his hand around her cheek. "Calista."

Hands pausing, she lifted her eyes to him.

"Forgive me," he said.

"Yes." She blinked. "Yes." She came to her knees, reached for his shoulders, and climbed onto his lap. Straddling him, she kissed him. "Make love to me," she whispered against his mouth. "Make love to me now, before it's too late."

There was an urgency to her plea he could not ignore. Lowering her to her back, he shucked off his breeches and moved between her legs. Her breaths were fast as he bent his head to take one taut nipple into his mouth. But his cock was hard and aching, and her whimpers signaled her readiness. With his fingertips he stroked her. Lodging himself at her opening, he thrust into her.

"*Ohh.*" Her eyes squeezed shut, her fingers gripping his arms.

Dear God. It was too good, too hot and wet and thoroughly perfect. Biting down on his need to move, to feel every tight, glorious clench of her body as he satisfied his hunger, he stroked a lock of silk from her brow. She was no virgin, but it was clear that this was not a woman accustomed to taking a man inside her.

"Open your eyes, Calista."

Lashes fluttering, her eyelids lifted.

"How long has it been since you last did this?" he said, trailing his fingertips along her cheek to the quick beat of her pulse in her throat.

"This is happening," she whispered, her gaze traveling over his face, her palms flattening on his arms, then slipping smoothly to his sides. "It is real. I haven't woken up."

"This is real." He kissed her lips and her hands tightened on him. But he held tight to his control. He had waited six years for this. He could wait another few minutes. "Are you ready?"

Upon a glorious smile she said, "I was ready weeks ago," and thrust her hips into his.

It was a toss-up as to who took whom.

With her hands on his back and buttocks she caressed him and pulled him to her, sending his self-control to perdition. With her body she begged for him, shifting and rocking to find her pleasure, and drawing him deeper into her upon each wild coupling. And with her whimpers and gasps she told him she wanted more, until he was driving into her, the intensity of each deep thrust beyond pleasure. He held on, and on, and on, and held back, fighting the pressure, the burn to release until it gripped him in the ballocks.

"Calista." He struggled for control. "I've got to—"

"I never knew it could be like this." She strained to him, her hands on his chest, then lower, making him insane. Her eyes were closed and she was working him with her body, her thighs a cradle of sublime strength. "It is *bliss*."

"Bliss that's shortly to end," he choked out. He snatched her hands away from his skin. "You must slow down. *Now*." But it was too late; his release came, surging and seizing his cock. "*Calista*."

And he lost himself in her.

Pleasure swallowed him. She was moaning, calling out words, pulling his mouth to hers and gasping against his lips as her body shook beneath his.

And then she was laughing. And laughing and laughing in unrestrained joy. And holding him tight and covering his neck and shoulder with kisses from her sweet, sweet mouth.

"Blast it, woman," he said upon a great inhale. "You mustn't fall into hilarity at a moment like this." He scooped his hands into her damp hair and seized her lips for a deep, satisfying kiss. "Laughter like that, even a minute earlier, could have put period to the entire thing."

Eyes brilliant, she was struggling for breaths. She bit her lips together and he wanted to kiss them apart.

"That was lovely, my lord," she said tightly. Her fingertips did an exuberant dance across his jaw. Then her mouth split into a brilliant smile. "No, no. That was *spectacular*."

His smile was slow and breathtakingly masculine.

"No doubt because I am Dare," he said, and lifted a brow.

Calista fell into laughter again and he kissed her, now lingering, cupping her face in his palms and drawing long, deep sighs from her.

When finally he lifted his head, he gazed at her for a silent moment. His Adam's apple jerked beneath smooth skin.

Longing to ask him his thoughts, instead she stroked a fingertip along his jaw. "How did you come by this scar?"

"Pirates. On the high seas. Nasty battle. Too shocking to share the details with a lady."

She grinned. "Oh, really?"

"Not exactly."

"How exactly?"

After a pause he said, "They say I acquired it fighting for the woman who stole my heart and then ran off with another man."

Her heartbeats skipped. "Do they?"

"Yes. But what do they know?" His hand came around her shoulder and stroked down her arm. "I am crushing you," he murmured, and drew away.

She watched him as he settled beside her. From shoulders to calves he was all taut skin, contoured muscle, and dark hair where it was most intriguing. His beautiful eyes were watching her study him.

"Do you approve?" he said in a sober baritone, but the corner of his lips that had kissed her entire body was smiling. He had always looked at her thus, as though he knew her wayward thoughts. Now she found it difficult to endure the intensity of it.

She glanced at the muscles in his arms again. "Do you make a pastime of chopping wood, or some such thing?"

"If I said yes, what would you think?"

"That you are the most peculiar lord this kingdom has ever seen."

"That is the third time you have called me peculiar since last night. Or perhaps the fourth."

Old Mary rattled the lamp as she commenced her midnight tolls.

"Rather, the night before last," he amended.

"It is tomorrow." She had stayed awake past midnight enough nights to know it meant nothing. But this time was different. This time she had gotten what she wanted. She had won.

"It is indeed tomorrow," he said with that same quiet pleasure upon his lips. "No response to my comment about peculiar, then?"

"Oh. Well ... You *are* peculiar."

"You think that because you have accompanied those
words with your smile that turns me inside out, I shan't take
offense. But I have, in fact."

"My smile turns you inside out?"

He touched her chin tenderly with his fingertips.

"It always has." Then he leaned forward and kissed her.

It was a simple kiss, brief and soft. It was followed by
another, slightly longer kiss. And then by another kiss even
longer, and considerably deeper, his hands circling her face as
she reached for his chest.

Then they were in each other's arms. Damp skin became
hot skin again as they touched and explored, their mouths
seeking, teasing, and promising. Finally they came together,
their bodies joining in decadent intimacy. This time there was
no urgency, no desperation, only the profound pleasure found
in heat and desire.

When it was over and she was sitting in his lap, exhausted
and hazy in his embrace, she smiled. Arms wrapped tightly
about his shoulders, she set her lips to the intoxicating
depression she had discovered beneath his ear.

"You may not disappear," she whispered through her
smile.

"You are in my bedchamber." He bent to kiss her
shoulder, then her neck. "I am not the one of us in danger of
disappearing."

There was such contentment in his voice. But a shaft of
worry pierced her satisfaction.

"I daresay," she murmured.

His fingers stroked her hair back from her brow. "I would
like you to stay," he said. "You may go now if you wish, of
course. But I would very much like you to stay until the
morning, Calista."

She buried her face against his neck and breathed him in.

"I want to stay. I want to stay," she said muffled against
his skin. And then again a bit louder, in case she hadn't been

heard, "I want to stay."

"Good. Good." The quietly spoken words vibrated against her cheek. "And good."

He laid her down and took her in his arms. She had never slept with a man like this, unclothed, embracing. But she found it as natural to curl her body into his as it had been to let him inside of her. He felt right—his skin, his warmth, his strength holding her. He smelled right, good, *so good*. Even his measured breathing sounded right, peaceful. If there were a heavenly kingdom, she was certainly standing in its forecourt now.

All she lacked was her son. And tomorrow she would have him again.

Closing her eyes, she let sleep claim her.

Chapter Twenty-Two

CALISTA AWOKE TO THE TOLL of the church bell barging through the wall and jarring her heart into frantic beats. Popping her eyes open, she reached out with both arms, searching, hoping, *praying*.

But she did not need to feel the mattress, flat and cool beneath her palms, to know the man she had gone to bed with was not now beside her. She did not need to see it.

Rain pecked at the windowpanes of her own bedchamber and made the dawn as gray as the storm of despair in her heart.

Aphrodite's cool white eyes stared at her from across the room.

Turning over, Calista pressed her face into the pillow, and for the first time in six years she wept.

~o0o~

She arose only to admit the cat, who curled up in a ball at her feet and purred loudly enough to match the rainfall's clamor. When the tears subsided, weary numbness crept into her blood and overcame her. Breakfast in the taproom would be unbearable. But if she remained abed, Mrs. Whittle would worry and use her precious time to ensure she was not ill.

She was not ill. Only without hope. And in love.

When she was a girl, Calista had heard fairytales of falling in love, and she had always imagined it a magical, splendid thing, full of blooming flowers and shooting stars. In London, she had looked for that magic in every handsome face, and she found eagerness to please and admiration. But no magic, no flowers, no stars. Snatched back to Dashbourne after only three weeks, she had stewed and groused at the unfairness of it.

Until the Marquess of Dare appeared.

Handsomer than all the rest, he had been uninterested in pleasing her, only Evelina and Gregory. And yet he had come to court *her*. So she teased him, and every afternoon after he drove them back to the house, she stewed and groused more.

It was only in the moment that she begged him to escape and the intensity in his beautiful eyes dimmed—the moment he said he would not help her—that she suspected she had perhaps been wrong about falling in love. That perhaps it was not magical flowers and stars. That perhaps it was something quite different from those. Because in that moment, for the first time in her life, she had felt her heart actually ache.

Remaining in bed until the bell tolled nine, finally she made herself rise and she dressed. She could not avoid seeing him; when she tried to avoid him, he found her anyway. The nasty goddess probably inspired him to worry about her.

Today, though, she would go somewhere he would not worry about her. It was the only place she could imagine going, anyway.

Dressing and descending to the kitchen, she found breakfast for the cat and tea for herself. But she had timed it poorly. When she stepped out into the foyer to gather her cloak and an umbrella, the constable was taking his leave and Lord Dare stood at the doorway of the taproom.

"Good morning, ma'am," Mr. Pritchard said. "Have you heard the news? The ford's five feet high if it's an inch, and the north road's flooded out. I'm sorry to say, Swinly is an island today."

"Yes," she said, pinning her gaze to his white whiskers, anywhere to keep it away from the man who had worshipped her body for hours and now knew nothing of it. "Mrs. Whittle has just told me."

"Lady Holland," Lord Dare said, "may I introduce you to Mr. Pritchard, the constable of Swinly?"

"My lady." The constable gave her an energetic bow. "Welcome to Swinly. I apologize for the rain that's delayed your travel. There's Mother Nature for you, upsetting everybody's plans. Good day, my lord." He donned his hat and went out into the rain.

Calista fumbled with the cloaks, searching for hers beneath Penelope's gorgeous green wool and all the others as if she hadn't found her cloak in precisely the same spot two dozen times already. But her eyes were clouded and her hands would not seem to function properly.

"Allow me," he said at her shoulder, and reached around her to pull forth her cloak. As on every morning, he was polite and mildly distant. This was the gentlemanliness of slight acquaintance, the man she had insulted the previous night, and it tore her apart inside.

She did not look at him as he laid the cloak over her shoulders and she caught a whiff of his scent that had made her drunk when he held her.

"Thank you," she mumbled. Grabbing an umbrella, she fled.

The church was quiet save for the echo of the rain on the vaulted roof high above. Old Mary would shortly sing her favorite song, this time to the tune of ten. Calista could practically feel the moments before the bell tolled each hour now, like the prickle of hairs rising when lightning was about to strike.

She sat in a pew in the front of the nave, as far as possible from the seats where she had shared a night with the Marquess of Dare. Bending her head, she swallowed back the tears again threatening.

"Ma'am?"

Her head jerked up. A young man possessed of straw-colored hair and a slender frame stood before her. Dressed all in black and holding a book, he peered at her from the aisle.

"I could not help but notice you appear in some distress. May I assist you?"

"Who are you?" She knew everybody in Swinly, but this man she had seen only once. Indeed, she had forgotten she'd ever seen him that night in the first frenzy of her determination to destroy the bell.

"My name is Charles Curtis. I am a guest of Reverend Abbott."

"How do you do, Mr. Curtis. I am waiting for him to finish—" *writing his sermon.* "I should like to speak with him, but I don't wish to disturb him."

"Reverend Abbott likes nothing better than to be disturbed from writing his Sunday sermon. Between you and me, I don't think he likes retirement. I half expect him to return to London any day now, God and the bishop willing, of course." He chuckled. "If you'll come with me, I will be happy to take you to him."

She followed him.

"Mr. Curtis, how do you spend your days here in Swinly? Do you ... Do you go out often?"

"Last week I walked to the next village each morning, to greet the children at the schoolhouse there. But the rain has kept me from it today."

"The schoolhouse." The world beyond Swinly. "Are you fond of children?"

"'Suffer the little children to come unto me.'" They passed from the church into the vicarage. "They are the most vulnerable among us, and our hope and future. Would that we gave them everything they need to thrive." He knocked on the door of the vicar's study.

Reverend Abbott opened it.

"Good morning," he said with a smile.

"Good morning, sir," Mr. Curtis said. "I discovered Mrs.—"

"Holland. I am staying at the Jolly Cockerel. May I speak with you, Reverend?"

"Of course." He gestured her in and took up a stack of papers from the desk. "Charlie, I have just been sketching out my thoughts on the annex. They are nearly complete, so you may as well take a look at them now."

"Ah, very good, sir." He bowed to her. "Good day."

The vicar closed the door. "How I wish I were twenty-six

again and setting off for London. I don't suppose a man of my situation ought to admit to jealousy, but I do envy that young fellow."

"You are fond of London, I guess?"

"Not of London, in particular. But of the work he is commencing, indeed I am." He gestured her to a seat before the fireplace in which a cozy fire crackled, and settled down across from her. "Before I retired several months ago, I directed a program to assist the indigent poor in acquiring shelter and gainful employment. Mr. Curtis was recently appointed to the position of assistant director of that program. He has come here to seek counsel from me on how they might begin to integrate the care of children into the program." He cocked his head and studied her face. "But you don't want to hear about that, I suspect. How may I be of help, Mrs. Holland?"

"Reverend, what do you think Hell is?"

He set his palms upon his knees. "You would like to know what the church teaches."

"No. I want to know what you think it is."

"Hell is the absence of love," he said without hesitation.

"But ..." She felt love now, in her chest and belly and every part of her. She twisted her hands together. "I have a son. He is five years old. He is my angel." Tears prickled at the backs of her eyes. "He was taken from me. I have not seen him in weeks. Reverend Abbot, I cannot *bear* it. I miss holding him. I miss the sound of his voice and his laughter. Every day missing him hurts more than the last."

"I am so sorry, Mrs. Holland."

"I thought ... I thought perhaps that I could distract myself from it until I see him again, then I would not feel it so acutely."

"Did distraction bring you comfort?"

"No." She stood and went to the window. The rain was beginning to ease. Within an hour it would end, and another hour later the river over the ford would begin to fall. Too slowly for her.

"There is a man," she said with her teeth together. "I am in love with him. But no matter what I do, to him I will always be little more than a stranger." She turned to the vicar. "I love them both, yet I cannot have either of them. Is that not Hell, Reverend Abbott?"

"It would seem so, yes," he said, folding his hands, "if love were about possessing another person."

"Possessing?"

"You said you cannot have either your son or this man, and that this is Hell to you. But have you considered that true love does not seek to possess, rather to give?"

"I don't want to possess them. I want to *be* with them."

He nodded. "My dear, it is clear that you are suffering. I wish I had a cure I could give to you, as Dr. Appleby at the other end of the village dispenses medicines."

"I have lost hope, Reverend Abbott. I don't want to *live* any longer."

For a minute he simply regarded her, his face thoughtful.

"Do you wish to end your life, Mrs. Holland?"

"If I could, I think— I think I would." She pressed her knuckles against her lips. She'd said it now. Aloud. The thought she'd had for days already. She could not retract it. "This existence is simply too painful to endure."

"Then why do you continue to try to endure it?"

She swiveled to face him. "What?"

"Why don't you end it?" he asked.

"I could not while my son lives."

"I see." The lines at the corners of his eyes bespoke decades of care. "Perhaps, then, another distraction is in order."

"Another distraction," she said with empty laughter. "There is no other man to whom I can lose my heart." There never had been. "Certainly not in Swinly."

"I meant that perhaps you should consider a different sort of distraction."

"Like dancing in the mud or shepherding a flock? I've already tried those. The pleasure in them was short-lived."

He smiled, but it was a kind smile. "I daresay it was." He stood up. "I have seen many destitute souls in my years, Mrs. Holland. You, however, strike me as a woman determined to overcome obstacles."

"Rather, determined to endure them." She had done so endlessly, first with her father and then with Richard, imagining a better day, a day free of him. "Or to escape them," she added.

"No. To overcome them," the vicar said firmly. "God gives us each day as a gift, Mrs. Holland. But it is ours to make of that gift what we will. I believe you will discover a way to overcome this grief. It might not be today. But your hope of seeing your son again is a foundation for it. You must have faith."

She could not tell him that the only day she had was today and the only faith she had was in the Goddess of Love's evil nature. She should have known she would find no comfort in a house of God that denied the existence of ancient pagan deities. She should not have come.

Days ago, Lord Dare had told her she would conquer this. He had told her it was in her character. But neither of them knew the truth.

The vicar was wrong. She had no hope. She would never see Harry again. And she would never look into Tacitus Everard's eyes and see her love returned.

Walking to the inn, she went swiftly to her room. She needn't eat today if eating would mean seeing him again, and she could not go out and about in Swinly without him finding her and speaking with her and unknowingly taunting her with what she could never have. Better to hide. At least today. At least until that indomitable woman he and the vicar seemed to see in her decided to arise and slap Aphrodite in the face.

But not today. Today she had only a heart for grief. Tomorrow would be plenty of time to try for hope.

One thing was certain, after all: tomorrow would always offer her exactly the same useless gifts as today.

Chapter Twenty-Three

TACITUS SET THE FULL BREAKFAST TRAY on the kitchen counter and gave the screw of paper to the innkeeper.

"This was lodged in the door."

Mrs. Whittle read aloud the words scribbled on a blank page torn from a book: "'To Mrs. Whittle, Molly, and Anyone Else It Concerns: I know about the flood. I do not wish to be disturbed today by anyone. Do not knock. Do not call through the door. Do not bring me food or drink. Please leave me alone until tomorrow. Thank you. Sincerely, Calista Chance Holland.' Good gracious, milord," the innkeeper said. "Did you knock?"

"I did not."

"What am I to make of it?"

"That Lady Holland prefers not to be disturbed today, it seems." He took the paper from Mrs. Whittle and stared at it again. Even in pencil, Calista's hand was firm and graceful, with a certain daring flare. It suited her. Rather, it suited the girl he had known six years ago. The words, however, were more suited to the terse, sharp woman he had encountered the night before when he had arrived at the Jolly Cockerel, the woman who wanted nothing to do with him. Again.

"She was ..." He should not share his concern with strangers. But the innkeeper's face was flushed with worry. "She was distressed over her son's departure last night, I believe. Perhaps she needs time alone to come to terms with it."

"The poor dear."

Dropping the note on the counter, he returned to the taproom and the men waiting for him to play cards.

So much for hoping to extend an olive branch to her after so many years. If he were honest with himself, so much for wanting to fill his senses with her again—his senses that remembered her so acutely, richly, as though his memories of her laughter had been made only yesterday, as though the dream of her that had woken him at dawn was real.

Memories and dreams. Irrational fancies for a grown man to act upon. But some men, he supposed, never learned.

~o0o~

The cat mewled.

"If you want to go out, then go out," she mumbled, turning over in bed and pulling the covers over her head to block out the sound of the rain. "But don't scratch on the door demanding to be let back in again immediately. Today I shan't oblige."

It mewled again. And continued mewling.

Behind the mewl, Calista heard footsteps in the corridor.

She opened her eyes and stared at the window. Climbing out of bed, she moved on wobbly knees to it, threw up the sash, and let the rain patter onto the floor and the hem of her nightgown.

"Five days?" she said to the cat. "Six, perhaps?" She looked over at it sitting by the door on its haunches. "Can you count?" She pivoted to the statue. "Can you?"

Every day she heard the footsteps. Sometimes they were his. Sometimes they were Molly's or Mrs. Whittle's. Sometimes they were other guests'. No one ever knocked. The note she stuffed into her door hinge every morning at seven o'clock was serving its purpose.

Leaving the window open to fill the already cold room with icy air, she went to the bed and fell upon it. She did not bother drawing up the coverlet.

In the morning when she awoke, the window was closed.

Chapter Twenty-Four

CALISTA INTENDED TO TIME HER RETURN from the stable to the inn so that she would not encounter anyone in the foyer. But Jackson lingered especially long over dictating the letter to his son because of the unusual diversion he had taken in telling his story. This morning she had asked about his wife.

She didn't know why she had. Perhaps because after a sennight alone in her bedchamber with a cat she craved human conversation. Perhaps because she felt guilty for having left her coachman to his bottle for so many days; never mind that he didn't know she had. Perhaps because she wanted to understand how a man could give his heart so thoroughly to a woman that even years after her death he still loved her. Perhaps it was simply because the cat wanted feeding and after accomplishing that she could not think of anyplace else to go.

For ill or good, she had risen, dressed, and sped past the taproom to come here to the stable. Now, eyes alight, her coachman filled her ears with praise of his Bess.

It made her late in returning inside. Old Mary had tolled ten o'clock long ago. Lord Dare would be in the foyer now, becoming acquainted with the Smythes. He would invite Alan to make up a fourth at the card table. But George would keep them chatting in the foyer for at least a quarter hour while Mrs. Smythe grumbled over the lack of milk and chastised Penelope for no apparent reason.

She could not avoid encountering them. *Him*. Even if she tried to evade him, he would seek her out. He always did.

If she had known weeks ago that he would not leave her alone even when she tried to stay away from him, she might have proceeded through the first of her endless days differently. But she had not known it weeks ago.

Now all she wanted was to forget him, forget how his arms felt around her, how his hot skin and hers came together, how he had carried her along into pleasure even when he had lost control. She wanted to forget how easily he laughed with her, smiled at her, and forgave her.

She wanted to escape.

But there was no escape from her fate. She understood this now.

She understood.

She paused in the middle of the inn yard shrouded in mist, and abruptly her head felt perfectly clear. Clearer than it had in days. Brilliantly clear.

There was no escape. Not from her pain. But she was not the only soul in Swinly suffering. Glancing back at the stable where she had left her grieving coachman in better spirits than she'd found him, she counted her quickening heartbeats.

She knew what she had to do.

Making her way down the street to the alley between the bakery and Elena Cooke's shop, she crossed the soggy path to the sheep field where the gate stood open. Closing the gate and latching it, she walked along the fence until she came to the first farm. A broad-chested man with a thick ginger beard was leading a draft horse out of the barn toward a pasture surrounded by a fence.

"Good day, Mr. Dewey."

He peered at her. "Good day, miss. Can I help you?"

"I understand that you once owned a herd of dairy cows."

His chest puffed out. "Best girls any man ever had."

"I have no doubt." She smiled. "I wonder, could you teach me how to milk a cow?"

He gave her cloak and bonnet a perusal. "You'd be wanting to milk? Yourself?"

"Yes. I know of a cow that needs to be milked today, and I would like to be able to do so, but I don't know how."

He offered her a skeptical eye.

"Is it very difficult?" she asked.

"Not for most folks." He lowered his bushy red brows. "Are you certain, miss?"

"Quite. In return, I will tell you the trick my housekeeper uses to wash coffee stains from wool. After that spill this morning in the taproom at the Jolly Cockerel, your wife will be thrilled to know it, I'm sure."

The eyebrows jerked straight up now.

"I will be glad to wait here until you have the time to teach me," she said with another smile.

"No one ever said Ned Dewey kept a pretty lady waiting." He unstrapped the horse's halter, released it into the pasture, and came toward her. "Lead on to the cow, miss."

~o0o~

She was milking a cow.

Tacitus stood at the window of his bedchamber and looked down into the inn's rear yard as the man perched at the beast's udder gave up his stool to the lady and she settled into the task. Occasionally the man interjected a word, and several times he pointed. But from where Tacitus watched it seemed that she was doing a remarkably good job of it.

He had never in his wildest imaginings imagined Calista Chance milking a cow.

But she was no longer Calista Chance. In six years anything could happen to change a person.

Taking up an umbrella, he headed for the byre. By the time he approached, the milk pail was nearly full. Tacitus recognized the fellow as the farmer who had been doused with coffee at breakfast in the taproom that morning.

"That's it," the farmer was saying with a smile as proud as a new father. "You've done a good morning's work there, miss."

She looked up, and the smile faded from her lips.

"Lord Dare," she said, her eyes retreating, but then her shoulders seemed to square. "You have come just in time to carry this pail into Mrs. Whittle's kitchen, for I'm certain Mr. Dewey must finally be about his own work again." Wiping her hands on her skirt, she stood. "Thank you, Mr. Dewey. You are an excellent teacher."

Dewey blushed ten shades of crimson, right to the roots of his red hair.

"You're a fine pupil, miss. A fine, fine pupil. The best I've seen in some time." He grinned at Tacitus like he'd taken the fox at the hunt. "Good day, my lord." With a jaunty step he went from the yard.

"Have you become a lady farmer since last we met?"

"This morning I have." She laid a slender palm on the cow's hide and stroked it, and Tacitus practically felt it on his skin. He had always admired her hands, and most everything else about her. And he fully suspected that if she smiled at him like she had at Dewey, he would turn into a blithering idiot too. He always had.

"But I cannot carry that." She stepped back from the animal. "So you must. I know you are strong enough to do so."

"How do you know that?" He handed her the umbrella and bent to heft the pail. "I might be suffering from a wounded arm or a hernia or some likewise debilitating injury."

"But you are not."

"Perhaps I don't wish to spill milk on my boots."

"You don't care about that. Come now, my lord. Mrs. Smythe is demanding milk for her tea." She preceded him through the rain into the inn, not bothering to open the umbrella, and raindrops settled on her hair like tiny diamonds.

In the kitchen she greeted the innkeeper with a brilliant smile and he nearly dropped the pail. At close range, she still slayed him.

"Mrs. Whittle, we have brought milk," she declared.

"Good gracious, milord!" Mrs. Whittle's cheeks were round and flushed as she stirred a pot on the stove. "Don't tell me you've milked Nell?"

"Lady Holland did the honors," he said. "I merely watched in awe."

"Well, I've never! The two of you are the most peculiar Quality I've ever seen. Now, milady, you've got to change out of that pretty gown that's all stained with milk and dirt, and I'll have Molly clean it up for you."

"Oh, well, I cannot change out of it. It is the only gown I have. But I will visit Mrs. Cooke and beg to borrow another for the day, so this one can be cleaned. Thank you, Mrs. Whittle." She glanced at him. "And you, my lord." She moved into the foyer.

"It seems you know this village well," he said as she took a plain brown cloak from a peg and drew it over her shoulders.

"Does it?"

"Mr. Dewey, the cow, and the dress shop. Have you come through this village often?"

"Only today." She buttoned the clasp.

Alan Smythe came into the foyer from the taproom.

"Good day," he said with a quick, keen eye at the lady. "Aha, you must be an adventurer, ma'am, to set out in the rain during a deluge."

"It has abated. And as I am not sugar, I shan't melt." She nodded to Tacitus and went out.

"Sugar indeed," Smythe murmured. "Lovely girl." He looked at Tacitus and his face went abruptly slack. "Is—is she your wife, my lord?"

"No." He could not even give the coxcomb a set down; his throat was too tight for more words.

He grabbed his coat and went after her.

"May I walk with you, my lady?"

"If you wish," she said, pausing to allow him to catch up to her. Then she set off along the edge of the muddy street and he fell into step beside her. Before they had gone three yards she said, "I am sorry for speaking of you as I did to my son last night. Please forgive me."

"You are forgiven, if you will forgive me for nearly running him over."

"It was an accident. You did not intend it."

"True. But I should not have been racing."

"I have no doubt it was Lord Mallory's idea. You were only being a friend to him to go along with it."

"There is some truth in that, at least the part about Mallory." He grinned. "You must know him well."

"I don't know him at all. But I know you." She halted and faced him. "I know you well. I know that you are principled and honest and generous. I know that you have an innate need to protect and help others. I know that your first concern is never for yourself and that you are truly a noble man, not only in title but in character."

"One might say that of any of the men of my rank." His mouth was insensibly dry. "It comes with the inheritance, you know."

"I doubt it. It certainly did not come with my father's inheritance." Her jaw was resolute, her eyes shining. "Anyway, you embody it. I know this from personal experience."

"People change," he said. "I am not the same man I was six years ago."

"You are right. You are a better man than you were then."

"You cannot know that."

"In fact I can. I …" She bit her lips together and started off again along the street. Almost immediately she stopped and turned to him. Across the expanse of puddles now glimmering in a ray of reluctant sunshine, she fisted her hands at her sides. "You …" She seemed to struggle to speak. "You like to read."

"Yes." He tilted his head. "I do."

"You like to read modern writers. Novels mostly, but also political treatises and agricultural journals because you wish to keep abreast of innovations." Her nostrils flared. "But your favorite authors are the ancients. You prefer the Greeks to the Latins, though you never admitted that to your parents because they preferred the latter, as evidenced by your name. Your favorite is Plato, and although you are reluctant to say so, you are particularly fond of his *Symposium*, especially the bit about lovers being like the two halves of a fish split down the center that must find each other to be whole again."

"How— How do you *know* that?"

"You will drink whiskey with Lord Mallory, but you prefer brandy. You liked school, you truly enjoyed university, and you occasionally nod off during lengthy speeches in Parliament, although never during Lord Ashford's passionate abolitionist arguments even though he is too darkly dramatic for your tastes. You always wished for sisters and brothers but never resented your parents for not providing you with them because your mother's health and their happiness was your greatest wish. The holiday that you took with them to the River Wye when you were fourteen is one of your fondest memories.

"You give your servants five fortnight-long holidays over the year, including Christmas Eve through Twelfth Night, because you believe they deserve it and because you are perfectly capable of taking care of yourself. You made a cabinet of walnut and cherry woods for your housekeeper that she won't use because she says it's too fine for her. Your valet, Claude, however, gladly uses the jewelry case you made for him in which he stores his collection of cravat pins. You rarely travel with him, which distresses him to no end, but you like your privacy. You have three saddle horses, Pilate, who is very naughty, and Herod and Melchior, who are excellent. But you only keep one pair of carriage horses and a single carriage because you would much rather ride than drive and anyway you rarely go to London anymore.

"After you discovered that Mr. Whittle had not returned last night, you offered Mrs. Whittle your assistance this morning, which is of course the first time a titled lord has ever been in her kitchen. You are suspicious of Alan Smythe's interest in me. Indeed, you are worried about me, about my parting with my son last night, and you still find me attractive—rather, desirable—and you want to kiss me." She blinked several times. "I know these things about you, my lord, and more. So ... There you have it."

"How did you do that?" *It wasn't possible.* "How were you able to tell me all of that?"

"I am living the same day again and again. I have lived this day with you, with everyone in this village, dozens of times."

"Right." He drew himself up. "I don't know how you learned those things about me. And I don't think I want to know. But this—" He gestured to her. "This teasing … I am not a fool. At least in that one manner I have in fact changed in six years."

She came toward him.

"I am not teasing you. I am telling you the truth. I am living the same day, repeatedly. This day. In this village. Everyone else is trapped here by the flood, but I am trapped here by an endless cycle of the same exact day. Think me mad if you will, but it is the truth." Her face was earnest.

"If you are trying to wrest something from me, it won't happen."

"What would I wish to wrest from you?"

"Money. Information." That sounded idiotic. "I don't know."

"I don't want money or information. I want to not be *alone* in this day one moment longer." Anguish sounded in her voice now, and panic. Her gaze darted aside. She grasped his sleeve and drew him toward a shop.

"Here is the dress shop." She opened the door and pulled him inside. "Good day, Mrs. Cooke. My lord, this is Elena Cooke. Like me, she is a widow, but her husband perished at Waterloo. After her husband's death, she had no funds so she came here, to the house he had inherited from his godfather, to make a new start of it. But her fashions are far too fine for a little provincial village like this one, and she is languishing, barely able to set dinner on her table each night. She would never complain, though. She is elegant and somewhat reserved and determined to succeed. She is considering moving to a city, but lacks the capital to make the change. And she sings beautifully."

He looked between the madwoman and the shop mistress. The dressmaker was staring at Lady Holland agape.

"Is that true?" he said.

"Yes." Mrs. Cooke turned astonished eyes to him. "It is all true."

"Have the two of you met before?"

"Not before today," Calista said.

"Not before this moment," Mrs. Cooke said. "Not that I recall."

Calista grabbed his arm and drew him back into the street. "There is Harriet Tinkerson's millinery. Her hats are very clever, especially a little plum-colored cap that I wish I could afford, and Mrs. Whittle's favorite, which is chip straw with taffeta in a lovely shade of sage green. But Harriet herself is something of a ninny and she has no sense of interior design and her shop is a bit of a mess, so she is unlikely to ever acquire the exalted patronage she desires." She opened the door to the shop. "Harriet?" she called from the doorstep.

A woman of brilliant yellow curls came from an adjoining room. Tacitus had seen her earlier at the inn, speaking with Mrs. Whittle. Now her eyes popped wide.

"Calista Chance? Lady Calista! Oh, my, it *is* you. What an absolutely delightful surprise!"

"Harriet, this is Lord Dare."

"Of course it is! I saw you two years ago in the Prince's review, my lord." She curtsied nearly to the floor. "It is a tremendous honor to meet you."

"Harriet, have I ever been in this shop before?"

"Upon my word, no! Why, Calista darling, I haven't seen you in years. But do come in and tell me how— Oh! Are you ...." She looked between them. "Are you Lady *Dare* now?"

Tacitus's heart stopped. And started again with a stumbling heave.

"I am not," she said. "Will you show Lord Dare the purple cap with the veil, please?"

Mrs. Tinkerson blinked like a fish. "It's just there." She pointed to a shadowy corner of the shop where a hat the color of ripe plums was nearly hidden by several others.

"Thank you." Calista tugged on his sleeve and he followed her again into the street. Mrs. Tinkerson came out behind them.

"Calista dear, you simply must return for tea later. Do say that you will!"

"Perhaps tomorrow," she said and grasped his hand.

"There is the pub where the fiddler does a fine rendition of 'Yellow Stockings,'" she said, drawing him along the street. "His 'Speed the Plough' is less enthralling. After he plays six dances, he breaks to drink a pint of ale and two fingers of whiskey, and in the interim Farmer Dewey tells a delightful tale about the herd of Hereford dairy cows he once owned. His account is embellished with all sorts of impossibilities, like the time one of the cows assisted a shepherd dog in herding a flock of geese. Still, they really do seem to have been extraordinary cows. And there is the smith's shop where Mr. Rhodes keeps an axe so sharp that it cuts through beam nicely. And there is the ford, of course. In approximately three hours the water will begin to drop, but too slowly for anyone to depart Swinly today. And at the other end of the street, of course, is the church where Reverend Abbott has just finished writing his Sunday sermon and is preparing to share lunch with his visitor, Mr. Curtis, who plans to annex an orphanage to the charitable foundation in London that he now helps direct. And of course you have heard Old Mary."

"Old Mary?"

"The bell in the tower. Mr. Pimly is just about to ring the noon hour. The hairs on the back of my neck are prickling. And ... *there*."

From the other end of the village, the bell's toll echoed between the buildings. He stared at the tower set against the parting clouds.

"If that is insufficient to convince you," she continued, "in about ten seconds a sheep will appear from that alleyway and walk into the middle of the street. Two minutes from now, another half dozen sheep will join her. Let's count the seconds. One, two, three, four, five, six, seven, eight—ah. There she is."

Tacitus watched the animal cross the muddy road to its center, halt, and release a pathetic bleat.

Calista looked up at him, her eyes entreating. "Do you believe me now?"

It was all too fantastical. Yet only one detail of the whole outrageous narrative shouted at him.

"You are a widow?"

She released his hand abruptly, as though only now she realized she had taken it.

"Yes."

"How have you done this?"

"I haven't *done* anything. In fact, nothing I *have* done has made a difference, not for many days. No matter what I do, I am trapped here in this village, in this flood, in this day. This day that never ends."

"And you expect me to believe this," he said slowly, "because I have been gullible with you once before?"

The panic had receded from her eyes. They were soft now with resignation.

"I don't expect you to believe it. I only hope that you will."

"Do you think me thoroughly addled?"

"Near the beginning of this, when I had only lived this day a few times and still believed I could escape it, you were trying to distract me from my determination to wait out the hours in the cold at the ford. Or perhaps you were simply being yourself—kind, patient, somewhat absurd," she said with a fleeting smile. "That night by the ford, you told me that six years ago you courted me because of my perfect teeth."

He had never told another soul that secret. Never.

"I admire you, Tacitus," she said. "I admire your kindness and generosity and, well, many things about you. If any good has come of this day, it is that I now know a man whom I can admire."

He took the step that brought him close to her—to her vibrant, sublime beauty that had always drawn him. Allowing himself to do what he had wished to do since he had seen her in the rain the previous night, he studied her features openly, slowly, taking in the shadowed crescents beneath her eyes and the crease in her brow that had not been there years ago. Then he looked into her eyes, crystal blue and bright and assessing him just as acutely as she had assessed him then.

"You don't look mad," he said.

"I'm not."

"What do you want of me, Calista?"

"I don't want to be alone in this endless day. Not for one minute longer."

He nodded. "All right."

She blinked. "All right?"

"You needn't be alone today. I will stay with you."

Relief came over her lovely face.

"You don't think I'm mad?"

"Let's not be too hasty."

Her partial smile revealed her white teeth. "If our positions were reversed, I would no doubt reserve some suspicions as well."

"If our positions were reversed, I would not have waited weeks to tell you about this."

"How do you know I haven't told you already?"

Ah. There was the spark in her eyes that he remembered.

"I suppose you might have. Now, what would you like to do today? I am at your disposal."

"Anything I want?"

"Anything you want." Predictably, his heartbeats quickened. If their positions were reversed and she offered the same … "Anything," he repeated somewhat huskily.

"I have an idea." She started off down the street, a decided spring in her step. "Come now, my lord. I've a mind to learn how to make a cabinet today."

Apparently her idea of *anything* was quite a bit different from his.

He went after her. "A cabinet requires many more than a single day to make, and skill far beyond that of a novice."

"Oh, don't be so stuffy."

"Ah, there. Now I am certain you aren't mad. You sound exactly as you did six years ago."

Laughter rippled back to him on the chill air. He watched the sway of her hips and the cascade of her hair and thought that if she was indeed mad, he wanted to be too.

Chapter Twenty-Five

"WHAT DO YOU CALL IT?" He stood in the open doorway of her bedchamber, peering down at the cat sitting at his feet.

"What do I call it?"

"What is its name?"

"It doesn't have a name. Not that I know, at least."

He looked at her curiously. "You have spent weeks in this animal's company and you haven't named it?"

"You don't believe I have spent weeks in its company."

"I might."

She laid the wooden spoon she had made at the carpenter's shop on the dressing table. Lord Dare had showed it off to Elena and Alan during their dinner at the pub as though it were a work of art. It was a simple thing, in truth, but it had been remarkably satisfying to make.

"Here she is," she said before the statue. "The author of my curse."

He came to stand beside her.

"She doesn't look too horrid," he said. "She's very attractive, actually. Are you certain she is to blame?"

"Why is it that if a woman is beautiful, men never expect evil of her?"

"Don't they?"

"I—" For the first time in days she thought of her husband's hard fist. "I suppose they do." She moved away from him, stripping off her cloak. A quick sheen of sweat had coated her skin at the recollection of Richard. She went to the open door. "Well, my lord, you have made good on your promise. You have not left me alone today, and I thank you for it. I am more grateful than you will ever know, in fact. But

I must say … I would like to say …"

He crossed the room until he stood very close. "What would you like to say?"

"I am sorry the day is over."

"It's not over quite yet."

Her heart did an abrupt little turnabout. "You cannot stay here. Now."

He reached out and closed the door. "Why not?"

She backed away until her calves came up against the bed. "Because you simply cannot."

"I won't touch you."

"That isn't actually what worries me."

His grin turned roguish. "Then you have much more faith in me than I do."

"This is unwise."

"Come now," he said, much easier. "I promised. And I am a man of my word, as you have said."

"Shall we go down to the taproom?"

He glanced at the bed. "Is this where you wake up every morning at seven o'clock?"

"Yes."

"Then we are staying here."

"There is only the bed. Not even a chair. Do you intend to stand?"

For a stretched moment he just looked at her. Then he took the two steps to her, grasped her shoulders, and pulled her mouth against his.

Despite herself, she closed her eyes and let him kiss her, let him taste her lips, then urge them apart. Releasing the breath she held, she let herself feel him too, kiss him, adore the softness of his lips and his skill, and she touched him with the tip of her tongue and felt all the heat and pleasure even that simple caress made inside her. His hand came around her face, beneath her chin, drawing her up to him. Then he deepened the kiss, matching their mouths together fully.

He drew away slowly. She opened her eyes to see him taking a visibly hard breath.

"There," he said firmly. "That's done with. Out of the way. Now we can move on."

Her lips tingled. She bit his flavor on them. "You *are* absurd."

"Not precisely what I wish to hear after kissing a woman for the first time. But circumstances being what they are, I will allow it." His voice was decidedly uneven.

She did not tell him that they had shared so many kisses already she knew his kiss as well as anything else about him.

"Now," he said bracingly, "I am going to sit here on this bed—beside you, not touching you—and tell you everything there is to know about the goddess Aphrodite. And you will sit here—beside me, not touching me—and listen attentively until you nod off or murder me out of boredom, whichever comes first. Understood?"

"Understood." She kicked off her shoes and sat on the edge of the bed as he removed his boots. "But what if I want you to kiss me again?"

"I will resist you." He settled beside her and his gaze slipped over her body. "Valiantly. Despite the temptation. Someday someone will write an epic poem about my courage and fortitude this night."

"You don't want to take advantage of me."

"Given the circumstances, I think it's best."

The circumstances in which she had told him the truth and he thought she was mad.

Old Mary's song rocked through the wall. They waited until the ninth ring faded into silence.

"All right," he said. "I will begin with the story of the Trojan War. Are you familiar with it?"

"I think there was a very big horse involved. Wasn't there?"

His brow wrinkled almost comically. "Hm. Do you know where Greece is?"

"Somewhere in the Americas?" Her lips twitched.

"Yes," he said with narrow eyes. "That girl from six years ago is most certainly not gone."

"I am testing your arrogance."

"I gathered as much."

"But I beg your pardon." She folded her hands in her lap. "I promise to be good now, my lord."

He took her right hand and lifted it to his lips. Softly, he kissed her knuckles.

"I told you that I have changed too in six years," he said. "Be exactly who you are, and I will be content."

"Even if who I am is a woman who believes she is reliving the same day over and over again?"

"Even then."

She looked at their hands. "You are breaking your own rule."

"I noticed that." His fingers tightened around hers as he rested them, still clasped, on the mattress. "Now where was I?"

"The Greeks and Trojans."

"Ah, yes. Once upon a time, in a land far, far away—"

"In the Americas."

He nodded. "A trio of vain, silly goddesses intent upon besting one another at any cost took note of a mortal girl of such surpassing beauty that gods and men alike all wanted her. Which of course means that she was quite like present company."

Calista smiled, leaned back against the headboard, closed her eyes and let his hand surround hers and his voice lull her into contentment.

She started awake.

"—Mr. Smythe, didn't you?'

She blinked and saw his coat right before her eyes and felt her cheek pressed against something much harder than a mattress. With a gasp, she pulled back.

"You needn't move," he said. "Either you use me as a pillow, or the cat does. And I much prefer you."

She pushed up onto her elbow. Legs crossed at the ankles and a book propped on his waist, he was lounging in apparent comfort, with her, apparently, sleeping on his arm.

"I am sorry."

"Don't mention it. You dozed off at the start of chapter two, though I've no idea how you could have. I am enthralled by the rapaciousness of this Prince Manfred. But I think you've read it already. You were mumbling something about the valiant Theodore in your sleep, and I haven't got to him yet. I suppose he might be one and the same as this heroic young peasant."

"He is." She pushed hair from her face. "Now I remember; you ran out of Aphrodite stories. Is it midnight yet?"

"Soon, I expect."

She settled back down on the mattress and tucked her hands under her cheek.

"I cannot believe I fell asleep. I thought I was too full of nerves to do so. I have never ... Well ..."

"You have never slept fully clothed before?" He turned the page as though he were still reading. "I can remedy that for you, of course."

"Now who's teasing?"

"I would like to tell you that you are beautiful when you sleep, but from this angle I could not see your face. The top of your head, however, is quite taking in slumber."

She smiled. "What did you say about Mr. Smythe that woke me up?"

"When you invited him and Mrs. Cooke to dine with us tonight, you already knew he admired her, didn't you?"

"I did."

"Perhaps you have a bit of Aphrodite in you, yourself."

"Please don't compare me to her."

"Still, it was good of you to allow them opportunity to come to know each other before he departs tomorrow."

"It was not only for them that I did it. I thought you might like the company of others."

He turned his head to look at her. "Other than you? Today?"

She nodded.

He laid the book on his chest. "Your company is entirely

sufficient for me, Calista. More than sufficient."

The hairs on the back of her neck prickled.

"Midnight," she whispered, and Old Mary's toll boomed through the wall.

As the twelfth ring died away, he frowned. Then the frown disappeared.

"You are still here," he said.

"I am." She sat up. "Oh! Were you waiting for midnight, thinking—"

"Certainly I was."

"It doesn't work like that. It doesn't matter what I'm doing at midnight or any time of the night. I always wake up here at seven o'clock."

"I see," he said gravely. Then he swung his legs over the side of the bed and stood up.

"You are leaving," she said, the ache of loss already spinning through her.

He shrugged his coat off his shoulders. "If I'm to be here seven more hours at least, I would like to be a bit more comfortable."

She swallowed again and again over the constriction of her throat. "You needn't stay."

"Of course I will stay." He untied his neckcloth and removed it. "But there won't be any more falling asleep. Is that clear?"

"Then perhaps I should read aloud instead of you, to keep me awake."

He passed the book to her. As he settled beside her again, his shirtsleeves tugged at his shoulders and arms, and Calista did not know which flustered her the most: the memory of his flesh beneath that shirt, or his intention of staying through the night in her bed.

"You mustn't allow yourself to be distracted by my breathtaking state of masculine undress," he said, casting her a sideways glance as he propped his arms behind his head. "I'd thought you made of stronger stuff."

"Usually I am," she mumbled. She opened the book and

began to read aloud.

He fell asleep in the middle of chapter four. Calista folded the book closed and curled up on her side and watched the even cadence of his breathing lift his chest.

"I wish I could see this every night when I fall asleep," she whispered. "You beside me."

Emotion rose in her, thick and hot.

"I wish I knew how to make this day end so that in the morning you would know me as you do now. I wish I had your kindness and decency and humor and faith in people. I wish I were as good a woman as you are a good man. But most of all, Tacitus Caesar Everard, I wish you were mine. I wish with all my heart that you were mine, and that I was yours."

She watched him sleeping until her eyelids grew so heavy that she could not hold them open unless she got up and walked around the room. But remaining awake would not make tomorrow come. It would only delay the inevitable return of today.

Still, she struggled against sleep, trying to take into her senses as much of him as she could, and knowing that it would never be enough.

Chapter Twenty-Six

NO CAT WAS CURLED AT THE END OF HER BED when Calista awoke to the tolling bell and the patter of raindrops and the gray dawn. No man lay beside her on the mattress. No wooden spoon rested on the dressing table beside the statue.

Closing her eyes, she drew in a deep breath.

Then she climbed out of bed and prepared to meet the day.

Alone.

By dressing swiftly and hurrying past the breakfast room, she arrived in the stable so early that Mr. Jackson was still seeing to the horses' morning needs. The inn's ostler whistled pleasantly to the beat of the rain on the roof, and the boy shoveled straw from a stall at the speed of Ian's favorite thoroughbred.

She had never seen the stable boy in the morning before, and she greeted him. He didn't even glance at her.

"I would like to have a word with you, young man," she said.

He seemed to start into awareness, and turned to her. He was perhaps eleven and had a sweet face with drooping eyes that made him look like the puppy.

"Good day, mum."

"Why is it that, when you were charged with delivering a letter to me last night, I must come here and ask for it today?"

His puppy eyes popped wide. "On my gram's honor, I plumb forgot!" He plunged his fingers into his waistcoat and produced the letter from Mr. Baker. She accepted it and tucked it into her sleeve.

"Thank you."

The ostler appeared and frowned at the boy.

"What're you doing here, Tommy? I told you to be off."

"I'd to finish mucking out this stall, sir."

"I'll do it, lad." He grabbed the shovel. "Now, be off with you."

The boy tugged his cap and ran out into the rain.

"Milady," the ostler said, "this is no place for that pretty dress. Least not till I've got this cleaned up."

"I don't mind." She thought of Mr. Curtis visiting the school in the adjoining parish. "Is he off to school, then? I thought the flood had blocked the way."

"No. Tommy doesn't attend school." He dug into the dirty straw. "He's got his orphaned brother and sisters to care for."

"But he is so young!"

"God doesn't measure a boy's years when He takes his parents. Only his heart."

"If I had known I would see him this morning, I would have brought a coin for him." She hadn't on previous days; she had been too irritated with him for forgetting about John and the letter. "Where is he off to now? I could take it to him there."

"His grandmum's ailing something fierce. He's gone home to tend her."

"Oh, *no*. Where is the house?"

Calista knew the nearby farms of Swinly well by sight, and had no trouble recognizing which place the ostler described. After writing Jackson's letter, she returned to the inn, collected the coins from her purse and an umbrella, and set out.

More of a shed than a proper house, it had a forlorn aspect, cheered however by quilted curtains. Not wanting to track mud inside, she remained at the door as three tiny children stared up at her. One looked about Harry's age, although the cheeks of all three were even gaunter than her son's, and their eyes were round with astonishment. She had the most powerful urge to grab them all into her arms and hug them until she woke up.

"Is your brother in?" she asked.

Tommy came out from behind a curtain drawn across the back of the room. "Mum?"

"Tommy, I neglected to thank you properly for delivering the letter to me." She took his grubby hand and pressed the coins into it.

He scrubbed his other fist across his brow. "Thank you, mum." He tucked the coins into his trousers pocket.

"I understand that your grandmother is ill. Has Dr. Appleby paid a call on her?"

"No, mum. We can't afford the doctor's fee."

"I see." She glanced at the three little ones again. "You poor things. Tommy, may I visit with your grandmother?"

He screwed up his nose. "D'you know how to treat ailments, mum?"

"Some." Her husband's gout, principally. But she suspected this woman was not suffering from too much cheese and Port wine. "Let me see if I can help."

He went to the curtain and opened it to invite her in.

The woman lying on the cot was much older than Calista had imagined a grandmother of these children would be.

"She hasn't eaten in six days," Tommy whispered, touching his grandmother's hand with the tenderness of an adult. "I can't even make her take broth."

The woman was little more than skin over bones. There was no odor of sickness, though. Calista put her palm to the woman's brow. It was cool. Alarmingly cool.

"When did she take to bed, Tommy?"

"Twelve days ago."

"And there is no one to nurse her, or to care for your sisters and brother now, except you?"

"No, mum. Papa went off to find work in the mines months ago. We've not heard from him."

Calista unclasped her cloak. "I will tend to her now. Show me where you keep tea, and the broth. What is your brother's name?"

"Fred, mum."

"You or Fred must run to the village and fetch Dr. Appleby. Tell him Lady Holland from the Jolly Cockerel requests his presence here."

Three quarters of an hour later, Fred returned without the doctor.

"He's not at home, mum."

Untying the apron she had found, she squeezed her patient's fingers gently and handed the bowl of broth to Tommy.

"I will go the village and fetch him myself, Mrs. Cochran."

The old woman's half-closed eyes seemed to flicker.

Calista stood up. "Tommy, I will let your employer know that you won't be returning to the stable today. There is little to do there, anyway, with no one coming or going." She spoke quietly to him. "Fred and your sisters are frightened now. You must distract them. Keep them busy straightening and sweeping the house and washing those linens to hang out now that the sun is shining. Tell them she will like to know they're helping. And promise them a special treat if they do it well. I will return later."

"Yes, mum." His face showed profound relief. "Will my gram be all right?"

"I hope so, Tommy."

She walked from one end of Swinly to the other, directly to the doctor's house. He did not answer her knock. She supposed he must have other patients, even in this tiny village. He had been available to the marquess, although that had been hours earlier in the day. Holding tight to her impatience, she went into Elena's shop to beg of her paper and a pencil to write a note, which she then left on the doctor's stoop.

The herd was milling about the street by the time she started back to the inn.

"Oh, move, you silly creatures," she muttered to the pair that always blocked the least muddy stretch of verge, and tried to nudge them aside. The sheep remained steadfast while she soaked her skirt in oily water and felt cross and helpless.

"This is not how I wished this day to go," she said, her

throat too tight. "Not in the *least*. Not after yesterday. Not this failure." She pushed past them and hurried to the inn.

She entered just as Molly exited the private parlor wringing her hands.

"Good day, milady."

"Good day, Molly." She removed her soggy cloak and set down the umbrella, remaining close to the doorway where she could not be seen from the taproom. It was well past two o'clock already. He was there now, graciously allowing men with one ten-thousandth of his income to best him at cards, and entirely oblivious to the fact that he had spent hours reading to her in bed the night before. Even speaking with him briefly today would be painful—too painful for her to bear just now, at least.

"Mrs. Smythe is unhappy without milk for her tea, isn't she?"

Molly's brows went up. "Yes, milady. How did you know?"

"Oh, you would be astonished at all I know." She turned to arrange her cloak on the peg so it would dry before she ventured out again in search of the doctor and gifts for the children. But food must come first. She felt wretchedly faint. "I will see to milking the cow shortly. In the meantime, would you like me to go into that parlor and tell Mrs. Smythe to take her endless demands and stuff them up her pointed nose? I can take the opportunity to also firmly recommend to her that it is a terrible, tragic mistake to force her daughter to marry a man she cannot care for, and that it would be a much wiser thing to allow her to marry for love. For that, Molly, I know *quite* a lot about."

She turned to see Molly's face blank with shock and the Marquess of Dare paused three steps up from the ground floor on his way down. The knuckles on his hand gripping the stair rail were white.

"So … *not* in the taproom at present, it seems," she mumbled, snatched up her cloak, and fled outside.

She'd thought she had already lived through the worst this

day could bring, many times over. But the more she fell in love with him, the more she realized she had barely scratched the surface of misery.

~o0o~

The serving girl's eyes were as round as Tacitus's, and she seemed just as paralyzed. Then she curtsied, offered him a quick, "Milord," and scurried away.

But he could not move. A jarring sense of déjà vu was seizing him.

Sharp, direct words.

Flashing eyes.

The passionate candor of her voice.

The gleam of her mischievous smile that retreated the moment he met her gaze.

She was the same girl he had known six years ago. Six years during which he had wondered if she had found another man to help her run away to London …

And a year after that, when he discovered she was married and wondered if that man had been the Honorable Richard Holland …

Eighteen years her senior, but not a bad-looking fellow according to reports, the youngest son of a baronet and thick in the pockets, Holland might have taken the fancy of a spirited girl on the town for the first time. He might have made promises that a young lady with laughter in her eyes and adventure in her soul would not have been able to resist.

After years of wondering, Tacitus wanted to know. He wanted to know about the man who had won her when he could not. And he wanted to know which of the marriages she had spoken of to Molly was hers: a forced tragedy or marriage for love. Serendipity had trapped him with her in this inn in this village for an entire day. He would not have another opportunity like this.

He went after her.

She strode swiftly along the edge of the muddy street. As she turned into an alleyway between two shops, he caught up to her.

"Did I hear you say that you intend to milk a cow today?"

"You did," she replied immediately, as though she had expected him. "She needs to be milked and someone must do it. Why are you following me?" She halted and faced him, her brow tight. "You mustn't, you know. It won't do either of us any good."

"I know." This was insanity. He hadn't spoken to her in years, and barely the night before. Yet standing here, facing her, it was as though no time had passed.

"I must do an errand now," she said, not meeting his gaze. "Excuse me—"

"Wait." He grasped her arm. The sensation of familiarity pressed at him with such force, as though he had held her like this before, though he knew he hadn't.

"I must know something. You will think me a madman for asking, but I find I must."

A spark came into her eyes. "Have you had another dream?"

"Another dream?"

"I thought perhaps— Rather, I must have been mistaken." She seemed to realize he was holding her and tugged away. "What do you wish to ask me, my lord?"

"Just now," he plunged in, "when you spoke to Molly, you said you knew the difference between being forced to marry a man you did not care for and marrying for love."

She blinked rapidly, repeatedly. "You were not supposed to hear that."

"Which is your marriage?"

"You should not be asking me this."

"Yet I am. And as peculiar as you may think me for believing it, you owe me an answer."

Her eyes, now round and rimmed with distress, seemed to seek purchase in the region of his chest.

"I am no longer married. My husband died not long ago. So, you see, the issue is moot. Good day, my lord." She turned and continued up the alley.

"Which was it?" he called after her. "Tell me."

She pivoted. "You *are* the most peculiar man I have ever known. What sort of person asks a woman recently widowed, whom he hasn't seen in years, whether she married happily? What do you hope to accomplish by asking me this?"

"I ... I think— I want to know that you were happy." It was the truth, though he only understood that now. "I want to know that you were loved, and that you loved him in return. It isn't my business, certainly. I recognize that. But seeing you again, and with your son last night, it has made me— That is to say ... I have wondered for years whether you are happy. I wanted you to be happy."

"Well, you might have done something about it *then*. For it doesn't help me now, you know."

Her words hit him like a slap.

"I did do something then," he said. "I courted you for a month. *Every day* for a month. I own three houses and a castle, yet I lived at an inn because that was the only way to see you. I spent thirty days engineering entertainments for a girl of sixteen and a boy of fifteen in order to be with you. So in fact I think I did do something then to try to make you happy."

"It wasn't *enough*."

"For God's sake, what more could you have demanded of me?"

"You didn't ask me to marry you!"

"Of course I didn't. You disliked me!"

"I was *infatuated* with you."

Tacitus stared.

The world was abruptly a vastly different place.

"Say that again?" he forced out upon a thin breath.

"I was infatuated with you," she repeated, spots of red high upon her cheeks. "Beyond telling. Sometimes it was so difficult to be with you without declaring my feelings that I had to leave abruptly. My mother had convinced me that a lady does not express her deepest feelings, that she must at all times remain pacific and modest, that true gentlemen expect this. I knew you disapproved of me, of my teasing and overexuberance. I was terrified that if I allowed you to see even a part of what I felt, you would revile me. Most days I was beside myself with the urge to pour out everything battling with the certainty that I must not."

"You ran away from me." He shook his head, as much to force into it the words she was speaking as to deny them. "Every time I came close to you. Again and again."

"I wish I hadn't. I should have spoken immediately. I should have told you at the beginning how strongly I felt, how immoderately. That would have swiftly turned your disapproval to disgust. Then you would have left at once, and my feelings would not have grown to the extent that they did."

"To what extent?"

"To what extent?" Her hands fisted at her sides. "What have I done to you, then or now, that merits this inquisition? Will you force me to speak of the greatest moment of shame and regret in my life? Do you need to hear me say it aloud? Is it not enough that I am equally ashamed of it now as I was then?"

He went to her and stood so close he might touch her, and his heartbeats thundered against his ribs. *To what extent?*"

"To what *extent?* I begged you to elope with me!"

Holy Hell.

He struggled to breathe.

"I did not understand," he could only manage.

"I suppose you imagined I did such things regularly. My father told me often enough that my manner with gentlemen was far too open, that it was bound to be misconstrued. My mother was so demure, so subdued. I *wanted* to be like her. I wanted to be good. Perhaps if I had been, my husband would not have—" She halted her words. "My father was a beast and my mother was a wet rag. I understand that now. I didn't then. Though it was not in my nature, I tried to behave as she taught me to. But I failed. I teased you about your reserve because I knew it was my fault, that you were only trying to show me your displeasure. How could you admire a lady you could not respect, after all?"

"Until that morning, I found only pleasure in your company." His tongue could barely form words. "I thought you wished me to drive you to London to meet another man."

Her eyes widened, and she became very still.

"No," she only said. And then: "No."

"You ..." This was unimaginable. Unbelievable. A miracle. "There was no other man?"

"The night before I came to the inn without Evelina and Gregory, my father told me he was selling me to Richard Holland to settle a debt of fifteen thousand pounds. He said you would expect a large dowry while Richard would pay him for me, and that anyway since you had not offered for me after so many weeks you never would. But I wanted you. That morning, I wanted you to take me away."

"To London?"

"To anywhere you wished. I would have gone. I would have gone with or without an offer of marriage."

And then, without a plan, without another thought, without asking her permission, he was kissing her—wrapping his hands around her arms, drawing her close, and taking her mouth beneath his. She was soft and sweet and she tasted like berries and tears and, swiftly, desire. Her lips parted for him and her hands swept over his shoulders to grip his neck and slip into his hair. She was delicious, warm and vibrant and *his*. She was his now. She had always been his, had he but known it, had he not been such a colossal fool.

He pulled her against him as he had dreamed so many times, and she was perfect, her curves and supple strength against his body, perfect as he had always known she would be.

Dear God, he hoped she hadn't changed too much in the years since he had fallen in love with her. Because this time, no matter what came now, he would not let her go.

Chapter Twenty-Seven

HIS KISS WAS A NEW KISS. A first kiss. Testing, questioning, seeking, and overflowing with an urgency that Calista recognized well.

But she already knew the texture of his lips and the flavor of his kiss. She knew the strength of his hands on her. She knew the need that arose in her, so hot and desperate, when he made love to her. She knew how it felt to want him, to be touched by him, and to have him satisfy her. She knew the joy in spending all night talking with him, adoring him without even touching him. She knew that she loved everything about him.

And she knew the depth of pain that her heart would descend into tomorrow when she looked into his eyes and saw that he had never kissed her before, never touched her, never made love to her. She could not bear it one more time.

She dragged herself from his arms.

"No. I cannot do this. I cannot be with you."

"Calista—"

"*No.* Don't. Please." She started up the alley again, her steps faltering.

"If it's too soon after your husband's—"

"It isn't too soon. It's not that. I simply cannot—"

"Who in creation do you think you are?" His voice grated.

She swung around.

"This is not acceptable, what you are doing here," he said in harsh, short syllables. "Do you even know that? Do you even know that you cannot treat people like this? Perhaps when you were eighteen you had the excuse of naïveté. But not now."

"You followed *me*. I tried to avoid you—"

"And yet you managed to pause long enough to tell me a story that has altered history for me. You are entirely duplicitous. What story will you tell me tomorrow, I wonder? That you never felt anything for me years ago and I imagined this entire conversation?"

Tomorrow.

"No. No." She returned to him swiftly and when she placed her palms on his chest he remained still. "Tomorrow," she said. "I will explain everything tomorrow. Everything that I cannot explain now."

"Tomorrow?" He did not lift his hands to touch her, but his heartbeats were swift and hard beneath her palms.

"I promise it. Tomorrow. I will not retract what I told you about the past. It is all true. But you must allow me until tomorrow to explain." Tomorrow that would never come. "Today ..." She lowered her arms. "Today you must let me be."

"The locals say that the ford will be low enough to cross tomorrow. Will I awake to discover you already gone?"

"No. I will be here." Every day. Forever. "Believe me, I long for tomorrow. If there were anything I could do to make this day end quickly, I would."

His eyes seemed to search hers. "Something isn't right. I don't know if it is your doing, or otherwise. But ... Allow me to help you."

Even *now* he offered this. Even hurt and angry and confused, he was kind. She closed her eyes.

"Tomorrow," she said. "Not today."

She went away from him, and he let her go.

She found Dr. Appleby and bade him hasten to Mrs. Cochran's bedside. Then she searched the village for gifts for Tommy and his brother and sisters. Returning to the inn, she went into the rear yard, found the pail, and milked Nell. Then she ate a piece of toast and cheese in the kitchen and went to her bedchamber to feed the cat. Walking out again, she crossed the village to Tommy's house, sat with his grandmother, and gave the gifts to the children.

She did not see the Marquess of Dare again.

When night fell she turned the key in the lock on her door and curled up on the bed and pretended that she could not go to him now and be with him, for even a few hours. And she pretended that it was better this way.

A soft knock came at the door and her heart jerked into a gallop. She unlocked it with unsteady hands.

Tommy stood in the corridor, his shoulders slumped.

"Gram's passed," he said, and his face crumpled.

He thanked her for what she had done for his family today. When his words broke into a sob, she took him into her arms and cried with him.

~o0o~

"Lady Holland, you must come away now."

Sounds seemed to come through a tunnel, the doctor's words echoing from somewhere very far away.

"This cannot be happening. Not again. Not today." She swung her gaze around the tiny cottage lit by the fading sun, to where the children sat huddled and weeping. "Not today," she repeated.

Dr. Appleby lifted the blanket to cover Mrs. Cochran's face.

"She cannot die today," Calista said to him.

"Lady Holland—"

"What was it, Doctor? You must know what illness took her. Are there medicines in your office that might have helped, had she been dosed earlier in the day?"

"You summoned me at sunrise," he said gently. "I gave her all the care I could today."

"Then why is she gone?" she whispered. "Why has she left these children all alone?"

"She was old."

"No older than my mother, who is perfectly hale."

"I suspect your mother has lived a different sort of life than Mrs. Cochran."

"But—"

"The human body does not last forever, Lady Holland. Sometimes people simply die." He set his hand on her shoulder. "Tommy tells me you have been here all day. You must return to the inn and take a meal before Mrs. Whittle closes her kitchen for the night. I will walk back with you."

Calista told Tommy she would return in the morning and went with the doctor.

"What of the children?" she asked him as they trod the path to the village center in the falling light. "Who will care for them now?"

"I will write to the mine and inquire after their father. If he cannot be found … We must wait and see."

"Thank you for your help today."

"I did what I could. In truth, the children seemed more comforted by your presence than mine. Tommy is a strong lad, but sometimes a boy needs a mother. Here we are," he said, opening the door of the Jolly Cockerel.

"Doctor." She touched his arm to stay him. "What if you had only one day to heal others? Only a single day. What if tomorrow never came, as it will never come for Mrs. Cochrane?"

"If tomorrow never came? I suppose I would do my best to help those who needed me today." He patted her hand atop his arm. "You have done a fine service to your fellow man today, Lady Holland. Do not allow grief to deny you the satisfaction of helping others. Good night."

She ate dinner in the corner of the kitchen, feeding bits of meat to the cat and absently listening to Molly and Mrs. Whittle chatter about this and that—dirty dishes and tomorrow's meals and the new cow Mr. Whittle would bring home as soon as the ford could be crossed. And she thought of her son.

Back in her bedchamber, she undressed slowly, crawled under the covers, and invited the cat to join her at the pillow.

"Why do you disappear each night, like everything else, when I know you are living these days just as I am?" she mumbled as she stroked its round belly. "Is it because I haven't named you? Was he right to think me odd for that?"

It purred.

"I don't understand what that purr means. But I suppose I shall have to accept that."

~o0o~

Old Mary's boom resonated through the little bedchamber. Calista slowly opened her eyes.

"Well," she said to the ceiling swathed in shadows. "Here I am."

She sat up and the patter of rain filled the silence between the tolls. Then she set her feet on the floor. With a simple curve of her lips, she drew in a long breath.

"Let the day begin."

Chapter Twenty-Eight

CALISTA PACED THE DISTANCE from the millinery's front door to the parlor.

"Fourteen feet … and a half. Which means this room is not actually rectangular. Harriet, who built this shop?"

"Oh, dear, I've no idea. My husband will know. Shall I go ask him?"

"No. I think we can do well enough here without his assistance, despite the disadvantages of the space. When we are finished, people will come to Swinly expressly to visit Tinkerson's Millinery." She set her hands on her hips. "Are you prepared to trust me?"

"But of course, Calista darling!" Harriet's curls bobbed. "I am ever so grateful you would do this for *me*, after so many years. How wonderful it is that the flood has trapped you in Swinly."

"How wonderful indeed." She pursed her lips. "All right. Let us begin."

~o0o~

"Well, my lord, I'm not right clear about it," the carpenter murmured. "She said she's just learned the lathe today. But she cuts the neatest bead I've ever seen, I'll tell you."

"Mm." Tacitus watched from the doorway, the drone of the rain and the scrape of the turning tool louder than their whispers. "It took me three months to learn the best technique for cutting a candlestick. And she is making a—what did you say she's making?"

"A decorative hat stand."

"And she claims to be a novice?"

The carpenter bobbed his head. The woman inside the shop, bent over the table, worked the blade while turning the wood as though she had been born to it.

"Mayhap she's a natural," the carpenter mumbled.

"It seems so," he mumbled back.

Lady Holland straightened, detached the wood from the lathe, and ran her gloved hand across the grain. As she tucked a loose satiny tress behind her ear, she noticed them.

"Good day, Lord Dare," she said with a smile that made his lungs melt. "Look at this hat stand I've made. Isn't it marvelous? I am especially proud of these coves." She hefted the piece, then grabbed up an umbrella from a table and came toward them. "Thank you for the use of your tools, Mr. Briar. You were kind to halt your work to allow me to do this. Mrs. Tinkerson will reimburse you for the wood, of course."

"Allow me," Tacitus said, taking the umbrella from her full hands. He opened it. "May I escort you ... somewhere?"

"Oh, thank you, but no. I am in something of a hurry. Good day, gentlemen." With another bright smile, she took the umbrella from him, went into the downpour, and strode swiftly up the puddle-strewn path.

The carpenter shook his head. "Women."

Tacitus was inclined to say instead, "Calista." But he didn't know the fellow well enough.

~oOo~

Calista wrapped the knitted wool around the boy's neck and tucked the ends into his coat.

"There you are, Fred. I hope you realize this is a momentous occasion. That is my first completed muffler. If it does not unravel immediately, it is because Mrs. Elliott is a superb teacher."

"It's wonderful warm, mum. Can I go now?"

She smiled. "Yes. You too, girls. Mrs. Elliott's greens need you to defend them from the sheep."

They scampered out the door, and Calista returned her attention to the old woman on the cot. With a kerchief she wiped a tear from the corner of Mrs. Cochran's eye and took her emaciated hand gently into her own.

"There now," she said softly. "The children will be well. Reverend Abbott has made a place for them in the vicarage, and Dr. Appleby will write to everyone he must until he finds your son."

The bony fingers twitched in hers.

"I know, dear," Calista said softly. "I have a son too. I understand."

~o0o~

"It's good of you to come along, my lord," Smythe said as they traversed the street that was finally empty of sheep.

"My pleasure, Smythe."

"I could be wrong, but you don't seem the sort to hang about in ladies' dress shops."

"I will take that as a compliment."

Smythe chuckled. They came to the shop door. A bell tinkled and a mild scent of roses came to him as they entered.

"Mr. Smythe, I am so glad you are here." Lady Holland moved toward them. "Mrs. Cooke, here is Mr. Smythe from the inn today. He has been in London for several months and has a great lot to tell you about what everybody is wearing there."

Tacitus watched her take Smythe's arm and lead him toward the dressmaker, then release him. As the others began talking she turned to him.

"Lord Dare. What a lovely surprise. Have you come dress shopping, too?" Her eyes assessed his clothing, a spark of mischief in the clear blue.

"Why, yes," he said. "My riding habit has a tear in the skirt, you see. I think I've got to have a new one."

"Then you are in the right place." Her eyes danced. "Do you have a preference as to color or fabric?"

"Not really." He set down his hat on a counter. "It might surprise you to learn that I have never done this before."

"Is that so? I admit myself astonished, really," she said

with another perusal of his clothes, and, he supposed, *him*. She was as bold in her teasing as she had been years ago.

"Until now, of course, I have typically preferred breeches."

"I see. Then I recommend this." She went to a bolt of cloth and stroked it so slowly that he saw the ripple of the fabric beneath her fingertips. "Gray velvet," she said in a hush.

"Aha." His voice felt as tight as the fall of his breeches. "Is that especially fashionable?"

"I've no idea. I chose it to match your eyes." Then her attention seemed to shift away. "There is the hour. I must be going." She took up her cloak. "Mrs. Cooke, I hope to see you later to discuss that idea I have. Good day, gentlemen."

Her smile hit Tacitus like sunshine in the chest. As she opened the door and departed, the toll of Swinly's church bell could be heard clanging along the street.

~o0o~

"Oh, Lady Holland, it is perfect," Penny said reverently. "But it is so mysterious. What does it mean?"

"It means," Calista said, setting down the sketchpad, "that I should like to introduce you to an acquaintance of mine, a gentleman who shares your interests in helping those in need."

"In London? Papa does not intend to return to London until the autumn."

"The gentleman is here in Swinly. The trouble is, I don't think your mother will approve of him."

"Why not?" Penelope touched her fingertips to the drawing of herself surrounded by children, with the silhouette of a man coming toward them. "Is he not a nobleman?"

"He is the third son of a very fine gentleman. But, no; not a nobleman."

Penny darted a glance across the parlor and then leaned in and whispered, "Mother told me that I must fix Lord Dare's attention, but I think he admires you. He has been watching you all evening, despite my father prosing on and on about politics."

"I don't know about that. But I do have a strong feeling that you and Mr. Curtis will like each other very much."

"We are continuing on to Leeds as soon as the road is open again." Penny's shoulders drooped. "Mother insists I must marry well before I've lost my bloom, and I'm sure she means to make it so this spring. I try to tell her I don't care about carriages and parties."

"But she won't listen. I understand."

"Does …" Penelope's cheeks glowed. "Does Mr. Curtis like children, do you think?"

"In fact I know he does. We simply must find a way for you to become acquainted without your mother intervening."

Like the oncoming toll of the church bell, Calista could sense the marquess's gaze on her now. She looked across the room at him, and could not resist smiling.

"Penny," she said. "I have just thought of the ideal plan. And I know the perfect man to help us."

Chapter Twenty-Nine

"THAT WAS CLEVERLY CONTRIVED." Tacitus watched Miss Smythe and Mr. Curtis continue along the path, walking side by side a proper distance apart yet entirely oblivious of the drizzle and puddles and everything else around them.

A smile of pure satisfaction curved Lady Holland's lips as she stared after them.

"How did you know they would be so swiftly compatible?" he asked.

"Oh, anybody could have seen it. Thank you for wresting Penny away from her mother. I suspected Mrs. Smythe would not deny her daughter a tête-a-tête with *you*."

"I am Dare, after all," he said mildly.

Her smile burrowed straight beneath his waistcoat.

"I wonder," he said, "how you guessed that I would play along with this subterfuge."

"Knowledge of your character, of course."

"Hm. I don't know whether to consider that a compliment or not."

"You certainly should. Now, my lord, I must bid you good day. Again, thank you." She pivoted on the path and started off, her umbrella swiftly obscuring his view of her. Too swiftly.

He'd spent no more than an hour in her company this morning and he wanted more. More of her sparkling eyes and blinding smile. More of her agile hands that still captivated him and her laughter that intoxicated him.

It did not matter that she was married. He had no dishonorable intentions—*none that he would act on.* She drew him now just as she had six years ago. But there was something different about her, something he had not seen in the foyer the night before, something he could not fix on and yet he wanted more of it. God or fate or who-knew-what had trapped him with her in this tiny village for a single day. He had lost his chance of having her years ago, but he could not allow this opportunity of simply being with her to pass.

"Where are you off to, Lady Holland?"

She paused and turned her shoulder to peek at him around the edge of her umbrella.

"Church," she said.

"May I accompany you there?"

Her lips seemed to flirt with a smile.

"That would be lovely, my lord."

The church flanking the inn was a modest building, featuring a tower from which the loudest bell in Christendom had woken him almost five hours earlier.

"May I enquire as to your purpose in going to church on Saturday?" he asked as he opened the door for her.

She offered him a grin full of mischief. Then her attention turned to a man walking up the aisle toward them.

"There you are, Mr. Pimly." She went toward him. "Thank you for this."

"Good day, ma'am." The man was all sinew and bones, and seventy if he were a day. "Are you ready?"

"Ready and eager. And here is Lord Dare to laugh at my attempt."

"My lord." Pimly nodded, but his attention was all for the lady. Tacitus didn't blame him. She practically glowed with anticipation.

"I think I should like to know what I am to laugh at before I decide whether or not I shall," he said.

"Oh," she said, her eyes alight. "I am going to learn how to ring the bell."

~o0o~

And she did.

"There you go!" Pimly shouted over the deafening throb of the first toll emanating from far above in the belfry. "Put your back into it! Brace your feet. Now pull! Yes, yes. That's it. Hold on tight!"

Gripping the rope with bare hands, she rose to her toes with the swing of the bell, her mouth and eyes and entire face laughing.

"Don't let go," Pimly called out. "Keep those arms—yes!"

"She won't hurt herself?" Tacitus said across the clamor. His stomach was knots, his heartbeats a steeplechase.

"She could," Pimly said. "It don't seem to be worrying her, though. Mighty strong for a lady. Wouldn't have thought it."

The bell's toll pounded through the tower again.

"Won't everybody in Swinly be horrified that the rings are uneven?" she shouted breathlessly as her heels again left the ground.

"They might," Pimly called back. "But the Lord Almighty'll only hear the music."

"Well said." Tacitus was torn between enjoying the shape of her legs revealed by her clinging skirts and worrying over her hands slipping on the rope.

"I don't think I can do this for much longer," she called over the reverberations. "But you forgot to teach me how to stop!"

"How d'you think you should, lass?"

She pulled and the rope hauled her arms upward again.

"I don't know!" Her eyes were wild.

"You'll know it."

"Before she breaks an arm?"

"Yes!" And then she was stumbling away from the rope as it danced in the air and snaked across the floor. Tacitus lunged forward and caught her up in his arms. Laughter shook her and she clung to him, her lips parted and cheeks bright. She pulled away from him and they watched as Pimly got hold of the rope and resumed the ringing.

When the twelfth ring finally faded to a hum, Mr. Pimly complimented her on both her form and courage, and he saw them to the door.

"How did you release the rope?" Tacitus said as they walked toward the inn, wishing he had another excuse to hold her, even briefly.

"All at once. It bit into my fingers and burned my palms horridly, so I tried to readjust my hold. But I realized that my arms simply were not strong enough to sustain it. So I let go, all at once. And the pain disappeared." She lifted her reddened palms and flexed them. "That is, not entirely. But I suspect this will fade soon enough." Her smile now was simple.

"You were remarkable. Are you disappointed that you did not pull all twelve rings?"

"No. I only wanted to pull seven." She halted and looked at him. "Here I must part with you, my lord."

His heart had not ceased its swift pace since they descended from the tower. He thought perhaps that in her presence it might never.

"Off to do another errand?"

"I am indeed. Good day." She strode away and he tried with every ounce of his imagination to devise a justification for continuing with her. Nothing occurred to him that did not shout *roguish scoundrel,* which was a clear message in itself.

Approaching the inn, he heard Mrs. Smythe in the foyer before he saw her. He'd no idea if Miss Smythe and Mr. Curtis had finished their stroll. Retreating from the door, he retraced his steps and continued down the street to the pub. After the activities of late morning, the book in his pocket seemed poor company. But he was accustomed to solitary pursuits. That such pursuits now paled violently in comparison to even the few minutes he had just spent with Calista Holland was a penance he must, as before, learn to endure.

~o0o~

When he returned to the inn hours later, it was bustling with activity. The men with whom he had played cards until a lady had employed him in her matchmaking scheme were at work draping garlands formed of paper loops from one corner of the taproom to another. Three threadbare children sat a table contriving the garlands. An elegant, compact woman with a pretty face directed a fashionable fellow in arranging brilliantly colored cloths on all the tables, followed by a woman in a spectacular hat placing bouquets of flowers planted in bonnets in the center of each.

The whole place smelled of baking—cake, he thought. He was rewarded for this guess when a trio of flour-smeared people he could have sworn were guests at the inn paraded into the room with plates loaded with sweets.

Someone bumped his shoulder from behind and abruptly his knee was scalding hot.

"Oh!" The innkeeper's serving girl covered her mouth with her palm. The other hand held a dripping pot of coffee. "I'm that sorry I am! And with Lady Holland making that special glove for me, now I've gone and forgot to use it."

The knee of his trousers was bathed in coffee.

"That's quite all right," he said and her face relaxed. "What's going on in here?"

"A surprise party for Mrs. Whittle! Lady Holland thought since Aunt Meg's always taking care of everybody else's needs, we could use the flooded day to give her a party, to thank her. Mr. Pritchard took her away to the pub for what he told her was a very important meeting so that we could prepare now."

"What a splendid idea. How may I assist?"

The elegant little woman presented him with a length of shimmery fabric.

"As you are the tallest here, sir, except for Mr. Dewey, who has gone to milk the cow, you can hang this on that curtain hook."

"Good heavens, George," came the voluble whisper of Mrs. Smythe behind him in the foyer. "She doesn't even know who he *is*."

"Oh, come now, Capricia," the fashionable fellow said. "He's offered to help." He extended his hand. "Alan Smythe, sir. And this is Mrs. Cooke. With whom may I have the pleasure of becoming acquainted?"

"I am Dare." He bit back a grin and wondered where the

instigator of these party preparations was.

"When the children have completed those links, sir," Mrs. Cooke said, "you may hang them from the picture frame in the foyer."

"How did you enjoy your stroll with Penelope, my lord?" her father asked. "She's a good girl, isn't she?"

"A fine young lady," he said. "I wish her all the best in her work with orphans."

Mrs. Smythe gasped. "She did not tell you about *that,* did she, my lord?"

"She did, and I am deeply impressed, Mrs. Smythe. These days all the great ladies are devoting their time to caring for the poor, of course," he drawled. "Why, only a fortnight ago the Duchess of Hammershire told me that she plans to found a school for orphans not a half mile from Hammershire Hall," he invented. Then he nodded soberly to her husband. "I recommend that you find your daughter a suitor dedicated to such work, Mr. Smythe. Together they could be the toast of society. Now, Mrs. Cooke, where was it that you wanted me to hang this?"

Chapter Thirty

THE COOL BREEZE FROM A WINDOW cracked open set candles to dancing like the villagers and travelers capering about the taproom to the fiddler's sawing. Cakes had been consumed, as well as a fair quantity of wine and ale, and tables pushed against walls to make space for the dancers.

"I don't know when I've had such fun!" Mrs. Whittle exclaimed as Mr. Pritchard swung her across the floor. Cheeks rosier than ever, she paused to take Calista in a quick embrace. "I never thought a grand lady could seem like a daughter to me. Bless you, dear!" She danced away, and Harriet took her place at Calista's side.

"That green hat is positively ideal for her. And I simply adore the alterations we made to my shop today. *Dear* Calista, what an eye you have for everything."

"Oh, I don't know if I have an eye for everything." Mostly for the handsome lord across the room, now in conversation with Penny and Charles. He smiled at something Penny said, and warmth filled Calista. She had wished that warmth away so many times she'd lost count of the wishes. But it happened every time, nevertheless. She could spend a lifetime seeing him smile and never tire of it. "I am happy you like the changes we made to your shop."

"Is my new business partner sharing our news, my lady?" Alan said, coming to stand beside Harriet.

"Business partner?"

"Mr. Smythe wishes to sell my hats and bonnets in Leeds and London," Harriet exclaimed. "We are going to open two shops together!"

"They are ingenious creations," he said. "More taking than

any other designer's I've seen in England. I've no doubt we will turn a tidy profit."

"How thoroughly wonderful." Calista grasped Harriet's hands. "I congratulate you both."

"Oh, there is Elena Cooke now," Harriet said and wiggled her brows at Mr. Smythe. "I suspect *she* will be positively in alt over your plans to stop in Swinly regularly, sir." With a bob of her bright curls, she twirled away.

Alan looked after Harriet with an unusually tight jaw.

"She will ruin the thing before it's even gotten started," he muttered.

"Hasn't it already gotten started?" Calista ventured.

His usual devilish grin resurfaced.

"It has, my lady. And I am grateful to you for making the introduction this morning. In fact it was Mrs. Cooke's idea that I should visit the millinery shop today. She has a very fine eye for fashion." His words trailed off as his hungry gaze sought the dressmaker across the room.

"And yet she does not wish to have her own fashions sold in Leeds or London?"

"She does, indeed," he said. "She intends to remove to Leeds within the month. Permanently."

"Does she? How delightfully—"

"Convenient." He smiled fully now. Then he took her hand and lifted it past his splendid neckcloth to his lips. "Thank you, my lady. I am eternally in your debt."

He went to claim a dance from Elena, and Calista let the merriment ebb around her. But she had one final task to perform tonight: her most important task.

Slipping into the foyer and taking her cloak, she went out into the night that glistened with starlight and walked past the sheep pasture and along Mr. Drover's field. Opening the latch on the door to the little house, she peered around the shadowy room lit only by the glow of dying embers.

"Tommy?"

"I'm here, mum." He sat on the empty cot, his palms cupped around his knees.

She sat down beside him.

"Your brother and sisters are already tucked in bed at the vicarage," she said. "You have been very courageous these past weeks, and I know you are worn out. Will you come have a cup of tea and a cake now, and then some sleep?"

"I'd like that. It's only that … It's …" A tear trickled down his cheek.

"It is difficult to leave here, isn't it?" she said softly. "It feels as though you are leaving her."

"Yes, mum. I know I've got to be strong for Fred and my sisters. It's tough going, though."

She put her arm around his shoulders.

"I know, Tommy. But this part is supposed to be hard. If it weren't, it would not be love."

As they walked the soggy path to the center of the village, gradually his steps grew lighter and soon he launched into a description of Mr. Smythe's top-drawer carriage horses. Youth and vitality disliked loitering in sorrow, she had learned. By the time they arrived at the vicarage he was almost smiling.

"Here you are," Reverend Abbott said as he opened the door to them. "Your brother and sisters have been waiting for you to arrive before they eat their bedtime cakes, Tommy." He gestured the boy inside. Tommy offered her a game tug of his cap, and disappeared into the house.

"Lady Holland, you were a godsend to these children today," the vicar said. "You can sleep well tonight knowing the good you have done for them."

"I am happy they are in your care and Dr. Appleby's now. Good night."

She went around the church to the inn yard. Music and light spilled out of the inn's open front door. Lord Dare leaned back against the hitching post, watching her.

"Good heavens, my lord. What are you doing out here without your coat? You must be frozen."

"And yet I am not," he said, coming toward her. "Perhaps due to the oven of seventy people all dancing in one small room. Or perhaps it is the wine I've drunk."

They halted face-to-face. Starlight glimmered in his eyes.

"Are you foxed, Lord Dare?"

"No, Lady Holland. Merely bemused. Who would have imagined so many people lived in this tiny village?"

"You mustn't forget the guests at the inn."

"How could I? Especially one guest who escaped the party she herself engineered, without a word to anyone."

"Oh!" She glanced over his shoulder at the doorway. "Has someone needed me for something?"

"Yes."

She moved around him. "Who?"

"Me." He touched her sleeve and Calista closed her eyes. It was best when he did not touch her. Tumbling into his embrace in the tower earlier had been a sweetness she no longer allowed herself.

But she could not resist this temptation; she turned her face up to his.

"For what did you need me?"

"I wonder if you would care to stroll with me. To the ford. They say the creek has already dropped half a foot. I thought to see it for myself."

"That does sound more pleasant than an oven. But you must first don your coat."

"Wait here," he said as he backed toward the doorway.

She spread her hands. "I've nowhere else to go, my lord."

A moment later he reappeared, pulling his coat over his shoulders.

"You don't dress like an arrogant lord," she said. "Did you always dress so …"

"Unfashionably?" He gestured her in the direction of the high street. She tucked her hands into her pockets before he could offer his arm.

"That isn't what I hear," she said. "I haven't been to London in an age. But according to Mr. Alan Smythe, a true arbiter of style, you dress in the height of austere fashion, in fact."

"Do I? I shall have to thank my valet for that. Claude is a

clever fellow, three steps ahead of me in most matters, I'm afraid."

"Did he dress you in the past?" She cast him a quick glance and wanted to swallow whole the image of his silhouette. "That is, when—"

"When I visited Dashbourne six years ago? Yes, he did."

"His taste is understated for a man of your rank. It suits you."

"On his behalf, I thank you."

"Of course, *you* are understated for a man of your rank."

Their footsteps splashing through puddles and the fading sounds of revelry from the inn were their only companions for some minutes.

"I dressed myself that morning," he said.

"That morning?"

"The last morning of my sojourn at the inn at Dashbourne. Six years ago. You see, I wished to look my best that morning. My most lordly and consequential."

Another silence stretched, the burble of the swollen creek ahead growing louder while Calista searched for her tongue.

"Did you?" she finally managed.

"Yes. I intended to call upon your father that morning. I wished to make my authority and power indisputably clear to him, and I was determined to be admitted." He spoke without haste. "I think I even pinned the House of Dare emblem somewhere on me, on my lapel, or someplace or other."

They had come to the edge of the ford. The night wrapped around her as she let the music of the rippling water seep into her senses.

"In your cravat," she said into the silvery blackness. "You wore a gold pin of the Dare crest in your cravat."

In the corner of her vision, she saw him turn his face to her. Another moment passed in silence.

"You remember that? That detail?"

"I remember every detail of that morning. I ruined your plans." She offered him the only smile she could. "What a very foolish girl I was."

His gaze swept over her features. "You have changed, it seems."

"Oh, I don't know about that. I am still foolish enough to do things like walk in the frigid cold outdoors at midnight."

Upon the word, Old Mary struck the first of her final twelve rings for the day.

"Shall we return to the inn?" he said.

"You must first assess the level of the creek." She went forward and down the slope. "That was why you wished to walk over here, after all."

"Was it?" He followed her to the edge of the water sloshing up the bank.

"What is your opinion? Six inches?"

"Perhaps. Still far too high to cross, even on horseback." He offered his hand and she took it, twitching her skirts aside to mount to the street again. "The rains were excessively hard," he said. "Perhaps it will not drop swiftly enough to allow for travel tomorrow and we will all be trapped here another day." He did not release her hand and she did not ask for it back. Not yet. "What would you do with your day then, Lady Holland? For it seems you have done all that could be done in this little village already today."

"I daresay I would find some project to keep me busy." Drawing her fingers from his, she moved toward the street. "Now, however, I find I am excessively sleepy. It has been a busy day, indeed."

They walked back along the street in companionable silence. As they passed the alleyway, Calista heard a shushing sound, then soft, masculine laughter followed by a sigh in Elena's alto tones.

She smiled and quickened her pace.

Within the inn, the merrymakers had dispersed, all except Molly, who drooped over a broom in the middle of the room strewn with the remnants of the festivities.

"Dear me, Molly," she said, whisking the broom from her slack fingers. "You have been awake since before dawn. You must go to bed at once. This can wait."

"But—"

"Molly," Lord Dare said, "Do as her ladyship requests."

"May I make up the fire in milady's room first, milord?"

"You may."

Molly dropped a grateful curtsy and disappeared.

Calista twisted her lips. "You are certainly not understated when you wish to be, my lord."

He bowed.

She looked around the room. "What a catastrophe. Ah well. I've nothing better to do."

"Mere minutes ago you mentioned sleep."

"That was before this." She set the broom to the floor. "Good night, then, my lord."

"What a shabby gentleman you must think me, to leave a lady to sweep and clean by herself." He pushed a table toward the center of the floor where it belonged.

"I think you a vastly peculiar gentleman to assist anyone at sweeping and cleaning, actually."

"Yes, you have called me that before." He pushed chairs into place. "Twice, I think."

"Certainly more times than that." She pulled a linen from the table and began folding it. "You are, after all."

"Clearly that girl from six years ago is still alive and well in you, Lady Holland."

"Thank you, Lord Dare. I think we should leave the garlands. The children made them in honor of their grandmother. I imagine Mrs. Whittle won't mind it."

"The doctor told me what you did for those children today."

"I did very little, in truth. And anybody would have, I'm sure."

"Not anybody. You are an exceptional person, Calista."

"I'm not, really." She took up another cloth and folded it into a neat square. "I miss my son. Dreadfully. It was the least I could do for those children."

"Say what you will, but— Well, good evening. Who are you?"

Calista's head came up to see him watching the cat leap into the room. It bounded onto a balled-up wad of paper and batted it under a table.

"That is Plato." Her cheeks warmed, ridiculously. "He lives here."

"Does he?" He bent to pry the ball from where it had lodged under a table leg. "What a fine name you have, sir."

"Mrs. Whittle doesn't have any idea where he came from, or why he does not live in the stable as all respectable cats should. But she says she hasn't seen a mouse in the place in two days. I know, however, that he is partial to bacon and eggs. He even drinks tea. Without milk. I have never seen a cat drink tea before." She laid the last table linen on the pile and glanced up.

Lord Dare stood perfectly immobile, a sheet of crumpled paper spread open in his hand, his eyes fixed on it. Plato sat at his feet, flicking his tail back and forth across the floor.

Strange, hot fingers of tension crept up her back. Finally, the marquess lifted his eyes. The candlelight caught in them like stars on fire.

"What is that?" she said.

He came toward her and extended the paper.

"It is yours. Forgive me. Once I began reading it, I could not— Forgive me."

She accepted the paper from him and recognized it in an instant. Her eyes darted to the floor, but Plato had disappeared.

Folding the letter from Mr. Baker, she tucked it into her sleeve and reached for the broom.

"I am sorry," he said. "I offer you and your son my deepest sympathies, and my apology for reading what was not mine to read."

"It's fine. Truly." She plied the floor with the broom bristles, sweeping debris toward the door. "It is an old letter."

"How old?" He remained where he stood.

She set aside the broom.

"Months old. But had I received it yesterday it would not matter. My husband was cruel to me, and he beat our son. He did it because Harry wished to spend time with me, but *he* demanded all of my time. Every minute of it. So he struck my little boy, often and brutally. I am glad he's gone, for now he cannot harm Harry again. So, you see, my lord, you mustn't be sorry for my loss. I'm not."

"My God, Calista," he whispered harshly. "I—"

"It's all right. Really."

"How can it be *all right?*"

"Harry is free. I am free. It is over. In the past. Now I am here, living in the present. And I have had today, a beautiful, perfect day. I am so grateful for it. That is enough for me, whatever comes tomorrow."

He stepped toward her, his face severe. "He struck you too, didn't—"

She pressed her fingertips to his lips. "Today, Tacitus. Only today matters."

He grasped her hand and turned his lips into her palm. The heat of his mouth scored every corner of her body, and a sigh escaped her. His arm came around her and he pulled her to him, and he found her mouth with his.

She twined her fingers into his hair, letting him kiss her and covering his lips with kisses of her own. It was so good to feel him again, delicious and dizzying. Swiftly she wanted all of him, this kiss, his hands, his skin and heat and embrace. They sought each other, closer and closer with each kiss. His arm tightened around her waist, his hand on her face, his thumb urging her lips apart. He lifted her onto her toes and she clung to his shoulders and made herself drunk on the flavor of him.

"I want you," she said. "Now. Tonight. Make love to me tonight."

His lips hovered over hers. "Only tonight?"

"Tonight is all I have. It is all I want. Help me make it perfect."

"Tonight it is, then," he said with glorious huskiness.

He did away with cloak and greatcoat, grasped her hand, and led her swiftly up the stairs. She pulled him to a halt at her bedchamber door.

"Here," she whispered. "I want to have the memory of you in my bed."

He bent his head, brushed his lips across hers, and then captured them in a kiss that rocked her to the soles of her feet. She gripped his waist and his hands came around her face. Then he was pressing her back against the door and his body to hers, and kissing her like there was in fact no tomorrow. Laughter tumbled through her throat.

He drew away only enough to look into her eyes, then his gaze dropped to her lips.

"If you are laughing at my kiss," he said, "I think I will go ahead and perish here immediately."

"I am so happy." She held him tight. "So completely happy."

"Ah, well. That is a relief," he murmured, pressing a kiss onto the corner of her lips, then her jaw, then her lips again. "Laugh all you wish, then, my lady."

"Don't stop kissing me."

"I believe I can comply with that demand." His palm circled her face, his thumb stroking over her lower lip. "I have had so many dreams about these lips." His voice rumbled very low. "These perfect lips."

"Not my teeth?"

"I cannot as easily kiss your teeth. But yes." He touched his lips to hers again, then again, then he parted her lips and ran his tongue over the edges of her teeth. She invited him into her, and the ache in her exploded into fire.

"Your teeth are perfect too," he said with urgency against her lips.

She reached for the door handle behind her.

"Come inside and let me show you what else is perfect." She opened the door and he dragged her inside and into his arms. The door closed with emphasis and his hands swept down her body to lodge around her behind and force her hips against his.

"Sweet Calista," he whispered, his lips moving to her throat. "You are perfect everywhere." With his hands bracketing her hips, he ground her against his arousal and she gasped and could not control her shudders.

Her fingers found the buttons of his waistcoat, unfastened them. Then he was helping her, pulling off his coat and waistcoat, drawing up his shirt, and baring his chest and his arms, and she got weak all over with need. By the amber glow of the fire, he was so beautiful.

"Yes," she whispered, running her hands over his hot, smooth skin and taut muscle. "*Perfect.*"

After that, removing her clothing seemed to become his priority: first her gown, then her petticoat, stays, shoes and stockings. Her shift was plain linen, suitable for winter travel. But he stared as though it were the finest French lace.

"Remove it," she whispered.

He did not move.

Nerves spiked in her belly. "What is it?"

"I am having a moment."

"A moment?"

"Of disbelief. You have ordered me to remove your clothing. I'm feeling dizzy. I think I might swoon."

"No! You *must* not try to make me laugh." She laid her palms on his chest as he gathered the hem of her shift and drew it upward.

"Your laughter is ambrosia to me. I could drink it and be drunk for days. Good God, this is a beautiful body. Calista, how—"

She pressed her mouth to his and his hands came beneath her breasts, then he pulled the garment over her head. She leaned into him, wrapping her arms around his neck.

"I am wretchedly torn," he said, his palms smoothing over her waist and hips.

"Between?" she murmured against his jaw, his roaming hands and the brush of her nipples against his chest driving her truly mad.

"Between holding you at a distance so that I can feast my eyes upon this beauty, and holding you close so I can touch it."

She trailed kisses on his throat and ran her palms up his

arms and around his shoulders. "Why don't you do both? Alternately."

"I have a solution." He went to his knees before her and she felt the caress of his palms and fingers from her thighs upward to her breasts. He cupped her breasts in his hands and covered a peak with his mouth. They groaned together, and she sank one hand into his hair and gripped his shoulder with the other as he kissed her, again and again, and her need throbbed. As though he knew, his hand surrounded her hip then caressed inward, and his thumb dipped to stroke her intimately.

"*Oh.*" Her knees buckled. He caressed again and her eyes closed as she felt it in her breasts and thighs and everywhere in between. He touched her until she was so tightly coiled inside with pleasure, so hot and without breath that she could hardly stand.

"*Please,*" she begged, thrusting into his touch. "More."

He looked up and his fingers strummed her. "More of what? This?" The tip of his finger slipped inside her.

"Oh, *yes*. Everything. More of your hands. Your mouth. *You.*"

Rising to his feet, he removed his remaining clothes. Then, taking her waist in his hands, he turned her back to him and drew her against him.

"What are you doing?" she whispered as he bent and kissed her shoulder with open lips, then her neck, sinking delirious heat into her.

"Giving you more." His hand smoothed down her abdomen, the other to her breast, and he gave her more. Considerably more. From her throat that he kissed, to her legs that bowed, she felt alive, needing, and craving his touch everywhere, before and behind and inside her. He took her breast into his palm, her nipple between his fingertips, and she ached for his mouth there again. He stroked deeply between her legs and she wanted him there even more desperately. His arousal was hard against her behind, between her buttocks.

"*Calista,*" he uttered against her neck, the rhythm of their bodies unbearable, too good, *too good.*

"Now." The word came upon a moan as she pressed down on his hand. She was shuddering, convulsing inside, gasping, wide open and reaching for him. *"Now."*

He swept her up and onto the bed, and then he was between her legs, probing, entering her, then thrusting hard and deep. She cried aloud. She was frantic, her body seeking his as he rose in her again. She bucked beneath him, spreading her legs, urging him, and he gave it to her. It was wild, all skin and wetness and hot urgency to be as close, as tight, as connected as her flesh and his would allow.

When her release came, it was hard and sudden, and immediately intensified by his.

Neither of them spoke.

Arms bracketing her, chest heaving against her breasts, he bent his head beside hers and set his lips to her shoulder. Lifting her knees to clasp his hips with her thighs, she trailed her fingers down his back that was damp with sweat, and she felt all of his strength.

Drawing away, he rolled onto his back. "That was—"

"Perfect," she panted.

He reached for her hand and drew it to his lips. "Entirely perfect," he said against her palm.

"Let's do it again," she said.

"Right."

He pulled her into his arms and their mouths came together, his fingers in her hair, her hands gripping his buttocks.

They did it again.

And then again.

The third time, they took their time. He invited her to touch him, and smiled when she did so tentatively, noting that this approach surprised him, given her usual style. But he was obliged to choke back groans when she showed him precisely what she thought of that commentary. She made him beg and had a deeply satisfying time doing so.

Touching his hard male body, kissing it, was a new world

of pleasure to her. Looking at his masculine beauty had always made her feel things in her own body, powerfully, even years ago. Now she allowed herself to revel in the feelings. Indeed, he demanded it, and seemed to take pleasure from her moans as she caressed him.

Finally he took her onto his lap and she took him into her. She loved how he filled her entirely, and she loved how each deep kiss seemed like an act of worship and lust at once.

The way he held her after it all, tenderly, stole every word she knew. He kissed her brow, then her lips, then her brow again, and stroked her cheek gently. She curled up against him, breathing the scent of his skin into her.

"Calista." The word rumbled beneath her palm upon his waist. His eyes were closed.

"Tacitus?" Her lips brushed his shoulder.

He reached for her hand and entwined their fingers, but he said nothing more. She tucked her cheek against his arm and closed her eyes.

Chapter Thirty-One

OLD MARY'S RING CRASHED through Calista's dream and dragged her into waking. Drawing in a long tunnel of air to fill her lungs, she let her eyes remain closed, savoring the images behind her eyelids.

A smile stretched her mouth as far as it could stretch.

"Glorious day," she whispered, turning onto her side and pressing her face into the pillow on the empty side of the bed. "Glorious night."

Her body was deliciously sore. A brisk walk this morning would serve her well. Later, though. Now she would linger abed for a few precious minutes and remember the night. Time enough today to venture out into the rain—

The rain that sounded ... *strange*.

Her body was *sore*?

Her heartbeats jolted. Quickened.

Between the bell's tolls, the rain seemed distant. And broken. Splashing. Not rushing. Not droning.

Not possible. She was still dreaming.

A cow's plaintive low broke through the reverberating pause.

Calista sat bolt upright, her eyes flying open.

And discovered herself entirely naked.

Her breaths jerked out of her, little puffs of shocked air. She took it all in: dry windowpanes, the pale yellow hue of a clear morning, her gown and undergarments strewn across the floor, a cow mooing in the rear yard. Not only the cow, people talking too.

Heart pounding in her throat, grabbing up the blanket to cover herself, she flew to the window and jammed it open.

"Thank you, Uncle! Thank you!" Molly was exclaiming to a man standing beside a cow covered in mud. Hefting a pail of water, he threw it over the creature's back, and the animal complained loudly as water cascaded off its sides into puddles.

"I did a good left-handed milk of her before I bought her." He patted the animal's back and said gruffly, "She'll keep Nell fine company. Now you go tell your aunt I've returned, while I clean the rest of this muck off Peg here. Just like a contrary female to wallow in mud when she could have been chewing grass." He crossed the yard to the water pump and Molly disappeared into the house.

Calista shut the window and clasped her shaking hands together as Old Mary broke into her seventh toll. Slowly the sound faded.

She held her breath.

The bell boomed.

"Eight," she whispered. "Eight," she said more loudly. "Eight. *Eight.*" she shouted. "It is Sunday! It is *tomorrow.*" She threw herself onto the bed and buried her screech of joy in the pillow. It smelled like *him,* like the man who had spent the night in her bed. She inhaled the scent, clasping the cushion to her face and hugging it so hard her arms hurt. "It is tomorrow. Harry, it is tomorrow!"

Mr. Whittle had arrived with the new cow. The road must be open. Today she would see her son.

Leaping from the bed and dragging the blanket about her body, she danced around the room. Aphrodite watched her impassively. She swept over to the statue, planted a kiss on the top of her stony head, and laughed.

"Thank you! Thank you, thank you, thank you!"

Tossing the blanket aside, she washed up with the basin of cold water and swiftly dressed. She took some care arranging her hair with hands that were not entirely steady. What did one say the following morning to a man one had made love to for most of the night? This was new territory.

Everything was new territory. Tomorrow had come!

Descending to the ground floor, she looked for Plato, but

no cat waited on the stairs for his breakfast.

Molly hurried from the kitchen, hands filled with a stack of cups and a coffeepot. Calista smiled. Some things remained the same every day, even when the day did not.

"Good morning, milady! The creek's down. You'll be traveling home now, I expect?"

"Yes." Her smile widened. "Home." To her family. To Dashbourne, finally.

"I'll bring you a nice cuppa tea as soon as I've poured these." She curtsied and went into the taproom. Calista hadn't any appetite; her stomach was sour from too many cakes the night before and agitated with nervousness. She paused in the taproom doorway.

Several of the other guests were breakfasting, but no handsome lord. Still asleep, no doubt.

Taking her cloak off the peg, she went out into the morning. A silvery-blue winter sky spread across the roof of the earth. The yard was softly muddy and pocked with hoofmarks, but straw had been strewn across it. Entering the stable, she greeted the ostler and went along the corridor to her carriage horses' stall.

But ... Something was ... *missing*.

She halted, then retraced her steps several paces. The stall before her stood empty. The stall that had housed the Marquess of Dare's horse.

"Mornin', mum."

She pivoted around.

"Tommy. What are you doing here? Shouldn't you be at the vicarage?"

He shrugged. "There's work to do here. And my sisters were scratchin' at my temper somethin' awful." He offered her a little grin. Then he reached into his pocket and withdrew an envelope. "His lordship bade me give you this."

"Has he left already?"

"Afore the sun was up, mum."

Tommy returned to work and Calista stared at the envelope. Her head felt light, her stomach bunched up like fingers fisting. But that was to be expected, she supposed. She sat down on the bench and unfolded the message.

Thank you for the night, my lady.
T.C.E.

She slipped the note into her sleeve and went to find her coachman. It was time to leave Swinly behind. Time to start living each day gratefully, whatever gifts each day gave her.

Time to start living one day at a time.

~o0o~

The creek that had been a river twelve hours earlier looked unremarkable from the other side of the ford now. Calista drew her head back into the carriage and tilted it against the seatback, her eyes on the wooden box on the opposite seat.

After packing her scant luggage and saying good-bye to Mrs. Whittle, Molly, and Penelope, she had nearly left the statue behind. But it wasn't hers to make that decision. Her mother wanted it. Her mother would have it.

And she would have Harry. That was enough. That was more than enough.

~o0o~

The four people that descended along the gangplank to the dock were not garishly or slovenly dressed. Nor were they haughty or vulgar or obnoxious in any manner when Tacitus introduced himself to them and welcomed them to England. Instead, his aunt took his hands warmly into her own and smiled with eyes exactly like his mother's.

"Dear nephew," she said, the smile crinkles on her face wonderfully familiar. "I have waited thirty-one years for this. Too long. How good it is to finally meet you."

His aunt's husband, a man of sturdy frame and an honest face, shook his hand.

"We're glad to be here, lad," he said with a light brogue that bespoke his Scottish origins. "Thank ye for the invitation." Their daughters, girls of perhaps eighteen, smiled shyly and offered their hands to shake as well. None of them curtsied or even bowed. None of them used his title. They were thoroughly American and entirely refreshing.

As they made their way through the press of dockworkers, sailors, and other travelers to the inn where he had arranged for lunch, his aunt and her husband told him of the crossing. By the time lunch was served, his cousins had thrown off their shyness and launched into tales of their month at sea. The younger, Cecelia, had hazel eyes that glimmered when she spoke of the ship's first lieutenant, and a brow that scowled prettily when her sister Anne choked on a chuckle.

All four of them were delightful: warm, well mannered, and interesting conversationalists. They were modestly appreciative of the meal, his servants that moved their luggage from the docks to the carriage, and his hospitality.

Tacitus could barely comprehend his good fortune. *He had family.* Family to fill his big, empty house with happiness and laughter. He was no longer alone.

Mounting Herod as the carriage set off loaded with relatives and traveling trunks, he felt a deep satisfaction in his chest he hadn't known in seven years. He hoped it would suffocate the sharp, gripping ache that had lodged there the moment he rode out of the Jolly Cockerel's yard two days earlier, and had not abated since. But he doubted it.

One night. Only one night. That was all she had, all she wanted, she'd said. She had made that indisputably clear. After her years under the control of a vile man, Tacitus could not blame her for wanting freedom.

Before leaving Swinly, he should have waited for her to rise and then said a proper good-bye. But the flood had already stolen too many hours from his journey between Peyton's estate and Bristol. He'd known that his carriage traveling from Dare Castle would arrive at the port on time; his servants were always punctual. But while his coachman was perfectly capable of attending to his guests, he had wanted to greet his relatives personally when they disembarked.

And he was not without pride. He simply could not have chanced saying good-bye to her in person. He hadn't trusted himself not to beg her for another night.

Nights.

Days and nights.

Forever.

Urging Herod onto the road behind the traveling chaise, he knew it could be worse. He could still be living a life of reluctant bachelorhood, but without the memory of one perfect day and night to sustain him.

~oOo~

"That cluster of stars is Hercules. He was a very great warrior in his time." Calista pointed into the black sky glittering with points of light. "And there is Ursa Major, the great bear, like your Mr. Bear. And that one, the brightest star, is Venus."

"Who was Venus?" Harry said sleepily. Tucked against her side under a thick blanket to ward off the night's cold on the terrace, his eyes were curious. But his little body drooped with weariness. The moment her mother had written to her elder brother about Richard's death, Ian had hastened up from town to Dashbourne. Today he had taken Harry on his rounds of the breeding stables and pastures awaiting the new foals, and then for a long ride in the cold across the estate. Accustomed to days alone and indoors, Harry was worn out. And rosy-cheeked. And deliriously happy.

Calista's heart was full of joy for him.

After a fortnight with him at Dashbourne, surrounded by her family, she wished her heart weren't aching so fiercely for someone else.

With Richard gone, she could begin anew. She would sell Herald's Court, find good positions elsewhere for the servants, and relocate to Dashbourne. Ian was focused on building his stables now; the possible threat of being thrown out by a new Lady Chance seemed distant, and even then she could move to the dower house with her mother and Evelina.

Settled in a safe home, the rest would be easy to arrange. Richard's investments were extensive. She would have plenty of funds to hire a tutor, a kind, intelligent person who would treat Harry with respect and compassion. And she would ask Ian and Gregory to teach him riding and fencing and boxing and all the other activities gentlemen learned as boys. She would depend upon her brothers to help raise her son, and Harry would grow into a good man.

She would do the same with Harry's younger sibling.

At first she had thought Aphrodite's game delayed her monthly menses. Other than when she had carried Harry, she had never been late, but circumstances in this case were extraordinary. With every day that passed, however, that theory disintegrated bit by bit. The full tenderness of her breasts and her consistently unsettled stomach told a clear story.

"Venus was the wickedest of all the gods of the ancient Romans, darling." She wound her arm more snugly about him. "They called her the goddess of love and beauty. In fact she was a terrible tease."

"But love is the best thing in the universe, Mama," he said in his sweet, soft voice.

"Yes." She pressed her lips to his forehead. "Yes, it is."

"Then I like Venus the most of all the stars."

She did not correct him. He was already half asleep. Hopefully one of the mares would give birth to a foal that her horse-mad son could name Pegasus or some such thing, and he would come to prefer those stars instead.

She uncurled from beneath the blanket, gathered him up in her arms, and carried him into the drawing room.

"Callie," Evelina said from the table where she was writing in a notebook, then lifted her head and saw Harry's sleeping face. She bit her lips together and followed Calista out. "What do you intend to do about that letter from Richard's solicitor?" she said in a hush as they started up the stairs toward the nursery. "It has been three days already. You cannot ignore it."

"My late husband would not have failed to write a will,"

she whispered. "He was too obsessed with his money to leave that sort of thing to chance." They reached the second story. "When I return to Herald's Court, I will find it, and all will be settled to Harry's advantage."

"When will you go?" Evelina opened the door to the nursery and Nurse came forward with outstretched arms.

"There's a dear," Nurse whispered as Calista transferred him into her round arms. "We must get this little one into his nightgown and tucked into bed with his bear."

Handing over the beloved rag doll, Calista let her son go reluctantly. But Nurse was as dear and capable as when she, Evie and Gregory were children. Her son was in good hands.

Anyway, in a few hours she would steal up here and cuddle next to him for the rest of the night, just as she had done every night for a fortnight already. She told Evelina and her mother that this was to allow Nurse more time to sleep, now that she was elderly. But she fooled no one. She had missed him so deeply. She could not tell them why, but they could see it.

Upon the first day of her return to Dashbourne, she had decided to tell no one of Aphrodite's game. They would think her mad, her mind turned by the misery of her life with Richard. Forever after they would imagine her unstable. Out of love, they might even take Harry from her.

She could never tell anyone.

Including the father of the child growing inside her.

If she went to him now and told him about the baby, she would have to tell him all. The baby would come far too early, yet healthy and whole, and he would know something was not right. More importantly, she could not live with him without telling him the entire truth; to lie to him would tear her apart. He was an extraordinary man, but he had already suspected her of madness. And she could never risk losing her children.

She closed the door softly. "I don't wish to take Harry away from here so soon after he has arrived. He is so happy."

"Leave him with us," her sister said. "Mama and Nurse and I will look after him. He is already a favorite of everyone here. And today Ian said he plans to remain in residence through the spring."

"Forsaking his merry widows in town for so many weeks?"

"For the foaling. And *must* we speak of our brother's wanton women aloud?"

"Some of our brother's wanton women are influential socialites, Evie. If you ever hope to design gardens beyond Dashbourne—"

"I already do."

"For someone other than our immediate family members," Calista added, "you must come to know at least some of those socialites. Gossip is how most things happen among the rich and fashionable." As well as among the residents and guests of a tiny village, she had discovered.

"You are lecturing me to avoid making a decision. Harry will be content here with us while you are gone. And when you are finished at Herald's Court you can return here permanently."

Only the ache she now felt every moment marred that happy prospect.

"I will go the day after tomorrow. I hope to be able to return within the month." It had to be done. It was the first step to beginning her life all over again. No desperation to run away. No need to escape. Simply life on her own terms.

Chapter Thirty-Two

THE CORRIDORS OF DARE CASTLE echoed with laughter, conversation, music, and so many comings and goings that Tacitus had difficulty keeping up with it all. Delighted with his home, his cousins swiftly made it their project to fill it with activity.

Cousin Anne had a passion for music. An invitation to a renowned violinist to perform at the castle was soon followed by a stream of fiddlers, harpists, guitarists, flutists, quartets, and soloists.

Cousin Cecelia has a passion for every other form of entertainment, as long as charming young men were involved. Prevailed upon to offer his opinion of the local stock of eligible bachelors, Tacitus turned the task over to the Viscount Mallory. Short on funds—which made London uncomfortable—and rusticating at Dare Castle temporarily, Peyton was happy to escort the cousins to all the parties, picnics and balls in the neighborhood. After each event he declared that American maidens were head and shoulders above English ladies, and if he were the marrying sort he would snatch up one of Tacitus's cousins and make her Lady Mallory. In response, Tacitus pulled his dueling pistols out of a drawer and dusted them off in his friend's presence. Peyton laughed. The cousins giggled. And that was that.

His aunt and uncle were excellent company, too, as industrious as their daughters though less gregariously so. His uncle hunted and fished in the estate's coveys and ponds, and his aunt spent hours in the kitchen trading American recipes for English recipes with his cook and housekeeper.

They were all thrilled with their visit to England.

He would never get rid of them.

But he did not particularly wish to. He liked them. Very much. Soon enough they would head off on their tour of Europe, and continue home from there. He would miss them. He was no fool: he realized that they were a substitute for the woman he truly wanted in his house. But they were a good substitute, and he was content.

He was not, however, happy. He had made a grave mistake in speaking to Calista at that inn. He had made an even bigger error in seeking out her company during their day of entrapment. And he had made a vastly monumental blunder in taking her to bed.

Above all, he was confused. She had changed since he courted her, but she still felt so familiar. He had spent less than twenty-four hours in her company, yet she was embedded as deeply in his thoughts now as all those years ago. The sound of her laughter and the sensation of her touch were so acute in his memory, he could practically taste them.

The dreams weren't helping matters any. Vivid dreams. Astonishing dreams. Each night with damnable regularity they filled his sleep, often waking him and leaving him hot and bemused for hours.

He *missed* her.

She was a widow and a lady. Despite her feelings for her late husband, she was now in mourning. He couldn't very well go after her like a randy bull. More importantly, she had said only one night. Quite clearly.

"You are thinking about her again."

Peyton sauntered across the parlor toward him, dangling a glass of whiskey from his fingertips.

Tacitus blinked to clear away the images in his head. "I beg your pardon?"

"Since I walked into this room five minutes ago—and spoke to you, by the way—you haven't turned one page of that book."

He closed the volume and set it on the table at his side. He hadn't read the *Symposium* in years, but the dream he'd had just before dawn had put it into his head. Or perhaps it was that cat at the inn, the one playing with the letter that had revealed to him she was a widow *when she had chosen not to*.

"I am having a moment of privacy, if you will," he said with ridiculous stiffness given the company.

"Privacy, in this house these days? Good luck to you."

"Are you drinking whiskey at ten o'clock in the morning?"

"No. This is for you." Peyton shoved the glass into his hand and took the chair across from him. "Drink it."

Tacitus set down the glass. "What do I look like to you, a sot?"

"Actually, you look to me like you've just lost your new puppy. Did she run away from you or did you run away from her?"

He considered telling his friend to sod off.

"Both, I think," he said.

The viscount lifted a black brow. "Back to her husband?"

"Her husband? How do you—"

"The woman at that inn. The one with the harridan-tongued sister and the boy. It's her, isn't it?"

He shook his head in wonderment. "How you know that, I won't ask."

"I might not be the marrying sort myself, but I would be a thorough ass not to suspect you've been wearing the willow for a lost demoiselle for years. I did not, however, realize she was still *alive* until we stopped in that little inn and you fell apart."

"You know, those dueling pistols are still on the sideboard in the drawing room."

The viscount smiled. "I am quaking in my boots." He took up the glass of whiskey and drank it in three swallows. "Ah. Thirty years in sherry barrels and … perfection. How I do enjoy sojourning at your house."

The hairs on the back of Tacitus's neck were prickling. Several nights ago he had dreamed about drinking whiskey with her.

"You should go," Peyton said. "I'll stay here with the

cousins and entertain them."

"They are not your cousins."

"Six of one." He waved the empty glass about. "The girls like me better than you anyway."

"I'll leave the pistols with their father."

"Splendid. When are you departing?"

"I'm not."

"If you take the dueling pistols with you, her husband won't be a problem any longer."

He stared into the fireplace. "She is a widow."

"Good Lord, Tass. What in the blazes are you waiting for?"

He didn't know. A sign from heaven? More dreams? Another happenstance meeting in an inn on some godforsaken road in a rainstorm?

Her. He was waiting for her to tell him she wanted only him as he had always wanted only her. Which was ridiculous.

And yet …

He came to his feet and headed for the door.

"Don't drink all the whiskey while I'm gone," he threw over his shoulder. "I will need a bottle to toast with on my return."

~o0o~

He went to Dashbourne. It was less than two days' ride away, and he had no idea where she now lived. He hoped her family would tell him. He had no good excuse for begging the information except the truth, but he couldn't very well share that with them before he shared it with her.

Not pausing at the inn at Dashbourne, he went straight to the earl's mansion. A servant came from the stable and took his horse. Tacitus walked up the steps to the front door and knocked, his heart pounding heavily and his tongue tied in twenty knots.

He managed to untie it sufficiently to announce himself to the manservant who answered the door.

"Do come in, my lord. May I take your overcoat and hat?"

"Dare, old man, is that you?" The earl was walking from the rear of the house into the broad foyer that Tacitus remembered like he'd been here yesterday. "What are you doing here? Passing through?"

"Not precisely," he bowed. "Good day, my lord."

Chance grinned. "Don't be such a stiff fool. Come, let me pour you a brandy and you can tell me what's lured you out of your hermitage. The last time I saw Mallory, he said you rarely ever venture forth these days. And I haven't seen you in town in an age."

In the drawing room appointed very sparely, but with taste, Chance uncorked a decanter and splashed brandy into two glasses.

"What brings you to Dashbourne?" He offered a glass.

Tacitus took the brandy and swiftly swallowed a mouthful. He'd given speeches in Parliament that had been easier than answering the Earl of Chance at this moment. He hadn't seen Ian in some time, and he'd forgotten how brother and sister shared the same crystal blue eyes. Those eyes now assessed him curiously. He had also forgotten how Ian had not recouped most of his father's enormous losses in six years by luck alone. The care-for-nothing Earl of Chance rarely lost at the card table not because he was particularly brilliant, but because he could smell a bluff ten miles away.

There was no way around it. Tacitus set down the glass.

"I am looking for your sister. Not long ago I encountered her while traveling. I should like to pay a call on her now, but I haven't the address of her permanent residence."

Ian did not even blink. But his jaw became noticeably tighter.

"Evelina?"

"No. Lady Holland." He'd no idea if Ian knew that he had courted Calista years ago. Until the old earl's death, his heir had been tearing up the less respectable haunts of London and nowhere near his ancestral estate.

Now the new earl studied him carefully.

"She recently lost her husband," Chance said with such

calm that it was almost a drawl. "Very recently."

"Yes, I am aware of that. Several months ago, I believe she said."

"*Weeks*, Dare. Three weeks ago. It happened the day before she found herself trapped by rains in a flooded village not two hours from here."

The *day* before?

Chance swiveled his drink casually but his gaze had grown sharp. "I don't suppose you encountered her in that village." Another swivel. "Did you?"

"I don't like the way you are looking at me, sir."

"And I don't like the way you're sniffing after my newly widowed sister, *sir*."

Tacitus blinked. "Did you just suggest that I am a dog?"

"If the shoe fits."

"Well, I say this is a fairly striking example of the pot calling the kettle black."

"Don't try to tell me you've never grazed in abandoned pastures before, Tacitus."

"It's none of your business whether I have or haven't, Ian. Although how any other fellow could even *try* when you're feeding off all those pastures yourself, I cannot fathom."

"Are you certain you want to go down this road with me, Dare?"

"Are you certain you want to cross wits with a man of twice your intellect and three times your character, Chance?"

"For God's sake, man, we're talking about my *sister*."

"And I'm in love with her!"

The words echoed across the empty room. Tacitus steadied himself and met Ian's surprised regard.

"I love her," he said. "I have been in love with her since before she wed that villain. Now that she's free of him, I want to ask her to be my wife—which, frankly, I had hoped to say to her before saying it to anyone else." He raked his hand across the back of his neck. "But there it is."

"You've loved her since *then*?" Lady Evelina stood in the doorway, eyes wide.

"Yes," he said, because everybody might as well know now.

"Then why didn't you ask her to marry you?" she demanded.

"I intended to. But I had the impression she didn't care for me. At all."

"You had the impression she didn't care for you?" She shook her head. "She was madly in love with you. You broke her heart when you left here so abruptly. You didn't even say good-bye to me and Gregory. He and I were disappointed, to be sure. But Callie walked around here like a ghost after that, until our father forced her to—"

"Evelina," Ian said, and Lady Evelina's lips snapped shut.

The countess appeared beside her in the doorway.

"What in heaven's name is going on in here? I heard shouting." Her features went slack. "Lord Dare?"

He bowed. He could hardly think. *Madly in love with him?*

With a tilt of her golden head, the countess glided into the room, Lady Evelina following.

"Good day, madam," he managed to say. "I was—" He glanced at Ian. "I was just asking his lordship's permission to court your daughter."

Her brows popped up.

"Your other daughter, Mama," Lady Evelina said. "I was right all the way back then. He was in love with her. I wish I had made a wager with someone about it. I would be rich now."

"Hush, Evelina. Lord Dare will think your jesting vulgar."

"Probably not. He likes Callie, after all. But even if he did take offense at my jesting, he would never say so. For instance, my lord, would you rather we simply tell you where my sister is and then all go to the devil?"

He smiled. "I would be very glad to know her present whereabouts."

"You see, Mama? Always the gentleman."

"Calista has gone to Herald's Court to settle her late husband's estate," Ian said. "I will have Taylor give you the direction."

Tacitus nodded. "Thank you."

"I trust in your intentions, Dare. But if I should hear anything that puts the lie to what you've said here, I won't take it well."

Ian Chance was a thorough hypocrite; his favorite paramours were other men's widowed sisters, after all. But Tacitus had to appreciate his protectiveness in this case.

"Understood," he said. "But the decision, of course, will be hers and her—"

"Lord Dare!" came a piping little voice across the room.

"—son's," he finished as the boy bounded toward them. "Good day, Master Harry, and … I don't believe I am acquainted with your companion."

"This is Mr. Bear. He is the second son of an earl, like Uncle Gregory, so I don't call him 'lord.'"

"Aha. Of course. How do you do, Mr. Bear?"

"How did you escape from Nurse?" Lady Chance said.

"Missy told Nurse that Lord Dare was here and I told her how he saved me from a wild horse in the rain and it was bang-up smashing so she let me come." He tugged on Lady Chance's wrist and she bent so that he could put his cupped hands over her ear. "Mama says he is peculiar," he said in a voluble whisper.

"I see you have your work cut out for you, Dare," Ian muttered.

"But *I* like him," Harry continued, sotto voice. "I think he's top of the trees." He lowered his hands and looked at Tacitus. "Have you brought your splendid horse?"

"I have. Would you like to see him?"

"Yes, sir!"

"We will first offer Lord Dare refreshment, Harry," Lady Chance said. "He has been traveling. But let us remove to a cozier place for that."

"I must see to a matter in the stable," Ian said. "I will rejoin you in a moment."

The countess invited Tacitus to follow her. Lady Evelina's

eyes danced quite like her sister's could. Undoubtedly she knew
he would rather be on the road heading toward Calista than
drinking tea. But they followed Lady Chance into a parlor that
was indeed cozier, with cushioned chairs and a merry fire to
dispel the chill.

"Oh dear, Evelina," Lady Chance said and went to a table
strewn with drawings. "I did not realize you had been in here
today."

"I don't do portraits, Mama, only landscapes. These are
Calista's. I was showing them to Harry this morning."

An object on a side table grabbed Tacitus's attention: a
statue of a woman carved from milky white stone. That statue
had been in Calista's bedchamber at the inn.

"Aphrodite," slipped through his lips.

"Isn't she beautiful?" Lady Chance said. "She is fourth-
century Attican. B.C., of course. And such superb artistry."

"My mother is collecting Greek sculptures for an
exhibition someday. Calista brought it from up north," Lady
Evelina said. "Do come look at these, Lord Dare. My sister is
a remarkably talented portraitist. Just see."

She held the pencil sketches before him, each drawn with
extraordinary skill, but also obvious affection for her subjects.
They were of the people of the little village of Swinly. There
was the constable as he announced that they were flooded in.
There was Miss Smythe with her earnest chin, blushing as she
took Mr. Curtis's arm. There were Mr. and Mrs. Smythe, his
good cheer and her pinched disapproval rendered perfectly in
pencil. There was the stable boy who had lost his grandmother,
and the vicar, and the doctor. And there was the innkeeper and
Molly, and even the cat.

"But this one, I think you will agree, is the best," Evelina
said, and offered him another.

It was a picture of him, drawn with such tenderness that
he was at least ten times handsomer than in reality.

"It is fantastically accurate, don't you agree?" Lady Evelina
said. "When I first saw these I recognized you, of course. But
I do wonder who all these other people are. Probably the

residents of the village near Herald's Court."

He did not correct her. Calista must have drawn these people from memory, but how she had done so after spending only a day with them was astonishing.

"Ah, Harry, tea is here." Lady Evelina went to the footman entering with a tray. "Did you bring the poppyseed biscuits, Lloyd? They are Harry's favorite."

"Rather, they are Lady Evelina's," the countess said with a fond grin.

"I like the lemon tarts," Harry said stolidly.

"Well, I can't fault you for liking fruit, can I?"

"My lord, do come help yourself to biscuits before my daughter eats them all."

Tacitus dragged his eyes from the Aphrodite statue.

"Did any of you just see that— That is— I thought I saw—" For a moment the stone had *glowed*.

They were all staring at him. Then Harry came forward and thrust his plate at Tacitus's waist.

"If Aunt Evie eats all the biscuits, my lord, you can share my tart." He held it forward with a hand that quivered a bit, his chin resolute and eyes guardedly hopeful. Tacitus's ribs abruptly felt too small to contain his heart.

He smiled. "Thank you, Harry. I would be honored."

Biscuits and tarts and tea were consumed. Ian returned with news that the first foal of the year would drop soon. Evelina showed them a design she was making for the garden behind her brother's house in town, and the merits of lily ponds and trellises were considered. It was all so enjoyable that Tacitus might have accepted their invitation to remain overnight if he could even momentarily consider lengthening the time before he would again see Calista.

Bidding them adieu at the earliest opportunity, he set off to find the woman of his dreams.

Chapter Thirty-Three

CALISTA THREW THE GIG'S REINS into the ostler's hands, said, "I won't be more than five minutes," and strode toward the door of the posting house. According to her servants, Mr. Absalom Grange had returned to town. And last night, in her late husband's cigar case, she had finally found what she was looking for.

Light rain pattered on her hair and cloak, but she was already half-soaked from the mad dash from her house, and entirely livid. And a little rain never harmed anyone.

Few patrons as yet peopled the taproom. Only three stared at her as she entered.

"What is the meaning of this?" she demanded, and shook the soggy document clutched in her hand.

Harry's solicitor stood up, his eyes darting guiltily to the document, then back to her face.

"You see, my lady, your husband—"

"My *late* husband, Mr. Preston."

"Your late husband instructed me to draw that up in the event that he perished while you were not in residence at Herald's Court."

"While I was not *in residence*? That is nonsensical. Why would he leave a will that stipulates I must be in residence at Herald's Court upon his death or Harry would receive none of his liquid assets?" In six years he had rarely allowed her to go anywhere. "I was *always* in residence."

"That's what you wanted him to think," the man to his right smirked.

"Mr. Billicky, you are no longer my late husband's lackey and no longer in my employ. Your opinion is not wanted here."

"I find Mr. Billicky's opinions very useful," the third man said.

"And you, Mr. Grange, may go to the devil," she said. "I've no doubt that you engineered this implausible program in order to cheat my son out of his inheritance. What were you and Richard quarreling about the morning you called on him? Your commission on this scheme?"

"Good guess," he said with smug grin.

"I will see you in court before I accede to any of this."

He rose to his feet. "I've another idea, my lady. You run back to your scoundrel of a brother and let him know I'll be suing you for the house, carriage, and horses too."

"Mr. Grange, I will have you know that my brother is a Peer of this Realm—"

"With plenty of troubles of his own to manage, I hear, and not much blunt in the coffer. Do you want to be dragging him into your little infidelities, my lady?"

"My *infidelities?*"

"No one need drag Lord Chance into anything," came a deep voice behind her. "I am here for you to threaten instead, gentlemen. And also to wipe the ground with your faces, if necessary."

She pivoted around and her shock warred with perfect joy.

"What are you doing here?"

"Staring down these fellows menacingly. Go along with it, hm?" Lord Dare spoke with ease, but his eyes were wonderfully warm upon her.

Mr. Grange glared. "Who's this, then?"

"This is—"

"I am Dare." The three clear words declared pure aristocratic authority and sublime confidence. "Also a Peer of the Realm, however with plenty of blunt in the coffer, and actually standing here before you rather than seventy miles away. So, who would like to threaten me first?" He looked at each of them. "Anyone?"

"In point of fact, they were threatening me," she said and turned to her late husband's henchmen while butterflies played tag in her stomach. "I will not accept your insults and untruths. If you wish to accuse me of misdeeds, do so before a magistrate and bring proof against me if you can find it. In the meantime, I will be sending these documents to my brother's legal counsel, who will certainly make mincemeat of them. And if you step one toe onto my property until this is settled, I will shoot the whole foot off. Have I made myself clear?"

Mr. Grange's face bunched into a scowl. Billicky sneered.

Mr. Preston cast the marquess a terrified glance and stepped forward, pulling a sheaf of papers from his coat.

"These are the only other copies of the letter, Lady Holland," he said. "The—ah—copies that Mr. Holland actually signed."

"Damn you, Preston!" Mr. Grange lunged forward. "You won't—" And then he was flying backward, tumbling over his chair and onto the floor in a great clattering sprawl of shouts and splitting wood.

Beside her, Lord Dare flexed his hand and frowned a bit.

"Haven't done that since third year, when that scoundrel Abernathy stole my Aristophanes to use as a doorstop. Not without a glove, at least." His eyes glimmered. "Smashingly satisfying, though admittedly painful."

She laughed and thought perhaps that she had just fallen in love with him again, if that were possible after falling in love with him so many times already.

"Thank you for your assistance," she said, and then snatched the papers from Mr. Preston's hand as he stared in shock at Mr. Grange on the ground and Mr. Billicky backed toward the rear door.

"I think you've broken his nose, my lord," Mr. Preston warbled.

"I daresay," the marquess murmured.

"L'msten dere," Mr. Grange mumbled through the bloody neckcloth crushed to his face as he struggled to his feet. "Dou cand do dis."

"I'm fairly certain she already has," Lord Dare said. "My lady, are you finished here?"

She tossed the documents into the fireplace and watched the flames consume them.

"Now I am," she said. "Mr. Preston, I am grateful for your honesty."

"Truth is, I'd hate to see the little master cut out of his rightful due," he said, clutching his hat and darting wary glances at the marquess.

She went out of the inn to the street and retrieved the gig from the ostler. After a delay, Lord Dare appeared.

"What were you doing in there?" Her fingers were unsteady on her horse's lead as he walked toward her. "Breaking Mr. Billicky's nose as well?"

"I was paying the innkeeper for that ruined chair."

"You are …" She was full of heat and tingling that made her want to melt against him.

"I am …" He stepped close to her. "Peculiar?"

"Wonderful," she said upon a smile that arose from her heart. "Thank you for helping me."

"You had it in hand already," he said, his gaze scanning her features slowly. "But I am glad I was here to see you prevail. You truly are a most capable woman. And courageous too."

"I haven't always been. I used to try to run away from my problems."

"But no longer?"

"No longer. Why have you come here?"

"I must tell you something." He looked about the street and then returned his gaze to her. There was intention in it. "But not here."

"There is a path to my house just over there that avoids the road."

He told the boy who held his horse to take it to the posting house's stable. Then they started along the dirt trail, drawing the gig along as they walked, the sun battling with the remnants of clouds and rain making everything brilliantly green. He spoke as soon as they were clear of the village.

"I am sorry I left Swinly as I did, without speaking to you.

Without saying good-bye."

"I had no expectations. I told you that."

"I know. You made that especially clear. But you deserve more than a man who shares your bed without benefit of marriage."

"What I do with my body is my choice. No man will control me again."

He halted, and the gray of his eyes was like storm clouds.

"I understand," he said. "At least, I think I understand. And I respect your wish for freedom. But, Calista, will you allow me to speak now? Finally?"

The air seemed to sparkle. "Finally?"

"I have spent the past three weeks composing speeches, rational speeches of argumentation worthy of Parliament, of Thucydides and Cicero. None of them suffice. None make clear what is in my heart." He stood very still. "This is the sum of it: You feel like home to me."

"Home?" she whispered.

"You will undoubtedly think me mad. I suspected it too. But I'm not. Dear God, I am not." He stepped forward. "I know you so little, only your beauty, your spirit, your kindness with the people of Swinly, and what you yourself have told me about the past six years. And I knew the girl years ago, that girl who rebuffed me when I would have given her everything, despite my intention of wedding without attachment, despite my fears. Everything—my name, my fortune, my heart. I would have reached into the heavens and battled the gods to pluck down the stars for you, one by one, if you had asked. And I would again, now. I don't understand this. I only know that you are no stranger to me. And here is the most insane part of it. For three weeks now, fantastical dreams have filled my sleep, visions of your laughter, stories that I know you never told me, things I know we have never done together but that feel so real, so true. I have never seen you dancing in the street in the rain, covered in mud. And yet that image is emblazoned in my mind's eye, and the sensation in my chest of laughter as I watched you dance. There is that image, that feeling in me, along with dozens of others I cannot explain. The sensation of your hand in mine is *acute*. It is to me as though we had made the memories together, as though these six years had not been lost to loneliness and unhappiness. I don't believe in reincarnation or whatever the spiritualists call it. I believe I have only this life to live. But though we have not lived any of it except a few weeks together, and those weeks years ago, I know you." He spoke deeply. "I *know* you."

"Tacitus—"

"Calista, for six years I have held the memory of you locked in my heart. Three weeks ago when I held in my arms a different woman, a woman so altered from the girl I knew before, still she seemed the same to me. Everything and yet nothing had changed. I cannot shake this and I don't want to. I will never shake it. You feel like home to me."

"This is not a dream." She barely breathed.

He took the final step that brought them together and his hands came around her face, strong and tender.

"Tell me you feel this too," he said. "Tell me I am not alone in this madness that is no madness."

"You are not alone in it. You were never alone. Not then. Not now."

His eyes shone. "Not now?"

"Never. I love you."

"You love me," he said roughly.

"I love you."

"Will you marry me? Please. I will never harm you, never seek to control you or shackle you. You may have your freedom, however you wish it. But be my wife. Marry me and make your son mine to love as well. Please, Calista. Make my dreams come true."

A sob of happiness broke from her. "This is *real*," she whispered.

"Yes," he said upon a gentle smile. "Can you give me an answer now, or do you require time? I will wait. I will wait with extraordinary impatience and I will probably be cross with everyone I know. But if it means you will be mine in the end, finally, I can wait."

"Tacitus, now I must tell *you* something," she said, backing away from him and clasping her hands tightly together. "You won't believe it. But I must say it. And if you cannot live with it ... Well, I don't want to imagine that."

"Does it concern the matter discussed at the inn just now, the accusation Grange leveled against you?" He spoke with such calm. She wanted to throw herself into his arms and never release him.

"You heard that accusation, yet you have asked me to marry you."

"I have waited six years for the privilege to do so. Give your news to me quickly, plainly, Calista, and I will be the judge of whether I can live with it." His face was very serious.

"It is not exactly easy to explain."

"Allow me to make an attempt, then. You are actually a French spy. There. It is out in the open now. And it's perfectly all right. I don't particularly care for half of those fellows in Parliament either, not to mention the king, and I've always thought tariffs on brandy were a crime."

She cracked a laugh and her heart ached with love. It seemed she would never stop falling in love with him.

"You are *absurd*. I am not a spy."

"All right. You are not a spy. But you have robbed a bank. Several banks."

She tried not to smile. "No."

"Of course not. Bank robbing is not nearly adventuresome enough for you. Therefore, you must be a highwayman. How positively thrilling. But I would rather you retire now. Dangerous life, that."

"No. Tacitus, *please*—"

He seized her and kissed her. His hands went into her hair and his mouth drank her in. She let herself touch him, and adore his lips and scent and body that she craved for a few precious moments, praying that they were not the last she would ever have of him.

He lifted his lips from hers.

"There is nothing, *nothing* that you could do that would drive me away from you. Believe me, Calista."

"I *didn't* do it." She broke out of his arms. "Someone else did."

"All right." His jaw was taut. "Tell me."

She told him.

"I am not insane," she said after a lengthy stretch of silence during which he only stared at her, no readable expression on his handsome face, and the sunshine battled with the rain for preeminence around them.

"This is …" He inhaled heavily.

"Unbelievable."

"I was going to say interesting."

"Interesting?" She stared at him. "That's all?"

"Well, it's not *all*. Of course." His brow furrowed. "I should probably ask you to furnish proof. I suspect that unless I do, you won't be satisfied."

"*Tacitus*. You are not *that* peculiar. You cannot simply shrug this off."

"Calista, I am who I am," he said simply. "Now, tell me something about me that I did not reveal to you during that day in Swinly. The day that I remember."

She could not shake her disbelief. "You are not running from me. You are not looking at me as though I am a madwoman. You trust me."

"I told you of the dreams I have had these past weeks," he said quite soberly. "In my mind, in my *heart*, they do not feel like dreams. They feel like memories. And two days ago at Dashbourne, I saw that statue glow."

"You *did*?"

"It glowed as though lit with a lamp from within, yet no one saw it but me. Now tell me something. Anything."

"I love you."

"Yes," he said, smiling. "Yes, I am just becoming accustomed to that."

"I love you."

He laughed and took her hand and laced their fingers

together. "Anything. Now. Satisfy my curiosity and your disbelief so that I can return to kissing you as soon as possible."

"I don't even know where to begin. I know you so well, I think I have memorized you."

"That puts me at something of a disadvantage, doesn't it?"

"A disadvantage?"

"I shall simply have to consider it a challenge. Rather, an opportunity to spend my time learning about you, exclusively."

She looked down at their entwined fingers. "When I asked you to run away with me, you thought I was asking you to take me to another man."

"But you were not?" he said quietly.

She met his gaze. "I think I have loved you since the moment you stood in my mother's empty drawing room and said, 'I am Dare.' I had never wanted any man until then and I have never wanted another since. Do you— Can you believe me? Or is it too fantastical?"

"It is fantastical. And yet—"

"I'm pregnant. Two months pregnant. The child is yours."

Abruptly his eyes became very bright.

"Mine?" he said deeply.

"Yes. I will understand if you cannot believe this. I— I will have to understand. But I could not lie to you."

"Two months?"

She bit her lips together. "Actually, probably closer to three. Or possibly four. After a while, when I thought it would never end, I stopped counting the days."

"We made love before that night? The night before we left Swinly?"

"Yes. Once. But it was toward the beginning of my days."

"Was ... Was there— That is ... Did we— That private parlor at the inn, the room Smythe hired for his family ... One of my dreams, it is— it is *remarkably* vivid. There was a table, and you—" His breaths seemed to catch and his gaze grew as beautifully loving as she had ever seen. "You asked me to take you into tomorrow."

"*Yes.*" She threw her arms around his neck and pressed

herself to him. "Yes! Although technically it only began in the parlor."

His hands curved around her waist. "Began?"

"It continued in your bedchamber. Quite nicely." She stroked his jaw. "Afterward, you told me the rumor about how you acquired this scar, which I have to assume is a false rumor since you never fought anyone for me. I am the only woman who has ever stolen your heart, aren't I?"

"Yes. What sort of glutton for heartbreak do you think I am?"

"No longer, my lord." She nuzzled the scar.

"Good God, I made love to you in my bedchamber and I don't remember it? How unutterably tragic."

She twined her fingers through his hair. "Would you like to repeat the experience now, this time so you will remember it?"

"Yes. Immediately would be best. It might encourage more dreams, after all."

"You believe me," she whispered.

"It seems I do." His arms encircled her and he drew her snugly to him. "And we are to have a child," he murmured, kissing her neck. "Another child. A brother or sister for Harry. Excellent."

Heart overflowing, she ran her hands over his back and gave herself to his kiss.

Abruptly his mouth lifted from her skin. "Three months?"

"Or so." Her fingers played in his neckcloth, wanting it gone, wanting every piece of his clothing gone, and a bed and bliss. "I think."

He grabbed her hand and moved toward the gig. "We don't have time for this yet."

"We don't? What—? Why?"

"We are getting married." He dragged the horse onto the path. "Immediately. As soon as we can reach the border. There's no time to waste."

"I don't care about that."

"I don't either. But many people do, and I don't wish our

child to be poorly affected by it. And also I am using this as an excuse to ensure that I get to keep you this time."

She laughed.

He pulled her into his arms.

"In other words, my lady," he said upon a gorgeous smile. "Will you run away with me?"

Epilogue

SEVERAL MONTHS LATER, the Marchioness of Dare gave birth to a daughter with beautiful stormy gray eyes.

The miniature lady's brother, who had grown very fond of the Venus Star (as he called it), insisted that his baby sister be named after the goddess of love. For he had an inkling that Venus had been the reason for the journey that resulted in his superb new father, not to mention his sister, and he wished to thank the goddess in this manner.

There was no living with him until his parents bowed to his demand.

In a tender, joyful ceremony in the chapel at Dare Castle, the infant was baptized Venus Mariana Dare, despite her godmother's skeptical brow and her godfather's wicked grin.

"With that name you have condemned her to a lifetime of inane teasing," Evelina told the radiant mother at the party after the ceremony.

"With that name she'll be hounded by all the worst scoundrels," the Viscount Mallory told the proud father moments later. "As her godfather I will, of course, defend her honor at sword point or pistol barrel as necessary," he added with a noble sniff that was entirely ruined by the gleam in his eyes.

Neither radiant mother nor proud father, however, was actually listening to these comments. In the midst of their guests, across the room from each other they were engaged in a silent communication regarding how swiftly they could slip away from the party unnoticed.

Five minutes turned out to be all their mutual impatience could tolerate. With their children safely in the care of every relative they had, separately they departed the festivities and shortly united in an empty room nearby. In moments, she was in his arms and he was pressing her up against the locked door and devouring her neck with his lips.

They did not require a bed to do what they then inevitably did. With Tacitus's American family again in residence, and Calista's family too, the newlyweds had already become experts at finding useful locations—not to mention postures—for consummating their happiness whenever the inspiration occurred, which it frequently did.

After all needs had been enthusiastically and ecstatically seen to, and Lady Dare was enjoying a lingering final taste of her husband's lips, he drew back and regarded her curiously.

"Where is the statue?"

She nibbled his jaw. "In Mama's personal chambers at Dashbourne. Next week," she added, kissing his neck, "she is taking it to London. She still hopes to mount an exhibition at the museum someday."

"You have no concern that Aphrodite will work her tricks with another unsuspecting victim?"

She looked into his eyes. "How could I begrudge anyone else the gift she gave me?"

He smiled and touched his lips to hers. "Gift, indeed," he murmured, and kissed her again.

A Note to My Wonderful Readers

I HOPE YOU ENJOYED Calista and Tacitus's love story. Many of you will recognize the inspiration for Calista's journey toward happiness: the film *Groundhog Day*. I adore *Groundhog Day*, and I loved turning the story of an individual fighting against life into a full-fledged romance set in Regency-era England.

History is chock-full of fiction, and myth and legend intertwine with fact so thoroughly in human culture that oftentimes the two are inseparable (except to folks with little imagination). For my readers interested in these sorts of things, here are a few mentioned in *Again, My Lord*: In ancient lore, souls were ferried across the River Acheron to reach Hades, although the River Styx was also a boundary between Earth and the Underworld. The philosopher Plato's *Symposium* is a fictional conversation between real friends gathered together to drink and to share theories about love. The theory quoted in the Epigraph here is attributed to Aristophanes, a comic playwright. Finally, the novel Calista and Tacitus read aloud to each other is *The Castle of Otranto*, a fantastically dramatic tale of magic and heroism published first in 1764, and hugely popular. (I like to think Calista borrowed the book from Harriet Tinkerson.)

Though I don't ever intend a moral to any of my stories, the message of Calista's journey is inescapable. Living with gratitude *in* the present *for* the present is a Truth I certainly need to remind myself of daily. Living with gratitude is, of course, not the same as passively accepting one's lot in life, especially when that lot includes emotional or physical abuse. In gratitude for those who help victims of domestic abuse, I am donating a portion of the sale of every copy of *Again, My*

Lord to nonprofit, nonsectarian organizations dedicated to helping women and children escape from abusive relationships.

Again, My Lord is part of my Twist Series of historical romances. As Tacitus suspects, Aphrodite's interference in the lives of misguided lords and ladies is far from over. The rest of the Chance siblings (and a few of their friends) are in for a ride! Look for Evelina's book coming soon. And turn the page here for an excerpt from *My Lady, My Lord*, my 2015 RITA® Award-nominated Twist Series novel starring Lord Ian Chance and Lady Corinna Mowbray, a rake and a bluestocking like never before ...

Turn the page for an Excerpt

from

My Lady, My Lord

A *Twist* Series Novel

Excerpt from My Lady, My Lord

MURMURS OF INTEREST AND FEET SCUFFLING on the wooden floor attended visitors as they moved from one objet d'art to another. The familiar sounds and the bubbly drink softened Corinna's fidgets. She circled the exhibition chamber, greeting friends and enjoying their remarks about the statuary, which were exceptional examples of the Classical Period carved from smooth white marble. One table-top-sized rendering of Aphrodite had been wrought from a single block of creamy alabaster.

Corinna stared at the supple creation. The goddess's graceful arms, shapely hips, and legs draped with a sheer suggestion of fabric, her hair flowing down her back and across her shoulders and over her rounded buttocks, suggested movement, fluid and sensuous. Appropriate for the Goddess of Love.

But something beyond that drew Corinna closer. The statue seemed to glow from within, a golden hue suffusing its curvaceous surface as though from hidden fire. In contrast, the goddess's almond-shaped eyes seemed disappointingly hard.

"Envious?" A voice like fire-warmed brandy on a winter night came just behind Corinna's shoulder. She pivoted and met the Earl of Chance's gaze. As usual, laughter colored his clear blue eyes. Also as usual, that laughter mocked.

The hair at the back of Corinna's neck bristled. She turned her shoulder to him. "Why don't you go crawl back under the rock you were born beneath, my lord?"

"Because it seems you are currently using it to wash your clothing upon," he drawled. "It can be the only explanation for the constantly dismal hue of your gowns."

"Oh, how flattering," she cooed. "I never imagined you

would notice."

"I'm merely observing that you appear as though you are at a funeral, or at the very least en route to one."

She swung around to face him. "Where is your latest lightskirt— oh, pardon me—your latest *friend*? I noticed her earlier, attempting to insinuate herself into your mother's good graces."

"I daresay she's off somewhere taking in the exhibition."

"She is very beautiful. Helenesque, really."

"She is, isn't she?" He smiled with natural arrogance.

"Too bad she hasn't two sticks to rub together in her head. But then, you do make a perfect pair."

His crystal eyes narrowed. "Ah, yes, because the ability to dissertate upon the fourth satellite of the planet Jupiter and the metaphor of Shakespeare's thirty-fifth sonnet is much to be prized over beauty, charm, and good manners. You've certainly proven the two cannot coexist."

"What on earth are you doing here? Did you come solely to vex art patrons?"

"Not at all. I came to please my mother." He bowed, a graceful movement of his broad-shouldered frame entirely at odds with his taunting grin. He cocked his head. "Vexing art patrons is merely an accidental *coup de maître*."

"Perhaps you might consider enjoying the art, instead." If he didn't remove himself, she would be obliged to cut him. But his mother was a friend, and mustn't be insulted so.

"I could," he conceded. "But I don't know that cretins are capable of becoming connoisseurs of anything of real value."

Corinna tilted her face up to examine his features more closely. It did not seem that he teased now.

She pursed her lips. "You could make an attempt." She gestured to the statue. "This one is Aphrodite, goddess of love and beauty. You ought to be familiar with her, at least."

"All right." He appeared to study the piece carefully. His brow bent and one of his hands cupped his jaw—a square jaw of classical proportions not unlike the statuary about them. After a moment, his lips curved into a skeptical twist.

"What is it?" she ventured, an odd frisson of hope mingled with the usual wariness tingling in her stomach. She didn't know why she should care that he took some interest in the alabaster figure, except that she was always happy to welcome a new member to the ranks of art devotees. But she held her breath. "What do you see?"

"Well, I don't know that I should say ..." His brow creased beneath a thick fall of overly long black hair. He never bowed to fashion; he was far too indolent and self-satisfied. "But it seems to me that ... No. No, I shouldn't."

"Shouldn't what?" She glanced at the statue. "No comment proffered from a standpoint of true respect for the artist, his medium, or his creation lacks merit."

The earl's mouth curved up at one edge and he shifted his gaze to her for a moment before returning it to the Aphrodite.

"Then I should feel free to say anything I wish about this statue? To you?"

"Of course. There is no critique of art I have not already heard more than once, I daresay. You cannot surprise me."

He slanted her a quick glance. "You sound proud of that."

A warning tingle scurried in where hope had briefly dallied. "Merely confident."

"Well, then, I shall forge ahead and offer my observation."

Something wasn't right. Her heart beat too quickly. She had known this man since they were both in leading strings. On the surface his attitude now seemed perfectly reasonable. Some instinct forged in her during childhood must be in operation. But what if her instinct was wrong? What if he had finally grown a conscience? And a cerebrum? His mother was a woman of great intelligence, after all. He could not have entirely taken after his father.

"Yes. Do," she forced herself to say.

"You say these all came here from Greece?"

"Of course. Attica, mostly, drawn from private collections throughout England and elsewhere."

He scratched his jaw with two long fingers. Corinna watched in sick fascination.

"Ancient Greece?" he said. "Are you certain of that?"

"Quite. Your mother never would have had them installed here if she and the experts at the museum were not completely convinced of their authenticity."

He shook his head. "No. I'm afraid that's impossible."

"But why on earth?"

"This one must be a recent production. Very recent, I'll wager."

She scrunched her eyes to peer at the piece more closely. "Why do you say that?"

"Well, you see." He gestured to the Aphrodite. "Just the other night Drake had this very girl up to his rooms on Piccadilly. She wore precisely this same shift. Had her hair somewhat differently arranged, but I know Drake would swear she's the one. Grace would, too. He saw her first, of course. Always has a quick eye for the sweetest beauties. But Stoopie stole the march on him." He leaned close to her ear. "Tells them he's going to be a duke someday. They can't resist it."

She stepped back, stomach churning. "You and your friends are barbarians. Hedonistic heathens. You don't possess an ounce of character among the lot of you."

As though a curtain lifted, from sober and thoughtful his features turned cool.

"You believe that your prosy, stiff-necked politicians and scientists are better?" he said, the drawl much more pronounced now. "I think not. At least Drake and Grace know how to enjoy themselves."

Corinna fisted her hands. It simply was not fair. At least when they were children she usually anticipated this. But over the past decade he had perfected his skills in dissimulation, probably to help him waste away the Chance fortune at the gaming tables.

"That is all they do," she snapped. "Enjoy themselves to the detriment of those around them and society at large."

"Oh," he grinned, but there was no real mirth in it, "we tend to keep our amusements rather closer to home than that."

"And that's another thing. You are ruining your brother."

What was she saying? She should walk away. What did it matter if anyone saw her cut him? He deserved it—he and his grotesque mockery of civility. But her tongue knew no curb. "I saw Gregory the other night at William Lamb's house. He conversed with several of the most prominent men in government with ease. He could make something of himself, but you won't let him."

The earl shrugged. "My brother is a grown man. He does what he likes."

"You should be ashamed of yourself, dragging poor Gregory into debased behavior, as though he weren't worth five of you. Ten. If I were you I wouldn't be able to sleep at night for the guilt of it."

"I haven't the foggiest idea what you're blathering about, Corrie dear. I sleep exceptionally well, deep and untroubled, whether inebriated or stone sober, accompanied or alone." He paused. "My conscience does not distress me, as obviously yours does." He tipped a fingertip toward her chest.

"You are despicable. That you even mention such—such accompaniment in a lady's presence is despicable."

"I seem to recall someone speaking of lightskirts a moment ago. But you are correct, of course." He smiled, a slow, wicked curve of his lips. "After all, generally ladies prefer not to hear about my accompaniment, but rather to live it."

"You are astoundingly arrogant. Despite what the society rags claim, not all women fall under your spell. Exceptions to the rule do exist." It was like staring at a carriage accident in progress. She could not seem to halt her tongue, draw her gaze away, or move her feet.

He gave her a slow perusal up and down, from the crown of her head all the way along her skirt. Spine shivering, she regretted not fleeing before.

Fleeing?

"Oh, I doubt it." His odious confidence fairly oozed. "I've long suspected, Corrie dear, that you put on this prickle with me for safety's sake."

"What on earth are you talking about?"

The smile deepened at one side, a dent appearing in his smooth-shaven cheek. Other women might call it a dimple. Corinna called it horrid.

He spoke beneath the hum of voices. "You want me to bed you."

Scalding heat rushed into her cheeks and her mouth dropped open.

His eyes flared with satisfaction. "Ah, I am not off the mark, I see. The blush of the virgin reveals all." He tapped a fingertip to her cheek.

She flinched back. "Perhaps your powers of observation are as poor as your judgment of character and your capacity for rational thought, Lord Chance," she said through gritted teeth. "Members of the human species color in the face from anger as well as embarrassment. But since you don't belong to that species, perhaps you simply do not know that."

"No, I don't think so," he said smoothly, regarding her with lazy intent, as though he were reading her thoughts and finding them singularly uninteresting. "I believe you have had a secret *tendre* for me all these years. Haven't you? Poor little Corrie. It would explain your attitude of contempt, a contrivance to protect your fragile self-esteem in the face of my continual disinterest."

"My self-esteem is far from fragile, and actual contempt for you explains my attitude of contempt."

"I think not."

"Is that all you can say? You think not? Is that the extent of your ability to debate a position upon which you feel so fully secure?"

His crystal blue eyes danced. "The only position I feel fully secure in, my dear, is atop a naked woman."

"You are disgusting," she spat out.

"And you are a cold fish."

"Reprobate."

"Bluestocking."

"Rogue."

"Prude."

"Dissolute."

"Ice queen."

Corinna's head spun from the champagne. "I despise you," she lashed out.

"The feeling, my dear, is entirely mutual."

"I beg your pardon?" A thin voice sounded at Corinna's elbow. "Could you help me?"

With a breath of relief, Corinna pivoted around. An elderly woman stood beside her. Garbed entirely in dove gray silk and chiffon, carrying a silver-tipped walking stick, with a gray silk hat sporting an enormous brim and a profusion of gray feathers, she looked to be about a century old. From within her face, lined to nearly caricature, a pair of soft, moist gray eyes entreated.

"Yes, certainly," Corinna said. "How may I assist you?" They must have already opened the exhibition doors to the public. She would certainly know of a matron of these advanced years if she came from one of the families of the *ton* that Lady Chance had invited to the preopening soirée.

"Oh," the woman tittered, her voice stronger than her appearance suggested, "it seems I have lost my reticule. I am here every day, you see, and the place feels so much like home that sometimes I leave my belongings about." Her paper-thin lips smiled around surprisingly even, white teeth. "But I cannot see very well any longer. My eyes haven't got the sharpness they used to."

"Let me help you find it," Corinna said.

The earl moved to the woman's side.

"Madam," he said in a steady, gentle voice Corinna did not recognize, "allow me to escort you to a chair while Lady Corinna looks about the place for your property." With great care, he grasped the old woman's hand and slid her arm through his elbow. The top of her outrageous hat barely reached his shoulder.

"Oh, you are very kind, young man." She patted his coat sleeve. "And your lady is beautiful. The two of you make a lovely pair."

Corinna's gaze snapped to Ian, but his attention remained on the woman.

She pointed her cane at Corinna. "You will have charming children, I am certain." She touched Corinna on the sleeve.

A jolt of heat coursed through Corinna from brow to toe. Her ears went cottony, the sounds of people moving through the chamber, talking, all abruptly muted. She blinked and gasped a hard breath. The earl's hand hovered over his brow, his eyes half closed.

With a single shake of his head he seemed to recall himself.

"I will return shortly," Corinna said, blinking again to focus her vision, and hurried off.

She found a little gray reticule tucked behind a life-sized statue of Ares, the god of war. She looked about for the earl and the old woman, but the hall had grown crowded. Instead, she followed the wall around the perimeter until she saw him ahead. He was taller than most of the men in the place, and she followed the sight of his glossy black hair until she reached them.

The old woman sat in a fragile heap on the stone bench, so thin beneath the gray gown that her bones protruded.

"Here you are, ma'am," Corinna said and offered the reticule. The woman clutched it with gnarled fingers and smiled.

"Thank you, dear girl." Her eyes glistened. "And thank you, my lord. I enjoyed hearing about your mother's projects."

He made an elegant bow. "And I about your grandchildren." He took her arm and drew her up from the bench. "May I escort you to your friends now?" he asked.

"Oh, no. I am here with my son, but he's somewhere about the place nearby, I suspect, and shall find me soon."

"Then to your carriage?"

She chuckled. "What a fine gentleman you are." She patted his sleeve again, then turned to Corinna. "You keep this one close, dear. Men like him don't grow on trees."

Corinna resisted choking on her tongue as the woman

tottered away into the crowd, reticule clasped tightly to her bony breast.

The earl moved beside her. "A lady of great taste, obviously," he said, laughter in his voice again.

Corinna's bemusement scattered. "More likely blind, and certainly deaf," she replied, then looked up at him.

She should not have. Where quiet pleasure had shaped his handsome features in the presence of the stranger, now cold aversion shone.

"You would know about an existence deprived of the senses, wouldn't you?" he said. Without awaiting her riposte, he turned and disappeared into the crowd.

~o0o~

Damn and blast his mother.

No. That wasn't just. Ian had enormous admiration for his mother. She had a fine character and a formidable mind, both of which she'd been obliged to hide for years because of her husband's ignorant, intolerant cruelties.

But since the death of his father nine years earlier, his mother had finally made her life what she wished, filled with projects and people the late earl would never have allowed in his home. Though she never asked more from him than her widow's jointure, Ian always supported her projects. He cared for her deeply.

But that run-in with Corinna Mowbray at the museum was enough to have a man damning Saint Mary if he thought she was even partially to blame for it.

Corinna Mowbray. The burr in his memories of childhood. The bane of his youth. Even Christmas held a blot because of that female and her ceaseless superiority, the same nose-in-the-air, better-than-thou attitude she still cultivated.

He couldn't have been more than twelve, she a few years younger. The house overflowed with guests for the holidays. He'd been in the stable brushing down his horse after a ride. Even as a child he'd liked several hours alone each day with the horses. The muted sounds of snuffling and chewing, and the scents of straw and animals comforted him. The morning was clear and cold, the stable warm, and he was content.

Then she appeared at the door and his happiness evaporated.

He'd told her to go away. She responded by informing him that he was an imbecile—as usual—and he was doing it all wrong.

At that age he already knew considerably more about the care of horses than any other boy around. But something about Corinna Mowbray always dug at his belly like a sharpened stick. The way she peered at him with her mossy eyes and spoke in short, chopped sentences as though addressing a simpleton never failed to crowd his chest with anger. For Ian, mild-tempered and amusement loving, that sensation felt like death.

She'd stood there in her little white frock with pink roses sprinkled across the sleeves and skirt, her golden-brown hair bound by thick white ribbons, so tight-laced, starched, and prim … and Ian simply left all reason behind.

He taunted her, teasing that she knew nothing of horses or anything worthwhile, only about baby things. The day before she'd showed off her insect collection in the drawing room like no girl he'd ever met. Privately he had been impressed. But faced with her alone in the stable he told her it was nothing but a jumble of dead bugs, most of them wingless and without the correct number of legs. She'd probably ripped them off when she killed them. As his pièce de resistance he said that a person couldn't ride a dead beetle anyway.

She turned every shade of red until finally she boasted that she might not be able to ride a beetle, but she could ride any horse in his father's stables.

He mounted her on Storm.

Even now, so many years later, Ian cringed at the image wedged in his memory of the little girl's twin braids flailing out behind her as the half-broken colt took off across the yard. He'd known then that he shouldn't have done it. But no one had ever been able to goad him like Corinna Mowbray. Guilt prickling at his insides, nearly as awful as the anger she roused in his young breast, he'd grabbed up his horse and followed.

He discovered her in a ditch beneath a hedge a half-mile from the stables. Storm had disappeared.

Her ankle protruded at a peculiar angle beneath her dirtied skirt and she wept, great heaving sobs, tears staining her pale face, her nose running. But even through her pain and wailing, she managed to tell him in no uncertain terms that he was a cretin, unfit for human company, and she hated him. She refused to allow him to place her on his horse and carry her home. Ian had scowled, mounted, and rode like the devil to fetch the head groom.

He spent the next week standing up at the dinner table, the caning his father gave him left such welts. But he vowed to never again allow Corinna Mowbray to get beneath his skin.

He had, unfortunately, failed at that many times in the succeeding years. He didn't see her often, and when he did he had every intention of behaving well. But he simply couldn't seem to hold his tongue with that female. Today's spitting match was no exception.

Disgust with himself cloyed at his skin. He never treated women with less than the honesty and respect they deserved. Now Corinna Mowbray had him squabbling in public and insulting her as though he were the worst sort of lowbred scoundrel. As though he were his father.

"What's the trouble, Chance?" Stoopie clapped him on the shoulder. "You look like your five favorite horses just lost at Newmarket one right after the other."

Ian looked up from his scowl. He'd ridden all the way from the exhibition to Brooks's already. He supposed he'd left his horse in the care of the club's groom outside from sheer habit.

He shrugged out of his friend's grasp. "Must've been in a brown study, but it's passed now," he said and gave his greatcoat and hat to a footman.

"You wouldn't know what studying was if it bit you in the arse," Stoopie chortled. "But I wouldn't either, so I don't blame you for it, old chap."

Ian's stomach clenched. She'd always told him he had porridge for brains, that he would amount to nothing. Once, when they were older, she'd said he was so lacking in intelligence he would even have to resort to cheating to win at cards, just like his father.

The clench turned to burning.

He'd done well for himself, of course. He enjoyed good friends, the ample proceeds of a smoothly running estate and a superb breeding stable, and the company of the most beautiful unmarried women in England. And he had never cheated at the tables. Not once. He worked hard to make certain he would never be tempted to do so.

"Care for a bite to eat?" the marquess asked, patting his rotund stomach. Ian nodded, casting his eye about for Jag and unreasonably glad he didn't find the baron amongst the club's patrons tonight. Jag was far too sharp, and Ian was in no humor for deflecting more questions.

They settled at a table and Stoopie ordered beefsteak and onions. Ian took the same, and a bottle of brandy. Those consumed, he ordered whiskey. Its pungent aroma curled into his nostrils like twin pincers, and the recollection of Corinna Mowbray's furious face faded slowly from his mind's eye.

After that, he was too far aloft to recall much of anything.

~o0o~

Ian awoke in unusual discomfort. The bedclothes twisted about his legs and arms, immobilizing him. He tried to stretch but cloth cinched up beneath his armpits. After the club he must have returned home more disguised than he'd realized. He preferred to wear nothing to bed, but his valet, Andrews, liked him to wear a nightshirt—damn his meddling. The wretched thing seemed heavier than usual, though.

He lifted a hand to rub his face awake.

Ruffles? Since when had he purchased a nightshirt with ruffled sleeves? Or satin ribbon wound about the cuff? Since when had he allowed any garment even vaguely resembling this into his house? Andrews had gone too far this time.

His palm smoothed across his cheek, and arrested. Andrews couldn't have possibly shaved him when he'd come home near four o'clock, could he? His manservant needed a stern dressing down just as soon as he brought his miraculous morning-after tonic: one part coffee, one part blue ruin, and one part secret ingredient. Andrews refused to tell him the mix, probably because he knew it was the sole reason Ian put up with his mother hen routine year after year.

The door opened. Ian slewed his sleep-fogged eyes toward it. A maid entered bearing a silver tray with a teapot and a sprig of flowers in a small vase. The tray was wrong; Ian took breakfast in his dining room, no matter what hour he rose, and he never drank tea before the evening. But the maid, apparently a new girl, was a pretty thing, so he didn't chastise her.

In his younger years he'd dallied a bit with willing servants, but categorically never his own. He appreciated a fine set of cat heads as well as the next fellow, though. The maid's jutted out over the tray like a pair of money bags ready for Midas to fondle. Her attention was fixed on the contents of the tray, so Ian looked his fill. He generally liked slightly smaller breasts, but it was still early in the day yet, and the maid's attributes weren't to be dismissed out of hand.

A niggling sense that something was not quite right pricked at the back of his neck. Something missing.

"Good morning, milady. Chocolate, toast, and the post." The maid smiled, set the tray upon a stand on the empty side of his bed, and departed.

Ian barely heard the door close.

This was not his bed.

He always slept in his bed. Always. He took his pleasures with beautiful partners wherever he wished, but never in his own bedchamber. It was the one place, the single spot that he could return to each night—or morning, as more often the case—and be at complete peace. He didn't even allow his friends into his private chambers.

He'd spoken the truth to that blasted prim bluestocking Corinna Mowbray the day before. He slept well every night of his adult life because he kept his own bed sacrosanct, unmarked by the scent of a woman's perfume, strands of long hair left behind, the impression of a head in the pillow beside his, and bits of feminine clothing lost within the bedclothes. It was one of the two rules he ever held to. No matter how tempting a siren's feathered boudoir seemed at three, four, or five o'clock in the morning after a satisfying interval of mutual pleasure, no matter how exhausted or inebriated, he always returned home. Otherwise, he simply did not sleep until the next night.

But this was not his bed. His bed was solid, smoothly fashioned mahogany, its deep blue draperies lacking even a suggestion of trim. A man of simple tastes—honest play, fast horses, and beautiful women—needed no more.

This bed was far from simple. Covered in lace-edged linens and frothy pink and white pillows, draped with a striped pink, gold, and white satin canopy, gold tassels trailing the painted white bedposts—this bed was clearly a woman's creation. A woman who enjoyed her femininity to the utmost. Ian had made love to plenty of women in beds like this, though few so opulently light of character. But he'd never slept in one.

Again, a peculiar lack tickled at his senses. Something was not right. Something was missing. Something . . .

Something he should have felt as he stared at the maid's breasts. Something that should have at least suggested its existence when he recalled the last few women with whom he'd shared this sort of luxuriously feminine couch. Something that was with him every morning at waking, more faithful than the most loyal hound, more reliable than the finest Swiss watch.

He slid his arm beneath the coverlet and brought his hand to his waist.

His heart slammed against his ribs.

He pressed his fingers into his abdomen. Through the thick linen nightshirt, soft flesh sprang back. He held his breath, and his hand stole lower.

Oh, God. No. No.

No.

No.

No.

Pulse racing faster than his latest Ascot winner, he bunched the fabric beneath his hand to his waist. Sucking in air like a drowning man, he reached downward.

He yanked his arm back and bolted upright. His chest jiggled. He slammed a palm over it and cupped a supple mound. His other hand slapped up, encompassing an identical shape. Breathing fast now, he pulled at the laces of the nightshirt, barely seeing the pink satin ribbon and rich embroidery, until the fabric gaped.

His head spun. His stomach roiled. He gripped the nightshirt and tore it down the center.

Two perfect female breasts, their beautiful pink tips velvety, perched gracefully above a smooth, slender waist, a delicate navel inches above a thatch of soft brown hair. Thighs any man would pay to put his face between, creamy and round, stretched along the counterpane, the torn nightshirt falling to either side.

Ian kicked his feet free. They were small, shapely, with narrow ankles and, like his legs and chest, devoid of hair.

Dear God. *What was happening?*

He lifted a trembling hand. The fingers were slender and long, the nails carefully manicured but not painted, the palms tender and uncallused. A woman's hand. A lady's hand. He knew the difference. He'd enjoyed the touch of plenty of both.

But not this one. He would remember a ring like the one on the third finger of this left hand if it had come anywhere near him. The sapphire was set in the gold at such a sharp angle that he would have insisted a lover remove the piece before commencing pleasing activities. Ian liked his sport lively, and occasionally outré, but bloodletting didn't interest him—though some of his friends found that sort of thing appealing. Not Ian. When he made love to a woman, the fewer accoutrements involved the better. The female body was plaything enough.

Something about this ring seemed familiar, though. It

wasn't in the current fashion. He'd bought plenty of baubles for women over the years, but he'd never seen anything like this in a jeweler's shop. It looked vaguely like a weapon.

He lifted his hand to his face. His fingertips brushed smooth cheeks and brow, full lips, a lilting nose, thick lashes, slender brows, delicate earlobes. He reached up and touched more linen.

A cap.

He pushed it off. A long braid of satiny tresses met his touch.

His chest filled, thick and itchy and sharp all at once, like a scream forming. But Ian had never screamed in his life, except on that one occasion when he fell out of the old oak and broke his arm. He'd been ten. He still had the bone-scar on his wrist to show for it. His father had said thank God it wasn't his right arm, a gentleman couldn't wield a sword properly with such a handicap. After that comment, Ian worked especially hard to get the wrist fully mobile again, left hand or not. It had hurt like the devil, but he'd done it. As with his university studies later, he'd had to save face.

A face that seemed to be no longer his own.

He choked, dragging in air. This couldn't be happening. It must be a dream. He pinched his thigh hard.

"Ouch!" His voice came forth light. Rich. Familiar.

No. Oh, no.

Not a dream.

A *nightmare.*

Leaping from the bed, legs tangled in the ruined nightshirt, he tripped toward the dressing table. The mirror, gilt-edged but not showy, was long and narrow, an oval that captured nearly his entire image as he stumbled to a halt before it.

No!

Ian squeezed his eyes shut.

Nightmare. Nightmare. Nightmare.

It had to be a horrible nightmare. Or a wretched jest his friends were playing. Stoopie was wealthy enough to fund something this elaborate, and immoral enough to invent it. They'd dosed him with a strong drug to put him into some sort of reverie, a terrifyingly real reverie, designed to make his stomach heave and his legs shake.

He didn't feel the thick pull of the poppy seed in his blood, though, nor the heavy stupor. But he'd only indulged in that messy pursuit a handful of times, and years ago. He preferred brandy. Perhaps there was something new he hadn't yet heard of. Another drug much stronger than opium. Something imported from the Orient. It must be. He cracked his eyes open and peeked at the mirror again.

The eyes that stared back at him in horror were not Chance blue, passed through nearly every male in his family since the time of King Harry. Instead they were muddy. Greenish-brown with a hint of gold if a man had to be decent about it.

But Ian didn't have to be decent about it. He'd never been decent to the bearer of those pond-colored eyes. And his anger was mounting. This was going too far. Drake and he had traded pranks since their school days, but neither of them had ever stooped so outrageously low. Ian's friend could not have chosen a more painful torment to impose upon him, a worse penance for the wrong Drake obviously imagined he'd committed—whatever it was.

He would exact retribution. As soon as the effects of this wretched drug wore off and he had his proper senses back, he would see to it right away. He'd no doubt that when he was in his right mind again he would remember the ruse. A man didn't recover from this level of terror so readily.

Stoopie would pay. And pay.

Staggering back to the frothy bed, he fell upon it on his face, releasing a shuddering breath into the feather quilt.

A scratch came at the door. This time another maid entered. He couldn't summon the enthusiasm to examine her breasts.

"Milady." Glancing swiftly at his torn garment, then away, the girl extended a silver dish bearing an envelope.

Ian reached for the envelope but his hand stalled. He leaned toward the tray. On the face of the paper, his monogram—the Chance crest—showed bold and clear. The address read *The Honble. Corinna Mowbray.*

This was wrong. He had never, ever sent Corinna Mowbray a letter. Categorically never.

Trying to still the shaking of his hand, he took up the envelope, nodded to the maid, and waited until she left. He unsnapped the wax seal—the Chance seal, stored in his dressing chamber table, to which only he possessed the key— and withdrew a single, folded sheet of his finest foolscap. Vaguely aware that his nostrils were flaring like a spooked horse, he opened it.

The writing was not his own, scrawled swiftly beneath the monogram, though with the weight of his hand and the angle of his script. Ian read the words, and his entire female body went cold.

You thorough scoundrel! What have you done?

Books by Katharine Ashe

Twist Series
Again, My Lord
My Lady, My Lord

The Devil's Duke
The Rogue (coming 2016)

The Prince Catchers
I Loved a Rogue
I Adored a Lord
I Married the Duke

The Falcon Club
How a Lady Weds a Rogue
How to Be a Proper Lady
When a Scot Loves a Lady

Rogues of the Sea
In the Arms of a Marquess
Captured by a Rogue Lord
Swept Away by a Kiss

Captive Bride (A Regency Ghost Novel)

Novellas
Kisses, She Wrote
How to Marry a Highlander
A Lady's Wish
How Angela Got Her Rogue Back
(in *At the Duke's Wedding*)
The Day It Rained Books
(in *At the Billionaire's Wedding*)

Fulsome Thanks

I am deeply indebted to some wonderful people for helping me bring this book to publication: Marcia Abercrombie, Georgann T. Brophy, Georgie Brophy, Caroline Linden, Mary Brophy Marcus, Miranda Neville, and Maya Rodale.

Special thanks for their work on this book to Lori Devoti, JB Schroeder, and Martha Trachtenberg, and to my editor Anne Forlines. Thanks also to my agents, Kimberly Whalen and MacKenzie Fraser-Bub of Trident Media Group for supporting me in every endeavor, and to Meredith Miller and Mark Gottlieb for putting *My Lady, My Lord* into the hands of foreign-language and audio book readers.

Thanks from my heart to The Princesses, the best street team an author could ever have. And thanks to all of my readers, who make it a thorough joy to write romance.

To my husband, son and little Idaho, I send up a gigantic, sunshiny "Hurrah!" in thanks for essential help with the story and for their love and enthusiasm through every moment of its creation.

~o0o~

If you enjoyed *Again, My Lord*, please consider leaving a review or rating of the book online. Reviews help authors find new readers, and I am indebted to each of you who have reviewed my books in the past. For links to review my books, visit the Quick Reference Booklist page of my website www.KatharineAshe.com.

Praise for Katharine's Novels

MY LADY, MY LORD

RITA® Award Finalist 2015
Romance Writers of America

I LOVED A ROGUE

"Passionate, heart-wrenching, and thoroughly satisfying."
All About Romance, *Desert Island Keeper*

"Katharine Ashe's historical romances are rich and inventive,
unexpected and smart, and she doesn't pull any emotional
punches. She writes with a wry, provocative, angst-y energy
that compels you to keep turning pages, even when it means
the thrill of a blissful read will be far too soon behind you.
Oh, yeah. This author rocks historical romance."
USA Today, A Must-Read Romance

I ADORED A LORD

"A riotous good time... Delicious."
Publishers Weekly

I MARRIED THE DUKE

"Historical Romance of the Year"
Reviewers' Choice Award nominee 2014

KISSES, SHE WROTE

"Smoldering."
Library Journal (starred review)

HOW TO MARRY A HIGHLANDER

RITA® Award Finalist 2014
Romance Writers of America

HOW TO BE A PROPER LADY

Amazon Editors' Choice 10 Best Books of 2012

WHEN A SCOT LOVES A LADY

"Lushly intense romance . . . radiant prose."
Library Journal (starred review)

"Sensationally intelligent writing, and a true, weak-in-the-knees love story."
Barnes & Noble "Heart to Heart" *Recommended Read!*

IN THE ARMS OF A MARQUESS

"Every woman who ever dreamed of having a titled lord at her feet will love this novel."
Eloisa James, *New York Times* bestselling author

"Immersive and lush. ... Ashe is that rare author who chooses to risk unexpected elements within an established genre, and whose skill and magic with the pen lifts her tales above the rest."
Fresh Fiction

CAPTURED BY A ROGUE LORD

"Best Historical Romantic Adventure"
Reviewers' Choice Award winner 2011

SWEPT AWAY BY A KISS

"A breathtaking romance filled with sensuality."
Lisa Kleypas, *New York Times* #1 bestselling author

Made in the USA
Columbia, SC
01 July 2020